𝔇𝔢𝔰𝔱𝔦𝔫𝔶 𝔑𝔢𝔳𝔢𝔯 𝔖𝔩𝔢𝔢𝔭𝔰
Deliverance

About the Authors
Bernadette Thompson Martin

Although born in Pennsylvania and raised in the charismatic town of Millville, New Jersey, I am a down and out Southern girl at heart.

In 2007, my husband Ken and I left the Sunshine state and moved to the homey, quaint city of Cottageville, South Carolina. We share our modest little farm with two rescue horses, one spoiled rotten mini donkey, three equally spoiled mini goats, three dogs, and two chattering cockatiels.

The soothing tranquility of country life feeds an active imagination and allows my pen to bring wonderful characters to life.

The story line began to take form at a *very* young age. Over the years, both it and I have grown expeditiously. Had I not endured the many wonderful and often bizarre experiences of life, these novels, part one and two of our trilogy, would never reach the level of realism and uniqueness presented. My aspiration for writing is insatiable. Knowing it brings joy to many others is my reward. I am presently retired and am a proud three-time NaNoWriMo award winner.

Jeannie Faulkner Barber

I'm a diehard Texan, born and raised in Marshall, now living in the East Texas piney woods of Kilgore with my wonderful husband, Monte. Our three sons, Joe Bryan, Adam, and Garry, and their wives, have blessed us with nine beautiful grandchildren. Monte and I share our home with our 'daughter', a Chiweenie (Chihuahua and Dachshund mix), Gracie Star (a little rescue).

"How 'bout them Cowboys?" Being a true-blue Dallas Cowboys fan, my mood depends on a win or loss…poor Monte.

My *two* passions in my life are writing and drag racing. My racecar, 'Connie', is a white 1981 Monte Carlo with pink racing stripes. Monte and I even met at the dragstrip. I've won more trophies and cash at the pulse-pounding sport than him, but he did teach me everything I know!

Presently, I work for the Overton-New London Chamber of Commerce as Office Manager and Executive Vice President, am a member and officer of East Texas Writers Association (ETWA), North East Texas Writers Organization (NETWO), and a 2007, 2011, & 2012 Award Winner of NaNoWriMo.

Other Works

By Bernadette Thompson Martin
Destiny Never Sleeps: Quest of the Two Queens
(with Jeannie Faulker Barber)

By Jeannie Faulkner Barber
Scent of Double Deception
(with Ann Alan)
Taste of Fire

Children's Literature by Jeannie Faulkner Barber
The Santa Coins
(illustrated by Denny Youngblood)

Destiny Never Sleeps
Deliverance

by
Bernadette Thompson Martin
and
Jeannie Faulkner Barber

Published by

Desert Coyote Productions
Longview, Texas

Library of Congress Control Number: 2017933533
EAN-13: 978-0-9986026-0-8
ISBN-10: 0-9986026-0-4

Typeset in 12pt Garamond
Printed in the U.S.A.
First edition 2017

We wish to dedicate this novel to a very special lady, Faye Summers. Her effervescent personality, limitless strength, and loving generous heart were the inspiration for a delightful new character.

Thank you for gifting us with a touch of your special magic.

A super big THANK YOU to the talented creator of our cover and back cover. Mr. Joe Jones of Longview, Texas Your incredible patience, kindness, and blessed friendship are appreciated and valued.

And another heartfelt THANK YOU to Don Martinez of Desert Coyote Publications for taking time out of his demanding schedule and lively home life to bring our novel to fruition.

Contents

Destiny Never Sleeps
Deliverance

Chapter One
The Little Rebel

Three pairs of teeny eyes, overflowing with fright, peered from under the lacey shamrock-green fronds of a giant hare's-foot fern.

Faye wrapped an arm around each of her quivering friends drawing the pair close. Kelsi and Tempi were much younger then she, and until today neither had ventured beyond the forbidden periphery of their small kingdom.

Nine Qergs were now a mere step away. The three young fairies dare not move a muscle lest they be discovered. Brittle leaves crackled under the massive creatures' pressing weight, which triggered a burst of panic in Kelsi. However, before she could let out a scream, Faye clamped a firm hand over the terrified fairy's mouth and shook her head no.

The fiendish soldiers grunted and began to sniff the air. The largest of the group came to an abrupt stop and scanned the area with his dark, lidless, serpentine eyes. "I smell fairy sweat. Check the underbrush." The others nodded and commenced to probe the dense thicket with their unsophisticated wooden spears. A powerful tranquilizing potion dripped like rancid brown slim from the metal tips. One scratch from the scalpel-sharp edge upon any living creature would produce instant paralysis.

Although sinister lances came precariously close at times, the three sprites remained undetected. Faye fought to control her breathing and remain steadfast for the sake

1

of the adolescent companions. They would surely be exposed if she were to falter.

After what seemed an eternity, the search halted. One of the soldiers swaggered up to the apparent leader. "You were mistaken, Gog. What you smell is your own stench," his voice was guttural and ruthless. "I say we move on. We're wasting time." A sudden death hold to the throat produced a startled look on the brute's reptile-like face as he gasped for breath.

"You dare question my word? I should crush your miserable neck like a brittle chicken bone." The insubordinate goblin was brought to his knees as Gog's iron grip tightened. "Unlike you, I have hunted these creatures for many seasons. Their scent is strong—they are near." He hurled the wheezing soldier to the ground and laughed as it gulped air. "Do not challenge me again if you value your life. A second grant of mercy will not be given. Now, continue the search. The full moon will rise two days hence. She must feed in its light, and I for one do not choose to be on the menu." As he took a step back, the heel of his muddy black boot nipped Kelsi's leg. The young fairy winced in pain and let out a shrill scream. "Ah, I told you the little morsels were here." A quick jab of the tainted spear tip had an immediate effect, and the tiny lass crumpled to the ground unconscious. "Bag this one while I gather the others."

The sight of their friend being captured caused the two remaining fairies to bolt from their leafy sanctuary. The twosome would be out of danger if they could scamper across the nearby waterway and enter the outermost border of their domain. Unfortunately, Tempi barely took two steps before she was seized.

2

Faye managed to elude the vicious onslaught for a few minutes, but nimble legs quickly began to tire. As she approached the water's edge, mounting exhaustion caused her to trip over a surface growth of river birch roots and tumble head over heels down the slippery embankment. Before the dazed fairy could recover, a Qerg charged forth and raised his noxious lance. However, the imminent assault was thwarted by the ill-timed intrusion of a large bird of prey. The great Barred owl swooped down at lightning speed, snatched up the defenseless sprite with a taloned foot, and sped off to the top of a nearby tree.

Angered by the provocative abduction, the Qerg slammed his burly weapon to the ground, grunted, and shook a scale-covered fist vindictively at the owl. "You no good clump of feathers…I should kill you."

Gog strutted up to the flustered soldier and gave him a harsh shove. "Forget that stupid bird. Get back to the search. Lord Tahl will not be pleased with a miserable yield of only two fairies."

The demonic militia dutifully continued a meticulous sweep of the area. At last, after a thorough search proved futile, they moved on and disappeared into the darkened forest.

Faye squirmed beneath the forceful appendage that held her body tight against the rough bark. "Ouch, your grasp is too tight. It hurts. Let go, Punk."

The majestic bird gave an airy chirp and immediately released its feisty booty.

"Wow. That was close." The teeny fairy brushed her soiled dress, wiped a sweat-drenched forehead, turned, and embraced the downy chest of her plumed knight. "Thank you, my plucky friend. You saved me from a horrible fate, but our precious Tempi and Kelsi weren't as lucky. We must hurry home and assemble a rescue team." She leaped upon the back of the massive owl and burrowed delicate legs deep into the dense olive-brown feathers for stability. "Okay, I'm all set. Fly fast as you can to Drealon. There's no time to spare. Queen Fallon must be informed of the attack."

Punk's powerful wings lifted them into the air and sped toward the fairy kingdom. Moments later, the distinctive green moss-covered roofs of the fairy settlement came into sight. Unfortunately, the owl's uncharacteristic high-speed approach triggered a community alarm. Panicked guards dashed from their barracks and sprinted to the palace courtyard. Villagers screamed in fear as they darted about to seek protective refuge.

Queen Fallon stood in the arched doorway of the earthen citadel while intense sea-green eyes remained fixed upon the rapidly descending life form. A smile soon replaced a frown on her ivory-skinned face as she recognized the enormous bird and its roguish rider. "Do not fire upon this creature. We are not under attack. It is only our Faye who returns home, although I do not understand, nor appreciate, the unrestrained swiftness of this flight. I shall speak to her posthaste."

Punk's feet had barely touched the ground before Faye leaped from his back and sprinted toward the Queen. "Your majesty, there's been a terrible attack. The Qergs have captured Kelsi and Tempi. We must gather troops and be off to save them. I'm sure they were taken to Odium

Manor. There's little time. A full moon approaches and you know what that means."

"Slow down, child. I find this frantic alarm a bit confusing. Everyone knows Qergs are forbidden to enter our kingdom. How could such a travesty transpire?"

Faye paused, lowered her gaze, and aimlessly kicked the dirt. "Uh, well, we sort of went a little beyond our border, Majesty. You see, while flying around on Punk the other day, I spotted a large growth of mushrooms near the water's edge. It didn't appear dangerous since the cluster was only a few yards outside the perimeter. Kelsi and Tempi learned of my plan and were determined to tag along. I told them no, but the two secretly followed me anyhow. Once they were discovered, I should have been more forceful and demanded they return home. Their capture is entirely my fault, Highness. Please, sound the alarm. There isn't a second to waste. We must quickly gather our militia. My friends will be killed if we don't hurry off to free them."

The Queen's expression darkened, and velvety red lips pursed. "I am disappointed beyond words, young lady. You, more than all others, know Drealon's most solemn rule. No one must *ever* venture beyond its boundaries for *any* reason. Because of such reckless disregarded of our laws, the blood of two innocent young girls will be shed. These blameless children shall soon suffer a death they were never intended to meet."

"No Highness, there's still time to save them. You gather the troops while I go get my weapons. Punk and I will be ready to go in two seconds."

She turned to dart off, but was stopped by a firm grip on the arm. "Stop, Faye. It is too late. Come inside, child. Let us talk."

5

The feisty fairy was perplexed by the Sovereign's compassionless attitude. How could this woman be so callous and allow her young subjects to be horribly slaughtered? "I don't understand, Highness. Cianest will not feed for another two days. We have time. What the bongles is wrong with you?"

"Faye, I will tolerate this insolence no longer. Go inside, young lady. Now!" The monarch irately raised her arm and pointed a finger at the door opening.

Thunderous anger boomed in Queen Fallon's voice which signaled the adolescent sprite to do as she was told without question. Once inside, the two entered a small drawing room and sat opposite each other.

Faye stared at the burnt-orange terra cotta floor and impatiently tapped the hard stone with her foot. She was obviously in a great deal of trouble and awaited the impending reprimand.

Suddenly, a velvety hand reached out and lifted her chin. "What am I to do with such an impetuous daughter? By rights, I should be furious and impose a most severe discipline, but cannot bring myself to do so. Your father's dynamic spirit lives in your heart and lessens my rage."

Faye gazed lovingly into the Queen's gentle face—her voice raspy with distress, "I'm sorry, Mother, and deserve every ounce of punishment you wish to inflict. But please consider my request to go save Kelsi and Tempi. They were completely without fault." Torrents of tears began to flow from vivid hazel eyes.

"It is not I who will impart suitable punishment, Faye. Forevermore, your heart shall endure righteous suffering, tormented by the preventable death of those sweet girls. Nothing more need be said. I suggest you try to rest. This is indeed a harsh lesson to learn, but hopefully it will prevent any such future tragedies from taking place. Now, I must fulfill my duties and offer condolences that shall do little to ease the pain of two families. Tomorrow, you will face them as well. I suggest you mull over the deed and carefully choose the appropriate words." She rose up, bent down, and tenderly kissed a tear-drenched cheek before leaving.

Faye sobbed bitterly into cupped hands. How could she have been so careless and shown such disregard of their laws. For several minutes, bloodshot eyes stared blankly into empty space. "No, it's wrong to simply sit here and let them die. I can't do it. If my mother won't try to rescue them, then I will." The impassioned young woman jumped to her feet, stomped the floor in defiance, and stormed out a side door. However, the swift exit came to an abrupt halt when she spotted Queen Fallon across the courtyard. Waist long, carrot-colored hair fluttered in the brisk afternoon breeze as the beautiful sovereign stood beneath the lofty boughs of a large oak with arms extended upward. "Punk, please come down." The giant owl took wing and gracefully descended to the ground.

Faye inched closer, curious to hear what was being said to her beloved pet.

Drealon's queen reached out and stroked the docile bird's head. "Thank you, noble Punk. Once again, you have braved danger and come to the rescue of my rebellious child." She drew a deep breath and shook her head. "I have tried without success to refine her behavior…to have her act the part of a royal princess. In time, this impetuous young lady is to rule in my stead. The one wish I cherish above all others is for Faye to mature and become a competent sovereign. Until such time arrives, please continue to watch over my daughter as you have so

7

proficiently done all these years. My heart would perish if anything were to happen to her."

Faye had never heard her mother speak in this manner. She leaned back against the hard earthen wall—an anguished mind awash in a sea of emotion. Part of her wished to conform to the system and become the princess so longed for. However, another part was wracked with guilt over the imprisonment and eventual death of her friends. *I'm sorry Mother, but once again, I must defy you. It's my responsibility, as a friend, and a princess, to save Kelsi and Tempi.*

After Queen Fallon walked off, Faye signaled to Punk by snapping her fingers three times—the duo's personal method of communication. Without hesitation, he flew to her side. She stroked the brown-striped cream chest and gazed into large, round brown eyes as she spoke, "I must travel to Odium Manor, Punk. The journey's going to be a risky undertaking, and I can't in good faith demand you take me there. It's a choice you have to make, my gallant champion…one from which we may not return."

The great owl lowered his head and nipped her hand gently with his golden yellow beak.

"We'll need every ounce of skill and courage we can rally, Punk, but I feel more secure knowing you'll be with me." Her tiny hand swept across a rather soiled dress. "Bongles, sure can't go like this….gotta find something more appropriate to wear. Fly to the edge of the Great Blue Meadow. I'll join you there soon as possible. Your excellent night vision might just be the one advantage we so desperately need to pull this off. Now, hurry away before we're seen." Faye watched in admiration as silent wings lifted the ghost-faced bird into the air and propelled him out of sight in sheer seconds.

8

She raced back to the palace and hurried to her bedroom. A quick flip through a mass of garments revealed all the wrong attire necessary for the endeavor. "This is ridiculous. I can't wear a stupid dress. I have to get my hands on a set of trousers. Hmm, I wonder…"

Convinced her mother would not return soon, she inconspicuously dashed to the monarch's private sanctuary. The young fairy looked around the spacious chamber and smiled. Queen Fallon, although regal and elegant, was a rather humble being. Unpretentious furnishings and fixtures were a testament to her modest principles. Scattered about the sunlit dwelling were several paintings of Faye's deceased father. The sight of the handsome fairy momentarily inundated her mind with a multitude of treasured memories. *I miss you so much, Poppa and know you would approve of what I'm about to do. I'll try to make you proud.* Hazel eyes scanned the room and soon spotted a large ornate wooden chest somewhat concealed under a skillfully embroidered linen throw. She pulled off the decorative covering, opened the weighty lid, and began to rummage through her father's aged hodgepodge of trousers and tunics. Most were too large, but at last, she found a deep burgundy set of leggings and a hunter-green tunic that seemed ideal. A bit more digging unearthed a pair of black leather boots, although some added stuffing would be needed to accommodate her petite feet.

Faye refolded all the strewn about garments, placed them back in the chest, and carefully positioned the loomed cover so nothing appeared disturbed. She scampered back to her quarters and dressed. Still, one unpleasant chore remained. Her silken, waist long, ash-brown tresses had to be cut short. Nothing could be left to hinder the rescue. Even a long braid might be grasped or entangled. The willowy girl stood before a mirror with scissors in hand. The sight of the eye-catching locks caused a moment of hesitation, but thoughts of Kelsi and Tempi alone in a dank, sordid dungeon awaiting death vanquished all reluctance. She grabbed a long thick strand and cut. Little by little, the striking mane dropped to the floor until only wisps of a pixie-like shag remained. "Hey, this doesn't look so bad after all. Splozits, I might even get to like it. Okay, time to get this body moving." The little fairy drew a deep breath, grabbed her bow and leather quiver, and took one last glance around before leaving.

It didn't take long to reach the specified location. The sight of the dense blue-carpeted meadow drew a gasp. "Golly, I'd almost forgotten how beautiful this was." The entire meadow was copiously carpeted with vibrant bluebonnets as far as the eye could see.

A loud hoot shattered the temporary daydream. "Hey Punk, fly on down and get me. I think we better lay low 'til dark." The obedient Barred owl swooped down, retrieved his small charge, and returned to an area of protective shelter deep within the dense green boughs.

Faye sat on a hefty limb, feet dangling aimlessly in the air, and watched as the sun disappeared on the horizon. "I'm really scared, Punk, but no one else is going to even so much as try to rescue our friends. It's all up to us." A trembling finger pointed across the meadow. "Over that distant hill is the outer boundary of Mantalac. I've heard foreboding tales of this kingdom. It's a horrible place…repellent and cheerless." The brave young warrior swallowed hard. "I'm not gonna give in to this fear." She rose up and climbed aboard her winged companion. "We better stay close to the tree tops. It may help veil our arrival. Okay Punk, what say we go save our friends?"

10

The great owl took to the air and headed in the direction of the evil kingdom. As they traveled along, the landscape began to transform. Vibrant green trees soon turned into a forest of macabre formations—barren and sinister in appearance. The lush valley meadow appeared desolate and uninhabited. Shadowed moonbeams spread a wisp of muted light across a frightening and inhospitable terrain.

Faye's eyes widened as they flew along. "Oh Punk, it's even worse than imagined. This land is dark as a dead man's dreams." The pair continued on until the black outline of the Manor came into sight. "I know you have to be tired after our long flight. Try to find a secluded nook that might mask us from fiendish eyes. We both should rest a bit. Think we're going to need every ounce of strength we can muster."

Punk flew to a partially hollowed tree trunk and quickly entered, providing a temporary haven. Faye stood at the entrance and looked out, her brow furrowed with worry. "The Manor is way larger than I thought it would be. How on earth will we ever find our friends?"

Before another word could be uttered, the great owl pushed her aside and took flight. She wanted to call out to him, but knew it would be unwise. Minutes felt like hours and fears began to mount. At last, Punk's dark silhouette appeared, and a breath of relief was drawn. "Where the podens have you been? I've worried ten years off my life." The owl nudged her and fluttered his wings in an excited manner. "What is it? What are you trying to tell me? Have you found Tempi and Kelsi?" The mention of their names caused an even greater flurry. "Splozits! What say you and I go snatch them out of that grubby fortress?" She leaped on board, and they rocketed into the murky night sky.

11

Soundless wings soared over the dank kingdom and circled the sinister walls of the palace. Soon, he came to rest on the narrow ledge of an iron-bared window. Strong talons grasped the slick overhang while the great bird struggled to maintain balance.

The little fairy's foot slipped on the slimy outcrop as she climbed off, and had it not been for the quick block of a well-placed extended wing, she would have tumbled to her death. "Whew, that scared the daylights out of me. Thanks, Punk." A glance through the rusty bars brought a groan. The mud-encrusted stone floor was at least ten feet down. How would she get inside? "Drat. Its times like this I wish I was older and had my wings. Jinglerajins, it's too far to jump, and I didn't think to bring a darn rope. Now, what in dinglesfreed am I gonna do?" She wrapped an arm around one of the bars for stability, drew a deep breath of disgust, and looked out into the night. "Hold on! I remember seeing a mass of thick vines twirled around the trunk of that hollowed tree. I'm sure they would work. Hurry back, Punk. Gather the longest length of grassy cord you can find."

The giant Barred owl released his grip and vanished into the midnight sky. Within moments, he returned—a bundle of cable-like vines clutched gently in his beak.

Faye secured one end to a bar then tossed the balance of the makeshift ladder inside. She tested the strength and felt it would suffice. "Well, it's not perfect, but will have to do." Hands trembled as she took hold and lowered herself down.

The damp, mold-covered floor was slippery, and the air reeked with the stench of rotting flesh. On both sides of the narrow corridor were barred wooden doors, the obvious entrances to several cells.

In the dim light, eyes squinted as she searched for any sign of life. No guards were visible and everything appeared safe to proceed. Being only a foot tall, there was no way to check inside the chambers from the top. However, a wide gap at the bottom proved effective. The bold fairy got down on hands and knees and began to peer under each door as she crawled along.

The first two cubicles on the right wall were empty, but she could see full-size feet move about in the next. Being too large for those of her companions, she moved on. There was a strange sound coming from first cell on the left wall, and a glance inside delivered a nauseous jolt to her stomach. Although the view was significantly limited, it revealed scale covered cloven hind hooves, and clawed feline forelegs as it slowly paced back and forth. This was the obvious lair of the legendary monster, Cianest.

As she moved toward the next compartment, a noise caused her to spin around. From out of the shadows sauntered a sleek-coated black cat. "Holy bongles, you scared the bejeepers out of me, kitty." Unsure of the creature's true intentions, Faye edged backwards. It was then something weird and wonderful happened. The cat sat down—its brilliant dark violet eyes fixed intently on the little fairy. Suddenly, Faye began to sense an unexplained connection to the striking feline. It was as though they knew each other somehow. She reached out and stroked the side of the animal's face, a gesture that caused it to purr. "Hey, seems you approve of my touch. Are you captive as well?" It gave off a semi-muted meow and rubbed her hand. "Well, we'll just have to rescue you too. I'm not sure if you can climb that vine over there, but it's the best I can offer."

13

Faye and her newfound friend then continued the hunt. At last, she peered in a cell and viewed two small bodies huddled together in a distant corner. "Psst, Tempi, Kelsi, it's me, Faye."

The two young fairies leaped up and ran to the door. "Faye, we have to get out of here. They will put us in with Cianest tomorrow. We'll be killed. Please, save us." They began to weep profusely and rather loudly.

"Shush, if you two don't be quiet we will all become dinner. Now, zip it. I need to get something to lift the lock lever. Just stay still and be quiet."

A quick search provided the perfect tool—the long wooden handle of a broom. It took a bit of strength and effort, but at last, the latch gave way, and the door cracked open. The two young sprites rushed out and into the welcome arms of their liberator.

Suddenly, a shrill, hideous cry from Cianest's cell pierced the silence. Faye spun around…her eyes teemed with fear. This surely would alarm the guards.

Almost immediately, the terrifying sound of heavy footsteps beyond the dungeon door was heard.

Faye grabbed each youngster by the arm and raced toward the improvised ladder. Tempi stopped at the base and began to cry. "I can't climb that. I don't know how."

"You will climb it, Tempi, and you as well, Kelsi, or we'll all become a meal for that beast. Now, get your behinds moving." They began to worm their way up the vine, and had nearly reached the window, when the beefy chamber door was violently flung open. Four Qergs rushed in and instantly caught site of the escapees.

As they neared the summit, Kelsi's tan suede boot slipped on a sap-coated leaf, and she tumbled downward, crashing into the others below her. The three sprites plummeted to the floor, temporary dazed by the unanticipated tragedy.

With spears raised, the Qergs charged.

Faye leaped to her feet and drew an arrow. It struck the first monster in the knee, but the miniature projectile had no effect on the massive brute. She fired once more, but the demons progressed and were only a few feet away.

The black cat arched his fur bristled back and hissed as it attempted to block the path of the lead beast.

Eyes intent on the fairy, the Qerg stumbled. "Blasted pest, get out of my way." He gave the daring animal a swift kick, propelling its small body into the stony wall. "If you weren't the Queen's pet, I'd kill you. Now, scat." Another vigorous kick was administered, which sent the feline running down the hall and out of sight.

The eldest fairy let out a whoop—startled by a sudden waft of wind. Her beloved pet owl had managed to wiggle through the bars and come to their rescue. Without a second of delay, the trio hopped on Punk's back. Faye closed her eyes and prayed he'd have the strength to carry all three away from danger.

With one mighty thrust, the noble bird lifted its massive body from the floor and sped to the window. As he reached the ledge, Faye directed the girls to dismount and go through the iron barrier. Punk struggled a bit, but at last managed to escape.

Once all were outside, the fairies again mounted, and the foursome headed toward Drealon and safety.

As the great owl circled above the enchanted compound, villagers screamed and pointed upward. Faye giggled at the antics, but then thought of her mother and the impending punishment. "Boy, am I ever in trouble?"

15

Tempi and Kelsi spotted their parents and started to yell and wave. "Momma, Poppi, we're home. Faye saved us." Punk gently landed, and the three riders leaped off. The two young ones scurried to their overjoyed mother and father who hugged and kissed them with passionate jubilation.

Faye stood by the great owl, her hand stroking his soft feathers. She noticed the crowd begin to part and knew the Queen was approaching. "Uh oh, I'm sure in for it now, Punk. You better get your feathered butt out of here before the yelling starts."

"Not so fast, " demanded Queen Fallon as she neared, "Neither of you are to move so much as one muscle. I have a few choice words to say."

Faye lowered her eyes and prepared for the lashing of a lifetime. She knew the undertaking was wrong, but could not allow Tempi and Kelsi to be slaughtered. Whatever punishment was issued, it would be gladly endured. The little sprite looked up, forehead wrinkled in puzzlement. No trace of anger showed on the sovereign's smiling face. "I'm sorry, Mother. It was wrong to disobey you, but I had no choice. Any reprimand could not compare to knowing those two little girls perished because of my foolishness."

The Queen rushed to her daughter and embraced a trembling body. "You are safe, my sweet daughter, as are your friends. For this, I am eternally grateful. What you did was indeed foolish, but also very brave. I cannot enact punishment for doing as your heart dictated. However, be warned. Never pull an imprudent stunt like this again. Do I make myself clear?"

Faye smiled and nodded, but knew, should an occasion arise where she was needed, the vow would be broken. Suddenly, she winced and pulled away from her mother. A

16

shooting pain tore through her back shoulders and ran down the length of her spine. "What's happening?"

Queen Fallon began to laugh, as did many of the villagers. "The transitory sting is brief. Now, feel the luster of your new wings, sweet child of mine."

A quick reach back brought an exclamation of disbelief. "Splozits, how on earth did this happen? I'm not old enough yet."

"That is true, but wings are not always granted to those of a particular age. They also are awarded for bravery and wisdom. You, dear daughter, have proven to contain both. Come, we have much to discuss." She placed an arm around her offspring's waist, and the two began to walk off.

"Oh my stars," the Queen exclaimed as she spun around. "In all the excitement, I have inadvertently ignored an enormously valued rescuer." The charismatic sovereign walked over and placed a hand on the head of the great owl. "Dear noble Punk, you are hereby granted the royal title of Sir Punk, our kingdom's most valiant knight."

The elegant bird puffed out his chest and gave off a rousing hoot.

Faye giggled and clapped, causing the entire village to follow her lead as the loyal guardian bowed…then took wing.

The sound of the large iron door slamming against the dungeon wall thundered throughout the Manor corridors as a furious Lord Tahl stormed in. He rushed up to the Qergs, his face red with rage. "What useless, incompetent dregs. How could the lot of you be outfoxed by three insignificant, amateurish fairies?" His livid gaze turned to

Gog. "Take your pick of these no account pieces of garbage and put them in with Cianest. She takes pleasure playing with her food before devouring it."

Although the chosen Qergs violently resisted, each was eventually hurled into the Lamiae's chamber.

Irritated and angry, Lord Tahl forcefully kicked a nearby wooden bucket and jettisoned the container against a distant wall. The crack of splintering timber did little to mask the bloodcurdling screams. "Enjoy the meal, angel," he scoffed, then arrogantly spit on the floor and walked off.

Chapter Two
Family Lies

Queen Adera drew a deep breath before turning the engraved golden knob to her chambers. The ultra feminine and spacious quarters, once solitarily occupied, would soon be shared with a soon to be husband. She felt a gender-neutral atmosphere would be more pleasing to both and had ordered a full-scale renovation.

Turquoise eyes glistened with satisfaction as they surveyed the room's elegant transformation. An ornate floral inlay of red, gold, and green intricately cut and polished stones framed the gleaming ivory marble floor, which continued throughout the royal abode. A fresh coat of delicate pale-coral paint breathed new life into once drab walls. Whisper peach sheer draperies embellished the study's palatial window, giving the room a warm and airy glow. Most of the elegant cherry wood furnishings remained, as did many colorful scenic tapestries. A large, hand loomed area rug of emerald green graced the floor's center, and all overstuffed chairs had been reupholstered in rich cream, dark peach, and hunter green stripped silk.

However, the most drastic alteration took place in the adjacent bedroom. From the center of a magnificent ceiling medallion, framed with diverse layers of delicately engraved ivory crown molding and trim, hung an enormous crystal chandelier. Fine silk draperies and a thick tufted spread matched the pale champagne hued walls. The mahogany furnishings had all been replaced with idyllic vanilla shaded pieces. Situated opposite each other were

19

two inviting peach sofas, strategically placed in front of the opulent black marble fireplace. Centered between them was a luxuriant floral designed carpet in shades of terra cotta, ivory, and green. The most outstanding feature, however, was the glorious box shaped four-poster bed cloaked with a striking silk canopy. Artfully gathered, and secured to each elaborate post with a golden sash, were rich champagne colored embroidered silk draperies. Matching ivory upholstered chairs, a night table, and a lush white sheepskin rug were placed on each side of the ostentatious bed. Scattered about the room were several ebony vases filled with brilliant coral, yellow, and blue flowers.

The sight of the romantic new décor took her breath away. "Ooh, everything is more stunning than envisioned. The enchanting ambiance truly captures our pure and gentle love. I hope he will find it pleasing."

"As long as you are within the walls, I'll find it more than pleasing, my beautiful bride-to-be." Randy wrapped both arms around his lady, who whirled around to face him.

Cheeks flushed as she gazed into electric blue eyes. "You were not supposed to view the room until our wedding night. Now, my surprise has been ruined. Whatever am I to do with you?"

He laughed and tightened his embrace. "Sweetheart, I seriously doubt an ounce of interest will be on the room's décor. Afraid these peepers are gonna be focused on a much more entrancing subject…you."

She gave him a playful kiss on the cheek and wiggled from his affectionate hold. Suddenly, her sparkling expression grew solemn.

"Uh oh, it's obvious something's troubling that pretty head of yours. Tell me what's wrong, sweetheart." Randy

20

took a porcelain-skinned hand in his and led her to one of the sofas.

"I have denied a vital truth far too long. It must now be told, yet the words elude me."

The handsome groom to be drew a deep breath and smiled. "Somehow, I feel it involves Kat, doesn't it?"

"Yes, but how did you know? I have thoroughly concealed this revelation. There are only a select few aware of the fact, but none who would utter a word unbeknownst to me."

"Guess you could say I've more or less sensed it my entire life, Adera. You see, there's always been a strange veil of mystery surrounding Kat…something that can't quite be explained…like the color of her eyes for example. Both Madeleine and Patrick had blue eyes, yet Kat's are golden yellow. Genetically it's almost impossible, unless brought about some rare mutation." He drew a breath. "Wanna fill me in on the problem? Maybe I can help fix it. After all, two heads are better than one. At least getting it out in the open might ease your mind a bit."

Adera nodded and began to tell the implausible story in great detail. Every so often, she would pause to allow Randy time for the incredible disclosure to sink in.

"Whew, always said you know how to drop a bomb, sweetcakes, and can see why you've been somewhat hesitant. Ironically, it sure as shoot clarifies a boat load of things." Randy scratched his head. "Look, I've known Kat a long time and more or less understand her. I'd say the best approach is a direct one. Just spit it out and tell her what you've told me. Let the blocks fall where they may. To be perfectly honest, I think she's gonna feel a sense of relief once the shock wears off. However, I sure as the dickens hope you have some evidence to back all this up, because I'll bet your buttons she's *not* gonna simply accept your word as pure truth."

"I figured as much and possess more than enough substantial proof which *should* erase any doubts. Perhaps you are right. The time has arrived to face my fears and deal with the task at hand. May I ask you to please find Kat and have her come to my, uh, *our* study?"

Randy nodded. "Sure 'nuff, my lady. Did my dumbo ears hear you right? It's *our* study?" He rolled his eyes and grinned. "Have to admit I plum like the sound of that." He chuckled, rose up, and started to leave, but stopped at the door. "Sweetheart, mind if I pull Tom aside and tell him? I'm sure when he finds out his mouth is gonna flop like a barn door in a windstorm. Plus, kinda think she'll need his grit to pull her through this."

"I agree. As you are to me, he is her strength." Once Randy left, Adera began to wring sweat infused hands as she paced back and forth across the room. *Please, guide my words Father.* A rap at the door brought all thoughts to an abrupt halt.

"Holy smokes Adera, this joint is absolutely gorgeous. I almost can't believe my eyes. Talk about a wow factor. Jiminy Crickets. Randy better dang well appreciate a wife with such incredible good taste." Kat rushed through the suite like an animated hurricane. "Oh my stars, the bedroom is beyond imagination. Maybe this sounds weird, but it somehow kinda looks like you and Randy." She giggled and faced Adera. "So, what's up?"

The Queen walked to one of the sofas and motioned for Kat to sit on the other. "I have much to tell you and regret it has taken so long. There is no simple way to say this, so I shall be blunt. Please, forgive my tardiness." She hesitated and drew a deep breath before continuing. "Kat, you are my—sister."

The bubbly country girl gave a quirky look and snickered. "Of course we are. I've always felt like a sister to you and hoped the feeling was mutual. Other than Tom, there's no one I love more."

Turquoise eyes briefly lowered. "You misunderstand, Kat. We are *actually* blood sisters. Our mothers were not the same, but my father is *your* father. You were born in Bowlandria."

At first, Kat sat motionless and silent, but then leaped to her feet. "What kind of sick joke are you playing, Adera? My father was a man named Patrick, not some alien godlike creature. I don't think this is one bit funny."

"Please Kat, sit down. Allow me to explain."

"No blasted way. I'm not about to stay here and listen to some ridiculous gibberish. Why are you being so mean, especially now when the wedding will be held in a couple days? If you don't want me in it then just say so, but don't feed me some cock and bull story about being blood relatives."

The situation was rapidly deteriorating into a nightmarish event. Both girls were now in tears and visibly distressed. "Kat, I beseech a moment to offer proof. Once it is shown, you *will* believe. We have been close for so long. I beg you trust me once more."

Although angry, Kat eased back down. "I doubt anything you can provide will change my mind, but give it your best shot. I'm game."

The Queen walked to a nearby corner and retrieved a strange rectangular object tucked in behind a large dressing screen. Once placed on the sofa, the covering was pulled, revealing an ancient painting. "Behold the likeness of Zuegas, our father."

Kat stared open mouthed at the portrait as tears tumbled down a taut face. She moved closer, and then glanced at Adera. "W-we have the same eyes. But, how's that possible? I don't understand. There's no memory of him or even of Bowlandria until I came here. My mother was married to Patrick. *He* has to be my father, not some stranger." She cupped her head in both hands and began to sob. "No, it can't be true, it can't be."

Unable to control rising emotions a second more, Adera rushed to her sister, and the two embraced, weeping profusely. "I wish there was an easier way to make known this fact, sweet girl. So often I desired to tell you, but the words would not flow. Please, do not close your heart to me. I love you so much. When we learned of your return, my soul leaped with joy." A glance at the empty table nearby offered a hint of relief. "Perhaps a bit of wine might help sooth our rattled nerves?"

In the blink of an eye, a chilled crystal decanter of a rich full-bodied white wine and two pewter goblets appeared on the glass table in front of them, the obvious handiwork of a talented yet invisible Brownie. Neither sister was exactly delicate as they downed the first beaker.

"Well, that kinda helped take the edge off," Kat declared as she leaned back. "But to say I'm shocked is bit of an understatement. As usual, my big mouth spurted out a few things it shouldn't have. I'm sorry and didn't mean to lash out in anger like I did, but this really rattled my brain." Trembling fingers rubbed a creased brow as though trying to wipe away the confusion. "Have to admit, I've felt an unexplainable close bond toward you from day one—sorta noticed it when we first went to Durmeleigh. Without you near, I was lost and uncomfortable." She reached over, poured each of them a second glass of wine, sighed, and took another hefty swig. "Okay, think I'm ready to hear more. For starters, I'd like to know just how on earth Zuegas became my father. I mean, he was here, and Mom was home in South Carolina. Or was someone else my real mother?"

"No, Madeleine was indeed your mother. Sit beside me while I explain the story from the very beginning. It is rather complex and a tad lengthy, so please be patient." Kat nodded, picked up her goblet, took a sip, and eased back into the thick tufted cushion.

"My mother, Adeanra, was a beautiful and gentle woman. Her portrait hangs next to the empty space in the hallway. She was tall, slender, with waist long platinum blonde hair. You have Father's golden eyes, while Mother and I share the same hue. She possessed many extraordinary talents including a weird and wonderful mental connection with animals. Pegasus was her most valued treasure. The pair soared among the clouds nearly every day. I would often ride along, but one afternoon I decided to remain behind and enjoy a cherished stroll with friends."

The Queen paused and eyes grew watery.

Kat moved closer and covered a trembling hand with her own. "This is obviously bringing back some pretty painful memories. Maybe we best forget it for now. You can fill me in a little here and there some other time."

Adera smiled and squeezed Kat's hand. "No, the truth must be told. My heart will be lightened once the secreted family lie is divulged."

She took a small sip of wine and proceeded. "On that fateful day, Mother failed to return as darkness began to

25

set in. Father sensed something was amiss and grew tense. He organized a group of friends to help scour the land in search of her. The following morning, they found Pegasus standing over Mother's broken body...the obvious victim of a fall. She was an accomplished rider and always made sure the safety braid was secured. Upon further examination, it appeared shredded as though chewed, and so Pegasus fell to blame. Father was so grief-stricken he wanted to destroy the great stallion, but when he saw the sadness in its eyes, he did not. I, on the other hand, felt bitter and no longer would go near the creature or even ride a regular horse."

"Holy crickets," Kat exclaimed. "The first time we all went on a ride, you mentioned the fact you hadn't sat a horse in many years. So, that's the reason. Now, things are starting to make a little sense. I ride Junar all the time and never saw one of the flying horses chew its braid. Something smells rotten there."

"I agree, Kat. We never understood how the mishap transpired and have often wondered if it was *indeed* an accident.

After Mother's death, Father grew increasingly distressed. He found solace traveling to the other region to mingle with humans. During one of these ventures, he happened upon an auburn haired beauty—Madeleine.

In time, the two fell in love, and she was brought into our world. A year later, the Castle was blessed with the arrival of a sweet baby girl named Kathleen. The following five years were perhaps the happiest we have known, until now. Laughter infested the halls from end to end."

"One afternoon, Father presented you a precious gift...McLachen. At the time, he was only a wee colt, but able to speak. Within days, the two of you became inseparable. Being a Bayard, he grew at an astonishing pace. You, my dear sister, took to riding as a duck would take to water."

Kat was now openmouthed, obviously flabbergasted by the revelations. "He was *my* horse? No wonder we were drawn to each other when I entered."

Adera smiled. "He was so excited to see you come home. When you left, poor McLachen mourned and eventually retreated into the great forest. It was a rare occasion when we would have the pleasure of his company, but even then, the jovial spirit was absent."

A frown crinkled Kat's brow. "I don't understand. Why was I sent back? Apparently, things were pretty darn good here. Did Mom or I do something wrong?"

"No, there was no wrongdoing. For reasons unknown, Madeleine grew homesick. She longed for her former land and family. Being a kind and humble woman, the intense sadness was concealed from Zuegas for quite some time. One day, he found her sitting alone in the garden, weeping. Upon questioning, the torment was uncloaked. Father adored this vibrant woman with a passion few ever obtain. He could not bear to see his beloved suffer. With a heavy heart, Father set arrangements in motion for her return and yours as well. Several trips were made to your world until a man was found who would cherish Madeleine until her death and care for you as his very own. Although Patrick was amply rewarded, his heart was pure and the love he held most sincere."

"Zuegas did all that for Mom and me? Wow. What an unselfish and gallant gesture. Not many would venture to insure someone else's happiness at the sacrifice of their own. Sure wish I could remember him."

"Your immature mind was thoroughly cleansed so no trace of our world would linger and obstruct this new life. At the request of your mother, she wished to retain the memory of Zuegas and Bowlandria—a wish affectionately fulfilled. Sadness was felt by all when the two of you departed. I cried for many days until no further tears would fall."

The two siblings were emotional and hugged. Kat reached over and poured another glass of wine. "Here, think we both need a bit more of this dang brew." Adera nodded as she took the goblet from Kat's shaky hand. "I never suspected a thing. Patrick was as close to me any father could be, and Mom never uttered a word. There *was* something, however, that always felt weird. I often sat on the pasture gate and talked up a storm to my horse, Red. Although I knew it was impossible, I actually expected him to talk back. Then, there were times I would dream of soaring high above on a magnificent winged horse. Did we ever go up on one?"

"No, but you did witness them in the air and relentlessly pleaded for a ride."

Kat chuckled and heaved a sigh. "Whew. Certainly is mindboggling, but also pretty darn romantic. What happened to Zuegas, I mean, Father."

Adera's eyes lowered and sadness draped her face. "He tried to remain strong, but his heart was broken and could no longer bear the pain of losing my mother, your mother, and you. Our race has the ability to determine their passing at will. When the time is chosen, they age until their bodies wither and fade. Such is the fate of our father. Prior to his departure, I was selected to reign in his stead. Father's bequeath was honored by all but one—his sister, Odiene. She believed the throne should be bestowed on her and eventually passed on to her son, Tahl. Several days later, Cook witnessed Odiene add a liquid to my morning juice. It was discovered to be a powerful poison. Incensed, Zuegas exiled my aunt and cousin to a distant land called Mantalac, where both currently reside. Over the years, the pair studied dark magic. Coupled with our mental and technically advanced capabilities, they have become immoral and malicious. Protocol requires all family be invited to the wedding. I pray these relatives will not accept, but do not believe my wishes shall be granted. It was imperative I reveal the truth at this time, for they would take exceptional pleasure in heartlessly imparting this guarded account."

"Hah, just let me at 'em." Kat slammed a fist into her open palm. "After tangling with a beast like Ios, I'll make mincemeat of those two."

Adera clutched Kat's hands. "No! You must not underestimate this duo. Although many of our kind remain, none are more powerful than Odiene and Tahl. I alone possess dominance over them. She is quite beautiful and he exceedingly handsome, but their appearance is deceptive. Be wary of our aunt and her vicious son."

Kat nodded and sat quiet for a moment. "Adera, so far I understand what you've told me, with one exception. What the dickens are we?"

The comment brought a wholehearted laugh from the Queen. "Oh Kat, I so love your robust personality. Our ancestors come from a planet called Sriebonia. It resides in a remote galaxy, unknown even to this day by your most advanced astronomers. It is similar to earth in many ways, but our superior civilization possesses many unique abilities, one of which is mass mind control. Their illusionary tricks are how they survived in your world and became known as gods. At times, one might appear to a human, or group of humans, as half beast and half man or appear as a monster of some sort. Many even took pleasure in performing such foolishness."

"So, something like a Minotaur or Centaur was not a real creature, but was in fact a hallucination?"

"For the most part, that is so, Kat. The ancients have never been nor claimed to be gods. They are merely travelers—scientists from another world. We are slightly different in appearance and incredibly stronger of will. I suppose you could say we are essentially humans with extraordinary enhancements. As these voyagers traversed throughout the universe, they would frequently allow intelligent and unique alien beings to join the expedition. On occasion, they would collect specimens, such as the flying horses or dragons. Many unearthly life forms and creatures were set loose upon the land after the intergalactic craft crashed. Once the Realm was created, the surviving animals were brought here. Other extraterrestrials, such as Merlin and the Elves, escaped persecution and voluntarily sought sanctuary."

A strange queried expression overtook Kat's face. "If I'm half alien, do I possess some sort of power? I've never realized any."

"There is little doubt a great power lies within you, but remains dormant for its need has yet to surface. Even my full potential has not yet come to light, so do not add a wrinkle to that pretty brow, my sister." She pulled Kat close and nearly squeezed the wind out of the confused girl.

Kat walked to one of the two large windows and fondled the soft silken drapery. "I'm not super upset, Adera, but would you mind if I go for a little stroll. I really need some time alone to sort things out in my wooden noggin. Things are swimming around like a cluster of tadpoles in a mud puddle."

Adera nodded and wrapped an arm lovingly around Kat as they walked together to the door.

The cool outside air felt uplifting as Kat meandered through the blossoming garden maze and headed toward the saltwater lagoon where the three mermaid sisters had taken refuge during the war.

A full-length white dress fluttered like bounteous yards of liquid cotton as she strolled along. Now and then, a puff of air would playfully flick her long raven-black hair. Near the water's edge, she spotted a gargantuan oak tree swathed in delicate winding ivy vines. The verdant turf softly embraced her body as she unceremoniously plopped down beneath the tree's massive boughs. With one arm propped upon an upright knee, she cradled her chin in hand and stared into emptiness. The rhythmic babble of flowing water allowed a troubled mind to plummet deep in thought.

"Mind if I join you?"

The unexpected sound of her husband's voice was startling and quickly ended the daydream. "Blast it, Tom. You scared the living daylights out of me. What do you want? Can't you see I wanna be alone right now?" A bit of blush rose in her face as she realized the unkindness in her voice. But his, or anyone else's company was not wanted at the moment.

He stood over her with hands on hips. "Feeling a bit sorry for yourself, Missy? Well, it's time to get over it. Randy filled me in on the whole story. I understand it's shocking to find out your life wasn't what you believed it to be all these years, but why not try to think of it as an incredible gift of luck. Most of us only get one father. You, on the other hand, managed to get two and one was a King."

She stood and faced him, mouth pursed. "Yeah, well at least your father was human. Just leave me alone, Tom. I need time to think."

"Listen to me, sweetcakes, I know it's a bit upsetting, but just because Patrick was not your blood father didn't make him any less a parent. His heart and soul adored you. No man could have loved a child more." Tom took hold of her arm, but she immediately jerked free of his grip. "Okay, Kat. You better dang well snap out of this mood right now or I'll cool that hot temper of yours off in the lagoon."

She glared at him and barked a reply, "You wouldn't dare!"

He threw his head back and gave a robust laugh. "Oh? Think again, precious." Before she could get away, he scooped her up and dangled her squirming body over the crystalline, tepid water.

"Put me down, Tom. This isn't funny. I'm not kidding. I demand to be put down this very instant."

Tom began to chuckle. "Do you *really* want me to put you down?"

Kat snorted in anger. "Yes. I've had enough of this blasted nonsense. I said put me down and I dang well mean it, Tom. Now put me the blazes down!"

"Okay, Princess. Your wish is my command. Down you go."

Amber eyes widened. "No-no-no….don't do it." Her exclamation preceded a high-pitched shriek followed by a thunderous 'kersplash'.

Moments later, a thoroughly drenched body surfaced, spluttering and slapping at the water's surface as though the clear liquid had committed the act. "You big dumb jerk. You think you're so smart," Kat bellowed and again slapped the rippled surface. "Well, at least be somewhat of a gentleman and help me out. My stupid dress soaked up this water like a day old sponge and is kinda weighing me down."

Tom stepped into the lagoon and offered a hand, only to yell out as his impish lady's stalwart grip yanked him into the pond beside her. Soon, the pair began to splash each other, and Kat's cheerless mood was replaced with playful laughter.

Randy and Adera, who were enjoying a leisurely stroll, heard the commotion and sprinted to the lagoon just in time to see Tom tumble head first into the salty shallows.

"Oh my stars," the Queen exclaimed as she caught sight of the frolicking couple. "What on earth and moon is going on here?"

"Hey Tom, need some help with that wildcat?" Randy was laughing so hard he began to choke. "You know, our joint does have bathtubs. Seen any water snakes, kiddo?"

Kat spun around and began a swift exit toward the shore.

At first, the dignified Queen joined in the madcap merriment and giggled like a young schoolgirl. Suddenly, she grew morbidly silent. Her face became pale and solemn, her brow furrowed.

"What is it, sweetheart? You look like you've seen a ghost." Randy grasped a quaking hand.

"It is Kat. An ill-omened aura surrounds her." Adera turned away.

Randy did not wish to alarm his two friends, so bid them a good afternoon and ushered the eye-catching sovereign into a nearby garden. "Okay, we're out of earshot now. Spill it. You saw something pretty bad to cause such distress. Was it death?"

For several minutes, Adera remained silent. "No Randy, I did not perceive loss of life. My vision was of something far worse—a torment that will make the recipient *desire* death."

At first, Randy was slightly rattled by the puzzling statement, but then began to chuckle. "Hey, you're probably just having a clear-cut case of nuptial jitters. I'm sure nothing bad is gonna happen to our gal. For whatever reason, all brides seem to go a little nutty as their wedding day approaches. Actually, it should be the *guys* who get the jitters." He snickered and planted a gentle peck on the cheek. "What say we get you out of the doldrums and go visit Cook? I'm a little hungry."

The Queen nodded and gave a feeble smile.

As the two lovers walked toward the Castle, Randy cast a quick glance back at his companions and felt an unexpected prickle of fear suddenly radiate down his spine.

Chapter Three
Celebration of Love

The first rays of sunlight revealed a kingdom bustling with energetic activity. A royal celebration, the likes never before seen, would begin at dusk. Today, Randy and Queen Adera would marry. Volunteers from far and wide had come to provide much needed and welcomed assistance in this monumental endeavor.

Preparation for the night's festivity was underway, and as expected, the kitchen was swarming with the clatter of pots and pans. Cook directed her staff like a well-seasoned General, barking orders right and left. The menu was an exceptionally ambitious one and presented an arduous challenge to the skilled Irish chef.

"Madam Cook, we have finished the cake." Two tall Elvin ladies, their faces smudged with icing, stood alongside the creative dessert.

A hush fell over the massive chamber as Margaret Mary walked to the table. "Oh, tis a grand thing you've made me' darlin's—a grand thing indeed. Tis truly the master of cakes, it is." Eyes filled with emotion as she scanned the baked masterpiece.

The elegant creation was immense….standing a good five feet tall. Each of the three smooth ivory frosted tiers was the size of a four-layer cake. A confectionary cluster of life-size peach roses and green leaves, garlanded by a sugary decorative ribbon, adorned each tier. The bottom layer hosted three dozen roses, the next layer held two dozen, and the top layer one dozen. However, the crowning glory to this stunning dessert was its topper. A pastry replica of the fairy tale Castle, complete with its towering spires, had been artfully sculpted and frosted. The magnificent pastry rested upon an ivory silk tablecloth, bedecked with strands of green ivy and real peach-hued roses.

"The wee pair of ya have created a cake the likes to never be seen again. I swear ya've put the heart crossways in me, and for that I'm thankin' ya." Cook took a crisp white linen hankie from her apron pocket and unceremoniously wiped a moist nose. "Enough of this lollygaggin' for now, it's time to be gettin' back to the task at hand. We've a great deal ta do, so no more ridin' out in me kitchen today, lassies. After all our hard labors, I'm thinkin' we'll be in for a wee bit o' swallyin' tonight."

The plump Irish woman tended to her oversized cooker a while longer, then decided to make sure the grand ballroom had been decorated as she directed and the tables properly set. The sight of the room brought a gasp. "Oh me' dear Lord in Heaven, tis somethin' of pure magic, it is. Sweet little Pudge, where are ya now?"

A small body promptly emerged from behind one of the tables. "Here I am, Mistress Cook. Here I am. Are you pleased? Have I done what you wished?" Wide-eyed, Pudge clasped two little hands tight together and waited for a reply.

The prodigious room had been transformed into a dreamland. Dotting the edges of the polished parquet dance floor were numerous round tables cloaked with gold brocade silk coverings. Each table was surrounded by eight chairs enveloped in the same lavish material. Pale-peach napkins sat atop opulent golden dishware complimented by ornamental matching utensils and striking gold-rimmed crystal goblets. A three-foot tall cut-glass vase, firmly

36

secured in the center of each table, was filled with a soaring grandiose arrangement of white and purple orchids. At the base of the arrangement, six white tapers sat in baroque porcelain candlesticks. Draped gracefully around the top of the room were strings of bulky green garlands interlaced with innumerable white and peach roses.

"Darlin' Pudge, ya have outdone yerself, ya have. Tis a wee bit of a genius ya are to create such a spectacle and a great deal more than I'd hoped it to be. Why, I swear ya've truly managed to bring a bit of heaven to earth. It is a grand sight—a grand sight indeed. "

A faint blush rose in the small gnome's face as a broad smile began to form. "Thank you, Madam Cook, thank you. Would you like to see the garden? Gleek and I have been blessed with an army of help, and we are nearly finished. It is a thing of beauty, a real thing of beauty." Before a word of protest could be uttered from Margaret Mary, tiny Pudge scampered out of the room.

Afraid to hurt the feelings of such a sweet creature, Cook headed for the nearby west garden. It was only a few yards from the ballroom entrance and would be used for the actual ceremony at dusk. Once her eyes adjusted to the bright sunlight, she stood in total amazement, mouth agape. "Holy Saints above! Surely I've left the earth and traveled to the blessed world of angels, I have."

The lush hunter-green garden lawn had been manicured to perfection. Flowers of every sort were in full bloom, saturating the air with a bouquet of heady fragrance. An archway of sculptured white pillars, flanked on each side by an ornate lattice fence and two smaller pillars, led the way to the wedding gazebo several yards away. Wispy sprigs of delicate white baby's breath dangled like flowery icicles from an oversized ornamentation of deep pink and lavender roses, which was artfully positioned across the top of the elegant arch. Matching arrangements adorned each of the two smaller columns and cascaded down the front of them to the ground. Countless white chairs were aligned on each side of the wide path. A decorative terra cotta vessel, overflowing with pink lily of the valley, hung from wrought iron Sheppard hooks placed at the opening of each row. In the center of each container was a solitary white candle. A magnificent four-poster gazebo, constructed of woven willow, stood at the end of the long path. Bathed among the sinuous branches was a prolific display of cream, peach, lavender, and pink roses. Multiple strands of brilliant crystal beading swayed gracefully below the fragrant boughs. In the middle of each side hung a glorious chandelier, artistically dressed in a highly crafted array of color refracting diamond-cut prisms. Situated on the tip of each graceful glass branch was a white candle, which when lit would create a whimsical spectrum of radiance aimed to delight the imagination. Suspended from the back of the handsome structure was a lavishly gathered cloud-white sheer covering which fluttered softly in the tepid breeze.

"Do you like what we've done, Cook, do you? Do you think her majesty will approve?"

Margaret Mary clasped her cheeks and shook her head. "Me sweet darlin', ya've worked a bit of magic here. Not a single Leprechaun or Fairy could have created such a feature. Twill be a sight none shall soon forget."

She bid good day to Pudge and began to walk back to the Castle. Suddenly, a blast of air from above nearly blew her over, followed by a rather robust laugh.

"Hey Cook, looks like a perfect day for a super wedding. Say, what the heck you doing out of the kitchen?"

Meeley waved both arms as she and Knox hovered overhead.

"Lord save us, girl. You gave me such a start. Come down here off that dragon a moment so I can have a word with ya." Cook straightened her tousled garments and hair while Meeley landed nearby.

The roguish pilot approached Margaret Mary with lowered eyes. "I apologize for the stupid prank, Cook, and know I'm well deserving of a good ol' fashioned scolding. It's just that I sorta got a bit overexcited like most everyone else around here today. Even Knox is more energetic than usual. To be perfectly honest, I'm a little surprised to see you out here. Figured you'd be knee deep to a turnip in food preparation."

Cook guffawed and gave Meeley a friendly slap on the arm. "Aye, me kitchen is a trifle hectic at the moment, but is under control. Pudge asked me to view the garden, and what a sight it is. Have ya ever witnessed such grandeur? The banquet hall is more than I'd hoped it to be, but this bit of landscapin' is a pure work of art, it is. May I ask what the likes of you and your flying-creature are doin'? I'd be thinkin' such a pretty lass would be fussin' and makin' ready for the grand ceremony. Shouldn't ya be gettin' on with it now?"

Meeley put an arm around Margaret Mary as they meandered toward the Castle. "I'm not actually in the wedding party. My contribution will occur at the *end* of the ceremony." The vibrant girl pointed up to one of the nearby spires. "Check out the big display being placed atop the tower over there. Well, the very second Adera and Randy kiss to seal their marriage, Knox and I will zoom overhead, and he'll send a stream of fire out to light those double rings. It will be spectacular."

Cook's round eyes widened. "Ah, t'will truly be a grand sight, lass. Just be sure yer wee creature burns the blasted rings now and not our sweet home." She wrapped her plump arms around Meeley and gave a hearty hug. "Oh, what a blessed night of splendor this will be, and I'm thinkin' there'll be a good bit of fun to be had by all, including me self." A flush tinted her cheeks, and she snickered. "Well, what are ya waitin' for? Be off with ya now. Let yer darlin' dragon rest a bit while ya go spruce up for that handsome lad of yours. He'll be wantin' ta share a dance or two with his lovely lady and maybe sneak in a little snoggin' to boot."

Meeley gave a playful wink, planted a tender kiss on the wise woman's cheek, and bounded off. Moments later, she soared overhead on Knox and was soon out of sight.

Cook returned to her kitchen as the final touches for a magnificent wedding event were set in place.

The Queen's chamber was a hubbub of activity as several attendants scurried about in preparation for the royal nuptials. Up to now, the nervous bride managed to maintain some form of regal composure. However, the sound of crashing glass caused the refined sovereign to put an abrupt end to the chaos. While rushing around the spacious bedchamber, two maids managed to collide. Now, a vial of perfume lay splattered upon the pristine marble floor. "Ladies, please. This must cease immediately. It is regrettable, but before my quarters are further destroyed, I implore everyone to leave. For the moment, I prefer to be alone," her voice was resolute. She walked to the door and tapped a foot impatiently on the floor as the as the room emptied.

40

Adera strolled to one of the large gothic windows, took a deep breath, and sighed. However, the tranquility was short lived. Below, the sight of a dark carriage entering the courtyard brought a shudder. *I prayed my invitation would be ignored, but it appears my dear aunt and her son have decided to attend after all.*

Troublesome thoughts were interrupted by Kat's boisterous entrance. The raven-haired girl blinked while a hand fanned her face. "Jiminy Crickets, it sure reeks of perfume in here. Smells good, but think you might be putting it on a bit strong. Whew."

Adera heaved a sigh and ungracefully plopped down upon one of the plush sofas. "A bottle was accidently broken a few minutes ago. I apologize for the overwhelming fumes, but it shall soon dissipate. Will you join me in a nice cup of hot tea? By the looks of things, it appears you could use a bit of relaxation yourself."

Kat nodded and nestled down alongside her elder sibling. Hardly a second had passed when an invisible source placed a brimming hot pot of tea and two cups in front of them. "Dang, our little Brownies certainly are efficient. It sounds ungrateful, but I chased all the ladies away prior to coming here. Just look at me. I'm a mess. Meon and Hoki can easily finish getting me ready. At least, *they* understand my needs without all the hassle."

"What an ingenious decision. I believe I shall do likewise, little sister. The same three Brownies have proficiently attended every need since childhood and precisely understand my dressing preferences."

The frustrated pair sat for a while, sipped their soothing brew, and chatted about Kat and Tom's wedding…held only six months ago. Although not quite as ostentatious, it had been magnificent in every aspect.

41

"Forgive me, but in all the confusion a family token was overlooked." Adera walked to a nearby night table and retrieved a small velvet box. "I hope you will like them."

Kat lifted the lid and gasped. Inside was a pair of gold, diamond-studded, lightning bolt-shaped earrings. "Oh my stars, these are about the most beautiful things ever! They're so unusual. Thank you." She leaped to her feet and gave the Queen a robust hug. "I don't *like* them...I *love* them."

Turquoise eyes danced with gratification. "I am delighted they are so enthusiastically welcomed. The lightning bolt was a symbol often linked to Father. He was somewhat melodramatic at times and took pleasure in making humans believe he had control of such an object. Of course, it was merely an illusion, but proved rather effective."

Kat rushed over to floor-length dressing mirror and clipped on the elegant baubles. "Oh Sis, they're beautiful. Look how the fiery diamonds sparkle and flash—almost as if the bolts are real. I will *never* take them off."

A knock at the door caused the two sisters to turn. Bagi entered and bowed. "Excuse me, Highnesses, but if preparations are not continued, you will be late for the wedding." The dignified nymph looked lovelier than ever. An emerald-green velvet gown was a perfect match to her striking eyes, while a woven wreath of white baby's breath highlighted the beguiler's floor length cardinal-red hair.

"She's right. Think we better move our backsides and dress." Kat headed for the door, stopped and gave Adera a thumb up. "I'll be back in a jiffy. Guess it's finally time to get this show on the road." She let out a whoop and dashed out the door.

The Queen laughed and summoned her three Brownies, Tabota, Brendalyn, and Chastena, who materialized and immediately began to groom and dress their mistress.

Honey-gold locks were curled and pulled back to accommodate a majestic bridal-veil tiara-crown headband…a gracious gift from Legar, King of the Merpeople, and his three daughters, Maris, Nerissa, and Romey. Above the base of petite diamonds was a gracefully arched row of large, satiny pearls set in a mysteriously unique manner which gave them the appearance of being suspended in air. Atop the string of pearls was an ornate layer of raised leaf like projections encrusted with blazing diamonds.

Once clothed in proper undergarments, voluminous layers of crinoline tulle were added to give the gown's skirt dramatic fullness.

"Oh Mistress, this is the most glorious wedding dress we have ever seen," Tabota exclaimed as tiny chocolate eyes scanned the entrancing creation.

The gown was fashioned from opulent champagne silk, which refracted the light at different angles to produce an incredible variance of hues. Sheer chiffon lace, lavishly embroidered in an elaborate floral design of gold, peach, and sparkling crystal beads, swathed the lucent sleeves and lustrous silk from the bateau neckline to the hem of the spectacularly full cut skirt. An immoderate profusion of jewel infused appliqués further enhanced the fitted bodice above and just below the silk ribbon belted waistline.

A ten-foot long ivory veil was attached to the tiara and an overgenerous cascading bouquet of white Calla lilies placed in the sovereign's hand. She walked to the floor-length mirror and gasped as tears filled her beautiful eyes.

"This wedding dress is consummate perfection. The Elvin seamstresses have created absolute enchantment. I shall never forget this moment for I shall never look as lovely."

"Wow," Kat exclaimed loudly as she burst into the room. "Sure can't wait to see the look on Randy's face when he catches the first glimpse of his bride. That dude's gonna plum soil his britches. You look…beyond beautiful, if there's such a thing. Geez, here I thought my gown was gorgeous, but it looks like a cotton-pickin' rag compared to yours."

A lone tear slid gracefully down the Queen's creamy cheek. "I am overwhelmed by the splendor of this garment. Hope my husband-to-be will find it pleasing."

Kat began to giggle. "Adera, I seriously doubt that bumpkin is gonna notice a dang thing of what you're wearing. Those blue peepers of his are only going to be focused on the true love of his life. It's kinda hard to explain, but there's a special glow surrounding you today that's pretty hard to ignore."

The noble ruler smiled and cradled Kat's hands in hers. "I will take your word for it. Now come, let me have a good look at you as well."

A slight rosy tinge appeared in Kat's cheeks as she twirled around. "Ya like it? The Elves wanted to use ivory material, but I chose this shade instead."

Kat's wide sweeping gown was splendid and flattered her in every way. Barely a silken thread of the strapless bodice showed through an obscene array of sparkling silver sequins and beads. Four voluminous ruffled tiers of crisp, shimmering, blush-apricot tulle intensified the skirt's profuse yards of pastel tangerine silk. In order to flaunt the beautiful new earrings, her long flowing, ebony locks were softly curled and somewhat pulled back. However, the

44

most outstanding feature was the impressive Princess crown, worn for the very first time. At her request, it was a relatively humble piece. Fiery diamonds dotted the wide gold filigree band. Dangling from the center of several open hearts were inserts of tiny golden teardrops, placed in honor of the miraculous Unicorn droplets that saved the life of her beloved horse. Hoki had already been advised to retrieve the cherished coronet after the nuptial ceremony and return it to a place for safekeeping.

"Wait until your handsome husband views *his* beauty," Adera exclaimed. "I predict Tom will be utterly captivated." The Queen's enlivened demeanor suddenly grew serious. "Please, forgive me for the necessity to blemish this unparalleled moment, but I must address a distasteful situation that has repulsively surfaced. Father's sister, Odiene, and her sadistic son, Lord Tahl arrived a short time ago. It was believed they would not attend, but we were in error. You will find the duo most attractive and extremely charismatic. However, do not be fooled by these outward appearances. Both are vile and cruel creatures who share love with no other life form. Never be alone with either of them, not even for a moment. You *must* keep Tom by your side—at all times. No matter what excuse either of these deviant creatures delivers, do not stray off unaccompanied."

Kat shrugged her shoulders and gave a nonchalant expression. "If you insist, but if dear auntie and cousin scamp were so detestable, why on earth did you invite them?"

Adera took hold of her sister's upper arms and gave a nippy shake—her tone humorless. "As previously stated, the choice was not mine to make. I am duty-bound by my noble station. Believe me when I say this, my sister, they

45

are not welcome. My advice must not to be taken lightly. Promise me to carry forth what is asked of you. Kat, *promise me!*"

"Ouch, okay. I promise. Don't worry. I'll be sure to keep a wide berth from that pair. Jeepers, not to change the subject, but kinda appears the sun's about to sink on the horizon. We better hustle. Sure don't want the bride to be late now, do we?"

The Queen glanced over at the window. "Oh my stars, I did not realize the hour. Yes, we must be underway. Kat, you *will* remember what we just discussed won't you?"

"Yeah, yeah, don't fret the small stuff. I'll keep Tom by my side the whole blessed night. Cross my heart and hope to spit. Well, that is unless I'm dancing with some other handsome dude, like Randy." She giggled and entwined an arm in one of Adera's. "How 'bout we get you hitched, lady?"

A rather dashing wizard and a courtly Elf stood at the bottom of the baronial staircase. Merlin greeted the two with a gallant bow. "Good evening, Highnesses. Never have my eyes witnessed a more lovely vision. The beauty that stands before me is beyond compare."

Adera trembled as she took the arm offered by the genteel man. "Thank you, my dearest friend. This is a day long dreamed of. I am grateful and pleased my request was accepted. There is no other more suited to take Father's place and escort me to my betrothed. Thank you as well, Horace, for your gracious acceptance to walk beside my sister on this blissful day."

The aloof warrior placed a hand to his heart and lowered his head in a chivalrous gesture of admiration. "Mistress Kat, may I offer an arm?"

"Of course you may, and I will cordially accept, Horace." She glanced over at Adera and gave a playful wink as she placed her hand on top of his.

The last rays of sun were nearly gone as the royal wedding party emerged from inside the Castle. Without a second of hesitation, McLachen and Nalay approached.

Kat let out a loud gasp. "Holy Moses, talk about decked out. Wow." She dashed up to the onyx-coated stallion and gave him a hug. "McLachen, you're wearing a saddle under this swanky blanket. Sorry, this is *not* acceptable. It must be removed immediately."

"No My Lady, please do not be concerned. Nalay and I have agreed to bear these contraptions while we transport you and the Queen down the designated path. Neither suffers an ounce of discomfort. The Elves designed our bindings to be rather bearable, and our plight shall only be for a short time. My Lady, you are royalty and must portray the part properly in front of our guests. Sitting sidesaddle is required, but to do such without aide is far too dangerous. We insist and will hear no more."

Kat sighed and submitted. "I can't believe how beautiful you both look, McLachen. Our horses back home would be pea-green with jealousy."

Ornate blankets of silk and lace had been draped over the back of each creature to protect the magnificent gowns worn by the bride and her matron of honor.

McLachen was adorned in a decorative covering of sparkling silver and a matching makeshift halter with a long silver lead line embedded with coral rose buds. Around his thick, muscular neck was a narrow garland of multihued orange roses. His lengthy mane and tail were artfully affixed with clusters of yellow and peach roses, silver ribbon, and white baby's breath.

47

A flamboyant jeweled covering, rivaled only by Nalay's prodigious golden horn, veiled the unicorn's brilliant white coat. Streamers of delicate white rose buds and ivory silk ribbon dangled from the corners of the golden halter and continued down the crystal-studded lead line. An immeasurable array of cream roses, and countless orange and black Monarch butterflies, dotted the creature's imperial mane and tail. It was unquestionably a breathtaking sight.

Adera nodded and moved toward the stately unicorn stallion. "Dear noble Nalay, it is known that no weight has ever been placed upon your back. To grant me such an honor is a blessed tribute that shall never be forgotten." She reached out and stroked the arched neck of the aristocratic equine.

"Ladies, a wedding awaits," Merlin exclaimed. "May I assist you aboard, my Queen?" The tall, powerfully built wizard took hold of the Queen's petite waist, lifted her off the ground, and set her gently in the saddle.

Kat giggled as Horace followed the identical procedure. After the gowns were tidied, Merlin waved his wand, and the shadowed garden sprung to life. Every candle glowed with brilliant light, while a myriad of lightening bugs illuminated the trees and flowers with an unparalleled twinkling display.

Several harps played as Horace took hold of McLachen's lead and began the procession down the rose-petal strewn path. Their movement gently coaxed the lily of the valley plants to permeate the air with the sweet combined floral scent of roses, jasmine, citrus, and musk. As they approached the magnificent wedding gazebo, Kat glanced over at the handsome groom, whose eyes were fixed solely on the vision behind her.

48

Tom left Randy's side, walked over, and lifted his wife to the ground. "If I wasn't already married to you, Kat, I'd do it all over again this very minute." After Horace led McLachen away, she and Tom took their places and watched as Adera made a heralded entrance.

Dressed in black velvet robes, Merlin wore a broad smile as he led the high stepping unicorn to the appointed mark.

Teary eyed, Randy rushed to Adera and gently lifted her from Nalay. The instant her jewel-covered slipper touched the ground, every butterfly posed on the Unicorn took wing. It was a magical dreamlike spectacle. However, Randy and Adera barely noticed….their entrenched gaze remained unwavered.

Randy led the Queen up two small steps and stood beneath the flowered arches, facing each other, hand in hand.

King Merneos inched forward and addressed the crowd. "As one of royal blood, I have been asked to preside over the joining of this incredible couple. Adera, I long knew your mother and father. They were as family to me. It has been gratifying to watch you grow over the years and mature into the striking sovereign you are now. Randy, although we have known each other for a somewhat short period of time, there is no other who is more worthy of this celebrated lady's hand. You have shown absolute courage, fortitude, and infinite love for our land, our residents, and most of all, this woman. It is my pleasure to anoint the two of you as man and wife. At this time, your vows may be expressed.

Randy cleared his throat, and his voice cracked slightly as he began, "My beautiful Adera, your incredible spirit, boundless kindness, and faultless devotion rescued a

49

wounded heart from a cheerless corner of darkness. Pure and gentle love restored blissful light to my time-hardened soul. There are no words that exist to describe the intense passion and adoration I hold for you...my Queen, my love, and forever more—my wife."

Adera swallowed hard, fighting back tears. "My darling Randy, for many eons, I dwelled in a secluded world of loneliness, dominated by my hereditary obligation to govern and protect our Realm. I possessed a core void of emotion. Deep within my body's shell resided an icy heart...barren of love. Then, *destiny* brought you into this world and into my arms. Your gift of true love energized my lifeless existence and ignited a dormant passion. I shall love you, my dearest husband, until the end of time...and a day more."

King Merneos placed a hand upon their heads and bowed his. "As all here have been witness to your testament of love for each other, I declare you Queen Adera, and you Randolph Carlton, husband and wife. Now, to quote a *human* term—you may kiss the bride."

Randy pulled his beautiful spouse close and kissed her. Suddenly, shrieks of fear erupted when a powerful swirl of air struck, followed by the whooshing sound of great wings above and a spine-tingling guttural roar. Seconds later, a stream of fire ignited the massive wooden rings placed upon the Castle spire earlier that day. The flaming presentation illuminated the subdued garden with brilliant intensity.

"Congratulations to my two best friends," Meeley yelled as she hovered overhead on the docile dragon. "Gotta take Knox back to his barn, but won't be gone long. Don't start the party without me. Okay Charlie, move your

50

fanny and come pick me up." Moments later, she and her dynamic beast vanished into the night.

The wedding party and their guests began to snicker. Red-faced, Charlie stood and turned to the crowd. "Sorry folks. Sure hope my screwball wife didn't scare you too bad. Guess I'd better head on out. If that fiery dame misses one second of tonight's party, I fear she might get her blasted dragon to turn me into toast."

Randy let out a robust laugh. "You might be right there, buddy. No problem. Go get that gal of yours. We promise not to start without you two."

The joyful couple greeted their guests for a few minutes then began to walk down the aisle and head for the Castle. Standing near the beginning of the second row was Odiene and Lord Tahl. The sight of them erased Adera's broad smile, and she winced as though an ominous arrow of terror pierced her heart.

Chapter Four
Dance of Doom

The lively sound of music trailed from inside the majestic palace and saturated the balmy night air. Kat's eagerness heightened as the royal gala neared. Little else had been spoken of for weeks—as this would be a celebratory event unlike any other.

She impatiently tugged at her husband's arm. "Hurry up. We're expected to join Adera and Randy in the reception line. Come on, Tom. Stop draggin' your darn feet."

They were about to enter the ballroom foyer when she caught sight of McLachen and Nalay off to the side being unsaddled and groomed. "Oh sweetheart, I have to speak with McLachen. He won't be able to share our merriment tonight, and I owe him a moment. Go ahead without me. Tell my sister and *brother-in-law* I'll be right in." Before he could utter a word, she planted a loving peck on the cheek and dashed off toward her beloved horse.

The dignified stallion gave off a low-key nicker as she approached. "My Lady, why are you not with the others? It is obvious the festivity has begun."

Kat stroked his coal-black forehead. "I wish there was a way you and Nalay could come inside. It just doesn't seem fair."

"My Lady, it would be most inappropriate for us to attend. You need not be concerned. Our lovely spouses wait patiently for our arrival. It is the perfect night for a serene stroll, wouldn't you agree?"

52

The unexpected comment caused golden eyes to brighten and brought a giggle. "Sounds as though you two will be well taken care of after all." She twirled a bit of his mane around her fingers. A gentle nudge to the arm caused her to turn. "Good evening, Nalay."

The majestic unicorn stallion nuzzled an outstretched hand. "The sight of you carrying Queen Adera down the aisle was one I shall never, ever forget. It was something only dreamed of in a fairytale. There are no words to truly describe the scene. Now, I suggest you two gentlemen get underway to meet your maidens. I have a pretty handsome escort waiting as well."

McLachen sounded a robust whinny and turned to leave. However, his departure came to abrupt halt, and he trotted back to Kat. "My Lady, a baneful swathe crosses the rising moon. It is a harbinger of impending peril. You must proceed with extreme caution this night. Never be alone for one second. Keep your husband and friends close at all times. Perhaps I should remain and stand watch."

"Geez, now you sound like Adera. All this gloom and doom talk is starting to scare the bejeepers out of me. I'll be perfectly *fi_*!" Kat let out a shriek as two strong arms suddenly enveloped her body. "Tom, you scared the doggone living daylights out of me."

He chuckled and tightened his embrace. "Don't worry, my furry friend. I'm not about to let this wildcat out of my clutches. You and Nalay go enjoy the evening."

The great stallion nodded, turned, and trotted off. Within moments, the incomparable Bayard and striking Unicorn vanished into shadowed obscurity.

"Let's head in, Kat. I'm hungry as a bear, and my feet are itching for a bit of dancing. Plus, if you and I don't help Randy and Adera welcome the guests, I think our two

53

friends are gonna be ripped. Let's go, girly. Your horse will be fine, and with me at your side, so will you, *my lady*." Tom laughed, and wrapped his arm around hers. Inside the Castle, they quickly took their place alongside the newlyweds in the lengthy reception line.

After all guests had been properly welcomed and seated, a blare of trumpet's signaled the foursome's entrance into the elegant ballroom. A hint of blush appeared on the Queens face as they were ceremoniously ushered to the royal wedding table. Once all were settled, the magnificent feast lavishly prepared by Cook and her staff began. White gloved hands proudly presented shiny, oversized silver platters of food as a literal parade of waiters entered the room. Glasses soon overflowed with ambrosial wine while the mirthful clamor of high-spirited gaiety permeated the festive atmosphere.

Absorbed in energetic conversation, Kat barely touched a bite of the scrumptious morsels. Joining the two royal couples at the table were Charlie, Meeley, Merlin, Horace, Nirage, King Merneos, and King Legar.

After the decadent dessert had been served, the talented orchestra began to play. Within moments, the polished dance floor filled with lighthearted partygoers. As would be expected, Merlin proceeded to ask every available maiden for a dance. Charlie and Meeley joined Howell, his enchanting wife, Wendy, and several other pilot friends in brisk conversation. Nirage and King Merneos, who disliked pointless frivolity, remained seated. Although the Mer-King's three daughters, Maris, Nerissa, and Romey, took to the dance floor among a bevy of drooling admirers, the oceans sovereign had not fully mastered maneuverability of his newly acquired legs. He chose instead to quietly observe the revelry with his friend,

Merneos. Ironically, it was the aloof elf Horace who surprised everyone as he gallantly shared a waltz or two with his human mother, Helen.

Kat, on the other hand, was not about to miss a single tune. "This has to be about the best party we've been at since we arrived here. Oh, they're playing another waltz. Come on."

Tom yanked her back down into the chair. "Kat, take a break for a second. I'm beat."

Randy escorted his new bride to the table and plopped alongside their best man. "I swear, this ole' boy has never danced so danged much. My feet feel like they've taken a short stroll on a long bed of thorns." He chuckled and gave his friend a playful slap on the back, "Looks as though you're in the same boat, buddy."

"Where the heck do these women get all the blasted energy? Kat's ready to twirl around the floor another time, but this guy's about ready to twirl right into bed."

Merlin teetered somewhat as he approached. "Master Tom, may I request the pleasure of your beautiful wife's hand for a dance?"

"You sure as heck can," Kat yelled out as she leaped to her feet. Tom cleared his throat and gave a disapproving look. "Oh silly man, nothing is gonna happen. I'll be right out there in plain sight, so don't fret a hair." Before he could respond, she pulled the great wizard onto the dance floor.

Kat was delightfully surprised at the wizard's ballroom prowess as they floated around the room to a serene waltz. "You're a mighty fine hoofer, Merlin."

"Thank you, Mistress. I have had numerous seasons to practice the art. Unfortunately, the toes of many ladies suffered a bit of grievance during the course of my

55

education." He chuckled and spun her around. "I must say, you are indeed a vision to behold this evening. Are we enjoying the festivities?"

"Jeepers Merlin, you sure know how to flatter a girl…and I accept." She smiled and gave his hand a playful squeeze. "For the most part, I'm having a blast, but there's a slight problem. I wanted to speak to Adera or Randy about it, but decided not to. After all, it's their wedding night and wouldn't seem right to throw a wrench into the gears."

Merlin gave a quirky look. "Your tool terminology puzzles me. Perhaps you might explain the statement in a more conventional manner."

"Sorry. I sometimes forget myself." She stopped dancing and pulled him off to the side. "When we were in the reception line, I greeted Odiene and her son, Tahl. When that guy took my hand, it literally raised the hair on my arm. I felt as though a jolt of electricity shot through me. He's extremely handsome, and she's a knockout with the most beautiful violet eyes I've ever seen. But, the two of them gave me the willies. It's really odd, because neither said or did anything to cause this feeling. Maybe I'm just being stupid, and it's nothing to be concerned about."

"No dear lass, most definitely be wary of those two. Obey your instincts, for they shall never lead you astray. Do not be deceived by that pair's appearance. They are treacherous and not to be trusted." He gave her a playful tap on the nose and smiled. "We shall have no more of this troublesome talk tonight. You are in safe hands at the present time, and we are denying ourselves the pleasure of this waltz." He led her back onto the polished platform. Soon, a tap on his shoulder brought the duo to an abrupt halt.

56

"Excuse me Merlin, may I cut in and share a brief moment with my exquisite cousin?"

The legendary wizard initially ignored the intruder, but stopped and addressed him upon receiving another tap. "I wholeheartedly frown on your request, but in order to not appear discourteous, Tahl, I shall allow the Princess to make the decision."

"It's alright, Merlin, he can *finish* this dance with me. I also do not wish to appear discourteous."

The ancient sorcerer coolly relinquished his partner, but before walking away, leaned in close to Tahl. "Be warned, my lad. I shall watch every move. It would not do well for you to transform this melodious waltz into a dance of doom."

Kat's breathing was rapid as the handsome aristocrat masterfully guided them around the ballroom. She avoided eye contact and was hesitant to speak at first, but soon curiosity overtook fear. "You dance divinely, Lord Tahl."

"I sense an air of uneasiness, Kat. Apparently, my rumored reputation has paved the way for needless apprehension. Rest easy dear lady, for I am not the depraved creature many believe me to be. Mother and I are aware of your existence and hoped one day we would be granted the pleasure of meeting. I must say, this is not a disappointment. What a lovely hybrid you are."

Amber eyes flashed and cheeks became flushed in momentary ire. "That comment is *almost* flattering, my Lord. It is true, many cautioned of your legendary devious traits. However, I tend to ignore the opinions of others and prefer to decide things based on my own observations. As of now, you seem pleasant enough, but my *hybrid* trust is far from gained."

He threw his head back and gave a robust laugh. "The Princess not only possesses Zuegas's eyes, but apparently his beefy fortitude as well. I could easily fall in love with such an outspoken, peppery woman."

The ardent remark instantly turned a smile to a frown. "How *dare* you say something like that? I'm very happily married and certainly not up for grabs, especially by the likes of you. Our dance has ended." She tried to pull away, but forceful hands held her tight. "Get your paws off me or risk getting knocked simple. This country girl might look delicate, but I can pack a punch like the kick of a mule."

His unnatural laugh echoed. "What a feisty little hell-cat you are. My proclamation was not intended to sound offensive, but to simply imply that a woman with such vigor might enrapture my surly heart. The words were never directly aimed at you. After all, Kat, we *are* cousins."

"I—I apologize. This dang temper has occasionally caused my big feet to be firmly planted in my big mouth."

"No offense has been taken, but I admit to finding you absolutely fascinating. Perhaps it would be best to change the subject to one less provoking. How do you like our Realm? It was created to somewhat mimic the home planet. In part, it is similar, yet remains dowdy in true comparison."

As always, insatiable curiosity surfaced. "No one has told me much about, uh,…oh blast. I'm afraid I don't remember the name of our native planet. Sorry."

"It is called Sriebonia. I would venture to say that one of the most outstanding features of our world was the intense luminosity of color. Earth's atmosphere does not support such light refraction. My mother's extraordinary violet eyes are a prime example. This globe's most intense amethyst would prove dull in comparison. However, in a human eye of the same tone, only a hint of lavender would be perceived. Had you been fully human, your beguiling amber eyes would be muted…more hazel in appearance."

Kat found these revelations captivating and desired to know more. "Odiene's eye color is certainly breathtaking and so is her beauty. I've often studied the portraits of the ancients that hang in Adera's tower hallway. Not only are the women gorgeous, but all of you men are more than handsome." The bold statement brought a rush of fire to her face.

Lord Tahl was unquestionably an impressive example of rugged masculinity. He stood about six four, with broad shoulders and muscular arms. A dapper, short-boxed beard, mustache, and wavy shag cut hair of cocoa-brown, framed an almost angelic face. Striking green eyes had a near hypnotic affect that literally tantalized the senses. Supple black leather garments effortlessly amplified a powerfully built body most men would covet.

"Have you ever looked into the heavens and wondered where our kind came from, Kat? Although the actual planet cannot be seen from here, the gateway is visible."

"Are you serious? Can you show me?" All fateful words of warning were now disregarded and ominous concerns dangerously put aside.

He smiled and offered a chivalrous arm. "Let us take up another glass of wine while we step outside a moment. The night is clear, and the stars shine bright."

Kat overflowed with anticipation as he escorted her through the open ballroom doors to the obscured granite terrace.

The handsome immortal placed his goblet on the waist high stone handrail and pointed upward. "If you look to the west, the Pleiades star cluster is viewable. Do you see it?" She shook her head no. "Here, allow me to better show you." As he raised his arm, the wine glass she was holding was accidently knocked to the ground. "What a clumsy oaf I am. Please, take mine. I shall get another when we return." Green eyes appeared enlivened as he handed her the goblet, causing a moment of hesitation. "Do not fear, Kat, I have not sipped a drop. It is perfectly untainted by my lips."

She nodded and took a sip from the crystal container. "Wow, this batch of wine is unusually sweet. Oh well, guess that is what Adera ordered. Now, show me again where Sriebonia is."

There are several hundred stars within the constellation, but most are not visible to the naked eye. Do you see the seven brightest stars in that cluster? Humans often refer to them as the Seven Sisters. Imagine, if you will, flying directly through the center of them. That would lead straight to our galaxy. Kat, you have barely touched your drink. Shall I return and provide another? "

Not wishing to seem ungracious, Kat took a couple more swallows. "What you're telling me is so darn interesting, Tahl. Sure wish Adera would reveal more, but for some reason she tends to avoid any conversation about the homeland. I often think the past causes too much pain. Still, there's so much to learn. The Travelers *are* part of my heritage, yet I know little about them." A sudden wooziness began to sweep over her, and she wobbled. "Yikes, think maybe I've had more than enough brew for tonight. Sorry. We better go in. I really don't feel v-very w-wel—" She collapsed into his arms and succumbed to darkness.

Distracted by a giddy pair of voluptuous ladies, Merlin momentarily turned his focus away from Kat. He suddenly realized the serene waltz had been replaced with a bouncy melody. Blue-black eyes darted about, but his quarry was not to be found. Panic began to overtake the wizard. He rushed out onto the dance floor and whirled around in hopes of catching sight of Kat and Tahl. "Zounds, how could I have been so careless? Perhaps she has been delivered to her husband."

Long black velvet robes fluttered as he hurried to the table where Adera, Randy, and Tom sat engaged in conversation. "Pardon the interruption, but has our Princess returned?"

Adera gasped and stood. "Merlin, do not jest. Until my aunt and cousin leave, Kat remains in danger. Where did you last see her?"

The great conjuror drew a deep breath. "It pains me to say I allowed Lord Tahl to cut in on our waltz."

"*You did what?*" Tom yelled as he quickly rose. "Is there no brain in that wooden noggin? You know he's dangerous, and she's his target. We have to find her, and do it quick before something happens."

"The lady remained in my sight and believed her to be out of jeopardy. Regrettably, a bit of distraction occurred. When I became conscious the dance had finished, she and Lord Tahl were nowhere to be found. Only a sheer moment had transpired. They surely could not have ventured far."

Adera tore from Randy's grasp and confronted the magician. "With the likes of Lord Tahl and his mother, more harm than you could possibly envision could easily take place in such a short span of time. My sister is in extreme peril and must be located without a second of

61

delay. For the first time in my existence, I am thwarted by such a thoughtless lack of duty, Merlin." She raised a hand to slap him, but was stopped by Randy's firm grip.

"Look Adera, I know it's easy to lay the blame on him, but we're *all* at fault here. I could have danced with her, or Tom, or anyone of our other friends, but we chose not to. Merlin loves Kat as much as anyone else. So, get over your anger, and let's go find them. This senseless squabbling needs to stop. Merlin, where did you last see them?" As always, Randy's persona appeared calm and levelheaded.

"The two of them were swirling around near the terrace doors."

Without hesitation, Randy and Tom bolted across the room and burst through the arched doorway. Adera, Merlin, and Merneos followed close behind.

"Kat, Kat where are you!" Tom yelled as he scampered about the spacious veranda. "She's not here." Fear was clearly evident in his expression.

King Merneos took hold of his arm. "I understand the concern and am in agreement, but panic will not serve us at this time. Others should be immediately alerted and asked to aide in our search, yet it must be done quietly so the guests are not alarmed."

Merlin stood alongside the Elf King. "He is correct, my lad. I claim full responsibility and will apply whatever powers necessary to return Kat safely. Merneos, will you kindly gather forces while I ask my tree friends to watch for her?" He placed a hand on Tom's shoulder. "I am sincerely sorry, my lad, but we shall locate your sweet wife and return her home safe." The wizard gave a reassuring nod and sprinted off. Mere seconds passed before he emerged from the night mist. "Word has been spread. When she is spotted, I will be alerted. Perhaps, my Queen, it might be best if you announce your honeymoon departure. I believe it should effectively disperse the festivities."

"That would be wise. Randy and I shall do so immediately. The thought of my sister in the hands of that malicious creature makes my skin crawl. Wait! Has anyone seen Odiene? Tahl would not leave without that sadistic woman by his side."

The Elf King turned toward her, his face unemotional. "Odiene has not been observed all evening, Adera. The elaborate carriage remains, but the four black horses have been unhitched and are nowhere to be found. I believe your aunt's role in this alleged abduction has been covertly executed."

Merlin's head spun around. "Did you say *black* horses? Do you recall if their eyes glowed red?

"Yes, as a matter of fact, they did," Merneos, replied. "I have never witnessed such unusual steeds."

"Nor will you." The distinguished sorcerer lowered his eyes. "Adera, this news is most distressful. Such animals are enchanted. They possess speeds greater than our Thunder Hooves and shall deliver their riders to Mantalac within hours. We have no time to spare."

All heads turned as Horace rushed up. "I noticed the wedding party had taken an impromptu leave. May I inquire to the evident problem?" The aloof Elf cocked an eyebrow as Randy quickly divulged the details. "I was uninformed of this imminence and overlooked the pair as they stepped out for a supposed breath of air. May I assist in locating our Princess?"

Merlin beamed and vigorously shook the Elf's hand. "Yes, my boy, yes indeed you may. Your assistance at the stables will be most helpful. Horses must be made ready. I

63

can place a similar spell on our mounts, but although they will gain great momentum, my powers are not as prolific as those of Odiene. Sadly, our pursuit shall take a few more days than theirs. Tom, please hurry off and gather Charlie, and Meeley. We must make haste."

Randy wrinkled his brow. "Why don't we just use the flying horses, Merlin? They certainly would be faster. Plus, we should be able to see more from the air."

"I understand your anxiety, my boy, but Tahl is a genuine Traveler...one with exceptional intuition and intelligence. He will suspect us doing such and plan accordingly. I fear our creatures might fall prey to his trickery. It will be a longer trek, but we must go in stealth by land animal."

"Sweetheart, heed his advice. You do not know the cunning nature of my cousin. Go Merlin, do what you must to ready our steeds. My husband and I shall exhibit an air of affectionate bliss as we thank our guests and depart." She turned to leave, but stopped and walked over to the frazzled wizard. "I am sorry for my unkind words earlier, dearest friend. You are not to be held accountable. I was in error to lash out as I did." The elegant Queen then delivered a tender kiss to his bearded cheek and squeezed a trembling hand. "If it is acceptable to all, one hour hence we shall rejoin in the drawing room." Heads nodded, and the group dispersed.

On the way to the stables, Merlin and Horace met McLachen. The wizard leaned close and whispered to Horace, "Do not inform the horse of this plight."

The dark brown eyes of the majestic equine scanned the duo with intensity. "Do not inform the horse of *what?* You forget, *wizard*, I have an acute sense of hearing. Has something happened to Princess Kat?" The great stallion

64

folded back his ears and moved to within inches of Merlin and Horace. "I shall ask one more time, and unless you wish to feel my anger, you will answer. Has something happened to Kat?"

The two men glanced at each other and drew a breath. Merlin reached out to stroke the great stallion, but was given a sharp nip. "Okay, I shall answer. Yes, something has indeed happened, but that is all we know. She has vanished and believed to have fallen victim to Lord Tahl." The heroic Bayard let out a bloodcurdling whinny, sending a chill down the wizard's spine. "We will find and return her safely, McLachen. A rescue party is in progress. You must calm yourself."

"I asked that she be watched over carefully, and this is how my request is rewarded?" The black steed reared and bared his teeth. "If a single raven hair on her head is harmed, you and the others will incur my ire. Chendar and I shall join the search. To leave the fate of My Lady to such incompetent creatures would be an obvious act of insanity." The harsh comment brought a huff from Horace. McLachen's gaze turned to him. "It is uncommon for one of your breeding to bear such a lack of responsibility, so I can only presume you knew little or nothing of what ensued. However, be warned master Elf. From this point on, failure is not an option."

The noble warrior placed a hand to his chest and nodded. "Rest easy, dear horse… I shall not fail."

Fiery brown eyes stared into those of Horace and Merlin before he gave a powerful snort and galloped off.

Merlin wiped his beaded forehead. "Whew. To say our McLachen was upset would be an understatement. I've never seen him like this. We must hurry, lad. I am certain Tom will be astride Chendar, and unless I am a total fool,

65

Queen Adera will sit atop McLachen. Six of our most fleet footed beasts must be quickly readied. I shall administer the spell to the intrepid stallion and his son when they arrive."

As predicted, once Queen Adera and Randy dismissed the reception, the elegant ballroom was quickly vacated. Only the clink and clank from the cleanup crew echoed through the halls.

The allotted hour passed like a flash, and the troupe now assembled in the empty drawing room.

Randy held his beautiful bride by the waist, her swollen, red eyes clearly indicating she had shed a tidal wave of tears. After she was seated, he cleared his throat. "On behalf of Adera and me, we wish to thank all of you for your support. Mantalac is a great distance from here, about four hundred or so miles. The journey is going to take the majority of us into unknown territory where we most likely will encounter creatures foreign to this kingdom. If anyone wishes to bail out, now would be the time. We will understand, and assure you that in no way would your absence hinder our profound friendship."

Charlie stood up and glanced around the room. "Each and every single one of us are your friends, Randy. Meeley and I consider you family. There's no way we would jump ship at a time like this. So, let's have no more blubbering nonsense. It's time to hit the road and go save our gal. The Deliverance Brigade is ready to roll."

Randy chuckled and shook his head, *"Deliverance Brigade?* You sure can name things, Charlie. Actually, I kinda like this title a little better than Merlin's Marauders. Guess in a strange way, deliverance fits. Certainly is a rescue operation. Okay, what say we get the show on the road and go kick Lord Tahl's butt."

Meeley jumped up and hugged her husband. "Darn tootin'. I'm ready. Just wish I could bring Knox. My little ol' green hunk of love would make fast work of that jerk, Tahl."

"Now, hold your wee britches a second. Not one of ya will be leavin' without a bit of nourishment ta take along." Cook burst into the room, followed by Jerome whose spidery legs nearly buckled from the weighty basket he carried. "I've prepared a bit o' food for each of ya. Twill be enough for the long jaunt ahead I'm thinkin'." She quickly gave each of them a large canvas sack and a perky kiss on the cheek, which brought an awkward frown from Merneos and Horace. "Now, be off with ya, and bring our lass home."

Outside they found six bay Arabians, all saddled and ready. Adera spotted McLachen immediately and went directly to him.

"My Queen, will you do me the honor to act as your steed?"

She buried her face into his lush ebony mane and sobbed. "Of course I will. You, more than any, have earned the right to rescue Kat." Randy walked over, gave her a kiss, and a leg up.

Tom and Chendar had grown as close as McLachen and Kat, so it was understandable they would team together.

The group was about to leave when Gleek darted out from the underbrush, puffing, and squealing like a stuck pig. "My Queen, my Queen. I found this just down the hill." Jerome rushed over and lifted the tiny Gnome up.

Adera shrieked as she viewed the object dropped in her hand. "Oh Randy, it is one of Kat's earrings."

67

Upon hearing the comment, McLachen went ballistic. He began to rear and whinny, nearly unseating his rider.

"Easy McLachen, she will be fine. We shall make haste to retrieve her." The sovereign's voice and easy touch was soothing and quickly calmed the distressed stallion. "My friends, this is a piece of the jewelry I presented to my sister earlier today. She would not have willingly parted with it. Our fears are incontrovertible. Lord Tahl has kidnapped Kat, and she is in grave peril. Let our trek begin."

A multitude of pebbles exploded into the air as the unique band of rescuers galloped off into the bleak darkness of night.

Chapter Five
Land of Lost Hope

A wispy tickling sensation caused Kat to brush her face and roll over. Goosebumps erupted on honeyed skin from an unnatural chill. She began to shiver and reached for the comforter normally strewn at the foot of the bed. However, in place of the velvety cover, icy hands touched the crisp tulle skirt of her gown. Long lashes fluttered as amber eyes struggled to focus.

Why is it so darn cold in here? We never have weather like this in Bowlandria. I'm freezing. She sat up, wrapped both arms around bare shoulders, and looked around. The room was dim and appeared unfamiliar. A tinge of panic began to creep up on her as she stood. *This isn't my room. What in blazing heck is going on? Where am I?*

A quick search located a half-burned candle and two matches. Once lit, the muted light revealed a dank and rat infested room. Other than a rag covered makeshift bed and small table, it was void of furnishings.

She rushed to the ramshackle wooden door, but found it bolted shut from the outside. Across the room, just above the bed, was a small barred window. A glimpse through it made her shudder with fear.

Muted sunshine shed a plethora of morbid shadows over a bleak land. Lifeless trees stood like deformed statues upon moldering soil. Dark clouds speckled an ominous gray sky, and the overwhelming stench of ebbing decay permeated the turbid air. Day was scarcely brighter than night.

69

Kat's mind whirled in confusion. Her head throbbed, and she teetered on the brink of being nauseous. The sound of approaching footsteps, followed by the distinctive clank of metal keys, brought a gasp. Her breathing grew rapid and eyes widened as the dilapidated door slowly creaked open. The sight of a tall, masculine silhouette standing in the rough-hewn doorway triggered a shriek of fright.

"It's good to see you have awakened. We were concerned the potion I added to your wine was perhaps a bit too strong." He took a step forward, revealing a familiar face.

"Tahl!"

"Who did you expect—your wimpy human spouse?" Lips curled in a sinister smile as callous eyes scanned the prisoner. "From this point on, Princess, I will be addressed as *Lord* Tahl." He took a step closer. "Welcome to the kingdom of Mantalac."

Kat momentarily stood silent, bewildered by his disclosure. Suddenly, golden eyes flashed with rage, and her body began to tremble in seething fury. "What kind of demented monster are you? I demand to be returned to Bowlandria immediately."

"You *dare* demand something from me? No one is given that privilege, not even my mother. In time, you will learn to respect and love me."

In explosive anger, she spat at him. "Love you? That will *never* happen. The very sight of you turns my stomach. Tom is ten times the man you are or could *ever* be."

"Is that so?" His face grimaced in anger as he rushed up and pulled her into his arms. "Allow a *real* man to tame that wild beast inside." He grabbed a clump of her ebony hair, pulled her head back, and forced a kiss.

70

Kat fought with combative ferocity and clawed his hand, causing him to wince in pain and hurl her to the floor.

"That outburst will prove incredibly costly, shrew. Perhaps your viper tongue will be distinctly altered and those feline claws dulled after spending a night in this icy dungeon without food or water. Be warned, half-breed, escape might prove to be a most unwise decision. Cianest is just across the hall and not someone, uh, *something* you would want to meet up with. But fear not, you shall not be alone. The *rats* will keep you company." With those odious words, he stormed out and bolted the rickety door.

Tears streamed down velvet cheeks as Kat stood in shock. *I'll never give in to you, Tahl—never! Starve me if you must, but nothing will break my strength of mind.* Boiling with anger, she streaked to the bed, yanked off the discolored, threadbare cover, and draped it over icy shoulders. Although the room was fairly dark, the candle was extinguished in order to provide some illumination when night fell.

Alone, frightened, and angry, she plopped on the straw mattress and drew shivering limbs up close to her body for warmth. The hours passed quickly, and as night drew near, the chill increased. She looked around for something more to wrap up in, but there was nothing else. A glance down brought hope. Her skirt's silk lining could provide a great deal of warmth. Cold-numbed hands trembled as copious yards of the luxurious material were ripped off and enrobed a chilled body. After several moments, the improvised cloak offered some relief.

Darkness began to flood the chamber which prodded her to light the candle. A moan from the hallway caused the hair on her arms to rise. "Who's there?" She swallowed hard and tentatively walked to the door. A minute crack revealed movement in the cell across the murky hall. "Hello? Are you Cianest?"

An eerie hiss-like 'yessss' was replied.

"My name is Kat. I'm the sister of Queen Adera of Bowlandria. I've been abducted by that thug Tahl and imprisoned here. Did he do the same to you?"

"Yessss, it was he who enslaved me. State your name once more."

"My given name is Kathleen, but most call me Kat." Although the ghoulish voice was fearsome, a noticeable undertone of sadness and compassion was detected.

For several moments there was only silence. "I know the name and the person, for the Lady Adera and I were once inseparable friendsss—our lives joyful as we shared happy days together. You were a mere child when last ssseen. The Queen risked all in an attempt to rescue me. Many times she tried, only to have countlessss souls lost in defeat. Tahl and Odiene are powerful, and the land well protected by Qergs. Please, do not hold fear, for unless we meet on the eve of a full moon, I ssshall not harm the sister of one so loved. However, heed my warning. You mussst avoid all contact on that solitary night, sweet child, for my odious thirsssst cannot be controlled. It is my curssse."

Kat was intrigued by this stranger's revelations. "I don't understand. If you and my sister were so close, why were you abandoned? That's not like her to give up."

The sound of hooves pacing a stone floor sent chills down Kat's spine. *What kind of creature is Cianest? Will I meet the same fate?* Her stomach lurched as a tinge of dread hit.

"Kat, you mussst not quarrel with Tahl. If given the opportunity, play to the devil's insatiable vanity. I pray you do not sssuffer his wrath as I have been made to do. There

72

is no essscape from this land of the lost. But hear what I say—Adera will never relinquish her quessst to rescue one so cherished. Never surrender hope. Now, try to ressst, child. He will return at dawn."

The comment brought a snicker. "Dawn? Is there such a thing in this forlorn region? I'm so thirsty. At least the brut could have given me water." The feisty girl turned from the door with head hung low. "Good night, Cianest, pleasant dreams."

Kat blew out what was left of the candle, curled up on the rudimentary cot, and leaned her head against the wall. Vermin could be heard scampering about, intermingled with occasional sobs from the cell across the hall. Little sleep would be had this night.

Doleful turquoise eyes gazed into nothingness. Adera had tried to rest, but the thought of Kat in the hands of their nefarious cousin tormented a weary mind. She leaned against a large boulder with her head on one arm and a rather sharp sword grasped firmly by the other. Brilliant shafts from the rising sun went unnoticed as dismal visions smothered consciousness. *Why did I act with such an unwary lack of judgment? The past has been repeated, and as before, I am to blame. Had we simplified our union, my repugnant relatives would have remained in Mantalac…securely enchained within its borders by father's banishment. Once before, I naively granted Odiene and Tahl a solitary reprieve so they might attend Father's funeral. My civility was rewarded with the despicable abduction of an innocent friend. Many lives were lost during our failed rescue attempts, and I fear this mission shall suffer the same fate.* Startled by a hand on her shoulder, Adera spun around with sword drawn.

"Whoa, I come in peace." Randy chuckled and gently pushed the blade aside. "In case you didn't realize it darlin', this sucker's a tad sharp."

She glanced at the weapon, gave off a soft agonizing wail, and hurled it to the ground. "Oh Randy, I am so sorry. You might have been injured by my hand. Please, forgive me."

He cradled the Queen's quaking body in his arms and kissed a troubled forehead. "You don't have to apologize to me, sweetheart. I understand what you're going through. We all love Kat, but that little livewire is a lot stronger than most realize. We're gonna get her back safe and sound, you'll see. There's not one of us here who isn't concerned and worried. Ironically, these emotions might work to our advantage. I've come to realize that intense resolve often overcomes implausible odds. Tahl and Odiene have only their wits and magical tricks."

Tom walked up and took her hand. "Don't torture yourself like this, Highness. Yesterday was your wedding day. Festivities rightfully overshadowed your sisters every moment. The responsibility to oversee Kat's safety didn't rest on either you or Randy's heads. If anything, the blame sits square on my shoulders more than anyone else. It seems we all appear to share a bit of guilt. Merlin's wracked with remorse, and I've had to do a good bit of talking to ease his anguish. Even poor McLachen feels he's responsible and should have stood watch over her. The hard truth is, not one of us is guilty of anything. That title, my Queen, belongs entirely to Tahl and Odiene."

Adera turned and hugged Tom. "I adore Kat as a sister, and the others care for her as a friend, but you and she are united by destiny—two souls bound to each other by divine love. It is clear your heart cloaks intolerable pain."

She caressed his hand and squeezed. "Should an ounce of harm befall Kat, believe me when I say Tahl and Odiene will pay the ultimate price. It is my *solemn promise*. Our land may never be altogether void of wickedness, but it will not be tolerated and shall be vanquished when encountered."

The handsome young man exhaled deeply and nodded. "It's almost unbelievable how one little ole country gal could touch the hearts of so many, but she has." He chuckled and glanced over at the group who huddled around the campfire. "Take a gander at our friends. There's not one of them who wouldn't give their life to save hers. A few years ago, McLachen pushed Kat aside and took the sea serpent's deathblow in order to spare his lady. Merneos and Horace could have easily traveled back to Durmeleigh after the wedding, but instead chose to come on this venture, even though it could deliver death. Meeley and Charlie never offered a split second of hesitation. That type of devotion will conquer all evildoing. As you've always told us, love is the most powerful force on earth, and lady, there is a bodacious amount of it flowing within this group."

Randy nudged his friend. "I couldn't have said it any better, Tom. You plum hit the nail on the head. Now, what say we all pack up our depression and hit the road?"

Within moments the horses were readied and the group mounted up. McLachen and Chendar were overanxious and almost left without their riders. As the group traveled along, Adera gazed into the clear sky. "Do not despair, dear sister. We are coming. You are not forgotten."

Kat paced the nippy cobblestone floor trying to infuse her body with a bit of warmth. Hunger pangs were intensifying, and her throat was parched from lack of water. She walked to the peephole window and looked up into the gloomy heavens. Suddenly, the faint whisper of a familiar voice permeated the still air. "Adera?" A glint of hope rose in misty eyes, but quickly faded to reality. *I must be getting weak and hallucinating.* "Please, don't forget me. This is almost more than I can bear. Help me, Tom."

Disheartening thoughts were curtly interrupted by a strange scratching at the door. At first, fear thwarted any attempt to discover the cause. But as always, curiosity overtook logic, and she slowly meandered over. The sound came from near the bottom so she kneeled down and peeked through the cracks. "Oh!" The sight of a deep violet eye peering back was startling and caused her to tumble backward. However, a weak meow eased the jumpiness. "Jiminy Crickets, it's a cat. What are you doing down here, little one? If you're prowling around for some big juicy rats, you've certainly come to the right place. This joint has enough rodents to feed a feline army. Wish I could let you in, but there's no way to open the door. Sure would be nice to have some friendly company though."

A furry black paw squeezed under the gaping threshold. Kat reached down and stroked the velvet-coated foot then gently caressed it in her ice-cold hand. Her touch brought a macabre moan from the small creature. "What's wrong? Did I hurt you in some way?"

Cianest hissed. "You did nothing wrong, Kat, it wasss the creature's way of stating his anguish over your imprisonment. He too is captive, but unlike you, his cell is within the body of thisss animal."

Kat frowned in confusion. "I don't understand, Cianest. How can that be?"

"Odiene possesses an instrument of horror. It can transform any living creature into sssomething of her choosing. I alssso am a victim of the article's grotesque enchantment. Our fur-cloaked friend is called Jypsey by all in thisss kingdom, but his actual name is Larc. In life, he wasss a Fairy King scheduled to be fed to me upon the rise of the full moon. At the last moment, Odiene decided not to grant him a swift death. Instead, the kind nobleman would sssuffer unbearable humiliation and be forced to live a torturous life as her pet. The poor thing cannot speak and mussst obey her commands. However, there are times it will endure severe punishment to offer a bit of comfort to other captives. Not long ago, he wasss injured while helping three fairy's escape. I observed his apparent unconventional familiarity with one of them in particular. Jypsey senssses your sorrow and weeps for you in the only manner possible."

Kat sat down on the cold stone floor and continued to stroke the warm paw. "Cianest, you said you are also a victim. Does that mean you were not always the creature you are now?"

Seconds passed in silence before Kat received an answer.

"I was once beautiful…my heart and soul unsoiled. Food wasss not needed for my kind. We obtain nourishment from the radiant light expelled by *any* sun. Tahl kidnapped me after the funeral of Zuegas. His intentions were far from honorable. When I refused his lussstful advances, he used his mother's devilish device to punish me. It was then I became this dessspicable creature. On the eve of a full moon, the thirst for blood and flesssh grows intense. There is no way to suppress the overwhelming desire. Without it…I will perish. Many

77

timesss I have fought to avoid the brutal ritual, but it is a curse that cannot be triumphed. I *mussst* kill and devour the victims. Often, Tahl and Odiene stand at the door and watch—their vile laughter mingling with the prey's screamsss. For days after, I weep over the deed, but it cannot be halted and will again take placcce upon the next lunar cycle."

Kat fought back tears of sympathy. Cianest was obviously a kind and gentle life form, compelled to execute the torturous ceremony for the sheer enjoyment of the poisonous duo. "I don't even know how to respond to this story. My heart is saddened. You say it is a curse? Is there a means to break it?"

"There isss a way, only one, but it is dangerous and nearly impossible. When the user of the implement is destroyed, the enchantment is dissssolved. Tahl is capable of performing a transformation, but rarely does so. Most captives are changed by Odiene. However, she is highly protected. No one can approach her at any given time. Also, the slaying must be fulfilled by someone who is not afflicted. If I were to destroy Odiene, the ssspell would be undone for all who were besieged by her hand. If by chance I destroyed Tahl, who cassst my spell, all changed by him would be freed, but in punishment, my damnation would remain."

"Wow, seems they've certainly covered all the angles. Suppose I somehow managed to destroy him, would you then return to your former self?"

"Such a task would indeed let loossse my bonds. However, it is a perilously unwissse concept to contemplate. Although I desire release from this hideous form, I forbid any attempt. Tahl and Odiene are equally devious and cunning. You will *not* sssucceed."

Kat rolled her eyes and exhaled. "Geez, now you're beginning to sound like Adera. Don't do this, Kat, don't do that, Kat…it's far too dangerous to try, Kat, but by the way, I have an eighty-foot titan I need you to slay. What the dickens gives with you guys? I may look young, but I'm far from being a little child. In reality, I have *many* rough years under my belt. Don't underestimate this little ole country girl's crafty talents."

The sound of an ancient iron door creaking open caused all communication to cease. Approaching footsteps brought a hiss from Cianest.

"Kat, Lord Tahl issss coming, do as I have directed. As much as it may disgust you, play to his vanity. Under no circumstance are you to crossss him. Promise me this request."

"Okay, you have my word, but I want it clearly understood, Cianest, if the opportunity arises, I will free you."

The clank of keys at the door caused Kat to quickly return to her makeshift bed. Slowly, the door opened. A masculine figure with arms on hips stood silent in the rough-hewn entryway, his face subdued by the dim light.

Kat's tone was highly sarcastic, "I presume it is you, Tahl? Or has one of your goons lost a lot of weight?"

"It appears a night in this hell hole hasn't altered your flippant attitude, dear cousin. Perhaps another week will temper that tongue."

Panic rose in amber eyes. Thought of remaining in the cold, moldy, vermin infested cell brought an instant apology. "I—I'm sorry, Tahl. These miserable conditions have caused me to be less than amiable. Surely you can understand that? Perhaps we should get to know each other on more *agreeable* grounds."

79

He moved into the light, revealing a smirking grin. "That's more like it, my pet." A gloved hand was extended. "Come. Allow me to escort you to *finer* accommodations."

She nodded and reached out in submissive acknowledgement of the gallant gesture. "I hope you will forgive my sullied appearance and rather unpleasant stench, my Lord. Might I be granted some water to bathe? My garment, however, is quite beyond repair."

Lecherous green eyes leisurely skimmed the tattered gown which now scantly cloaked a rather statuesque figure. "You have dressed better, but I actually find this present lack of attire remarkably stimulating. Nevertheless, I shall remain *for now*, a gentleman. A bath awaits and fresh garments are laid out in your room. It is my desire you dress in a more fitting color. Blood-red has always been one of my favorites as is the style I have chosen."

Kat remembered the promise to Cianest and drew on her womanly wiles to effectively manipulate his smug egotism. "It is an excellent choice, my Lord. I believe such a flamboyant hue might better compliment my black hair. Red has always been a color I thought to wear, but never have."

They ascended a lengthy spiraling staircase which led to a large open room. After spending several hours in obscure darkness, the abundant candlelight caused her to squint. "Tahl, may we stop by the fire a moment so I might warm my body. I'm very chilled."

His rough hand tightened its grip and jerked her forward. She wanted to fight…to kick and bite him in anger, but somehow managed to restrain rising emotions.

"No, I find your odor offensive and do not wish to be subjected to it any longer than need be." He shoved her away from him and clapped his hands. "Isabelle."

80

Immediately, a young woman, with head lowered in a subservient manner, entered and stood silent.

"Take this foul-smelling piece of rubbish to the arranged quarters. Bathe, perfume, and properly prepare her. Once she is made suitable, bring the wench back to me. Now, go. The sight of the two of you sickens me."

The docile maiden limped over to Kat, gently took hold of an arm, and led her away. Not a word was uttered as they traveled toward the intended location. Kat was astonished to find the chosen chamber quite spacious and immoderately furnished with lavish antiques. Several long narrow windows, obviously designed to thwart off any chance of escape, dotted the exterior wall. Although adorned with many unique garnitures, the atmosphere lacked cheer. Laden walls, draperies, and bedding, did little to brighten the setting, giving the room a funereal atmosphere.

"Your bath has been made ready, mistress." Isabelle's voice was timid—her eyes lowered.

Kat walked over and took the strange young woman's calloused hand. "You appear to be human. Where did you come from, Isabelle?"

"It is forbidden for me to say, mistress. Come, I will assist you to disrobe and bathe. Our master wishes you be prepared posthaste. I trust the scented oils chosen will be agreeable."

"Hold on just a dang second. That jerk is not my *master*. Now I get it…you're his slave." She lifted the girls chin and peered into terrified cocoa-brown eyes. A quick glance revealed a plain, but eye-catching face accompanied by a well-endowed body partially visible beneath the semi-sheer gown. "Do you have family?"

81

Although eyes darted about in near panic, Kat's soothing words seemed to ease the apprehension. "Yes. I come from the village. There are many of us within the walls. When the master views one he finds appealing, they are captured and brought to the Manor to satisfy any and all of his desires. None return once they enter the palace. Most vanish, never to be seen again. Please my lady, you must quickly wash. I do not wish to feel his fury."

"Don't worry, Isabelle, I'll cooperate. Sure wouldn't want anything to happen because of me. If truth be known, I'm pretty darn anxious to scrub away this stinking grime." Kat yanked off the tattered gown and slipped into the Jasmine-scented tepid water. "Isabelle, will you sit and talk with me a bit? I wish to know more."

At first the shy maid refused, but finally relinquished her fear and sat alongside the large sunken tub. "There is little I can reveal, mistress. It is forbidden."

Kat drew a breath. "I understand and won't force disclosure of something that might cause danger or distress. Whatever we chat about will be our little secret. No one else need know a thing. I wish to become a friend—not an enemy. Why haven't you tried to get away from this slimy jerk and return to your family?"

Tears began to form in Isabelle's eyes. She stepped back and lifted her gown, "Because of this, mistress."

The sight of the hideous clawed chicken limb brought a shriek. "Holy blazes! Did he do this to you? How?"

"I once refused his advances and later tried to escape. Lord Tahl had Odiene use the amulet to transform my foot and lower leg making any who would look upon me turn away in disgust. I was warned that should I make another attempt, more of my body would be altered."

Water speckled the gray granite floor as Kat leaped from the tub, wrapped a towel around her wet body, and embraced Isabelle. "He's a dang blasted monster. Apparently, poor Cianest suffered the ultimate punishment, and who knows how many others have succumbed to that pair's insane magic? Trust me when I say, if there's a breath left in this old body, I'll find a way to break these curses and free everyone. The first step needed is to gain Sir Warp-A-Lot's trust. What say we check out the *wonderful* attire chosen for me? Then, I'll go see the creep and put my womanly charms to work on that snake. Sure as heck won't be easy. Just hope I can restrain from vomiting."

The sight of the selected dress brought a wince. "You gotta be kidding. What a gaudy piece of rubbish." She held up the risqué frock and frowned. "Well, it's far from my liking, but at least the pitiful garb is clean. How the tar heel do you put this stupid thing on?" The floor length gown, the color of freshly drawn blood, had a strapless bodice and asymmetrical fitted top. Several semi-sheer panels, pieced together to form a lavish skirt, flowed from the gathered waist and revealed an immodest amount of leg as the wearer moved. A serpentine belt of gold and diamonds wound lustfully upward between her breasts, coiled around the neck, and rested its serpent-like head obscenely in the cleavage of her bosom.

Isabelle braided Kat's long raven hair and added a few finishing touches. Fully dressed, she walked over to the floor length mirror. The sight of the flamboyant image brought a yelp, "Leaping lizards, I look like some shoddy honky-tonk harlot." She sighed and shrugged her shoulders. "Well, guess it's time to see if this tawdry mass of material, or lack of it, might help beauty slay the beast."

Kat drew a deep breath, strolled to one of the narrow windows, placed both hands on the damp wall, and stared into bleak obscurity. "Merlin often said the woodland trees would carry words from one person to another in great times of distress. If what he proclaims is true, I beseech this plea be delivered to my beloved husband." The willful girl swallowed hard and fought back tears that begged for release. "My heart belongs only to you, Tom—always has and always will. Forgive me sweetheart…survival depends on what I must do. Please hurry. I fear time is limited." Velvet lips blew a kiss out the window and a forlorn head lowered. Immediately, a sudden cool wisp of air brushed her cheek, as though in eerie acknowledgement of the heartfelt request. "Thank you," she whispered.

She straightened her back, squared bare shoulders, and turned from the window. "Isabelle, what say we get this stupid circus on the road? Obviously, the demented *ringmaster* waits. Sorry to break the bad news, but if that idiot cousin thinks he'll tame this *Kat*, he's in for one heck of a surprise." Filled with a mere shred of hope, she proudly strolled from the room.

Chapter Six
Lovely Limbs

Queen Adera fidgeted in the makeshift saddle. To her, time appeared to progress at a frustratingly slow pace. Sheer minutes now felt like hours. She had wanted to reach Mantalac two days hence, but unfortunately the kingdom still remained a little over a hundred miles away.

McLachen stopped and drew a breath. "Is something amiss, My Queen?"

Adera reached down and gently stroked the stallion's silken mane. "No sweet friend. I merely grow anxious."

"Our concern is shared, Majesty. My Lady resides in a terrible place. I fear her very life dangles precariously at the vile hand of Tahl. If you so desire, I shall pick up the pace. My legs do not yet grow weary and can easily travel many more miles."

The benevolent matriarch smiled and gave a reassuring pat on his neck. "Although it is tempting, dear one, we must be considerate of the entire group, including the other horses. All are severely fatigued and require rest. Tomorrow we shall begin at daybreak."

The duel conversation was interrupted when Randy and Tom galloped up and flanked her sides. Randy reached over and caressed the Queen's satiny hand. "What say we call it a day, pretty lady? Our horses are about spent, and night is rapidly approaching. I think it's about time we make camp." The handsome newlywed looked around and sighed. "Wow, this area is completely foreign to me, and unlike any place I've ever seen. Sure wouldn't want to pick

85

the wrong spot and lead us into a nasty situation. I'm up to suggestions, *Mrs. Carlton.*"

Adera found the comment a welcome relief and giggled. "You always brighten my darkest moments…*Mr. Carlton.*" Turquoise eyes danced, and a blush rose on her face as she blew him a kiss. "We have entered the domain of the Gentle Woods. No harm shall befall us within these boundaries. If memory holds true, a crystal stream flows nearby. The water is cool, and the adjacent grass lush. Our horses will take pleasure in resting there and gain strength on the nourishing forage."

They traveled on about half a mile until the babbling brook she spoke of came into view. Within minutes, camp was made ready. The Arabians were unsaddled, watered, and turned out to graze while the two Bayards kept an ever-watchful eye to insure no steed wandered off.

Day quickly faded into night as everyone settled around the cozy campfire. After a brief and somewhat lively round of conversation, sleep descended upon the encampment.

Charlie propped against a blanketed saddle, closed his eyes, and cuddled Meeley who wiggled in beside him.

On the far side of the fire pit, Merneos and Horace made makeshift beds out of copious mounds of blanket-covered leaves.

Merlin, as usual, wandered off, vanishing into the forest's misty darkness.

Randy prepared a comfortable mat for him and Adera in the shadow of a large old, moss-laden log. With his beloved wife cradled safely in his arms, he quickly succumbed to exhaustion and drifted off to sleep.

Tom walked over to a large oak, sat upright, and leaned his head back against its rough bark. Suddenly, he leaped to feet and shrieked. "Hey, hey, hey, what the blazing dickens is going on? Who's there?" The commotion woke the entire troupe who immediately rushed to his side with weapons drawn. "I swear on my old hound's grave, it felt like someone just twirled their fingers through my hair."

Suddenly, from out of the giant tree, a pair of delicate hands reached toward the frightened young man. Soon, a voluptuous body emerged, followed by another. "We search for the mortal known as Tom."

Adera used dignified caution as she approached the duo. "The one you touched is who you seek. May I ask why he is of interest?" She extended a hand in a show of friendship. "I am Adera, Queen of Bowlandria. Our venture is peaceful. We travel to Mantalac to rescue an individual who has been wrongfully taken from us."

The two willowy figures gazed at each other before speaking. "We are nymphs of the woods and protectors of our land. My name is Leora, and this is my sister, Willa"

Adera smiled and bowed her head in a gesture of respect. "Tom, these ladies explicitly request an audience with you, although I do not yet know their intention."

He sauntered over and stood beside the sovereign. "I'm Tom. What is it you wish?"

Leora's bare feet scarcely touched the dew-kissed sod as she moved toward him. "We are kin to the trees. They have asked us to deliver a message. It is from a captive at Odium Manor."

Randy rushed up alongside his friend. "Tom, they must mean *Kat*." He then took a hurried step closer to Leora. "Okay, spit it out lady, what did she have to say?" The abrupt outburst caused the nymphs to swiftly retreat back into the oak.

Adera grabbed Randy's arm. "You must calm yourself. Do not cause fear." She edged close to the massive tree

87

and spoke one octave above a whisper. "We mean no harm and apologize for such explosive anxiety. The life of our imprisoned loved one is of overwhelming concern. She is my sister, the spouse of Tom, and lifelong friend of Randy. Please, return and convey her message."

Several moments passed as an eerie tomblike silence surrounded the camp. At last, Leora and Willa inched out from their wooden carapace of sanctuary.

Randy started to speak, but was instantly hushed by the Queen. "So we may prove true sincerity, all shall humble ourselves before you." She motioned for the group to kneel. Merneos and Horace frowned, but soon realized the token action was vital and followed suit.

Willa leaned over to her sister and raised her voice in a deliberate manner. "I'm still not convinced we can trust them. Talk about a mismatch of races. When did Elves begin to mingle with inferior humans? I've heard the elders speak of Queen Adera, but even one so great as she now appears to bond with these disgusting mortals. Do not venture far from our home, sister."

The two sprites had delicate facial similarities and were astoundingly beautiful, but that is where the resemblance ended.

Leora was an apparent creature of spring—her lithe body clothed in a fluid grass-green gown. Vivid emerald eyes and pouty coral lips complimented a sun-kissed complexion. Remarkable waist long tresses of colorful wild flowers appeared to literally grow out of wispy light auburn hair.

Willa, on the other hand, was an obvious representative of winter. Rosy cheeks and lips glorified flawless skin that was white as new fallen snow. An impressive shag mane of long-needle pine matched the stunning creature's striking

88

green eyes while a gauzy gown of scarlet seductively wrapped a statuesque body.

The snap of a brittle twig caused all heads to turn as a lone figure emerged from the ghostly darkness. Merlin casually placed a hand on the trunk of a nearby birch. "Why is everyone staring? Have my robes become soiled?" The great wizard snickered and strolled into the dim campfire light. "My woodland friends inform me you have been asked to deliver a message to Master Tom, my dear sprites. I suggest you dismiss the uncalled for wariness and get along with the assigned task. There's nothing to fear here. Now, please do as you have been instructed posthaste." Although his voice was mellow, significant undertones of irate forcefulness was detected.

Willa and Leora glanced at each other, shrugged their shoulders, and obeyed the judicious conjurer without delay. After Kat's words had been conveyed, Leora gently kissed Tom's cheek. "The lovely lady blew this token into the wind and prayed it would reach you."

Tom was visibly shaken by the disclosure and stared at the ground as though it might offer a miraculous word of comfort. At long last, he raised his head and looked over at Adera who burst out in tears as their eyes met. He rushed to her and caressed trembling hands. "It's going to be okay, Highness. We'll get to her in time. Kat's one tough cookie, and when backed into a corner, our little lady will come out fighting like a wildcat. Tahl is going to have his hands full." He drew a deep breath. "Now, how 'bout you dry those tears. That southern cookie has some mighty powerful blood running through those veins. She'll be fine. Hopefully, we'll get an early start tomorrow and gain some ground. I know it won't be easy, but try to get a little rest."

Adera teetered and stood on the verge of collapse. Randy moved close and wrapped a strong arm around her tiny waist for additional support. She quickly regained composure, glanced around, and blushed. "I apologize for a fleeting show of weakness. It has passed and my banner of fortitude returned. We will retrieve Kat safely. Tahl and his insane mother shall be destroyed. This foul act will be their last deed of evil upon our earth."

McLachen whinnied and pawed the ground furiously. "I suggest man and beast sleep well tonight. At dawn, Chendar and I will embark at a robust pace. Keep up or remain behind—I do not care. Our only concern is for the safe return of My Lady."

Adera pulled from Randy's grip and approached the majestic equine. She could clearly see anger in his dark brown eyes. "I beseech patience for a short time more, noble horse. Rage will not free my sister, but could hinder any chance of successful rescue. Our assault must be swift and well calculated or it is doomed to fail. You are aware of past events and know what I say is irrefutable. Tahl and Odiene are substantially protected. Never, for so little as a split second, can our guard be lowered. Nor should we underestimate their malevolent powers. It would bring about the guaranteed destruction of this entire group, and in retaliation, that of my sister."

The great horse snorted—then lowered his head. "Your words hold truth, Highness, and I shall obey. Forgive my restless outburst."

"Sweet McLachen, we share your pain. Kat is loved by all here. I believe this united assembly of friends attests to their unconditional devotion. These steadfast companions have willingly surrendered themselves to deadly harm for her sake. I have always stated there no greater force

90

stronger than love. All here overflow with such emotion, filling us with unmitigated power. Failure will *not* prevail."

Merneos and Horace edged up beside Adera. "You know the sanctified word spoken by an Elf is a bond that cannot be broken once it is given. Horace and I pledge our allegiance to this quest. Our every breath from this moment forward shall be dedicated to the deliverance of our friend—even if it is to be our last. We do not acknowledge defeat nor will we surrender to the evil from whence it came." The noble Elf King and trusty warrior placed a hand over their hearts and bowed.

Without a word being uttered, Meeley, Charlie, Randy, Tom, and Merlin stepped forward and mimicked the Elves' gesture of dedication.

"I thank all here for such stirring dedication." McLachen bowed in acknowledgement.

Standing wide-eyed in the shadows, the two wood nymphs shuddered in obvious wariness of the strangers. Slowly, the duo inched near the gathering.

"We have never before witnessed such remarkable resolution," Leora declared. "This bizarre assemblage of moderately mixed beings is beyond impressive. We would like to aid you in some way if we may."

Willa drew a long breath, gave a smirk, and put her hands on her hips. "Well, for holly bush sakes! Don't just stand there gawking at us with such silly looks on your faces. We're offering to help."

Merlin's blue-black eyes glowed. "We happily accept the gracious offer, my dears. I believe you might be of enormous assistance. Let us all sit as we discuss a further course of action."

Dead dried twigs were added to the fire and soon delivered welcomed warmth to night-chilled bodies. Once settled, plans were formulated.

"Merlin, is there a way you can get a message back to Kat?" Tom asked.

The wily wizard stroked his long beard. "I could send word through the trees, but Kat does not speak or understand their language, nor that of the forest animals. Such an effort would be futile."

Willa stood and spoke. "Do none of you possess a brain? I believe the answer is quite simple. Have a fairy convey the message. Most speak your language. They are quite small, winged, and unbelievably fast. An experienced warrior should have no trouble flying in and out of the manor safely." She gave a quirky look around at dazed faces, rolled her big emerald eyes, sighed, and sat back down.

Randy huffed. "Well, that would be fine and good, but doesn't exactly look like we have a bag of fairy's hanging from our saddles to choose from."

The unique winter nymph returned a sarcastic glance. "The fairy kingdom of Drealon is only a short distance from here, *mortal*. There is a protective spell guarding their land which makes it invisible to the human eye. We know the password and can take you there, as long as you promise to keep those clumsy big feet of yours from stepping on the poor wee things."

Merlin rose and placed himself in a guarded position in-between the fiery nymphs and the others. "I believe that shall be enough unnecessary banter. However, crude as this lady's comment may be, it is a valid solution. I suggest we put differences aside and work in a more suitable union. Our goal is not to determine the most superior among us,

92

but to save Kat." Dark wizard eyes glared with strong intent as he glanced around at each member.

Charlie stood up next to Merlin and put his arm around the conjuror's shoulder. "He's right, guys. This isn't the time for us to be bickering between ourselves. That's a definite recipe for disaster."

Meeley jumped up alongside her husband. "Right you are, sweetheart. I for one have about had enough of this childish quibbling. We better dang straight begin to work as a team, or failure will be imminent. Sure wish I had been allowed to bring Knox. We'd make fast work of that creep Tahl, grab Kat, and all head back home to Bowlandria."

Soon, the area around the campfire grew loud with tense voices as the group once again began to squabble among themselves.

Adera had been patient to this point, but the bickering pushed her to the limit. Her voice boomed as she abruptly stood, "This must end, now! Meeley is correct. If we do not set our differences aside, the outcome will bring defeat and death to each of us, including Kat. Leora and Willa, will you be so kind to lead us to the fairy kingdom when daylight appears? Your resolution is unfaultable. Kat *must* be informed of this rescue party. Knowledge of us will fill her with crucial optimism and allow dormant wits to surface. Without such hope, she is doomed. Randy, Tom, Charlie, and Meeley, we shall have no further bursts of ire, do you understand? Each could do well to take a lesson of tolerance from our Elvin friends. Meeley, you were not permitted to bring Knox as Tahl drools to capture such a prize. For the safety of your beloved dragon, I did not allow it. Tom and Randy, I share your anxiety, but it will only hamper our attempt to save Kat. Merlin, you are a

93

dear friend, but your incessant wanderings are becoming most intolerant."

She paused and drew a deep breath. "Dawn will soon be upon us. I suggest we try to obtain a bit of rest. Weary minds and bodies are most ineffective. Pleasant dreams my friends."

Her words were powerful and promptly calmed escalating tensions. A short time later, only the faint sounds of sleep was heard.

The sun had barely risen over the horizon as the group set out for the fabled fairy kingdom. Hours passed, and the once lofty forest road gradually became an almost impenetrable narrow path. Horses stumbled and nearly unseated their riders as sturdy legs became tangled in the thick underbrush. Soon, the forest grew even denser, forcing the riders to dismount and walk in front of their mounts in a futile effort to clear the way. Sinuous branches whipped their faces and tore delicate flesh.

Adera, entwined in a dense cluster of kudzu tendrils, took a nasty fall. Blood infused tears trickled down her honeyed cheek. "How much farther must we travel, Leora? We cannot endure much more of this, nor can our mounts."

The pretty nymph helped the Queen to her feet. "We are only a few steps away, Majesty." She pointed to a long cascading thicket that draped a ponderous stand of pines. "The entrance is through that coppice. It appears impassable, but will part easily once the words to enter are uttered."

Although the opening was only a few feet away, it took several minutes to reach due to the treacherous terrain. Leora placed a hand on one of the spiraling kudzu tentacles and uttered strange words barely conceivable to the human ear. Suddenly, the vines began to shudder and divided like living draperies pulled by a great invisible cord. Beyond was a picturesque landscape, open, clear, flowered, and spacious. The air smelled fresh with a tinge of floral fragrance. Hues were more intense than could be imagined. Greens, blues, reds, and yellows were stronger in tone than any ever seen by these new visitors and brought gasps of delight. Bountiful flocks of unusual and utterly brilliant birds, apparently unafraid and curious of the guests, freely landed upon outstretched hands. The trees were thick with masses of butterflies that glowed brightly as they fluttered about.

Leora and Willa began to chuckle. "Is this a sight unlike any other? Welcome to the fabled kingdom of Drealon. The city is not far, but it may be advisable we travel on alone. The fairies do not take to newcomers easily and will be terrified. Queen Fallon is a wise sovereign. After we explain your plight, I believe she shall graciously welcome you with open arms, Highness. We will return in a short time. 'Till then, please rest." The summer like nymph took hold of her sister's arm and the pair sprinted off.

The quaint fairy village came into sight within minutes. As predicted, many of the wee folk scattered and hid in fear as the two giants approached. Although they had seen the wood sprites prior, the sight of the 'tall ones' promoted an air of panic.

Separation from the outsiders apparently awarded Willa a bit of relaxation, and she began to giggle. "Look at those miniature inhabitants running around like a bunch of common garden ants. Wonder what they would do if I stomped my foot real hard and rattled the ground a bit. Hmm, might be interesting to find out."

Leora placed a firm grip on her mischievous sister's arm. "Willa, don't you *dare* do such a thing. These are our friends. Sometimes you can be such an impish vixen. If I didn't love you so much, I swear I would disown you. Now, behave." She leaned over and placed and tender kiss to the pretty nymph's ivory cheek. "We need to stop here and wait for Queen Fallon to approach. I hope she will grant our visitors an audience. They appear remarkably upset and desperate for help."

It wasn't long before a small, elegant golden carriage pulled by four teeny white horses hastened toward them and stopped a few yards from the sprite's feet. The awkward looking coachman immediately leaped down, opened the door, and offered a hand to the royal occupant.

"Good day, Queen Fallon. My sister and I come in peace. Might we be granted a moment of your time?" Leora spoke in a temperate tone.

The imperial fairy was dressed in a brilliant teal gown which intensified the vividness of her carrot-red hair. "You are always welcome in this land, my dears. However, for the safety of my people, we must insist you remain outside the village. If you will sit, we shall converse." She motioned to the soft turf.

Leora and Willa eased down which brought them closer to the Ruler and made conversation more effortless for all.

"We have not had the pleasure of our neighboring wood nymphs for many moons. What brings you to Drealon?"

"Your Highness, we encountered a group of travelers who are in desperate need of assistance. They come from Bowlandria. One is their Queen, Adera. It seems her sister

96

has been abducted by Lord Tahl. They are on a mission to free her. However, the task is futile. Alas, love for this hostage drives passionate fortitude. We thought perhaps you might meet with them and discuss the possibility of assistance."

The fairy Queen stood silent for several minutes and gazed off to the side. Finally, she looked up into their apprehensive faces. "I have heard of Adera…a kind, gentle, and noble woman. She is the daughter of a founding ancient I believe. Who accompanies the lady?

"She travels with four humans, two Elves, and uh, *Merlin*."

"Merlin?" The tiny monarch drew a deep breath. "He has not entered our region in many years. Last time was a bit of a fiasco. The wizard is quite clumsy…handsome, but never the less clumsy. Return to them and extend a cordial welcome. Regrettably, all must remain outside of town. I cannot put my citizens in harm's way. We will make immediate provisions to convene. I am *most* anxious to meet this queen. It will be a delight to hold court with another sovereign—especially one so renowned. Hurry off, my lofty friends. Inform those concerned they may enter."

The pair of wood nymphs rose, politely bowed, and ambled away. Echo's of thundering hammers made them smile at each other. It was obvious a platform designed to lift Queen Fallon up to a suitable height was already in the process of being constructed.

Willa nudged Leora as they walked. "What an idiotic idea. Those wee folk are too small to help. I cannot see where it makes a lick of sense for Adera to ask for their assistance."

97

"Oh no, sister, never underestimate these little beings. They are extremely clever, and their warriors are most valiant. I believe they could provide crucial information and that is ultimately what Adera seeks."

"Well, it's certainly a good thing these *foreigners* have their own mounts. Can you just see them trying to ride one of the fairy horses?" Willa quipped. The statement brought a robust laugh from the unique siblings as they scampered through the forest.

Crunching of dried leaves brought the group to their feet as the exotic sisters emerged from the woodland. Adera rushed over to Leora and Willa ahead of the others. "Did you meet with Queen Fallon? Are we able to continue? How far is it to their home?" Questions came in rapid succession causing the two sprites to stare in surprise.

"Yes Majesty, she will hold audience with the entire entourage and bids you welcome. Unfortunately, all must remain on the outskirts of town. Please understand, the residents are extremely small. Even when overly careful, the possibility of being accidently trampled raises trepidation."

Queen Adera nodded and forced a smile. "Understood...we shall graciously comply. Randy, Charlie, and Meeley, please gather our goods while Horace, Merlin, and Tom, ready the horses. Merneos, walk with me a moment. I desire a private conversation."

"Of course, Adera, I believe we share an equal concern."

Once out of hearing range, she turned and faced the noble King. "It is Tom. I do not know how he will react if any negativity is given. His love for Kat is profound. Please keep a close watch over him. I shall control my husband to avoid any further outbursts as witnessed a short time ago. It is critical we learn all we can from the fairies and perhaps gain a little insight to carry forth a victorious rescue."

"You need not worry. Horace and I will be vigilant and keep a watchful eye on the lad." He paused and momentarily looked away. "This venture may not end well, my lady. You must ready yourself for an outcome none of us wish to contemplate."

Adera sighed. "I am aware of what you say, Merneos, and have tried to brace for the worst. As you know, my failed attempt in the past cost the lives of countless brave souls. The thought of that tragic endeavor haunts me to this day. What is now requested is nearly inconceivable and most revolting, but you are my only hope. Neither I, nor any of the others, are capable of carrying out such a dreadful exploit. Should you choose to decline, I shall fully understand for the very thought of the deed sickens me."

King Merneos wrinkled his brow. "I shall do whatever is required, Adera, and do so without question. You must realize by now my loyalty is beyond reproach. We have been companions for many eons. Your command will be executed without hesitation."

She turned away from him, lowered her head, and began to weep into cupped hands.

My dearest Queen, speak the words that shall rid your soul of its distress." He walked around and stood before her, then gently lifted a quivering chin and wiped a tear-stained face.

"If our mission fails, and Kat cannot be saved, I beseech you to destroy her. I would rather she be dead than tortured like so many others at the hands of that vile demon. You are aware of what he has done to Cianest. My sister cannot be made to suffer the same fate. I seek an oath that you or Horace will not allow such a travesty to ensue. Your arrows are true and will quickly find their victim. Her suffering will be brief."

In a rare show of emotion, the noble king pulled Adera into his arms. "I vow to do as you direct. If no option prevails, her life will be spared from unspeakable agony. Death will be swift and painless." He looked into swollen turquoise eyes and planted a kiss on her cheek. "For now, let us not dwell on defeat, but embrace victory."

After gaining a brief moment of composure, the pair returned to their companions, who were ready to be underway. Kat's fate now rested in the hands of this small, diverse band of friends, and the unpredictable will of destiny. If successful, she and many others would be freed. However, if they failed, Kat would die.

Chapter Seven
A Fairy's Saga

As the unique hodgepodge of friends edged their way toward the designated Glenn in Drealon, Randy sprinted to catch up with Charlie and Meeley who shadowed the two wood nymphs. It had been decided the horses would be walked far behind the array to avoid the possibility they might accidently trample a wayward fairy. Horace and Merlin led the Arabians, while Merneos strolled alongside Adera and McLachen. Tom dawdled at the rear of the troupe…fully absorbed in a concentrated conversation with his Bayard horse Chendar.

"Hey guys, slow down," Randy huffed as he connected with the couple. "I've been hoping to get you two alone so we could talk in private. Finally seems that window has been opened, at least for a few minutes."

Meeley draped an arm around Randy's neck. "So, what's up, buttercup?"

"I'm not really sure how to address this, little britches," he replied with a slight chuckle, "It's kinda quirky. Has my wife mentioned anything about the rescue mission to either of you? That darling lady sure as shoot is not acting like herself and my gut says there's more to the dang picture than she's letting on. True, Adera would never callously deceive us, but wouldn't put it past her to hide a few bits of information in order to protect everybody. I'm pretty dog-gone sure a smidgen of truth is being intentionally withheld."

101

Charlie scratched his head. "Adera never confides much to me, or any other male figure, that's a bit understandable, but she might open up to Meeley, right sugar beet?"

Meeley took her arm down from around Randy's neck and sighed. "Well, now that you mention it, there was something I noticed earlier that seemed a trifle odd. Didn't want to say anything 'cause it seemed innocent enough and really was none of my business. I went to check on the horses and noticed Adera and Merneos talking in the woods. Wasn't able to hear the conversation, but she suddenly burst into tears. Now, here's the strange part, chaps. That high and mighty Elf took our queen in his arms and planted a kiss on her cheek."

"He did *what*?" Randy shrieked.

"Hush, you dodo. It wasn't *that* kind of embrace or kiss. More like one of comfort. Something obviously upset her big time. I think you are dead right, Randy. I'll try later to see what I can find out. I'll bet the barn it has to do with Kat. Haven't you noticed how distant her gaze is lately? That's not Adera. I haven't seen such a look in eons. Sure tells me there's a mighty big problem tormenting that brilliant mind. I suspect McLachen knows more than he's telling as well."

"Yeah, you women can be pretty secretive at times, but then again, who can figure out what goes through a female's brain." Charlie nudged Randy in the side and snickered. "Ouch, that hurt sweetie," he yelled after receiving a hard punch to the arm. "I was only kidding. Everyone has you figured out."

Meeley gave him another hard jab. "Yeah, well figure out how you'll treat those bruises." She gave him a wicked glance, turned, and strutted off.

Pent up emotions caused Randy to chuckle which quickly morphed into much needed robust laughter. "Charlie, when will you ever learn not to antagonize that firefly? She has a heart of gold, but the temper of a furnace. Let's hope that lady of yours can pull Adera aside later and get to the root of the problem. I'm pretty anxious to find out what the blazes is going on. Hey!" he yelled out— startled by an expected arm curling around his waist. "Adera, you nearly made me soil my britches."

She smiled and hugged him tighter. "If I may be so bold as to ask, what are you so anxious to find out about, sweetheart?"

He fidgeted a bit…worried his conversation may have been overheard. "Aw baby cakes, it's nothing. I'm just curious why we have to meet with the fairy monarch on the outskirts of town. Wonder if we're considered inferior and unworthy of their company?"

"They are tremendously skeptical of outsiders, especially humans. Few, if any, are ever allowed inside their borders. In your homeland, there was a time these gentle timid beings were hunted for sport. Many were even feared without reason. Sadly, when one was captured, it was cruelly treated and violently tortured, until death freed its suffering. Nearly all of their kind was destroyed. To save what remained of their race, they fled into our dominion. Although others live, Drealon is the last fairy kingdom to survive on this entire planet. Here they thrive, isolated from all others with the exception of a precious few."

Adera paused and took his hand. "Do not be concerned, darling. Fairies are not known to be pompous or hostile creatures. I believe Queen Fallon shall graciously extend every courtesy to us. You have always applied logic to situations. Please do so at this time. Our bodies are quite

103

large in comparison to theirs. The need to remain distant from their village is undeniably valid. So much as a little inadvertent nudge from one of our feet could cause extreme damage or death to many."

"Come here you beautiful goddess." He pulled her into his arms and embraced the love of his life tightly. "Not to worry, sweetheart. I will act as the proper spouse of the Queen of Bowlandria. We have had so darn little time to actually talk lately. Why don't you tell me more about the fairies as we walk along? Have you ever seen one?"

"Hey lovebirds, forget about me?" Charlie exclaimed. "Think I'll leave you two alone and go search out my own wife." He laughed, gave Randy a rap on the back, and left to join Meeley.

Adera and Randy looked at each other and began to giggle. They *had* momentarily put everything and everyone out of their thoughts. Even the concern for Kat was set aside, giving a welcomed bit of relief.

"I have never personally seen a fairy, but mother often made trips here. At that time, their land was ruled by a King. His name was Larc. She said he was a jolly soul...very kind and just."

Randy wrinkled a brow. "From the sound of what you're saying, he's no longer the monarch. Do you have any idea what happened to him?"

She drew a deep breath. "I do not recall the exact details, but it is thought the little King perished at the hands of Cianest. He and a small band of soldiers traveled beyond the secured border of Drealon and were captured by several Qergs. It was near the eve of a full moon and time for Cianest to feed. Neither he nor the soldiers were ever seen again."

104

"Holy blazes, what a horrible story. So, Fallon is his wife?"

"Yes. After months of searching, it was determined the King would not return. Fallon's coronation followed months later and she remains the current sovereign. I understand this Queen is wise, righteous, and dearly loved by her people."

Randy nudged Adera and chuckled, "Sounds a lot like the Queen of Bowlandria."

His comment brought a blush to her face. "Many of these magical creatures fly. Some do not have wings, either from being too young, or not achieving the desired character."

"Seriously, the little critters actually fly? I've heard all the legends, but never believed in their existence. Sure have to admit, nothing surprises me here anymore." He snickered. "I wasn't too overly excited about seeing this empire of theirs, but now I'm getting more and more anxious. Darn shame they disappeared from our world."

"Actually, meager groups linger in your world. They are drastically few in numbers and spread thin across the lands. Their habitats are progressively being diminished as humans develop more area. In time, all will cease to exist. Only our colony shall remain."

The pair continued conversing as they strolled along and soon arrived at the chosen site. A towering platform had been erected and the area appeared alive with activity. Tiny fairies fluttered about both on the ground and in the air. Although given short notice, the magical creatures created a dreamlike camp of captivating enchantment for the new guests. It was an astonishing feat.

"I believe your concerns might be laid to rest now, dear husband."

105

Randy looked around and shook his head. "Dang straight they are, honey bunch. No doubt remains. We are pretty darn welcome here. Say, you suppose that's Queen Fallon over there." He pointed to the middle of the tall stage where a foot high woman stood, flanked by many armored soldiers. A colorful rainbow gown nearly matched her delicate iridescent wings, while a cascade of orange-red strands fluttered in the soft breeze.

Adera walked over, knelt before the rustic pulpit, and bowed her head. "Queen Fallon, on behalf of me and my fellow companions, please accept our most humble greeting. We are grateful for your kindness and hospitality. I am Adera, Queen of Bowlandria."

The little fairy queen's voice was high-pitched, but amazingly audible. "It is our pleasure, Adera, to welcome such a noble monarch. Your illustrious reputation is renowned throughout the territory. We have endeavored to make these accommodations suitable and trust they will suffice. Unfortunately, our resources are limited and incapable of satisfying the nutritional needs for individuals of your stature. What can be gathered is all that can be offered. Please, be seated so we may all converse more comfortably."

Adera turned and motioned for the group to sit. The two aloof Elves drew a breath of displeasure, but relinquished and eased down. "Do not be troubled. We carry sufficient food and only seek refuge for the evening. Our mounts, however, will need to graze. I ask permission to turn them free. The magnificent black stallion is the noble Bayard, McLachen. His fame is known to all. He and his son Chendar will see the others remain at a safe distance to insure no harm shall befall your people."

106

"I have heard of this great steed and am privileged to have such a delightful creature visit our land. Permission is granted. They shall find our meadows exceptionally sweet and nourishing."

Suddenly, a small fairy rushed up the steps and hurried to the Queen's side nearly knocking her over. "Whoops. Sorry, Mother. Are these the travelers you spoke of? Wow, they *are* big aren't they? Hi, I'm Faye."

Queen Fallon pursed her lips and drew a very long deep breath. "Please forgive my rather unsophisticated and *impolite* daughter. I have tried to restrain this child's exuberance to no avail. Alas, she possesses more of her father's spirit than mine."

Randy, Charlie, and Meeley began to snicker at the incorrigible little sprite. Adera forced back a chuckle, turned, and motioned for the three to edge forward. "Highness, may I introduce my husband, Randy, and our dear friends Charlie and his wife Meeley." She then beckoned the Elves to approach. "It is with great pleasure I present another celebrated sovereign, King Merneos, ruler of the Kingdom of Durmeleigh. His companion is our talented Elvin friend, Horace." Adera spanned the area, but could not locate Merlin. "Somewhere nearby is the great wizard, Merlin, though only the trees can tell where he is."

Queen Fallon rolled her striking sea-foam green eyes. "Merlin we have long known and believe that is all need be said regarding the subject. On the other hand, I am particularly delighted to meet the exalted King of the Elves. Stories of your bravery and wisdom are legendary as are the escapades of your valiant warriors." The two Elves bowed their heads in respect, obviously content with the monarch's courtly recognition.

107

"My royal counselor and dear friend, Savah, will guide you to a location suitable to set up camp. Should there be other needs or requirements, please inform her, and all efforts will be made to facilitate the requests. As dusk falls, we shall meet again for an evening of mirth and conversation. 'Till then, I bid you good day." She walked to the stairs, spread her magnificent wings, and fluttered off, followed by the entire entourage.

Randy leaned over to Charlie. "Can you believe what we just saw? This is plum awesome."

"You said a mouthful and then some, Randy. Wish we could see the actual town, but they're right. Good thing Kat's not here. You dang well know she'd have to sneak in to get a peek. Probably get us all thrown out of here in an hour."

Meeley crept up beside them. "Guys, this might be a good time for me to speak with Adera. She's strolling with Tom. I'll go join them and see what I can find out while you set up camp. Maybe she'll open up, maybe not, but it's worth a shot."

Randy placed a hand on her shoulder. "Good thinkin' Meeley, just try not to mention much about Kat. If the subject comes up, fine, otherwise, clam up. Right now she's pretty relaxed, so whatever's causing her grief just might surface during a bit of lighthearted conversation. Thanks, Meeley. You're a good friend and glad you've come with us."

She smiled broadly, gave Charlie a playful slap on his backside, and sprinted off.

Horace strolled up to the two men. "Our words have been fleeting the past few days, and I apologize. However, it was crucial King Merneos and I convene so we might strategize tactics. Mantalac draws near. It is the Elf way and the key to successful endeavors. He has need of Merlin, and we must seek him out at the present. Will you require assistance to set the tents? I can lend a hand if need be."

"No, we can handle it, Horace. Not a problem." Randy smiled and gripped the aloof Elf's shoulder. "Miss you, old friend, but would rather plans be formulated to safely defeat the malevolence we'll soon encounter instead. Chatting about nonessential things is not the number one priority at the moment. There'll be plenty of time for idle talk later. Now, hurry and catch up to Merneos before he gets lost."

"*Lost*?" Horace cocked one eyebrow and cast a frosty glance. He then gave a slight nod of acknowledgement and hastened into the forest.

"Excuse me, gentlemen. I was sent by Queen Fallon to offer my services." The voice was soft, mellow, and came from above their heads. "If you would not mind, may I land on an outstretched palm so you can view me more easily?"

"Yeah, I suppose that would be okay." Randy wore a puzzled look as he extended his right hand. Seconds later, a small figure floated down and stood before him. "Well knock me down and drag me in the mud," he exclaimed as he viewed the pretty young fairy.

"I am called Savah." She pointed to their left. "If you will proceed through the willows in that direction, a secured area has been arranged for your encampment."

The diminutive sprite stood less than a foot high. A flowing gown of bright yellow perfectly complimented her short, wispy auburn hair. Breathtaking blue eyes illuminated a round flawless face while lacey white pearlescent wings lay folded tight against her back.

109

"Little lady, it might be best for you to sit. It would be more comfortable for sure, but also eliminate the possibility of falling. I'm Randy, and this here tall drink o' water is my buddy, Charlie."

Savah eased down as directed and sat with legs crossed. She looked over at Charlie and stared, then looked up at Randy. "Forgive me sir, but he does not seem to be made of water."

Randy began to laugh so hard that he nearly bounced the poor little thing off his hand. "I'm sorry, Savah, it's an old human saying and doesn't mean he's liquid. Truthfully, I'm not too sure what he's made of."

Charlie cast a fleeting offensive glance which quickly morphed into a snicker. "Don't tell her I'm made of puppy dog tails, or she'll fly off for sure. Hello, Savah, hope you'll forgive our crude remarks. It's been a trying time for all of us, and this little break is a much needed bit of relief."

She nodded and giggled, obviously amused by their rhetoric. "I can relate to what you say. When our king was taken, all shared the queen's grief. A period of overwhelming sadness drifted across the land. The slightest ray of light was considered a blessing during those long days of gloom. Sadly, they remained sparse for months on end."

Randy's eyes widened. He looked over at Charlie and gave an inconspicuous wink. Perhaps critical information might be gained from this tiny beings tale. "We know very little of what happened here. Can you tell us more about the disappearance of your king?"

"We have arrived at the designated site. There remains two more hours of daylight in which to tend to your chores. Are you in need of any further aid?"

Her avoidance of the question was more than obvious, but Randy was determined. "Yes, there is. Queen Fallon said *all* our needs would be provided."

"Yes Sire, that is true," she meekly replied.

"Good. We *need* to know about the king's demise."

She spread her wings and fluttered from his hand, but instead of flying off landed on a nearby stump. "Please lower your bodies and I shall fulfill the request."

They immediately plopped down in front of her and waited.

The little fairy looked away for a second, drew a breath, and began, "King Larc was a kind, gentle man. Our kingdom thrived, and the people enjoyed a peaceful, secured existence. One afternoon a group of young lads informed a royal knight about a sizable mushroom patch a few yards on the other side of the black stream. Unfortunately, the location is beyond our protected boundaries. You see, Qergs cannot breach Drealon's borders thanks to an everlasting, powerful enchantment. Only those who have become friends may pass—no other can do such. Many travelers believe they have entered our domain, but are unknowingly transported around the edges. A law forbids any fairy to stray beyond the protected perimeter, as we cannot liberate those who are captured and taken to Odium Manor. It is a dark, terrible place, where the very air reeks of decay and death."

She took a deep gulp and continued, "King Larc, and six companions, set off to collect some mushrooms…our most delectable and treasured food. All failed to realize the eve of a full moon drew near—a period of extreme danger. Cianest feeds during that lunar phase. This creature's food of choice is fairy flesh, and the hunt for victims grows intense. One brave soul survived the Qerg attack and

111

managed to find his way home. The others, including our King, were captured and scheduled to be fed to the vixen two days hence. None were ever heard from again."

Randy ran a hand through his wavy black hair. "Dang, it appears Adera was right about what happened. She claims no one actually knows if Larc perished. Possibly he survived and is a slave or something at the castle."

"No Sire, only a female has a slight chance to stay alive. Even then, it is doubtful they will receive mercy. Many scouts were sent forth at great risk, but no sign of our sovereign has been found. The Manor is nearly impenetrable and highly protected. If one travels by land, they will not exist long. A poisonous vapor flows over the land surrounding the compound. No creature can pass through the mist and live. Only by air can the fortress be infiltrated. Even then, the way is perilous. Eyes are everywhere."

A great deal of information had been inadvertently exposed by this fairy's saga. Randy and Charlie would expose their findings later when all the members of the group gathered. They thanked her and immediately set about their work.

After enjoying a cooked meal, a luxury that was unavailable until this night, the eight friends sat around the campfire and conversed about the days exciting activities. When Savah's disclosure was revealed, the robust banter screeched to an abrupt halt.

"Merlin, is there anything you can do to ward off this gas?" Randy asked. "Unlike our little friends here, we don't have wings."

The wizard stood and paced in a small circle, stroking his long dark beard. "Ah, yes. An ancient spell comes to mind. If the fairies will gather the necessary ingredients, I

112

can whisk up a potion to neutralize the poison. We and our mounts will breathe without incident. Sadly, I must state the taste is most unpleasant."

Adera rose. "It is time for us to go meet with the Queen and others. Merlin, I will ask Savah to join you and pray she finds a way to gather the needed items. Merneos, great tact must be employed to request assistance or none shall be given. Tom, we spoke earlier and I beseech you to use restraint. Any outburst will thwart all efforts. The aide of these marvelous creatures is desperately required."

Tom nodded. "I agree Adera and apologize for my aforesaid actions. It won't happen again. Suppose I just needed to vent. If anything happens to Kat, my reason for living is lost. She is my world."

Randy put an arm around his old friend. "We know, Tom. Think it's safe to say we each feel that way, maybe not as much as you, but to some degree. That little hellcat has wormed her way into all our hearts. Don't sweat it, buddy, we'll save Kat and destroy the monster and his harpy mother as well."

As they walked to the fairy meeting grounds, Meeley snatched hold of Randy and Charlie to pull them back from the others. "I wasn't able to uncover diddly squat. Adera and Tom were engaged in a pretty heated conversation. He was going off the deep end big time. Poor guy blames himself for Kat being kidnapped and put in danger. One thing did seem unnerving though. He outright yelled at Adera, saying he would rather be put out of his misery than go on without Kat. Adera suddenly burst into tears, which took the two of us by surprise. I'm not sure if it was his yelling or the statement, but something sure set her off. Tom instantly apologized and she settled down, but it was really strange. "

113

"Aw, it's probably just the tension of everything getting to her, like the rest of us. Thought of Kat being in such danger and then hearing Tom's harrowing declaration, obviously hit a raw spot." Charlie took Meeley's hand and squeezed it tight. "You did pretty good…for an amateur."

She spun her head around and snapped back. "Amateur? Why you miserable oaf, I can out do you any day. Wait 'til we get back home. I believe a robust session with Knox might refresh a bit of manners and respect." The expression on his face brought a roaring laugh. "I'm just kidding, honeybunch—honest." She gave a playful nudge and took hold of his hand as threesome trudged along.

They caught up to the others and soon arrived at the brightly lit area. It was dreamlike with tiny torches shedding a golden glow over the landscape. Hundreds of fairies fluttered about carrying lanterns, presenting an even greater infusion of enchantment.

"Good evening, friends." Queen Fallon rose to greet the visiting assemblage. She now wore a magnificent glittering gown of deep hunter green. Atop her cascading locks sat a tall spiky crown of jewels as magnificent as any ever seen. Faye stood alongside and fidgeted with the coral colored evening dress she wore, obviously uncomfortable with the frilly garment.

Makeshift seating had been formed out of mounds of grass swathed with layers of strange silk-like netting. Once settled, the Queen inquired of their intent.

"My sister Kat, who is also the wife of Tom, has been abducted by Lord Tahl and taken to Odium Manor. We have banded together to retrieve her."

Queen Fallon gripped the railing. "It is not possible. *No one* can be rescued from Odium Manor. The excursion

114

must end here, or you will perish. It is unfortunate this loved one has been taken, but she can no longer be saved."

Tom leaped to his feet, but was quickly subdued by Horace. "Easy lad, allow Adera and Merneos handle this." His tone was as firm as his iron grip.

Merneos sat tall and spoke with self-controlled confidence, "We are aware of the dangers, Majesty, but no one here is a stranger to such evil doings. Queen Adera is the cousin of Lord Tahl and familiar with his powers. She also posses such capabilities, except her heart is pure, not blackened by impiety as that of he and his mother. Do not underestimate our resolve. We ask only for information to assist us."

The fairy Queen eased onto her makeshift throne and stared into the heavens. "We have very little findings that may be of help."

"Wait! I've been in there and know a lot. Let me tell them." Faye leaped to her feet.

"*Faye*, sit down and *do not* utter another word…or suffer my wrath."

"Yes, Mother." The young fairy made a face, folded her arms in disgust, and plopped back into the chair.

"We must be underway at daybreak, Queen Fallon. If I and King Merneos may hold a private audience with you tonight, it will be greatly appreciated." Adera spoke benevolently yet maintained a definite royal presence.

The little sovereign paused in thought for what seemed to be ages. Finally, she rose and addressed Adera, "I knew your mother, Adeanra. She was a good friend and noble ruler. We will meet, and if possible, answer your concerns. For now, this gathering shall disperse. In one hour, you both shall return…alone. It is all I can offer, dear child. Our warriors are no match for the depravity that saturates

115

Mantalac. As sincere as your hearts may be, I fear you will suffer defeat."

While the others in the rescue team remained at camp, Adera and Merneos rejoined the fairy Queen. Several hours passed before they returned, but not a shred of happiness crossed either face.

Adera choked back tears as she addressed the group. "We have gained valuable information and insight. It appears the path ahead is grievous and deadly. Tom, Kat is your wife, and my sister. Only you and I are obliged to proceed."

He nodded and drew a breath. "I will *die* if need be, but I'll never abandon Kat."

Adera cast a faint smile. "If any of you choose to return to home, I shall not question the decision. What we face is a danger greater than presumed. Our victory will be difficult, if not impossible, to achieve. Think on this matter and disclose your answer at sun's light. My heart overflows with grief...I can speak no more this evening."

Randy rushed over and caressed his sobbing wife. "Well, my answer won't have to wait until morning. I'm going. Nothing in this world's gonna keep me away."

Meeley stepped forward. "I'm in, and so is Charlie."

Merneos cleared his throat, "Horace and I remain resolute until the end. We have never, nor will ever, back down from a confrontation with evil."

Merlin, who had been missing for hours, emerged out of the night mist. "Gadzooks! The gloom around this camp is as thick as a fog. Not to worry, dear friends, failure is not an option. Success is imminent for you have the greatest wizard of ages on your side. Need I say more?"

The table of providence had now been set.

Chapter Eight
Little Big Stuff

T he cadent sound of the horses pace echoed through the forest. Randy peered around at his comrades as a shadow of concern cloaked his face. No words had been spoken since the group set out at daybreak.

Tom was visibly taken aback by Adera's proclamation the night before. Meeley and Charlie rode alongside each other and barely made eye contact. Merneos maintained a composure of indifference as did Horace, although the Elves' almost inconceivable hint of a scowl indicated they too shared an air of trepidation. The legendary wizard, however, who dallied behind all the others, appeared surprisingly undaunted.

Randy finally pulled up his horse and spun around in the saddle to face his friends. "Okay, dudes, the morbid silence is driving me nuts and has to stop. We know the outlook is bleak, but our glumness is certainly not helping matters. If we don't snap out of this, you can dang well bet we'll fail. So, cheer the heck up and open those yappers. That's an order."

At first there was little response, except wide eyes staring at him. Bit by bit, frowns turned to smiles, followed by traces of laughter.

Charlie spurred his horse, trotted up beside Randy, and gave a salute. "Yes sir, are there any further *orders,* sir?"

Adera could no longer contain herself and burst out laughing. "At times Charlie, you bring a bit of Jay back into our lives. He always knew how to cheer us during the most distressing times. What a blessing it is to have you and that same delightful wit with us."

Randy looked over at his wife and winked. "Yeah, appears good ol' Jay contaminated Charlie's brain. Suppose we can conjure up a cure?"

Tom and Chendar, who led the group, turned back and joined the trio. "I don't recall a lot about Jay, but do remember him being upbeat most times. It was right to slap some sense back into us Randy. Our low morale will only exacerbate any chance of victory. Adera, have you come up with any plan? If we don't soon unite and form a perfect strategy, I'm not sure this rescue will work. We've been on the road now for about four hours. Why don't we take a break, give the horses a breather, and discuss some tactics? I know my butt is starting to wear."

"So is my back, Master Tom." The young Bayard normally had very little to say. "I'm also hungry."

Tom chuckled and patted his mount on the neck. "Alright Chendar, we get the drift. Think this pretty much seals the deal, Adera. We all need a little rest."

She nodded, halted McLachen, and dismounted. "Chendar is correct. It is time the animals were refreshed. We should also take nourishment to maintain our strength. It will soon be needed. Within the hour, the outer rim of Mantalac shall be breached. Let us gather and discuss a plan of action. The proper moment has arrived for none shall be had once we enter that vile prefecture."

"Have you ever been here before, Adera?" Meeley asked. "We're running blind and haven't a clue of what lies ahead. Might be helpful to know and somewhat easier to prepare for the upcoming conflict."

Randy plopped down alongside his bride. "Hi, sweet cakes, fancy meeting you here." He gave a playful nudge.

"Meeley's right. Better break the bad news and get it out in the open before things get out of hand. If we know what to watch for, adjustments can be made before a problem arises."

"I agree and shall speak of an incident my mind desires to forget." The beautiful Queen drew a long breath. "Several years ago, another loved one was abducted, much like Kat. A rescue attempt was made…a failed attempt. Many valiant souls perished. Fear of a similar venture weighs heavily upon my mind. I do not wish harm to befall any of you and will do what I must to thwart off danger." She lowered her head and sighed softly.

Randy reached over and took her hand. "You needn't tell us more of this occurrence. I can see it's tearing at your heart. Forget the past botched conflict. Just tell us what you can about the area and the castle. That's really all we need to know."

Merneos leaned forward. "You have married a wise man, Adera. Do as he suggests. Let the past act as a map to success. Because of it, we know what methods are unsuccessful. It is a valued opportunity not conceived by Tahl."

"My Lord is correct," Horace interjected. "Failure has granted insight into victory. Providence graciously provided knowledge of the gaseous barrier, but greater information, such as the internal layout of the Manor or number of guards and their location, would be most advantageous. We are also unaware of other deadly traps. If only there was a way to gain this data. Alas, there is not."

From out of Randy's brown leather saddlebag came a small voice, "Oh yes there is. I can tell you."

Heads swiveled as all leaped to their feet.

119

"Oh bongels, I'm stuck. Can someone help me get out of this thing? Hello? Are you still there? Hello?"

Randy walked over to the wiggling bag and released the flap. "There, it's open. Whoever you are, come on out." He started to reach for his sword, but realized the size of this intruder would be of no consequence, so slid the weapon back into the sheath.

A tiny head, wearing a rather large grin on its face, appeared. "Hi. It's just me." Seconds later, the effervescent fairy ungracefully fluttered to the ground. "Whew, glad to be out of there. Do you know that satchel smells rather bad? A sprig of lavender or two might help." She brushed off her garments and leaped up on a nearby stump.

Adera walked over and stooped down. "What is your name, little one, and kindly explain why you were hiding in my husband's pouch."

"Splozits, guess I didn't make much of an impression when you met me. I'm Faye, Queen Fallon's daughter. Now do you remember?"

Randy looked at Tom and rolled his eyes. "Well, this is just great. Now, we'll probably have the whole fairy world coming after us on top of things."

The tiny sprite stomped her foot at his comment. "I came to offer a bit of help, and this is how I'm rewarded? My Mother will not send anyone after me. She knows I can take care of myself and do pretty darn well at it. Plus, I have my protector with me." She pointed up into the tree behind her. There, perched like a feathered Cheshire cat, was the noble Barred owl. "It appears you don't want me around, so think Punk and I will just go rescue that friend of yours by ourselves. We've been to that wretched Manor before and managed to help three of our friends escape. At least I

120

can fly. Like to see you do that and get up above the poisonous gas."

Tom moved closer. "Well missy, I'd say we've underestimated your talents. How 'bout you spill the beans?"

"Humans are so weird. Why would I spill beans…they're for eating."

Kat's spouse let out a hearty roar. "Let me restate that—please tell us what you know about the Manor."

Faye gave him a sly look. "Oh no, you just want the information and then will send me on my way. Either I go along and help, or no deal. Figure it out yourself, *human*."

Charlie began to laugh and patted Tom on the back. "Think our friend here has your number, pal. Let's take a chance. If what she says is true, this tiny creature has already done more than any of us, and successfully. Sometimes powerful things come in *small* packages."

Horace strolled up and scanned the fairy. "She appears capable of handling the situation. I suggest we allow this child to join our band." He stretched out a gloved hand and offered assistance with the other. "If I may Princess, grant me the privilege to transport you to a more suitable location."

A scowl formed on her face as she climbed into his palm. "Don't try to pull any funny stuff. I know how to fight."

The aloof Elf warrior nodded and gently carried Faye over to a large maple log and set her down next to Adera.

The rescuers' clearly showed amazement.

Faye looked around at the giant strangers, her annoyed hazel eyes darting from one to the other. "Well, are you giants going to stand there gawking like I'm some sort of vermin or get on with the conversation? I'll share what I

121

know of the Manor, but don't try to fool me. Punk will peck your noses off."

Meeley began to snicker. "I really like this feisty little lady. Don't worry Faye, we girls are gonna stick together. You're now part of the team. Right, Adera?"

Turquoise eyes were dispassionate and velvet lips pursed. Soon, her glance began to relax and a smile formed. "Yes, she shall be a most valued member of this alliance. None will question my word. Welcome, Princess Faye."

Tom cleared his throat. "I'm not sure if you know much about our quest? My wife, the sister of Adera, has been abducted by Lord Tahl and that witch Odiene. We're determined to save her, as well as any other captives, and destroy those two villains once and for all. Think you can handle this task?"

Faye sat down and looked up at him. "You're rather handsome for a male human, although I've had restricted contact with your race. Actually, everyone is somewhat handsome, except the ladies—they're pretty. Even the Elves are mighty fine looking specimens. Merlin's face remains hidden under that bush of a beard, so can't tell what he really looks like. The wizard does have nice eyes though, so I can only assume the rest is attractive."

Adera briskly snapped her fingers. "Faye! Do not wander off the point."

Randy patted his bride's knee. "She's just a child, honey. Ease up."

Almost immediately the Queen's demeanor softened. "I beg forgiveness for such a bad-mannered outburst. We understand excitement obviously flows within, but prefer only the topic at hand be addressed without unnecessary distractions. Our hearts are heavy and time is limited. Danger lurks mere yards away. Please, do not take offense.

I assure none is intended. Any advice given shall be most appreciated."

The little fairy pouted while suspicious eyes searched the faces of each member. At last, her look mellowed and an impish grin began to form. "I sometimes, well most times, tend to ramble. Mother has scolded me for the very same thing. She often says I remind her so much of father and how he used to go on and on about nothing…uh oh…rambling again, huh? Sorry. I'll try to act more mature." She pulled up her legs and crossed them. "First thing you need to figure out is how to get above the gas. You don't have wings."

Merneos spoke, "The creature is correct. Unless we find a solution to overcome this first obstacle, the rest of the quest is futile." He cast a glance to the ancient wizard, who idly stared into the trees. "Merlin, have you been able to produce a remedy?" No response was given, bringing a look of ire to the Elf King's face. "Merlin," he yelled.

The legendary figure jumped. "My stars, Sir, one need not wake the dead. What is it you desire?"

"I desire you pay attention, *Wizard*. Have you produced an antidote for the toxic gas surrounding Odium Manor?"

Merlin glanced at the circle of friends. "Sadly, it is not complete. I lack one ingredient and fear it cannot be obtained. I search for an alternative, but none yet comes to mind."

Randy pursed his lips and frowned. "Well, isn't *that* just a dandy bit of information? Were you waiting to tell us after we all began to choke? Okay, Merlin, what's missing, and why the blazes can't we get it?"

"I require a bit of moss."

Horace stood abruptly. "You cannot obtain *moss*? The fungus is everywhere. What nonsense is this?"

123

The conjuror shook his head. "I beg forgiveness. The problem was not clarified. You see, the required fungus must be extracted from the moat bank surrounding the Manor. I need but a smidgen, however it is impossible to retrieve. A considerable distance must be traversed through the deadly barrier. No creature can sustain breathing long enough to get the through the noxious gas. The task is hopeless."

Faye sprung to her feet. "No it isn't—I can get it."

Adera frowned. "Your bravery is without question, but even one so bold cannot attempt such a feat."

Faye hung her head. "You're right Majesty, I can't. My new wings aren't strong enough yet."

Stillness fell over the encampment like the prelude of a storm.

Iridescent wings fluttered as Faye stood on tippy-toes. "Hold on, I can't do it, but *he* can." A petite finger pointed upward. Instantly, the giant Barred owl came to her side. "This is Punk, well, it's Sir Punk now. He's lightening fast and can easily hold his breath long enough to complete the mission. It'll take just a second for him to get the moss. Plus in the dark, he won't be detected. So see, it *can* be done."

Tom rose and strolled to Adera. "Highness, why not allow her to try. What she's saying is true. That owl can easily zip in, grab some moss, and get out before suffering any ill effects. What choice do we have? Not one of us can do this. I ask you give it a shot."

"To be fair, I leave the decision to our assemblage." The Queen took a breath. "My vote is...yes."

A unanimous verdict was reached. The courageous owl would be sent to retrieve the necessary element. Without Merlin's potion, Kat could not be rescued.

124

Punk puffed out a downy chest, as though proud of the intrepid venture asked of him.

Merneos coughed, "Ahem, perhaps this tenacious warrior might convey a message to Kat. It is imperative she not lose hope. Two problems may be solved by the duo's combined efforts."

"Absolutely not! I forbid such an endeavor and will not place this esteemed child in jeopardy." Adera sprung to her feet nearly knocking Faye off the log.

Tom's voice cracked, "Hold on Adera, think a second. She might be able to get through and be the salvation we've prayed for. What say we allow Faye to make the choice? Think you can safely handle this dangerous undertaking, little britches?"

She began to giggle. "Of course I can, silly. While Punk gathers the moss, I'll fly in and deliver the message. It's an easy mission, but I'd better hitch a ride to the Manor on Punk in order to conserve some wing energy." The little sprite reached over and stroked her friend. "Punk and I will be fine. Don't worry."

"It is with heavy heart I assign this task, my darling girl. Please, remain safe. No harm must befall you or this noble bird." Adera whispered the message and gently placed a kiss on the fairy's head.

The ancient magician walked to the courageous pair and addressed them on bended knee. "Sir Punk, I require gray moss from the bank of Odium Manor's moat. It is plentiful and will not be difficult to find. A pinch in your beak should suffice. You, my feathered colleague, are our only hope to acquire the ingredient." Blue-black eyes softened as he stared into the apprehensive face of the fairy princess. "Do not fear, little Faye. The stars foretell success and the safe return of such valiant knights."

125

Tom eased down next to twosome. "It's a brave thing you're attempting, little big stuff, and I'm more than grateful. Our hearts travel with you." He stroked the bird's soft head.

The tiny princess smiled, gave a quick wink, mounted up, and buried her legs deep into the owl's downy feathers. "I'm ready. Let's go, Punk. We should return within the hour everyone."

The noble raptor gave a soft hoot and shot into the darkening evening sky.

It didn't take the great bird long to reach the macabre palace and safely perch on a tree high above the deadly vapor.

"We don't have much time, Punk. Hurry off and get the moss. I'll go find Kat. Pretty sure I know where she's at. When you're finished, wait here. It might take me a little longer to do my chore." Faye gave him a hearty hug. "Oh Punk, please be careful and come back safely. I could not bear to be without my best friend." She quickly wiped away budding tears. "Circle high above the gas until you locate the target. Qergs are everywhere, so keep a diligent watch. Your night vision should be a great asset, as is your speed. When you feel it safe to dive, inhale as much as you can and under no circumstances breathe again until you are back in the clouds. Do you understand me?"

The great ghost-faced owl closed his golden eyes and nuzzled his tiny charge.

Her fragile voice was shaky as she turned away and prepared to dart off, "See you soon, Punk."

A soupy fog suddenly moved in and shrouded any hint of moonlight as darkness engulfed the land around Odium Manor. It was as if nature decided to assist the plucky winged warrior.

He located a tall decaying Poplar and perched safely near its top while scanning the nearby moat. Sharp night eyes spotted the moss, but the way was blocked by the presence of many Qergs. Precious minutes passed before the hideous fiends moved off.

It was now or never.

Punk took a deep breath and launched from the dead limb. Strong silent wings carried him swiftly toward the ground. He swooped down, snatched a clump of the fungus with his powerful talons, and shot back into the sky.

However, the moss was slimy and slipped from his grasp. Another attempt would be necessary.

Once again he perched high in the tree and observed the surroundings. Before a subsequent assault could be made, two Qergs appeared. They walked around a minute—then sat down and began to chat.

Time was running out. Punk had to act. He dove toward the monsters, clawing each on the head as he rocketed by.

"That pesky owl is about to become fodder," one of the guards grunted. "Hand me a big stone." He took aim and hurled it at the feathered assailant. "Get out of here you miserable hunk of flesh. Now, get."

The feisty bird acted as though it had been frightened off, but merely flew to a branch obscured from their sight. At last, the goblins swaggered off. Punk knew only one more chance remained to seize the valuable component. He drew a breath and plummeted toward earth, scooping a beak full of moss as he passed.

Without a second of hesitation, brawny wings propelled the plumed champion back into the clean night air. Although nearing exhaustion, the plucky little knight headed for the designated tree and sat in silence as he waited for his mistress.

Seconds later, the tiny princess perched gracefully alongside her hero. "Whew Punk, it was a lot farther than I expected, but got the message delivered. Kat's a pretty thing and seems sweet. Her gown is awful though. I would *never* wear something like that, nor would mother ever approve."

A nudge from the owl caused her to refocus. "Sorry. I really need to work on my rambling, don't I?" She giggled and stroked his chest. "Hate to ask this, but my wings are spent. Suppose you can fly me back?"

He gave a chipper hoot, she climbed aboard, and the pair began the trek back to camp.

Adera heard the flutter of wings and scanned the sky.

Nearing exhaustion, Punk crashed as he tried to land safely...his chest heaving.

Faye tumbled to the turf, but leapt to her feet and rushed to him before anyone could react. "Punk, please be okay. I can't lose you—I just can't. Merlin, can you do something to help him? Please, don't let him die."

The benevolent sovereign shoved Merlin out of the way and reached down to the heroic bird. A beckoning voice reverberated through the shadowy woodlands, "I call upon the power of my ancestors to heal this warrior." Ivory fingers trembled and emitted a soft-pink glow as she placed a quivering hand upon its fading heart. Almost immediately, the bird fluttered and stood.

128

All eyes focused on the Queen. Never had this secretive power been viewed. She looked into mystified faces and smiled. "I did not know if I possessed the miraculous talent of my mother, for it has never been summoned prior. The life giving force has apparently been bestowed upon me."

Randy walked over and knelt beside his wife. "What an incredible gift, but why didn't you try to use this power to resurrect Tanas?"

"It can only aide one who is but a step from death. Once the soul has departed, no force can return it. His life could not be saved—only revenged." She placed a kiss on her husband's cheek. "It appears our intrepid warriors were successful in one of the appointed tasks. Noble Punk holds the moss within his beak."

Faye caressed her best friend, and then handed the essential ingredient to Merlin. "Hope it's enough. You said we only needed a pinch."

The medieval sorcerer grinned and gave a playful wink. "It is indeed sufficient, little one, and I shall brew the potion posthaste. Thanks to our gallant paladin, the first barrier into Odium Manor is about to meet defeat. The elixir shall be ready by dawn."

Bright hazel eyes literally danced with glee as the ecstatic sprite stood proud alongside her beloved companion. "The message to Kat was delivered, Majesty. She's fine for now, but really anxious to be rescued. I can't wait to get started in the morning. When do we leave?"

Merneos stepped forward. "We shall depart before the sun rises over the horizon. You, my child, must return home. The dangers that lie ahead are no place for a fairy."

Faye's cheery expression turned to anger in an instant. She stomped her foot and raised a tiny voice, "How *dare* you send me back. If not for me and Punk, you would be

129

heading back to your own home and Kat wouldn't know what's happening. I'm going, and no *Elf* will push this fairy aside."

Randy slid in between the two. "Whoa, hold the pitchforks. No one is going home. Merneos, I think I speak for the whole bunch of us, and can honestly say this fiery package just saved the quest. She's earned the right to continue." A quick glance around verified the rest were in agreement. "Faye, your owl will have to fly on his own, but you are more than welcome to ride along safely tucked in my saddlebag if you like."

"I accept the offer, sir. However, there is one small request. Will you mind adding some herbs and lavender to that satchel. It has a most disgusting odor."

The small sprite's unanticipated remark brought a billow of laughs. After enjoying a warm meal, the encampment settled down so all could gain a few moments of sleep.

Rays of sunlight barely cleared the night darkness as the distinctive mix match of cohorts prepared to depart.

Merlin passed a vile of putrid gray-black liquid around, instructing everyone to take one hearty sip, with the exception of Faye who required only a drop. All the horses were given a share making the entire troupe invulnerable to the toxic fumes.

A short time later, the band of deliverers mounted and was underway. Soon, they would encounter the edges of Mantalac and view a desolate land of nightmares.

Chapter Nine
Tahl's Fury

Kat shivered and tried to warm her naked arms as she scuttled along behind Isabelle. Unlike the welcoming Castle in Bowlandria, the Manor's corridors were dark, cold, and cheerless. A morbid sensation flowed around her like a great vapor of despair. *I hate it here and long to return home. Did everyone forget me or is rescue underway? This is nearly intolerable, and I haven't a clue if a mission is in progress or my loved ones are even alive.* She sighed and swallowed hard. *No, blast it, I'm not gonna give in. Even if Adera and Tom were unsuccessful, Randy will never abandon me. I must remain strong to survive. This is all Tahl's fault. I'd give anything to sock that jerk right in his smirking face. He thinks he's so handsome, hah! I've seen a sweeter mug on a twenty-year old hog.*

The sight of the hefty oak doors leading into the throne room sent an icy tremor down her spine. Amber eyes widened as Isabelle pushed against them, and the ancient wood creaked. Fear gripped her momentarily and she stood frozen. *Get hold of yourself, dim wit. Do what Cianest advised. Turn on that country gal charm.* "Okay, Isabelle, let's get on with it."

The oversized chamber was shrouded by eerie shadows cast from sparse candlelight. A stifling odor of fetid mold permeated the air, causing Kat to retch. Fearing offense, she restrained the urge to vomit and somehow managed to regain a touch of composure.

Menacing eyes glared from veiled seclusion as she walked toward the waiting antagonist. The rhythmic rapping of fingers upon wood echoed throughout like

131

rolling thunder. Lips snarled slightly as she caught a glimpse of Lord Tahl who sat with legs draped indignantly over one of the stately chair's bulky arms. Her heart pounded and bosom heaved, as breathing grew rapid. Tiny beads of sweat began to form without constraint on a furrowed brow.

At last, she came to a halt and stood at the steps before him. Realizing uncontrolled anxieties would surely be detected she shrewdly bowed. "Lord Tahl."

He slowly rose, strutted to the edge of the marble stage, and towered over her with hands on hips. "So, you've decided to humble yourself to me. Good."

Kat kept eyes lowered as the depraved ruler orbited around her while scanning a scantily clad body. "Do I meet with your approval, my Lord?"

"Somewhat. The improvement is marginal, but it shall suffice for the moment." He drew up close and seductively ran a finger across creamy shoulders. "The gown is undeniably lovely. Pity it resides on such a mediocre body."

Blazing gold-brown eyes glared into his. "What a pompous skunk…the likes of you wouldn't know coal from a diamond. You've waddled in filth so long no amount of water would wash it away. My skin crawls at your touch."

Enraged, he raised a hand.

Kat stood firm with eyes intent, and braced for a violent strike, but instead received laughter.

"I find such bold human insolence both amusing and fervently stimulating. No punishment will be given at this time. More *favorable* plans flood my mind, and damaged goods are far from appealing. Isabelle, take this insubordinate wench to my apartment. I'll deal with her later—and enjoy the process. You will soon find out, dear cousin, I have *much* to offer. In time, no other will grant pleasure as I do. Now, get out of my sight."

The gentle servant girl tried to take Kat's arm, but was brusquely shoved aside. "Hands off, missy, I'm not a baby and can walk without help." The spirited princess abruptly spun on her heels and stormed off. Once in the hallway and out of earshot, she stopped, leaned up against the cold granite wall, and allowed pent up tears to flow. A quick glance at the meek maiden, who stood near with head hung low, turned anger to shame. She reached out and took the young girl's hand. "I'm sorry, Isabelle. My rude actions toward you were uncalled for. None of this is your fault. Please, forgive me?"

"No offense is taken, mistress, but I am fearful of Lord Tahl's fury. You do not know the extent of his ire. He was humiliated and surely seeks revenge. Please, do not further invoke more anger. Sickening as it may be, allow the master to have his way."

"This is one chick who will *never* concede to such sordid lust. My warped cousin can toss me back in the dungeon to rot for all I care. I'd rather die there than share one split second of passion with that deranged monster. Sure, he's handsome on the outside, but has a heart and soul blacker than a witch's hat. I don't wanna get you in trouble, so lead the way to the lowlife's boudoir. Just between you and me, his *jerkiness* is in for a bit of a surprise and about to get a heck of a lot more than bargained for. You can cut your teeth on that."

Kat felt the knot in her stomach grow as she walked alongside Isabelle through poorly lit corridors to Lord Tahl's billet. Befitting his ego, the cavernous room overflowed with an excessive collection of immoderate garish furniture. Covering the greater part of the lifeless gray walls were gigantic tapestries depicting morbid battle scenes and tasteless amorous depictions. A mammoth fireplace, along with an insignificant cluster of candles, provided ghostly illumination to the abhorrent quarters. Centered between two narrow windows was a significantly inelegant bed covered with copious animal pelts.

She turned slowly and looked around the entire room…her face wrought with anger and disgust. The only appealing feature she could find was the door leading out of it.

"Isabelle, where does his mother reside? I have yet to see her."

"The lady dwells in another wing. She prefers solitude and seldom makes an appearance. However, do not be anxious to meet with this malicious woman. Doom is Odiene's constant companion, mistress. It is said the sorceress takes great delight watching innocents suffer by her hand. Many do not survive the horrific torture long. For sheer amusement, mother and son periodically enjoy watching the beast Cianest feed. Piteous screams of the victims, mingled with the pair's laughs, echo throughout the manor. It is a night we captors dread. The sounds resonate in our minds for days after. Sadly, you will soon witness the event, for a full moon approaches."

Kat winced at the disclosure. "Why doesn't someone kill that low life hag and her miserable excuse of a man? Why is this allowed?"

The timid maiden edged close. "Mistress, the lady wears an unusual amulet around her neck. It is a peculiar, powerful item and can transform any creature into whatever she and her son desire. My leg is proof of its ability. Cianest is perhaps their most hideous mutation. It

134

is said she had once been an exquisite beauty with a pure soul."

"I spoke with Cianest while imprisoned. She also told me of the so-called *token of destruction* possessed by this deranged pair."

Isabelle took hold of Kat's hand. "Be very careful, mistress. Tahl is heartless with an overblown ego. He is easily insulted and will seek revenge. Please, do not allow him to inflict punishment. I implore you to accept his pleasure."

Kat whipped her hand from the tender grasp of this newfound friend and huffed, "He can turn me into a toad for all I care. This girl is *not* going to be his latest conquest."

"But, mistress…he…"

"No Isabelle, the book is closed. Drops of his alien ancestor's blood runs through these veins as well. My sister, Adera, has powers greater than those he or his warped mother possess. She told me a great force resides within me, but unfortunately has not yet surfaced. Maybe old dirt bag will be the catalyst to unleash my outlandish potential. Either way, he can go straight to Hades before I'll render myself to such a creep." She drew a long calming breath. "You better scadoodle out of here before the donkey's butt makes an entrance. Don't worry about me. I'll be fine. Now scat."

"Mistress, I was ordered to remain with you until his Lordship arrives." Penitent eyes gazed intently and quivering lips forced a smile. "I pray he will show mercy and respect your station. Try to make yourself comfortable."

The sound of the hefty door being pulled closed by the timid maid struck a nervous blow to Kat, who stood in the center of the room. *Well dummy, you've gone and done it this*

135

time. Could you listen to what Adera and the others told you? Oh no, not miss know it all Kat. You had to be the smarty-pants and deemed their concerns as nonsense.

Time seemed to crawl as Kat waited impatiently for the unwelcomed arrival of her captor. The raven-haired beauty strolled over to the stained glass window and stared out into dark infinity as a troubled mind drifted. Less than half an hour had passed since a miraculous message of hope was delivered. The remembered moment brought a smile.

She and Isabelle had entered Tahl's room and were scoping it out. Suddenly, there came a peculiar tapping at the window, startling both girls.

"Isabelle, have I lost my mind, or is there a *fairy* at the window?" Amber eyes blinked in disbelief.

The gentle maid hurried over and cracked open the window. "Oh little miss, surely you are lost. This is certainly no place for a fairy. Hurry away before you are captured."

Faye wriggled her tiny body through the minute crack, smiled, and looked around—large hazel eyes wide with wonder. "I'm not lost at all, but am searching for the one they call Kat."

"I'm Kat, but who the Sam-hill might you be?"

The tiny creature began to giggle and fluttered over to a nearby table. "My name is Faye. I was sent here to deliver a message. A whole bunch of people, well, most are people, some are Elves, and then there is Merlin who is anyone's guess."

"Ahem, it's nice to know my friends sent you, but do you mind telling me what they have to say before that idiot Tahl comes in?"

Faye rolled her eyes. "I really do need to work on my focus of things. Sorry. Queen Adera wanted me to tell you

136

that they are near, and salvation is at hand. Do nothing to anger Tahl or his mother. Remain safe at *all* cost. Rest assured, they have not forgotten." A blush rose in her face. "Tom also wanted me to say he loves you and will soon hold you in his arms, safe and unharmed. Then he asked I deliver a kiss from him, but think it best to simply say it, if you don't mind. I'm not old enough to kiss anyone, let alone a human. Mother would tear the hide from me if she knew I did something like that. I have to admit a kiss would be nice to experience though. It might be a couple years before such a feat is acceptable, unless it happens by accident of course, which actually wouldn't be so bad." A glance into the two girl's faces brought a wince. "Bongles, I did it again. Mother should have named me Rambling Rose."

The peculiar comment caused Kat to chuckle. "It's okay. I've been known to do the same thing. However, Isabell is right. You are at great risk of being discovered and need to be off. Please, tell everyone I miss them and am more than ready to get the tar out of this horrific place. I'm fine and not in any jeopardy, at least I don't think so. Also, tell Tom I love him. Now, hustle those wings and get going Faye. Danger lurks in every corner of this joint. Thank you. Be safe little one."

Moments later, the tiny sprite edged out the window, gave a wave, and fluttered from sight.

The sound of footsteps stripped her thoughts of the pleasant visit and snapped a fearful mind back into reality. *Sounds like my cousin decided to make an appearance at last. Little does that dopey slob know my resolve has been re-energized! Old Hot Britches is in for the time of his life, but not the one he thinks he'll have.* She lifted her head high and stood firm as the door creaked open.

Tahl stood with an arm on each side of the doorway then teetered forward, knocking over a chair in the process. He snatched up the ornate wooden fixture and violently flung it against the wall. "Gog, get in here."

Instantly the demonic warrior entered the room. "Yes, my Lord."

Angry eyes fell upon Kat, who remained silent. "Take this piece of garbage to her room. I'm too drunk to deal with such play toys tonight. I require sleep." The inebriated master stumbled over and harshly squeezed her cheeks. "You will not be granted the thrill of my *enjoyment* this evening, Princess. However, it will be soon…I promise." He laughed and pushed her to the floor. "Get her and that wretched maid out of here before I have nightmares."

The obedient brute yanked Kat up and led the duo out the door. She started to struggle, but soon realized it would be ineffectual so submitted peacefully.

Alone in her room, she began to shed tears of anger and frustration. "I hate that filthy tyrant more each minute. If that warped rapscallion believes I will ever yield to him, let alone enjoy it, he is totally bonkers. It ain't gonna happen." Kat angrily ripped off the lascivious gown, shredding every thread and flung the tattered pieces into the fireplace. "Here's what I think of your choice of garments. They're nothing more than lewd fire kindling." She scanned the room for something to put on, but no other clothing had been provided. "Well, if this isn't a fine kettle of fish. Now, I'm plumb stupid naked." Feeling foolish, she began to laugh. "One day my harebrained temper is really gonna get me in deep trouble. I suppose a makeshift robe of sorts can be whittled out of the crummy bed sheets." She stripped them off, grabbed a handful of window sash, and fashioned a crude but suitable covering.

138

Unable to rest, Kat paced the floor for the better part of an hour. Finally, she plopped in a dust-laden chair placed near the narrow slit of a window and drew a breath. Depleted of strength, she closed bleary eyes and drifted off to sleep.

A hand on her shoulder abruptly pierced her slumber. She leapt up in alarm and shouted, "What the blazing tar hill is going on? Where am I?"

"It is only me, mistress…Isabelle."

Kat swallowed hard and gathered her wits, as sleep infused vision cleared. "I'm sorry, Isabelle and didn't mean to yell. It's just that you scared the bejeepers out of me. Perhaps in the future you should stand back and simply call my name. Think that might be a tad safer."

The gentle servant eyed Kat and frowned. "Mistress, where are your garments?"

A quick glance to the side brought a snicker. "I burned the suckers. This sheet is more to my liking. Well, if truth be told, it's actually all I could muster up. Have any idea where I might obtain some clothes?"

"Oh goodness, mistress, Lord Tahl will be most angry. You should not have done that. I will search to see what might be found. Can I get anything else?"

"I'd certainly kill for a cup of coffee, but if it can't be had, then just a little something to eat and drink. Not much has been provided since I've been brought to this fabulous resort and I'm starving."

After Isabelle left, Kat walked over to the floor mirror and caught a glimpse of herself. A glimpse of the frumpy outfit brought a burst of laughter. "Oh my stars, if you aren't some sight."

The meek maid quickly returned, carrying an armload of clothing while tediously balancing a large pewter tray

139

with her other hand. "These were all the garments I could collect, mistress, but have a feeling you will fancy the foodstuff I obtained."

Kat dashed over and took the tray, placing it on the small table in the center of the room. The aroma of fresh brewed coffee tantalized her senses instantly, and she tossed the domed lid aside like a ravishing maniac. A sip of the hot brew brought a lengthy sigh of relief. "This is a drop of pure heaven in a cup." She took another mouthful, rolled her eyes, and checked out the other items on the platter. "Well, slap me simple—donuts. They are without a doubt my most favorite food."

After thoroughly satisfying an empty stomach, she eased back in the chair and relaxed for the first time in days. "Isabelle, I hate being called mistress and would rather be addressed as Kat. I understand you wouldn't wanna call me that in front of our egotistical egghead host, but in private, I think it will be okay. Do you have a nickname?"

A blush rose in the demure girl's face. "No, none was ever given, mistress, uh, Kat."

"Well, we're gonna remedy that right now. Let's see. How does Ibby sound? It's just a quirky take on your name, but a smidgen more personal. I like it and think it fits like a glove."

Isabelle sat and stared at the wall a moment. Slowly, her eyes brightened, and a smile formed. "I like it too. Ibby it is, but *only* when we're alone. The master would punish me severely if he knew."

Kat huffed. "Master disaster is more like it. He thinks he is the greatest gift to women. Well, hate to break the bad news, but the draconian brute is nothing more than a crummy booby prize."

Ibby frowned. "I do not understand. What is the prize you speak of?"

The innocent comment delivered a robust laugh from Kat. "It's a human slang word sometimes used to represent a really, really bad prize…one that is stupid and utterly useless. Think it pretty much suits him, wouldn't you say?"

Both girls giggled and continued to chat. It was a welcomed departure from the sadistic treatment Kat had received since she arrived.

"Kat, tell me of your native land. I have no knowledge of the outside world."

"You would not understand where I came from or even how I got here, so how 'bout I tell you about Bowlandria instead?" Eyes brightened as thoughts of home formed. "The temperature is always mild—never too hot or too cold. At times, the sky is so blue it boggles the mind. Brilliant sunlight flows like golden butter over flower-decked green meadows. Diverse wildlife scampers about, while songbirds perch in lofty trees and fill the air with their sweet melodies. The castle where I live is enormous…with pristine granite walls and towering white spires that appear to almost touch the heavens. There are many villages scattered throughout the kingdom, which is peaceful and happy. My beautiful sister, Queen Adera, is a kind and gentle. She is the anointed guardian of the entire Realm and does not *rule*, but prefers to simply guide and protect all who reside within it."

At first, Ibby's brown eyes danced with delight as Kat spoke, but slowly a shadow of sadness began to form. "It sounds so wonderful. You are lucky to live in such a place. Our land is a complete opposite."

Kat drew up close to Ibby and caressed the young maiden's hands. "Has your kingdom always been this way? Why do you stay?"

"The elders spoke of a time when our land was much like yours. It was a place of contentment and peace. Happiness and laugher filled the air. Our crops were bountiful…magnificent meadows were alive with beauty. One day, Odiene and her young son entered Mantalac. A proclamation was made, declaring her the royal sovereign and we her subjects. Fearing the worse, many fled. This angered Odiene who quickly put a curse on anyone trying to escape. If they so much as set a toe over the boundary, their bodies would burst into flames. A few residents did not believe such a feat could be implemented and sadly perished. The skies grew dark and the land withered as happiness gave way to misery. Slowly, our freedoms were purged—our people tortured and forced to do her biding. This filthy piece of architecture was constructed by the blood and sweat of hapless villagers. As Tahl grew, so did his viciousness. Driven by irrepressible lust, he captured countless women. If one caught his eye, she was brought to the Manor and never again seen. Their fate remains unknown." Eyes welled, and her voice cracked as she struggled to continue.

"My oldest sister, Jewell, was one of the first to be abducted. Unlike me, she was a striking beauty with flowing cocoa brown hair and eyes. I've searched throughout the Manor for her and several friends, but not a trace has been found. I can only presume they were sacrificed to Cianest."

Tears dripped from Kat's cheeks, and her heart teemed with revulsion. "It's okay Ibby, we'll find out what happened to them. I promise." She paused and drew a

142

breath. "Your plight is the inadvertent consequence brought about by my father. Odiene was his sister. She tried to poison Adera, and instead of being put to death, he banished her and her son. Regrettably, this was the land they chose. Somehow, I will make things right. If it is the last thing I do on this earth, I vow to restore the light to your kingdom."

The two girls embraced in a moment of consolation— a moment that was quickly vanquished when Tahl thrust the door open.

Kat leaped to her feet, hatred spilling from her eyes. "How *dare* you enter without knocking? I demand you leave immediately."

A snarl formed on his face. "You will demand *nothing* of me, wench. Where are the clothes I ordered?"

"I burned them." She stood nervy with head high.

Lord Tahl rushed at her, slamming Ibby against the floor as passed. He violently seized a handful of Kat's long ebony hair and dragged her over to the sizzling hearth. "The only thing preventing me from tossing your worthless body into this fire is the thought of tonight's activity. After my *need* is fulfilled, and I advise you to insure it is, princess, your future may well be at risk. However, this pitiful servant has betrayed my orders. Such jovial companionship was never intended or desired. I forbid it." He whisked out a mysterious object from his black leather vest pocket and held it up. The adornment appeared to be three interlinked rows of harmless ivory rings, bound together on three sides by engraved gold bands. "Now, you shall witness the true power of our kind first hand." He began to utter words in an unfamiliar language.

Kat huffed, "Do you seriously think I'm frightened of your mommy's trinket?"

143

His eyes blazed and lips curled. "Never again speak of my Mother in such a manor. She is ten times the woman you will ever be. Watch and weep, cousin. This creature's anguish is the product of *your* arrogance and unbridled belligerence."

The rings began to hum and secrete a pale blue luminosity which built in intensity as he continued the exotic chant. A sudden thunderous boom was followed by a blinding burst of white light infused with a piercing shriek.

Kat heard the sound of a door slam and fought to regain hazed vision. Slowly, the immobilizing dots began to fade and sight returned. A quick glance around the room revealed Tahl had left. "Ibby, where are you?" The unnatural silence stabbed her heart. What had transpired? "Ibby. Speak to me." She stood and twirled around, desperate to locate the benevolent acquaintance. An eerie noise from a darkened corner generated a flurry of goose bumps. "Who's there? Come out where I can see you."

Gradually, an adorable copper-feathered hen emerged from the darkened shadows.

Tears began to fill horrified eyes as Kat slumped to the floor. "Oh no, please tell me this hasn't happened."

The fluffy fowl walked over and nestled its head in her lap.

Kat reached down and gently stroked silken feathers. Her mind swirled in disbelief and confusion. When Isabelle first revealed her affliction, she mentioned the threat of being further transformed. Apparently, Tahl was a man of his word, and now this guiltless young woman had suffered his wrath.

The sight of the piteous animal was more than Kat could bear. She had tried to remain stalwart and not give

144

in to mounting fears. However, knowing the blame rested on her shoulders, tears burst forth like a great geyser. Sobs hammered a quaking body as salty torrents billowed down pale cheeks. Minutes passed, and soon anger replaced frustration.

Kat sat up and placed the docile hen in a nearby chair. "This is all my fault, Ibby, every stinking bit of it. I don't know how yet, but I'll free you from this curse. If it takes the last breath in my body to destroy Tahl and Odiene, then so be it. His Lordship will not be keen on the *pleasure* he's going to receive. I've never felt such hatred or unbelievable yearning to destroy as I do right now. Tonight, this meek princess is about to become a ferocious animal."

Little did she suspect, those malevolent words would be shockingly prophetic.

Chapter Ten
Transformation

Beads of sweat covered Tom's brow as he awoke with a start from the nightmare. "Kat," he yelled out.

Randy dashed to his friend and shook him. "Wake up, buddy. What's wrong? Are you okay?"

Tom blinked his eyes and drew a long breath. "I—I had a vision of Kat being tortured. Her screams of agony were horrific. I can't bear this much longer. We have to get to her soon. Perhaps it's not just a nightmare, but real. I swear to you right here and now, if anything happens to Kat, you may as well put me out of my misery and allow me to join my wife." His breathing was rapid and intense as the handsome man fought back tears of anguish. "I waited the better part of my life to be with her again and can't lose that girl now, Randy, I can't. She's my heart and soul."

Merneos walked over and took a firm grip on Tom's arm. "We will not hear of this talk again, for only one defeated can speak such words, and we will *not* be defeated. Do you understand?"

Tom stared into stone cold eyes and nodded. "You're right, Merneos, sorry for the outburst. Sure didn't mean to wake everyone. That stinkin' nightmare was so real. I'm telling you, the blasted thing rattled me clear to the bone."

"It was meant to do such, my lad." Merlin joined them and spoke softly, "We are only a short distance from Mantalac, and I suspect its influence has reached into your subconscious. The land is a dark place, filled with destructive magic. I must take a moment to ponder this

146

situation. Somewhere in the depths of my mind resides a counter spell to prevent further afflictions."

Meeley glanced at Charlie and winced. "I've been having horrible dreams the past two nights, but never said anything because I didn't want to upset anyone. Merlin, for the love of Pete you have to come up with something. These are really morbid images, and they're getting worse."

Charlie pulled her close to him and squeezed. "Not to worry, sweetness. I'll never let anything hurt you or our friends. Wizard, it's time to prove your worth."

Merlin nodded, turned, and vanished into the darkness.

Tom walked over to a large rock and propped up against it. Tender eyes were bloodshot and puffed from lack of sleep—his face pale and tight. He stared at the ground, deep in thought. Slowly, a shadow approached.

"I have visions of her as well, Tom, and bear similar fears. However, to ease your troubled mind, allow me to disclose something that is unknown to any other, not even to Randy." Adera glanced around and sighed. "My sister and I share an uncommon and somewhat imperfect means of communication. It is rather erratic and voiceless…more like a whisper in our minds. She remains unharmed, but fearful. I also perceive an incredibly abnormal and unimaginable volatile rage mounting within her…unlike any ever experienced. This, Tom, is where the danger resides. If provoked, Tahl's retribution may become lethal."

He reached out and took hold of the Queen's porcelain hand. "Adera, relate to her the importance she remain in control of erupting emotions. You know how easily Kat can fly off the handle."

"I cannot do as you ask, dear brother-in-law. Our telepathic link is significantly limited. Two days hence, we should arrive at the Manor."

"Two days might as well be two years." He began to pace, wringing his hands as droplets of concern poured down a vexed face. "I can't let something happen to her, Adera. It's out of the question. We *have* to do something."

The great Sovereign looked around as though the smothering night air might grant an answer. Her gaze fell upon the horses resting peacefully nearby. "Perhaps it is possible to push our steeds enough to eliminate a day. However, caution must be utilized to avoid injury."

"I agree, Adera," Tom replied. "There must be a way to travel along at a faster pace without harming the critters. We have to put our heads together and figure this out."

Randy joined them just in time to hear the last bit of conversation. *"We* need to figure things out? It appears you two have decided to simply take matters into your own hands and not consult with the rest of us. Well, that's not gonna cut it." He turned and yelled for the others to gather around. "All of us need to be on the same page and follow a distinct, unified plan. If not, we'll fail. Tom, you served in the military and know better. A group divided has no chance of winning."

Charlie stretched and yawned as he approached. "Dudes, can't we discuss things in the morning? I'm tired and would like to get back to my nice dream."

"Oh, and just what sort of nice dream were you enjoying, *darling*?" Meeley devilishly edged up to him and winked to the others. "Come on, spill it, big boy."

"For your information, I was dreaming of Cook." Apparently amused at Meeley's concern, he began to snicker. "Yeah, she and I were having such a grand time.

148

She cooked and I ate. Yep, best darn dream ever, and mighty good vittles too." He rubbed his belly and then burst into a robust laugh. "Don't worry my fiery aviator. *You* are the only woman of my dreams, other than where food is concerned, that is."

Merneos and Horace looked somewhat perturbed at the jovial antics being displayed. "Were we roused from our slumber to frolic?" The Elf King's tone of voice was filled with ire.

Randy cast a fleeting glance at his wife and friend. "No Merneos, a more serious problem has become apparent. Meeley and Charlie were simply releasing some pent up emotions, which we could all use if truth be told." He peered around at everyone then turned to face Adera and Tom. "Would you two care to explain things now that we're all together?"

Tom's voice cracked as he spoke, "We didn't mean to upset the apple cart. It's mostly my fault. I'm sick with worry about Kat. Sorry y'all, it was wrong of us to even consider formulating a plan without consulting everyone. I promise it won't happen again." He sighed and turned to the benevolent queen. "Blast it. I'm no good at explaining things and honestly not sure what to say. Perhaps it's better if took over."

She smiled slightly and nodded. "I shall divulge what I must."

Before a word could be uttered, Merlin dashed up, his sides heaving for breath. "My lady, I have received a vital communication from the trees. Leora and Willa overheard your concerns and took action. Much was observed. Kat *is* in peril. Tomorrow evening, Tahl will summon our princess to his quarters where he intends to have his way with her. She, however, is not a willing participant, and it

149

is feared he will retaliate in a most vile manner. We must indeed hasten the journey. Do not be concerned. Our steeds are well rested and nourished. They will not endure a moment of stress. I suggest we pack up and leave this night without an instant of delay. If we travel at a brisk pace with limited rests, we should arrive at our destination by morrow's nightfall. What say you?"

Tom heaved and gave a sigh. "Merlin, both you and Charlie know these animals better than anyone else. Are you absolutely positive they can travel safely at a quickened pace. I believe all are in agreement and won't sacrifice their well-being."

"Oh no, my lad, they are more than capable of such a feat. Remember, they have been enchanted. No harm shall befall them. You have my word."

Merneos stepped up next to the ancient conjuror. "It is settled. Ladies, if you would gather our necessities, we gentlemen will break camp. Merlin, Charlie, and Horace, will you prepare the horses, while I, Randy, and Tom tend to the other activities." He began to walk off, but abruptly stopped. "Tom, set your mind to rest. No harm shall befall Kat. She will soon be delivered safely." He and Horace placed a fist to their chest and bowed.

A smile began to creep on Tom's face. "Thank you. Thank all of you."

Within half an hour, all chores were completed and the riders mounted. The horses were unusually alive with energy as though they sensed the urgency.

Randy was nearly unseated when his mount reared and fought the reins. "What the blazes got into these guys?"

McLachen let out a loud whinny. "I had a hearty talk with them, Master Randy. Your steeds shall have no problem maintaining a brisk gait from this point forward.

Chendar and I will assure their pace. My Lady must be rescued at any cost."

"Hey, what's going on? Can't a fairy get some sleep around here?" Faye peered out of Randy's saddlebag and yawned. "Is it time to leave already? Feels like I just went to sleep"

Seeing the comical expression on the little fairy's face caused Tom to snicker. "How the dickens did you snooze so sound, little one? We made enough noise to raise the dead."

Randy raised an eyebrow and made a face. "Geez, in all the rush to get ready, I plumb forgot you were in here. Hope I didn't hurt you, Faye. We were in a bit of a hurry, and this old bag got slammed around when I loaded it up. Are you alright?"

The tiny sprite wiggled part way out and draped both arms across the edge of the leather satchel. "I'm fine, but why didn't you wake me. I'm sure I could have helped. Hey, did anyone tell my owl we're leaving. Punk, where are you?"

A sudden whoosh of wings answered her call as he plummeted from the treetops and landed unceremoniously on the Arabians rump, causing it to buck slightly. "Whoa, don't launch us into the dirt. Be careful, Punk, but stay close." She stroked his downy head and sent the great bird into the air.

Adera gave McLachen a pat on the neck. "If you are ready, noble friend, let us begin."

The mighty ebony stallion whinnied, reared slightly, and broke into a brisk canter, with the entire group following close behind.

"Sure is bright out tonight," Faye exclaimed. "Guess it won't be long before the moon is full."

Tom and Randy peered into the darkened sky and then at each other. She was right. The entire orb was almost completely illuminated. Cianest would soon feed.

Unable to rest, Kat nervously paced the floor in her room. She knew Tahl's advances would be impossible to thwart off much longer. A new gown had been delivered earlier by another handmaiden named Brandi, accompanied with a note saying she was to join him for dinner wearing it.

"Mistress, may I serve a bit of breakfast? You have been awake for hours without so much as a drop of water. Please allow me to bring nourishment."

Brandi was a sweet young woman, perhaps twenty years of age, with short dark hair, large round doe-like eyes, delicate features, and a well-formed figure.

Kat smiled and nodded. "I'm not very hungry, but would love some coffee."

"Of course, mistress, I will return promptly with a pot of the requested brew."

After the new maid had left, Kat walked to the window as tears trickled down her face. "Oh Ibby, I miss talking to you so much. Brandi is nice and all, but we had become friends. Somehow, I have to find a way to free you and all the others who have been transformed by that jerk. I hate the very sound of his name."

"No mistress, you must not think such thoughts. He is heartless and will not hesitate to inflict a devastating wrath upon you as he has done to me and others."

Kat spun around, her eyes darting about. "Wha—what the heck? Who said that? Who's there?" Slowly, a fluffy red hen skulked out from a shadowed corner. "Ibby?"

"Yes mistress, it is I."

"What in blazes in going on? How is it you can speak?" Teetering from disbelief, Kat plopped down on the side of the raggedy bed. Ibby leaped up and nestled beside her.

"I don't know what happened, mistress. At daybreak I discovered my voice had returned. It is somewhat bizarre because I can speak in a human voice, but also understand and converse with other animals."

"Oh Ibby, I'm so sorry. Please, forgive me. If only I'd kept my big fat mouth shut." Kat stroked the soft feathers as she spoke, "There has to be some way to break this spell. Wonder if Cianest would know what can be done?"

The timid fowl stood and looked up at Kat. "You cannot go to her, especially at this time. The night of feeding approaches. Do not blame yourself. This transformation was inevitable. I always knew that. Like so many others, once he discarded me, my time was limited. At least in this form, I may find out what happened to Jewell. Word has it she was transformed into a common house mouse which means she may still be alive."

"Promise you won't speak to another living soul, Ibby. This has to remain *our* secret. Do you understand me? If he were to find out, well, I don't know what the creep would do. Brandi will be back soon, so we have only a few minutes to converse. Tahl sent another piece of garbage for me to wear tonight which is unbelievably worse than the other. Actually, there isn't a whole lot to the dang thing. What's with that dude's warped mind?" She walked over to the chair and held up the garish garment. The sheer midnight-black gown was gaudily embroidered and dotted with sequins. Only a wisp of black silk covered her *private* areas. "Can you believe this piece of crap? Well, I'm *not* gonna wear it. Tahl can put the blasted get up on one of his goons."

"I understand your feelings, mistress, but if you do not favor him, he will bring harm. I know the thought is sickening, but please try to endure. He is not all that unattractive, which at least offers some consolation. Perhaps it might help if you close your eyes and pretend he is your beloved Tom. Hopefully, help is on the way and this suffering will be short lived."

Kat shrugged her shoulders, walked to the mirror, and held up the distasteful dress in front of her. Much as she hated to admit it, Ibby was right. The choices were slim to none. A multitude of emotions soared to the surface. "No! I can't do it, Ibby. I just can't. Thoughts of his hands on me sour my stomach." She dropped to the floor and began to sob.

Brandi opened the door and screeched, "Mistress, are you alright? What has happened?" She swiftly placed the tray on a nearby table and dashed to Kat. Kneeling beside the distraught girl, she lifted a chin and wiped away a flood of tears. "Oh sweet lady, do not torture yourself like this. I know what is expected and understand. Many have undergone the same agony. He is a not a man, but a beast in disguise—a predator of women. We permit such advances for fear he will turn us into a monster like Cianest. She was perhaps the most beautiful creature I have ever seen. Her revolting conversion is beyond cruel."

This was the first time anyone had mentioned knowing Cianest prior to being cursed. As usual, this disclosure tantalized Kat's insatiable curiosity. "You knew Cianest before the transformation? We spoke while I was imprisoned. She was once a friend of my sister, Adera. Please, tell me what you know."

154

Brandi paused, her eyes lowered. "I fear retaliation, my lady. The subject is forbidden."

Kat caressed trembling hands. "It's safe within the walls of my chamber. I truly appreciate your hesitancy and will not force you to do anything you do not wish." Suddenly, a cherished aromatic scent turned a distressed head. "Oh Brandi, you brought coffee. I so need a boost." She leaped up, scurried to the table, poured a cup, collapsed in a nearby chair, and savored the delectable brew.

At first the frightened maid remained in place, but suddenly stood erect and ambled over to Kat. "The time is now, my lady. Perhaps providence has sent you to free our land. I see great strength lies within, and somehow feel many prayers are about to be answered. I will reveal all I know." She sat crossed legged on the floor in front of Kat—her head held high in proud defiance.

"When Cianest was first brought to the Manor, she was wrapped in cloth and securely bound. I was one of those chosen to attend her. No others were allowed to breach the isolation.

After three days, Lord Tahl loosened the bindings, freeing her delicate hands. She never uttered a spoken word. Only the soft sound of piteous weeping was heard." Brandi paused and swallowed hard. "At last, the confinements were fully removed, revealing a magnificent celestial being."

Kat gasped. "Celestial? Isn't that a bit of a stretch on words?"

"Mistress, Cianest was as close to an angel as I have ever seen. Her skin, which looked like flawless polished alabaster, appeared to glow, even in subdued light. Sphere-shaped eyes complimented a glorious face, further enhanced by gilded lashes, brows, and pouty lips. Her waist

155

long wavy hair was like silken strands of lustrous sunshine. But two of the most impressive features were her glistening golden-feathered wings and dazzling rainbow colored eyes. Never have I witnessed the likes of either."

"Holy blazes! I've seen a likeness of such a creature before. In our Great Hall, there's an alabaster statue of an angel. It's so lifelike you almost feel she's real. Leaping crickets, I'll bet the dog gone farm Adera had the sculpture made as a tribute to her beloved friend. If our elegant monument is a true likeness, Cianest *was* absolutely magnificent. How could Tahl be so heartless to turn such a pure soul into some devilish monster?"

"Like you, Mistress, she would not yield to his lust. Time after time he tried, only to be rejected. At last, he grew angry and used the amulet to transform her into the hideous creature we now fear. Once under its spell, those afflicted must act as the creature they have become dictates. Their willpower no longer belongs to them. I have heard Cianest scream in anguish for days after a feeding. Killing, as she is forced to do, brings throbbing grief to such a benevolent soul. You will soon hear the heart retching cries of despair, for the night of slaughter approaches."

Kat eased from the chair and ambled across the room. "Thank you, Brandi. This revelation disturbs me more than you can know. Somehow, I must end this tyranny."

Brandi rushed over and grasped Kat's hand. "No, mistress, you must not think of such things. He and his mother are far too powerful and will destroy you. Many have tried, and all met a hideous death. No compassion resides in either of their black hearts."

"Well, I'll not be another of his *Louse-ship's* trophies. Unlike others, I am of the same ancestry and my sister is as strong, if not stronger, than either of them. Adera claims I also possess powers, but darn if I know what they are. Perhaps dopey will unearth more than he can handle." She spun around…eyes ablaze. "I have to go see Cianest. Is there some way we can sneak down to the dungeons without being detected?"

The docile hen that had been nestled on the bed, jumped to the floor. "I know a way, Kat."

"Ibby! No, I told you never to utter a word." Kat rushed over and scooped up the fluffy fowl. She cast a glance at Brandi, who stood with mouth agape. "You must swear to never reveal what was just witnessed to anyone. Pledge your word to me, n*ow!*"

"You have my solemn vow, mistress. I can only assume this is the former maid—the one I replaced."

Kat set the little bird back on the bed and plopped down beside her. "Okay, looks like we now have formed an unexpected and rebellious band of three." She giggled and stroked Ibby. "No matter what happens, we must keep everything to ourselves or risk extermination. Agreed?"

The two new friends voiced an overwhelming yes. Brandi then rushed over and sat alongside Kat. "Well, now what?"

"I still need to go speak with Cianest. Brandi, perhaps it's best you tend to another chore. That way, if we're caught, you'll be free from blame. Ibby, we must be quick and it's imperative neither of us are seen. Can you handle such a feat?"

"Of course, Kat, I've managed to sneak down there many times in search of my sister. Scores of rats were found, but no mice. If you remember, it is a dreadful place—clammy, unclean, and sunless, with air that reeks of death and decay. The only sound to be heard is that of

157

Cianest's hooves as the pathetic creature paces the floor. She's aware of the moon's cycle, so time grows short. In hours she will be unapproachable. This time of day the guards are seldom around. Best we leave now."

After Brandi departed, Kat eased open the bulky wooden door of her room, checked to see if the path was clear to proceed, and then followed Ibby through a maze of dark narrow corridors. Soon, they arrived at the stairwell leading down to the dungeons. At the bottom, the two companions quickly went to the cell where Cianest was imprisoned.

"Cianest, it's me, Kat. I haven't forgotten what you told me and know it's not safe to approach at this time. However, things are growing worse by the hour. I don't know what to do. Please, talk to me."

A hissing sound was heard as a clawed hand grabbed the bars of the cell. "I smell your blood, and my thirst is almost intolerable. You must leave, Kat. The craving is excruciating. I am struggling to contain it, but can do so for only a moment. No one is safe at this time, not even you."

Kat edged close and stroked the scaly hand. "I'm sorry you're forced to endure such lurid torture, sweet Cianest. One day, you will be unchained from this terrible bond. You'll see."

"Hurry and speak, child. My monstrous desire mounts. Why are you in this place?"

"Tahl will send for me tonight. What should I do about his advances? He's a nauseating, disgusting excuse of a man. I would rather be dead than submit to his twisted whims."

Just then a voice boomed out of the darkness. "So, I am disgusting, dear cousin. Well, perhaps I will not wait until tonight and take you here and now, in front of your grotesque friend." He rushed and grabbed hold of her arm, pulling her close to his body. "You will pleasure me, and perhaps again later, *if* I enjoy it." Before she could protest, he slammed her against the wall, his hands traveling over her body.

Cianest violently shook the bars and shrieked, "Stay away from her."

Ibby flew into a rage and fluttered into his face. She savagely pecked at his arm, taking attention away from Kat momentarily.

"How dare you try to disrupt my dalliance?" Tahl swatted the spunky fowl…the force of his powerful blow brutally hurling its small body against the hard granite wall, rendering her unconscious. "I should kill all three of you, but it would spoil my enjoyment. Perhaps your plucky maid would make a tasty morsel for Cianest tonight."

"No, she's innocent. Leave her alone." Kat moved between Tahl and Ibby. "Do what you want with me, but leave Isabelle alone." She edged close to him. "Spare this maid's life and I will openly submit to your wishes."

He scoffed, "My desires will be realized one way or the other, foolish girl. I make no deals with a common wench." Anger rose in her like a hurricane. "Do *not* call me a common wench. I am a Princess of the Realm and derive from the bloodline of one greater than you."

Apparently amused by this uncommon outburst, he threw his head back and roared with laughter. "At least you have some backbone which ironically excites me even more. Get into that cell where I will show you what it is to be with a god and not some wimpy mortal."

Afraid for the life of her friend, she obeyed and backed into the dank cell. Almost immediately, the ancient prince was upon her. He ripped her clothing and began to hotly kiss a bare ivory shoulder. This was more than Kat could bear. She pulled away, and clawed his face. "Get your filthy paws off me, you deviant piece of dirt."

Ire flooded his face as fingers wiped away beads of blood from torn flesh. His voice boomed in rage. "If anyone else did this to me they would suffer instant death, but my needs would remain unsatisfied. Another fate awaits, dear cousin. It appears you prefer to act like an animal, so perhaps it is time you become one." He reached in his vest and pulled out the mysterious instrument of transformation.

Eyes grew wide with fear, but Kat stood fast. "Go ahead, creep. None of this mumbo jumbo will compare to what my sister will do to you and that demon you call a mother."

A rough hand slapped her across the face…the force of the blow knocking her to the sullied floor. "Insulting my mother appears to be somewhat habitual. Well, it shall happen no more. Mother's pet is a puny black cat, so perhaps it is fitting I have one similar, only larger of course." He began to utter an incantation in the same unfamiliar language heard before. Without delay, the amulet hummed and commenced to emit a soft blue glow. Aware of the proceedings, Kat sheltered her eyes as a blinding light flashed, delivering intense pain. Moments passed before sight returned. At first, a quick glance around revealed nothing unusual. Then she looked down. Velvety black fur covered her body which was apparently no longer human. She tried to speak, but only a freakish guttural sound emanated from her throat.

Tahl edged into the corridor and snatched up the reviving chicken, tossing its body to the floor in front of Kat. "Here's your dinner, *Princess*. Enjoy it."

Ibby looked up, squawked, and backed away.

Kat glanced at the tempting morsel, turned, leaped up on the makeshift bed, and lay down. Round golden eyes fixed an angry gaze on Tahl, as lips curled, revealing a large set of white incisors.

"Your fortitude is strong, I see. Well, it will do little good. You will remain in this state until the decision is made to act more civil toward me. As for that scrawny thing you call a chicken, it will look a great deal more appealing when hunger sets in. Eat it, or die. I could care less either way. The choice is yours." He reached out, slammed the door closed, and laughed as he walked away.

Ibby cowered for several minutes, but eventually worked up a spot of courage to approach the fearsome feline. "Ca—can you understand me, m—my lady?"

The great cat gave a solitary nod yes.

"Thank goodness." The little bird exhaled and edged closer. Oh, mistress, without a mirror, it is impossible to fully comprehend what has happened. Lord Tahl transformed you into a large black panther."

The eye-catching feline gave off a piteous moan as Kat viewed what she could of her new body.

The copper hen trembled as it hopped up beside the ebony carnivore. "It seems I am to meet my end by your hand. Please mistress, make my death swift." She drew close to the head of the breathtaking panther and closed her eyes.

Kat looked down and nudged the loyal maid. Unable to speak, she began to purr. It was the only way to notify Ibby she would not bring harm, regardless of what Tahl demanded.

Cianest screamed from her cell, "Ibby, tell me what hasss happened to Kat. What did that monster do to her? Tell me thisss very instant."

"Our beautiful lady has been changed into a fearsome black panther. She was ordered to devour me, but apparently refuses. I do not believe speech is possible."

"No, the ability remains. Kat, lisssten to me, force yourself to vocalize. It will not be easy, but the power isss there. You are part immortal. The transssfiguration cannot fully engulf you. Your presence when Ibby was morphed ssshielded her as well. Please try, Kat."

Round eyes darted about as the altered girl struggled to talk. An hour or more passed without an ounce of luck as frustration set in.

"Don't give up, mistress. Keep trying." The tiny friend's persistence brought a moment of irritation. A blow from her massive paw rolled the tiny hen across the floor.

"Ibby, I'm sorry and didn't mean to do that."

"Kat, you can speak!"

The panther leaped from the cot and approached the fragile fowl. "Don't worry, Ibby. I sure as heck won't do as ordered. That miserable oaf gave me a choice, and I choose to die before I hurt you." She lumbered to the door. "Cianest, are you alright? Did he injure you in any way?"

"No harm has befallen me, but thisss eve I must feast. Please, forgive what I am compelled to do. I am powerlessss to contest Tahl's bidding. Be strong, my precious child. Adera shall never abandon you. Help will soon arrive." A loud hiss echoed down the dismal stone passageway. "The guardsss come. Please, dear one, shelter your ears. I do not wish you be subjected to the devastation

I must inflict upon the sacrificial innocentsss. Many times I have tried to avoid thisss disdainful travesty, willing to face death rather than kill and devour the guiltless prey. Sadly, all attempts proved fruitless. Do not think ill of me."

"No apology is needed, Cianest. I understand. My heart breaks for the cursed torture forced upon you. I swear if it takes my last breath, I will make Tahl, and his witchy mother, pay for these sins."

Ibby pushed against Kat, urging her to retreat to the back of the darkened room. "Strive to remain calm, mistress…what is about to happen cannot be avoided. It will not be easy to ignore the sounds, but you must try."

The great cat snarled, then walked over and curled up on the tattered cot.

Moment's later, petrifying screams began, followed by the sound of rushing hooves upon the cobbled floor, the crush of bone, and flesh being gruesomely torn apart.

Kat leaped from the bed and paced the floor in a futile attempt to avoid the resonance coming from the devastating carnage being inflicted. Without hands she could not shelter her ears. The sounds were beyond horrific—beyond any that could be imagined. Piteous screams mingled with the guttural cries of death. It was almost more than she could bear.

Soon, a tomblike hush filled the dungeon. Cianest had finished her meal.

163

Chapter Eleven
The Dark Kingdom

Bit by bit, corn-blue skies mutated to gray and grew darker with every step, as the group progressed deeper into the bewitched kingdom of Mantalac. Trees withered and became barren of foliage. The lush forest landscape gradually morphed into a dismal and haunting environment.

"Adera, hold up," Randy yelled, but his plea fell on deaf ears. His wife recklessly urged McLachen forward at breakneck speed, aggressively ignoring any attempt to slow down. At her insistence, the vigorous pace continued throughout the day, bringing the horses to the brink of exhaustion. Reluctantly, infrequent stops were made to give the weary equines a brief rest and allow them time to attain a bit of nourishment.

Randy remained silent as a quick breather was given, but kept a vigilant eye on his titled spouse who paced like a caged animal, anxious to continue the trek. He tried to smile when King Merneos walked up, but worried eyes overshadowed his ruse.

"Do not be troubled. Your lady will be fine, Randy. Adera has tremendous strength and fortitude within her. These anxieties are well founded and to be expected. She and Tom are astride inexhaustible Bayards. The four find any necessary stop a temporary annoyance. It shall pass." He leaned in close. "Let us walk. A subject most vital requires brief discussion."

Randy nodded, and the pair meandered out of earshot of the others. "What's wrong, Merneos. I see you're

164

sporting a rare wrinkle on that flawless forehead. Something sure as blazes has you concerned."

Vibrant blue eyes widened and one eyebrow raised slightly as a look of irritation crossed the noble Elf's face. He blinked a couple times, shook his head, and instantly returned to the more conventional superior expression. "Shall we have a discussion of eminent threats…or my *appearance?*"

The King's humorless tone of voice caused heat to rise in Randy's cheeks. He more than understood this was no time for frivolity. "I apologize, Highness. Your concern is definitely warranted. The situation is pretty darn grave, and it was wrong of me to act so improvident. It won't happen again." He drew a long, deep breath.

"We are about to enter the Cimmerian Forest…a sunless, mirthless place filled with venomous decay. It shall remove any feelings of happiness and replace them with intense malevolence. No human can resist this vile curse. Adera, Horace, and I, are the only members who will not be fully affected. Although basically immune, we will nevertheless endure minor afflictions which could prove somewhat dangerous."

"I had no idea something of this nature would be encountered, Merneos. There was warning given of the toxic gas, but nothing more mentioned. Sorta explains why everyone is so blasted touchy all of a sudden, and sheds a clue to Adera's bizarre behavior. We best call a group meeting right away before the effects take further hold. Let's hope good old Merlin will come up with something. The man might be a tad bit peculiar at times, but appears to be a significantly clever and talented wizard."

The pair hurried back to the campground and gathered the troupe. Randy swallowed hard and thought carefully of what to say. "Okay guys, I'll just let it fly and not gonna pull any punches here. Best to slap it on out and let 'er rip." He inhaled deeply and continued. "Seems we're about to enter a cursed forest. Some of us are already feeling the effects and been a bit edgy." He looked over at his wife, raised both brows, and smiled. "Unless we come up with a way to overcome this unbeknownst obstacle, our mission is about to come to an abrupt end."

Adera leaped to her feet and hurled a stick at Randy. "*No.* I will *not* yield. How dare you even suggest such a thing?"

All eyes widened and jaws dropped at the benevolent sovereign's combative outburst.

Randy gave Merneos a quick glance, lowered deep blue eyes, and huffed. He knew what had to be done and personal feelings must be set aside for the moment. His voice thundered as he pointed a finger, "*Adera, sit down and shut up!*"

Her husband's uncommon ferocity appeared to deliver almost instant submission.

"I'm sorry for the brusqueness, sweetheart. Riding ahead as you did caused the malicious spell to hit you first. My flare-up was necessary to thwart its hold. As y'all can see, this odious enchantment had an upsetting affect on Adera's temperate personality. What was witnessed is only a smidgen of the nightmare that waits out there. Being non-human, Merneos, Adera, and Horace, will only be partly influenced, and as you can see, that in itself is pretty darn intense. Unfortunately, the rest of us won't be near so lucky. We'll receive the full dose, and it's doubtful any can survive. The spell leads humans to madness. As it engulfs our minds, we'll begin to destroy one another. Unless a solution's found, each of us will fall prey to this devastation. Merlin, I hate to say this, but the success of this endeavor appears to fully reside in your hands."

"Allow a moment to gather thoughts, Randy. My mind is somewhat cluttered at the moment." The great wizard twirled a bit of his unkempt cocoa-brown beard in long nimble fingers as blue-black eyes searched the heavens. "Ah yes, I believe the answer is relatively simple. The only way to overcome this malicious spell is with a counter spell. One rarely used comes to mind, but feel it should suffice. Fate, once again, is apparently on our side."

He rose, walked to Adera, and took her hand. "Unfortunately, my lady, your early infection dictates the logical testing be applied to you before any other. May I have permission to try?"

Turquoise eyes looked up and delicate pink lips curled to form a soft smile. "Do what must be done, sweet friend. I also wish to apologize for the aforementioned eruption. In my haste, I foolishly failed to realize our location. The toxicity of this woodland was known to me. Had we proceeded, not only would failure follow, but most, if not all, would have perished." She reached out toward her misty-eyed husband, who quickly clasped hold and squeezed delicate fingers. "Proceed, Merlin."

The ancient mage nodded, closed his eyes, and began to recite an incantation in a strange and inconceivable language. When finished, he gently brushed the Queen's forehead with his right forefinger, causing instant collapse.

"Adera," Randy exclaimed.

Cradled in her husband's arms, lavish lashes fluttered as she slowly regained composure. "I-I feel fine. My mind is completely free…nary a smidgen of angst remains. Time and again your brilliance has delivered us from the clutches of doom. Our gratitude is boundless." She rose and placed

167

a tender kiss to the whiskered cheek of the dateless conjuror, which brought a slight blush to his cheeks.

One by one, each member of the troupe was given the invocation, including all the animals. After a brief rest, the group mounted and entered the nefarious canopy of shadows.

As they traveled on, only the cadenced plod of the horses was heard. The air reeked with the rancid stench of decay, filling the traveler's hearts with overwhelming moroseness. Luckily, the effects were negligible, thanks to the uncanny abilities of an unconventional wizard.

Hours passed and soon progress slowed to a near crawl. Horses' feet relentlessly became dangerously ensnared in an impassible overgrowth of thorn piercing bramble.

Randy dismounted and yelled for the others to follow suit. "We can't put these animals through anymore torture. Blood coats their legs like scarlet droplets of splattered paint. They have to be in agony. Unfortunately, looks like the balance of this trip is gonna have to be made by foot."

"It is a wise decision, my brother. After so many hours astride our mounts, a good stretch of the legs is rather welcome," Horace announced as he readily descended onto the inhospitable terrain. Groans of disapproval caused him to spin around with hands on his hips. "Have my valiant students all vanished and been replaced with a cluster of weak-kneed complainers?"

Meeley jumped down with a snort. "Don't get your panties in a bind, Horace. We're all just tired and grumpy—something that pompous Elvin brain of yours can't understand. Come on over here and say it to my face, and I'll show what weak-kneed is."

Charlie rushed over and stood between the pair. "Whoa, take it easy you two. I think a touch of this blighted forest might be influencing this silly agitation. How about we all take a deep breath and calm the heck down." He put an arm around Meeley and pulled her close. "Now face the facts, little britches, we did give out a grunt of displeasure when told to get off the horses. But, my pointy eared friend, you also have to understand her reaction was not a sign of weakness, but simply a normal human reaction."

Merneos walked over and stood by the flustered warrior. "He speaks truth, Horace. Our companions are humans and must react as such. Let the trivial annoyance be put to rest and allow us to continue. The sooner we emerge from this baleful place the better."

Horace approached Meeley and stretch forth a hand. "I ask forgiveness for my reprehensible outburst, dear lady. There are times I forget my station and expect too much. You and the others have never failed to prove your worth." He bowed his head and placed a fist to his heart in a gesture of respect.

"Aw heck, how could I stay angry at such a genteel bloke?" She let out a robust laugh and grabbed hold of the Elf, giving him a huge bear hug. "There, that should mend some bridges."

"Yes, I believe it shall," Horace replied as he straightened his vest. "Let us hope we have no more bridges to mend…at least not in that manner."

His flustered words brought a laugh from the entire group, with the exception of King Merneos, who as usual, remained expressionless.

Randy helped Adera off McLachen, while taking advantage of the moment to grab an opportunistic hug. "Ah, now I feel better." He chuckled and gave his new bride a quick peck on the cheek.

169

Charlie patted his mount as he spoke, "Dudes, we will need these buggers to get us back home and can't let them simply wander off, especially in such a miserable place. It's not safe. Heaven only knows what else is wandering around out here."

"Point taken, Charlie," Tom replied. "McLachen, do you and Chendar think you can lead these horses to a protected locale and keep them secure until we return?"

The great black stallion looked at his magnificent son and both began to snicker. "Sir, we are more than capable of such an undertaking. However, I wish to continue on. My Lady is in danger, and I must join in her rescue. Chendar can handle the appointed task."

Adera walked up and stroked the thick, arched neck of the great ebony horse. "No, my noble knight, you must not proceed. Travel back to Drealon where safety is guaranteed. Please, carry forth my bidding. Do not be troubled. I vow to return with Kat."

McLachen pawed the ground and vehemently exhaled. After a few seconds, he calmed and nuzzled the Queen's soft palm. "I hold great respect for you in every way, Majesty and shall fulfill the request. You have never broken an oath to any creature. My Bayard hearing is unparalleled. When you reenter the land of fairies, merely speak my name. We shall respond without delay. May the stars grant victory, gentle Queen, and bring My Lady back home."

The stunning sovereign cradled his velvety muzzle in her hands and kissed it gently. "Go now, great horse. Be at peace. You and your mistress shall soon be reunited."

McLachen turned and trotted over to his son, Chendar. "We must herd the mortal beasts to safe territory. I shall

170

take the lead while you keep them in tow from behind. Be diligent my son, for these animals are somewhat flighty and rather unpredictable."

"Yes Father, I will be exceptionally attentive. Concern weighs heavily in your eyes, but do not forget the Queen is a being of honor. Truth of her worth has been demonstrated more than once. Master Tom grows depressed by the hour. He rarely, if ever, speaks now. I feel increasing despair in his heart. The wellbeing of our princess burdens each of us in some form."

McLachen nickered softly and gently nudged his unequaled offspring. "I often fail to verbalize my pride in you, Chendar—a fault I shall endeavor to set right in the future. Not only have you become magnificent in appearance, a welcomed gift from your exquisite mother Darcy, but also cultivated a superior sense of wisdom for one so young. I suggest you bid Tom farewell for now, and wish him safe journey as the group continues on."

The steel-grey stallion's glorious silver mane blanketed an elegantly refined head as he bowed to his father in respect. "I will make my words of departure short." He turned and walked over to Tom, who leaned against a large boulder—eyes resolutely fixed in the direction of Mantalac. "Sir, I must be underway. Free your mind of the heavy burden it bears. Success depends on sharp wits. Princess Kat is unswerving and will not succumb to evil."

Tom gazed into the devoted eyes of his four-legged companion. "I hope you're right, buddy. Suppose if that wildcat of mine could stand up to that eighty-foot sea serpent, Ios, this disgusting shell of a man won't be much of a problem" He chuckled and stroked the colt's muscular neck. "Be careful, Chendar. We're not far from the stinking manor and at risk of peril. Hopefully this venture will end relatively soon and we'll all be returning to Bowlandria."

Moments later, the two Bayard's rounded up the other horses and herded them into the dense woods.

Randy wrapped an arm around the tiny waist of his wife as they watched their mounts trot off. "They'll be fine, Adera. You can bet your buttons McLachen will take good care of those critters. He'll have them come running full steam when he hears your beckoning holler."

"Yes, I have no doubt in his abilities or dedication. My concern rests in our outcome. I fear we may have already been defeated."

Randy spun her around and clasped her shoulders. "What do mean?" Her lowered eyes and silence sent a prickle down his neck. "Adera, what the blazes aren't you telling me." He gave her a gentle shake.

Turquoise eyes remained fixed on the ground. "I have sensed a terrible tragedy. There is great distress in the heart of my sister. She lives, but not as we know her."

"What? You're not making a lick of sense," Randy exclaimed as he lifted her chin. "Either she's alive, or she's not. Dang it woman, speak up."

Adera swallowed hard. "I do not know, Randy…it is merely an awareness. There was a fleeting moment of searing pain followed by utter confusion. Now, I sense intense hatred and overwhelming despair. I do not know what Tahl has done to her, but something horrific transpired. It is as though Kat's essence has been divided. The girl we love lingers in one part, but the other is almost—animalistic. There is nothing more I can tell."

The handsome groom drew a deep breath and embraced his wife. "It's okay, sweetheart. We're not far away and will soon find out what gives. At least we know she's alive." He peered over at Tom, who was chatting with Meeley and Charlie. "Perhaps it's best we keep this tidbit to ourselves for now. No need upsetting Tom more than he already is."

Adera nodded and looked into her husband intense blue eyes. "What would I ever do without your strength?"

He chuckled and lovingly kissed her forehead. "Baby cakes, hope you never have to find out. Now, how about we go join the others and get our fanny's movin. Looks like a nasty road ahead."

"Yes, from this point on, it becomes increasingly treacherous. We have yet to encounter any Qergs, but I believe that shall abruptly change."

Randy led her over to join Tom, Meeley, and Charlie, and called the others to gather round. "We need to go over a few issues before continuing. Adera recalled a few interesting details which might prove beneficial. How 'bout y'all take a seat and hear what the lady has to say?"

"At last we shall relish a sensible gathering of the minds." Merlin casually plopped down on a nearby rock and grinned as he looked around. "Well, must I conjure up chairs, or will each find a place to rest while we converse?"

Merneos gave the wizard a quirky glance before settling down on a moss-covered log alongside Horace and the others.

Faye fluttered over to Meeley and nestled on a protruding branch beside her. "Hi. What's going on?" She dangled her tiny feet and jiggled them playfully as she peered around.

173

"Shush," Meeley replied. "We're going to discuss some things. Adera's the only one who's been here before and has information on what might be encountered. Now, hush up and pay attention, little bit."

The tiny sprite's eyes widened, and she nodded. "Okay," she whispered which caused Meeley to snicker.

Randy glowered at the pair and cleared his throat, "We've been pretty doggone lucky so far and managed to overcome the dangers we stumbled upon. Merlin has thankfully kept us safe for the most part, and I for one am extremely grateful, but more pitfalls lay ahead. Think we all better pay strict attention to what Adera has to say."

The regal Queen rose, her face showing strained emotion. "I have traveled this path prior, and it is not a pleasant one. Danger lurks in every corner and shall grow more intense as we move forward. Thankfully, Qergs have yet to be encountered, but I trust this will soon change. They are disgusting and deadly creatures created from the nefarious mind of my aunt, and Tahl's mother, Odiene. Unlike the Shankquas, these creatures are quite large and possess a trickle of intelligence. Our swords will be of no use against such monsters. Arrows must be the weapon of choice. Avoid their lengthy spears at all costs for our armor will easily yield to their sharpness. Most hunting tips are saturated with a dreadful potion which will render you immobile and helpless within seconds should it pierce your skin. However, some may be infused with a lethal poison. Death is instantaneous. Shoot fast, straight, and aim for their heads. This is the only means to bring them down. Hesitate, and you shall surely perish."

She paused a moment allowing the words to be absorbed. "Qergs will not be our only obstacle. Odiene and Tahl shall be expecting us, and undoubtedly have plans set in motion. What vile traps lay in wait, I do not know. Be vigilant, for every step may prove to be the last taken."

Charlie slapped his knee, breaking the stony silence. "Well, that sure put a quiver in my liver."

Randy, who had been staring at the ground, looked up and began to chuckle. "Dang Charlie, you sound like old Jay more all the time. No one had a better knack of brightening the air at just the right moment. I've said it a thousand times before, but I'll say it one more time, sure glad a touch of him rubbed off on you 'cause we certainly need it now."

Questions quickly began to surface and shot forth like a bolts of lightning. Adera answered the best she could and finally laid most inquires to rest.

Faye suggested she and Punk might fly ahead to observe any potential dangers laying in wait. "We'll be high up and safe, but at least we can spot Qergs or anything else that might be out there. Early warning of an impending ambush might be a life saver."

Randy smiled and held out his hand. "Flit on over here, Faye." Without a moment of hesitation, she took to the air and landed gently in his outstretched palm. "You deserve this." He gingerly took hold of her tiny hand and gave a tender kiss to the cheek.

She giggled as a fiery blush rose on her face. "Dandelion dust! My first kiss and it had to come from a human. Splozits."

The little fairy's comment broke the morbid atmosphere and pulled forth a bit of laughter from each member, even the reticent Elves. Well-wishes erupted as the brave sprite climbed aboard her winged champion and took to the sky.

"Well, time to load up and get underway," Randy, declared. "Tom, how about you and I take the lead? Ladies, think each of you should walk in between two of the men for safety."

Adera began to object, but was quickly subdued. Merlin and Charlie walked with Meeley, while Merneos and Horace escorted the Queen.

As they advanced further into the cheerless kingdom, the landscape became more lifeless. Torturous brambles tore viciously into flesh. A syrupy mist rose eerily from the decaying forest, filling the air with a foul pungent stench. The path of soft earth hardened into a crusty loam delivering pain to weary feet as they trod along.

Suddenly, Meeley stopped and looked around. "Oh, I smell something sweet, like fresh baked brownies." Before Charlie could stop her, she darted off to the side.

Adera turned and screamed. "No Meeley. Do not go into that clearing. Charlie, stop her. It is a trap."

The dragon's aviator was just about to step into the open area when two hands grabbed hold of each arm and forcefully pulled her back. "My lady, you must not go forward. Hold fast, Willa. The human cannot escape our grasp or she will perish." The wood nymph sisters struggled as Meeley twisted and fought to free herself.

Charlie sprinted ahead of the others and reached his wife first. "Meeley stop, it's a trap."

"It is not. Don't you smell those brownies? I'm so hungry, Charlie, and they smell wonderful. Let go of me."

"I hate to do this baby, but there's no other choice. Hope you don't hold this against me. It has to be done." He winced and delivered a harsh slap to the face, then quickly caressed her.

176

The shock seemed to work as grey-blue eyes blinked. "Wha-what happened, and why the dickens did you slap me? Why, you big Palooka, I outta knock you from the North to the South and back."

Leora stepped forward and pointed to the mustard colored knoll. "Mistress, you were about to step upon that soil. It is a living type of quicksand and would have devoured your body in seconds. Salvation would be impossible. The fragrance it expelled was devised to entice a human. You were struggling and about to break our grasp. This gentleman did what was necessary to save your miserable life. Be grateful for his actions."

Charlie led his wife back to the others. "I'm sorry I had plant such a firm slap, but you were almost insane and trying to get lose. It hurt me as much as it did you. Forgive me?"

Meeley rubbed a reddened cheek. "Well, all's forgiven, but not so darn sure it hurt you more than me. Ouch. Did you have to hit so blasted hard?"

He pulled her close and gave a robust hug. "When we get home, I'll make it up somehow, sweetums. Cross my heart."

She snickered. "You sure as shoot will, ya big sap. Don't think I'll forget either."

Randy took hold of Adera's arm. "Yikes! That was too close for comfort. If it wasn't for those two wood nymphs, Meeley would've been killed. Not one of us anticipated something so sinister. From now on, we better stick like glue to each other and watch every step. I had no idea a snare of that nature even existed. Everything looked harmless. Another second would have done her in and probably Charlie to boot. Thought of such an outcome,

177

had she not been stopped, actually gives me the dang shivers."

Merlin strolled up to Leora and Willa. "Ladies, we are forever indebted. Your arrival could not have come about at a more opportune moment. I have often asked the trees of your whereabouts, but received no word. How did you find us?"

"Willa and I have never left your side. We remained cloaked by the forest, although we did find the decomposition of these timbers most unpleasant."

Adera walked up and politely bowed to the two nymphs. "Your quick actions and bravery saved the life of our cherished friend...a debt which shall never be fully repaid. I beseech you accept my most humble gratitude. As the sovereign of Bowlandria and guardian of the Realm, I bestow upon each of you the distinguished title of Royal Sentinel. When we return, my declaration shall be spread throughout the territories. All will respect and honor your station. It is the least I can do for such valiant souls."

Randy nudged Tom, his eyes dancing with delight, "She sure is something, isn't she? No wonder I fell head over heels." A glance at Tom caused a moment of joy to fade. "Dude, I'm sorry. I shouldn't have made such a stupid remark. It was plain dumb and thoughtless." He placed a hand on his friends shoulder. "We'll get Kat back. She's a tough cookie and will be okay. When we return to Bowlandria, we'll all enjoy a few hearty drinks, some laughs, and one heck of a lot of rowdy conversation about the things encountered during this insane adventure."

Tom smiled, but his eyes clearly showed deepening sadness. "Yeah, I suppose so. I know Kat will never give up, but pray we get to her in time. Tahl is the devil incarnate, and no telling what deviant things he can do to torture her. Until she's back safely in my arms, I can't be happy. Sorry, I don't mean to rain on your parade, but my heart's overwhelmed with worry right now."

Randy gave Tom an encouraging pat on the back. "I more than understand, buddy." He glanced over at his bride, who was happily chatting with the others. *I truly do know how the poor guy feels. If anything were to happen to Adera, my life wouldn't be worth another breath.*

An icy chill ran down his spine and he shuddered. What would his friend do if this endeavor turns tragic? Although he tried not to believe it, a harsh fear prickled his gut like a cancerous thorn.

Kat *may not* survive.

Chapter Twelve
A Traveler's Tale

Sounds of approaching footsteps roused the slumbering panther. Kat stared at the door, as lips curled exposing powerful white fangs.

"Ibby, we must not speak in front of Tahl. No matter what happens, remain silent.

The transformed servant nodded then glanced around the room. "Oh mistress, you were ordered to devour me. If the master discovers this has not happened, he will inflict pain upon you, and I shall surely be killed. What should we do?"

Golden eyes darted about in panic. Her little friend was right, and if found intact she would be sacrificed. "Ibby, pluck some feathers and scatter them around the cell. Hurry, we haven't a second to spare."

The fragile fowl did as she was told and spread a bounty of coppery down throughout the dank chamber. "What do we do now, mistress?"

"In order to make this believable, it's imperative I show a mouthful of feathers. He's nearly here." She bent down and snatched a copious amount of downy plumes from the back of the little hen.

"Ouch, that hurt, Kat."

"Sorry, Ibby, but I there's no time to be gentle. Now, tuck yourself under the mattress and don't move a muscle. I'll take care of the rest."

The former maid leaped on the bed and wiggled between the wooden slats and the makeshift covering. No

180

sooner had she done so, when the door was flung open and slammed thunderously against the wall.

Kat growled and backed up as the pompous ancient strutted in. Eyes glared as she kept a diligent stare upon him, while small feathers floated eerily from her lips to the floor.

Tahl smirked as callous eyes scanned the room. "So, it appears the beast in you took hold after all. Good. She was a pathetic specimen of a girl and needed to be eliminated. Hope the meal was enjoyable."

The great cat let out a shrill scream and pounced forward, stopping only inches from him.

"You insolent piece of lowlife—how dare you charge at me." He backed out of the chamber and pulled the door shut. "You will learn to obey, cousin, or *die*."

In an effort to calm the intense anger raging inside, Kat paced around the musty cubicle for several minutes before speaking. "Every bone in my body wants me to rip his throat out. It's all clear, Ibby. The perverted lump of garbage is gone."

A small comb-crested head peered out from under the tattered rags of the mattress. "Is-is it sa-safe, mistress?"

"Yes, at least for the time being, but there's no doubt he'll be returning. We have to think of some way to get you the heck out of here." Suddenly, the narrow gap between the bars offered a possible means of escape. "Listen, if I stand on hind legs and stretch, my head will almost reach the opening. Can you make your way up my back and squeeze through the bars?"

"I think so, Kat."

"Once you're free, hide until all traces of danger are gone. You must get as far away from this joint as you can. Be careful and don't get caught. I'm sure my sister,

181

husband, and friends are not far away. If you happen to cross paths, tell Adera what has occurred. Please, do not take any chances. At least my mind will rest easier knowing you are okay."

"I'll find your sister, mistress, and won't stop until she's located. It breaks my heart to leave you here like this. Please, do not further anger Tahl. He's unpredictable and can inflict great pain."

Kat nodded, and proceeded to stand up against the door. "Hurry, Ibby...get the tar out of here. Don't worry about me. I'll be fine. Now skedaddle before someone comes."

The gutsy captive fluttered up the panther's back to freedom's gateway. "I promise to return with your sister and the others. I'll not fail. I promise." She wiggled through the narrow bars and dropped to the stony dungeon floor.

Kat got down and began to circle around the tiny chamber. Worry flooded her mind. *I pray you remain out of harm's way, my brave little friend. If we're blessed with a bit of luck, Tom and Adera will be located quickly.* The sound of movement from across the hall altered dismal thoughts. "Cianest, you've remained silent. Are you okay?"

At first, there was no reply, only the sound of hooves clanking against the cobbled floor. "Yesss child, I am fine. It is painful for me after a night of feast. I regret you had to bear witness to this loathsome act."

"There's no need to apologize. It's not your fault. What kind of monsters are Odiene and Tahl? Those two come from the same planet as Adera, and are also my kin, yet they're as different as day is night. It tears my heart to shreds knowing you are forced to perform these atrocities simply for their manic pleasure. I swear to heaven, Cianest, if a door of opportunity opens, I will rip the life out of Odiene and that degenerate son of hers."

Cianest hissed. "You mussst not think such things, Kat. Odiene is more powerful than most realize. As for Tahl, he has transformed both of us. Should you end his life, I will indeed be released from these bonds, but you will never return to your former ssself. Another must perform the act. Tahl's demise cannot and must not be brought about by *your* hand."

Golden eyes lowered. "I-I could not bear to be bound in this body for eternity. My life would become a living hell. Tom would forever be without a wife and I without the husband I adore. Yet, you are hideously held captive— compelled to slay guiltless lives. At least the creature I am could be let loose from the confines of this imprisonment. That can never be your fate. No, I wouldn't be able to live with myself knowing you must endure this disgusting existence. If the chance arrives, I will liberate you."

A loud, woeful moan echoed down the odorous dungeon hall, followed by piteous sobs. "You are truly the sister of Adera, child. My icy heart is warmed by such compassion. The intent is more than honorable, but must be vanquished from your mind. I forbid further consideration of it."

Kat growled and glanced around the clammy walls of the morose confinement. "There has to be some way this miserable spell can be reversed. Perhaps Merlin will know a cure. He's the wisest and most talented of wizards. If anyone can cook up an antidote, he will. I know it. Don't despair, Cianest. We will find a way to free both of us. Hold strong and have faith." Frustrated and nearing exhaustion, she curled up on the tattered mattress and quickly drifted off to sleep.

183

Surrounded by the secured escort of their men folk, Adera coiled an arm around that of her friend as they strolled side by side. "Allow me to aide a quavering body." Meeley remained shaken from the close brush with death and was a tad unsteady on her feet. "I am pleased we ladies are granted this rare opportunity to freely converse. Such a moment is rather difficult to obtain."

"You're so right, Highness. We've been on a whirlwind ride since leaving the Castle. How are you holding up? And don't go saying you're just fine, because I can see stress tarnishing that pretty face."

The alluring sovereign squeezed Meeley's arm and smiled. "It appears one so astute cannot easily be fooled. It is true. My concerns and fears are countless." She tapped her husband on the shoulder. "Randy, we should rest a moment."

A sigh of relief was breathed by all as the friends formed a circle and eased down on a soft hummock of decomposing leaves. Faye and Punk joined the group, which also granted the weary owl a welcomed pause. Food and drink was passed around, providing each a nourishing respite.

Randy's brow furrowed. "Sweetheart, we've never really talked much about your aunt and her son. Maybe it's time we knew a speck more about this dirty duo. Y'all are related, yet there's a gap of difference ten miles wide. Considering no two humans are exactly alike, it's understandable your people could also vary, but *these* two are way out of the box. I for one would love to know what's up with them."

184

Adera realized all eyes were clearly focused on her and brushed frazzled golden locks from her face. "I shall try to explain as much as possible. You have every right to inquire."

She swallowed hard. "As you know, Odiene is the sister of my father. He was one of our planets most accomplished scientists. Along with two dozen skilled citizens, his sister was chosen to join a sophisticated exploration group. Their lengthy mission would navigate through time and space. Given father's superior knowledge and leadership qualities, he was appointed commander."

"Our society is significantly advanced…ten thousand years more than the existing human populace." The ancient ruler paused briefly to gather thoughts.

"Many of the participants, such as my parents, were wedded. Odiene was accompanied by her spouse, Kram. They were happy and deeply in love. While exploring a newly formed and highly unstable planet, my mother wandered off to gather a few rare and vital medicinal herbs. She was about to be crushed by a landslide of loosened boulders when Kram reacted and valiantly pushed her out of harm's way. Sadly, he perished. Odiene, who only days prior had given birth to their son Tahl, grew insane with grief. She blamed mother for Kram's demise. No words of clarification would alter her assessment. As the days progressed, so did her angst, hence the fury toward my family commenced."

Meeley gasped. "It's a tragic story for sure, but geez, his death wasn't your momma's fault. Darn thing was a bloomin' accident."

Adera nodded. "Yes Meeley, it was simply a mishap, but Odiene did not see it as such. She attributed Kram's death to an act of reckless irresponsibility. Mother was guiltless

185

and tried in vain to appease Odiene's dolefulness. Alas, lividity intensified in my aunt's soul—a bitterness that would never cease and steadily drive her to the brink of madness. Many times, Zuegas was forced to confine his sister to secured quarters."

"Months passed and soon I was born. Being the only two children on board, Tahl and I were inseparable and happily played together. But as my cousin matured, Odiene's influence transferred his personality. Time and again, Tahl would try to cause me harm. At length, we were separated."

"When Cianest decided to join our travels, I was elated. My solitary life was re-energized and overflowed with days of laugher and joy. She and I formed an indissoluble sister-like bond. Tahl watched us from afar as a vile jealousy darkened his heart. He vowed to one day destroy her."

Charlie gasped. "Hold on, you knew Cianest? She's a bloodthirsty fiendish beast."

"No Charlie, she was not a monster, but the purest of creatures. Her beauty was incomparable as were the special gifts only her kind possessed."

The great sovereign halted briefly as distraught eyes stared downward. "After our ship crashed on this planet and functional items salvaged, many specimens were inadvertently set loose upon the earth. Most were harmless, but regrettably feared by humans. A number of these creatures perished before they could be saved. When this protectorate was created, those which remained alive were brought to Bowlandria and released."

"I knew how you came to be here, but never the rest. What specimens were dispersed?" Randy's gaze was intent.

"Most, but not all, you have already encountered. Meeley, you possess the last dragon that exists. Knox is the lone survivor of many. He hatched the very day you arrived and was immediately deemed guardian of our world."

Meeley shook her head. "Well I'll be a son of a gun. I'm totally flabbergasted. I've always known Knox defended us and Bowlandria, but the whole blasted Realm? Wowzer."

Adera smiled. "It should also be noted he chose a lifelong companion—Meeley. Until you arrived, gentle Knox hibernated, tucked safely away within the hardened shell of a massive green egg. A special bond exists between you and he that none shall ever break. It might be suitable to retain this information, Charlie, lest you rile your wife's precious pet."

"Uh, yeah, I sure as the dickens will." He cast a quick look over at his beaming wife and wiped a sweaty forehead. "I love you sugar plum, just remember that."

The flustered comment brought a bit of cheer to the group and some needed laughter.

"Okay, y'all, calm down. Let the lady continue," Randy declared.

Adera nodded. "After our majestic home was built, peace reined for eons. During these days, many of our kind chose to visit your world, curious to witness its progression. Some, including my father, would often toy with the humans they encountered, proliferating mysterious tales that would last throughout the ages. Unfortunately, during one of Odiene's visits, she happened upon two very evil magicians, Yiema and Kaiva. They were the twin offspring of a dark Elf sorcerer and a human witch. She enchanted the pair, coaxing each to reveal every morsel of their vile craft. Coupled with superior intellectual capabilities and a few of the ships salvaged items, Odiene and Tahl soon grew lethal. Once all knowledge could be

187

obtained from Yiema and Kaiva, they were brutally murdered by Tahl."

Adera rose and strolled over behind Randy, placing a both hands on his shoulders.

He turned and stood up beside her. "It's okay if you want to stop, baby cakes. I had no idea things were so intense. How 'bout we just drop it for now."

She lovingly ran a lone finger down his cheek. "No, sweet husband, my traveler's tale has progressed this far, and it is time to unmask suppressed exploits. I am fine."

Merneos stood and bowed to her. "I have known you since childhood, Adera, but now discover my eyes were blind to these happenings. Accept deep gratitude for your deliverance of these unknown events."

Charlie jumped to his feet and nearly knocked Merneos over. "Whoops, sorry, Highness." He steadied the flustered Elf who returned a glance of disapproval. "See, told you dudes the Deliverance Brigade was the right name for this motley bunch." A look of disbelief and ire crossed everyone's faces instantly and turned the buoyant outburst to silence. "Uh oh, think maybe I'll just sit my fanny back down and work on getting both feet out of my extra large mouth." With those words, he dropped to the ground and gave a queried look.

Horace huffed and frowned at Charlie. "Now that the rude interruption has been dismissed, please continue, Your Majesty."

"There is not a great deal more to tell, dear friends. In time, Odiene and Tahl were banished to Mantalac. It was once a land of beauty and tranquility, but now grows desolate. Father took pity upon his sister and chose a suitable location. After viewing the carnage unleashed by the duo, he chastised himself for the devilish infliction set

188

upon the meek, hapless residents, but nothing could be done. Our race is forbidden to kill one of its own. It is the strictest of our laws. Although Odiene and Tahl held little regard for this sacred rule, Zuegas remained bound to it. That is why they were banished and not destroyed. When father decided to rest, I erroneously allowed my aunt and cousin to attend the funeral. It was during this time Cianest was captured by them and eventually turned into the creature she is. An attempted rescue developed into a grave debacle. I foolishly underestimated the powers of my relatives and soon became overwhelmed. Nearly all of my army was destroyed. The unspeakable death of those brave warriors weighs upon my soul to this day."

Merlin interrupted. "My lady, do not cast blame upon your person. Please, shed such a torturous burden. You were a mere child at the time with limited powers and juvenile wisdom. It is clear this nightmare of a past failure is what you now bear."

Tears began to well up in her eyes. "Yes, it remains my worst concern, Merlin. Because I did not succeed in the rescue attempt of Cianest, she suffers a fate worse than death. I could not continue life should my sister experience comparable horrors. Failure is not an option."

Randy cradled the sobbing queen in his arms. "Let it go, sweetheart. You've been holding this in for days now. Once you release the frustration, your mind will clear up, and we'll all be better off."

Tom walked over and tenderly rubber her back. "We're not going to fail, Adera. See, unlike the prior attempt, we possess a highly sophisticated weapon, and they'll be completely powerless to fight it—love, dear sister-in-law, love. Not a blasted thing on this planet is stronger, and it will end their reign of terror."

189

She turned and stared into his warm, mellow brown eyes. "Your words are uplifting, Tom, and hold much truth. I have always stated love is the most powerful force on earth. Thank you, dear one, for reminding me. Our meager group contains more of this miraculous emotion than all the army's of the world combined. My loyal friends, we will soon fight an indispensable battle against evil, and our fortitude shall lead us to victory. Although it is against the laws of my ancestors, for the protection of our homeland and the citizens who reside within it, Odiene and Tahl must, and shall be, destroyed."

Tom gave Adera a hug and soon the rest followed his lead. After a brief period, they regrouped and once again began the perilous trek toward the Black Castle.

Hours passed, and what was left of the treacherous path vanished. Now, hardened earth gave way to a cadaverous smelling swamp. Each step became more difficult than the next. Often they would have to halt as lethal vipers passed precariously close. One bite would be fatal.

Meeley was in tears, her body quaking in apparent pain as she trudged through the odorous muck. "I don't know if I can continue, Charlie. My legs are nearly numb, and every bone in this body aches."

"I'm right here with you, baby. Hold on to me. We'll make it out of here before long, right Adera?"

"Yes, we shall soon be free of this quagmire. Solid land is but a few steps ahead. However, it is near the Manor and well patrolled by Qergs." She looked up and waved. "Faye, what danger lurks on the horizon?"

At his mistress' bidding, Punk zoomed down and skillfully perched the pair in a nearby tree.

The tiny fairy pointed a finger ahead. "I have not seen a living soul, Majesty. There are no Qergs in sight. Around

190

that curve is high land and the path appears clear. I'll go check again though. Sure wouldn't want something to pop out on you."

With a might whoosh of powerful wings, the great owl, and his rider rocketed into the air.

Exactly as Faye stated, high land soon came into sight. Everyone, including the airborne scouts, crumbled to the ground as solid footing was obtained. After quenching their thirst, the party cautiously moved on.

The landscape had become even bleaker as they drew closer to Odium Manor. Shrouded starlight cast eerie shadows as the sunless sky dimmed.

Adera's eyes widened and a frown formed on her brow. "Something is amiss, Randy. We should have met resistance by Qergs long ago. It is as though they have been intentionally recoiled. I am troubled by what I see, or should say, do not see."

"Yeah, kinda feel the same, sweetums. I've never been this route before, but have to admit something sure smells rotten. Those fool relatives of yours surely would have a ton of their fiends out hunting for us. What the heck's going on?"

Merneos edged up to Randy and Adera. "It is obvious you each sense the unsettling atmosphere. There is little doubt a trap awaits. Dare we send Faye on ahead to scope the terrain?"

The Queen nodded and signaled for the brave little fairy. "Faye, we are uneasy about the lack of opposition. Yet again, I entreat your aid. Is it possible to safely take wing once more and view our footpath? However, I do not wish to place you in danger. If this cannot be achieved unscathed then the venture must be terminated. Do not

191

agree unless it is viable. I hold your honor as a princess of Drealon to speak only truth."

"We *can* do it, Majesty. Don't worry. Punk will fly high enough to keep us free from harm. The Manor is just ahead. I didn't see a thing around it before, but this time we'll make a closer pass. It does seem a bit odd, doesn't it? You suppose it's a ploy to ambush us?"

"It would seem so, little one." Adera smiled and stroked the downy head of the great owl. "Keep your rider safe, noble Punk. Do not allow a foolish mistake to deliver disaster."

The large Barred owl lovingly mouthed the Queen's fingers. Seconds later, he shot into the sky carrying his spirited charge.

Adera watched until they were out of sight. She turned her glance toward the Manor and shuddered as a prickle of impending doom engulfed a troubled heart.

Chapter Thirteen
Band of Obedience

Morning arrived, and Lord Tahl was anxious to see if Kat had at last decided to surrender. Upon arrival, he was disappointed to find the great panther even more agitated. "It appears your refusal to yield remains. So be it. I can wait. When you grow hungry enough and become sick of these surroundings, maybe then you'll realize what I have to offer might be rather enjoyable in comparison." He strutted over to her and pompously attempted to pat the ebony feline on the head.

Instead of submission, he received a violent swat across the cheek and yelled out in pain as sharp claws tore flesh.

Eyes blazed. "You will pay dearly for this," he screamed. A stream of blood gushed from between his fingers as he held a hand over the fresh wound. "I should kill you now, but to die by my hand is sadly forbidden. However, be warned dear cousin, if submission is not obtained by the next full moon, Cianest will enjoy a 'royal' meal."

Tahl stormed back to his room, slamming the meaty oak door behind him as he entered. The might of the vehement action echoed down dim corridors like a rolling blast of thunder.

"I cannot believe this insubordinate half-breed had the gall to again strike my person in such a brazen manner. She will soon pay for that impudent act." He kicked a small tapestry covered wooden footstool across the room, shattering the insignificant object against the rigid granite wall.

"I am a prince…a god among men and more than worthy of her paltry charms. Perhaps a few lashes of the whip will alter such defiant behavior." He looked in the mirror at the disfiguring scratches to his unspoiled face and winced. "If these mutilating lesions even nominally impair my entrancing appearance, I vow that odious hellcat will suffer a fate worse than death."

After tending to his wound, he flopped across the bed and stared up at the deep scarlet canopy. Anger, and a highly bruised ego, caused his muscular body to tremble with agitation. Suddenly, a perplexing thought entered a deranged mind. Odiene had tutored him in the art of transformation using the mysterious amulet, but had never revealed the method used to reverse its effect. Although a scorching passion hungered for Kat, she was never the less his blood cousin and part traveler. The abhorrent actions he had recklessly taken so far were against all laws governing his race. Fear of retribution by Adera, as well as his mother, delivered an uneasy quiver to his stomach. "Dear Auntie is indeed a powerful force to reckon with, but Mother is equally daunting. I'm not sure she will approve of what I've done to her niece."

The stymied Prince rose and began to pace the floor. A knock at the door caused a spike of panic to creep down his spine.

"My son, are you up and about? I would like a word."

Eyes darted about in dread, but there was nowhere to run or hide. He had to face Odiene and suffer what wrath she might inflict.

"Please come in, Mother." He dashed over to the window and plopped down in an overstuffed sage-green chair. Fearful eyes widened as they watched the door ease open.

The stunning monarch entered, leisurely walked to Tahl, and cupped the handsome man's taut face in her silken hands. "Your enviable eyes overflow with distress, child. What bothers you so?"

Tahl drew a deep breath and stared into Odiene's uncommonly beautiful face. "I fear a great sin has been committed—one that violates the commandments of our ancestors. My covetousness has trounced compliance and brought about an immoral deed. Forgive me, Mother. In heated anger, I performed a misdeed."

Odiene strolled to a nearby chair and gracefully eased down. Surprisingly, hint of a smile began to form on her luminous face. "So, she is stronger than anticipated." Intense violet eyes glared at him. "You need not concern yourself, my darling. This insignificant creature is no match for our noble ancestry. Tell me, what wrongdoing has been performed."

"After enduring numerous humiliations, I used the amulet to transform Kat into a black panther. I hoped the metamorphosis, coupled with confinement in a dungeon cell, would alter her attitude. Apparently, my assumptions were incorrect. I dropped in on the beast a short time ago…curious to see if the dear princess had at last amended her way of thinking. However, instead of a pleasant greeting, that harpy clawed my face." He turned his head revealing the bloodied scratches. "This is the third time that pitiful half-breed has struck me and it shall be the last."

"I am pleased you chose to freely reveal what has transpired, for this tarnished exploit has not gone unnoticed. Do you not realize by now, nothing escapes my

195

attention? Had deception been selected, severe punishment would have been inflicted. I commend your truthfulness. Regarding Kat's demise by your hand, such a feat toward our kind *is* forbidden. But perhaps the day has arrived to lay aside the old diktat. It is time the house of my brother is brought to its knees. Adera draws near. However, any attempt to free her sister will meet failure. When she is destroyed, you, my son, shall be declared King. Our rightful station in Bowlandria will at last come to pass. I shall not object should you decide to keep your new *pet*. Cage her, kill her…it matters not to me. Together, we shall locate a more worthy bride."

Lord Tahl rushed to Odiene and knelt on bended knee before her. "Thank you, Mother. Your words relieve a great bind. Throughout the empire, my masculine charms are legendary and desired by all females who come in contact with me. No woman has ever dared refuse such a reward. Unfortunately, I find this wench challenging, almost to the point of obsession. Somehow, I must break her spirit. Kat ignites an inferno within…one I have never felt prior. I do not know how to undo the spell, but when the time is right, will you perform this task for me?"

She reached out, gently stroked his injured cheek, and whispered unrecognized words. When her hand was removed, the wound had vanished. "Of course I shall, precious. Her current form would make it impossible to indulge unrestrained pleasure. Once you have had your fill, we can properly *dispose* of this thorn." The exotic vixen rose, slowly walked to the door, then stopped and turned. "Allow one hour to pass, Tahl. Come to my quarters at that time. I shall grant assistance in controlling Kat."

Tahl attempted to question Odiene, but his voice fell on empty space as she departed without hesitation. *Could*

Mother have a device of control I know nothing about? If so, and it works, perhaps I could use it on others to give more complete dominance. This entire situation may be providence in disguise and eventually grant me ultimate jurisdiction over all residents of the Realm, including the meddlesome Elves.

Feeling excited about the possibilities that could arise, he meandered to the window and stared into the murky sky. A ruthless smile formed as thoughts of unconquerable sovereignty danced through a despicable mind.

An hour felt like days as Lord Tahl impatiently waited to hear the clock chime the appointed moment. At last, the longed for melodic ding sounded.

Odiene's suite resided in another wing of the enormous manor. Powerful limbs propelled the anxious young man through a maze of candlelit corridors. Slightly winded, he paused in front of the ornate golden-handled door to gather composure.

"You may come in, Son."

Queried eyes widened as he turned the knob and entered. "How did you know I was here, Mother? I hadn't yet knocked."

The noble beauty stood facing the fireplace. She gave off a meek laugh and slowly turned to greet him. Rich green robes accentuated vivid violet eyes, including those of the black cat cradled in her arms. "You deem my perceptive powers to be limitless, but in this case, the dead might have been roused by the boisterous bound of feet as they stormed down the hallway. Come, join me." She gracefully eased into one of two chairs situated in front of the toasty, roaring fire.

A slight blush rose in Tahl's face as he walked over and sat facing her. "Sorry for the rushed approach, Mother, but your tantalizing declaration fueled at bit of curiosity. I'm

197

more than anxious to see what you have to offer." He edged up in the chair.

She reached down and picked up a black velvet bag…its top secured by a braided gold and silver cord. "Kat is stronger than most you have ever encountered, for the powerful blood Zuegas courses through her veins. On our home planet, this instrument was created to overcome those few who became unruly. Unsure of what might be encountered, your father wisely smuggled it aboard. Should a situation arise, he felt it might provide added protection. When he perished, it became my possession and has been secretly hidden these many years." Odiene untied the binding and opened the satchel. Ivory hands trembled slightly as they retrieved the item.

Tahl gasped as he viewed the gem-infused black leather choker. "I don't understand. It looks like a fancy animal collar. How can such a ridiculous item be used for control? I'm not in the mood for trivial jokes, Mother."

A trace of annoyance surfaced as she frowned and nudged the black cat from her lap. "You *dare* question me? Perhaps my offering to such an unappreciative son is a mistake. This is not a toy. In our world, it is known as the Band of Obedience. It is one, if not *the* most powerful weapon we possess. No creature can resist once the article has been fastened around their neck. The directive of those who place the device upon another must be obeyed. No force exists powerful enough to overcome its ability. Kat will be defenseless. As long as this band remains in place, she must, and shall, obey your every command."

He took the object from her hand and studied it. "There are no hooks or clasps. How is it fastened?"

"None are required, my darling. The instant it touches the flesh, it will adjust to the victim's size and meld

198

together. It can only be removed by your touch." She lowered her eyes and sighed. "I once wished to use this on another as an act of vengeance, but the occasion never presented itself. Instead, I endured days of agony and waited. At last, the opportunity so longed for arrived. However, in place of this collar, the instrument of destruction was simply the slice of a sharp blade. Her death has to this day been considered an accident, but was in reality, retribution."

Tahl glared at this mother. "What did you do, Mother? Whose death did you cause?"

Odiene's eyes were coldly free of emotion. "You need not know. I will speak of it no more. Do you wish to use the device or not? I have matters to attend to and cannot waste time."

"Yes, I'd like to use it, but just how do you expect me to put this around that beast's neck? She'll rip me to shreds. It's a good idea, but cannot be carried out."

"Oft times I question if you are *truly* the prodigy of your gifted father and the jewel of my womb." A look of regret engulfed her face. "Forgive me, darling. Remembrance of the premature death of your father, inflames bitterness." She embraced his face. "You look so like him, sweetheart. Kram was my love, my life. Our marriage was idyllic…one to be envied throughout the galaxy, until that pompous shrew caused his death. My brother refused to see the truth, blinded by his wife's beauty."

"Adeanra!" Tahl grabbed hold of his mother's arm. "Did you cause her death? How? They said she fell from Pegasus. It was stated to be a freak accident."

Odiene yanked her arm from his grasp. "You needn't sound so righteous, Son. She deprived you of a father and me of a devoted husband. I merely weakened the safety braid on that flying beast." Tears slid down silken cheeks. "However, upon witnessing the sorrow suffered by my brother, I felt great remorse and wept. The greatest sin of our kind had been foolishly committed. Zuegas soon found comfort in the arms of that pitiable human, Madeleine. Eventually the pair brought Kat into existence. My regret began to wither as I watched him enjoy life and feel love, while my heart lingered in loneliness. One day, an injurious declaration was announced and my soul turned to stone. His oldest daughter, Adera, would follow in his stead. Anger rose within like a raging fire. You are the rightful heir, not her. I pleaded with my brother, but all appeals fell on deaf ears."

"Don't weep, mother. I understand. If truth be told, I loathed Zuegas. When he decided to pass on, I was actually delighted. The man was as weak as his brat. This land needs a real ruler. Once we eliminate Adera and Kat, our road to Bowlandria will be free of obstacles. Who cares about the archaic laws of our ancestors? We are no longer bound by those regulations. *This* is our world now. Together, we will govern and once again be worshiped as gods. Your revelation places Kat in another light. She needs to suffer as you have been made to suffer, and I shall personally apply the means. In short time, with your assistance of course, her human form will be restored, allowing my needs to be amply satisfied." He gave a crude smirk. "Can you offer a suggestion on how I might place this band around her miserable neck? I'm anxious for the fun and games to begin." He wiped the tears from his mother's face and kissed her forehead.

"It is a simple matter. Take Gog with you to the dungeon. Have him lightly scratch the side of the panther

200

with his spear. Its toxin will immobilize her instantly. Place the band of obedience around Kats neck and remove the beast to your quarters. When she recovers, all freewill shall be eliminated. You may then toy with her as you chose. Never detach the band, even upon transformation to her former self. With the band secured, the lady will be forced to obey and deliver the intense pleasure you desire."

"What would I ever do without you, Mother? This is a treasured gift beyond my wildest dreams." He planted a kiss on her cheek, turned, and exited the room. Once back in his quarters, Lord Tahl fondled the remarkable trinket. "No one, not even *you*, Mother dear, will ever again go against my will. I shall rule over all."

He set the velvet bag on a small oval table, poured a large tankard of wine, and guzzled it down. After consuming the intoxicating brew, he yelled for Gog. Without hesitation, the grotesque monster appeared in the doorway.

"Yes, master. What can I do for you?"

Somewhat inebriated by the rapid indulgence of the fermented beverage, Tahl swayed slightly as he walked toward the Qerg.

"Follow me to the dungeons. When I open the door to this particular cell, I want you to lightly scratch the panther with your spear. Do not injure it. Simply pierce the skin so the toxin will take hold. Are my instructions clear?"

The repulsive Qerg leader nodded then followed close behind the monarch as they headed for Kat's cell and kicked at the door.

Tahl unlocked the door and slung it open, revealing the large black cat standing on the cot. Gog walked around his master and edged close to the great feline as it snarled and bristled. With one quick motion, he touched the spear tip

201

to the ebony coat and pricked the skin. Immediately, Kat fell prey to the noxious venom and collapsed to the floor.

Tahl pushed the guard aside and quickly put the jeweled binding in place. The soft leather band no sooner touched Kat's neck when it expanded to fit and sealed itself closed. "Gog, carry this *thing* to my room and set it by the fireplace. I'll be up shortly."

The Qerg scooped Kat up in his beefy arms and trotted off.

Feeling proud and undaunted, Tahl walked to Cianest's cell. "Hey monster, wake up. Thought you might want to know, the princess is fully under my control now. Once her form is restored, I intend to do whatever pleases me for as long as it pleases me. How do you like that tasty morsel of information, beastie?"

Scale-covered claws grasp the bars and shook the door violently.

The sudden outburst brought a howl of unsympathetic laughter from the inhuman narcissistic jailer. "Once I see how this raven-haired relative fulfills my fantasies, perhaps I'll alter *your* appearance as well. Then, you and I will have an equally, or better, bit of enjoyment. Of course, noting will happen until after I tire of Kat. You see, angel, before we embrace ecstasy, you shall feast upon her." He threw his head back and guffawed as he paraded away, drowning out the terrifying screams from Cianest.

Paralyzed muscles began to shudder as movement returned to the ebony feline. Round golden eyes struggled to gain clear vision and legs wobbled as Kat attempted to stand. The sight of her fanatical cousin sprawled roguishly in a nearby chair ignited pent-up rage and sent a jolt of hatred coursing through her body. She snarled and crouched down, ready to pounce. However, the impending attack was thwarted by a sudden outburst of laughter.

"So, you are awake and desire to kill me, dear cousin. Well, think again. I demand you lay at my feet."

Kat suddenly felt her body drop to the floor and do as commanded. *I don't understand. Why did I obey? I-I can't move?*

Tahl rose, and stood in front of her with legs spread in a self-aggrandizing manner. "Having a bit of a problem? From now on, my dear, you will learn who is master of this palace." He kicked at her neck. "How do you like the new adornment, Kat? I believe it is rather attractive and quite suitable for such a miserable low life."

Eyes darted about in confusion. She could feel a binding article around her neck, but was unable to see exactly what it was. *Every bone in my body wants to tell him off in no uncertain ways, but I must not speak. Cianest is right. My life depends on maintaining this silence.*

"You will no longer make any attempt to do me harm." He reached down and patted the sleek cat's broad head. "That's a good kitty," he said sarcastically. "I see confusion in your eyes, precious, so allow me to relieve a bit of anxiety." He walked across the room and picked up a large hand held mirror. "Here, view the elegant necklace I've chosen."

Kat glanced into the reflective glass revealing the jewel-encrusted leather binding. Immediately, amber eyes shot back to her oppressor, and she let out a hiss.

"Oh no, pretty pet, you will not sound off in such a manner to me again. In fact, I demand you purr."

Unable to resist, the velvet-coated panther did as directed. *This can't be happening. What kind of contraption is this thing? Hurry, Adera, I don't know how much more torture I can bear. Please, don't forget me. Tom—I must think of Tom. The only thing that can save my sanity is sweet thoughts of you.*

The vile pseudo-prince strutted across the room and poured a large beaker of wine. After indulging in several more, Tahl staggered back to the chair and clumsily took a seat. Words were slurred as he spoke, "The adornment is known as the Band of Obedience, half-breed. Until I find all traces of your human free will have been thoroughly eliminated, it shall remain locked around your precious little throat. Resistance is futile. For now, you are to remain a subservient beast. Once I feel all demands are being obeyed without question, Mother will instruct me on how to alter this distasteful body into a more satisfying subject. Do not be fretful, Kat. Nights of overwhelming ecstasy spent with a *real* man will arrive before you know it." He forced a lengthy odorous belch, yawned, and laid a bobbing head back as the alcohol swallowed up his consciousness.

Kat looked around the room, her mind swimming with fear and anxiety. Was this to be her fate? Had she been abandoned? She glared at the loathsome captor. *I don't know how, but vow to kill you at first chance. No blasted collar is going to bind my will…never!*

Exhausted, she placed a tormented head upon crossed paws and closed her golden eyes.

Chapter Fourteen
The Black Castle

Gasps seeped through fetid air as the wearied rescue party caught their first glimpse of the Black Castle. Its ghastliness was beyond conception. Randy scanned the horizon and winced. "This joint looks like something out of a dang horror flick."

A frown crossed Adera's brow. "I do not understand, Randy. What is a flick?"

He began to snicker and gave a playful hug. "Sorry, sweetcakes. My slow-witted brain often forgets where we are. It's a slang term used in my world for a movie, which you probably don't know what the blazes I'm talking about either." He drew a deep breath. "Movies are kinda like a series of pictures that, well, move." A glance into mystified eyes told him this was not being properly explained. The handsome groom ran his fingers through thick, black wavy hair and made a face. "Perhaps it might be better for you to simply think of the term as another stupid human slang word." He leaned over and planted a cordial peck on the Queen's velvet cheek.

"We may never fully understand each other's terminologies, but it does not matter. Our love will forever bridge the language barrier." Adera beamed as a tinge of blush rose in her face. Suddenly, the jovial expression transformed to a more somber one as she caught sight of Tom who stood nearby, head, and eyes lowered in obvious despair. "Oh Randy, please go to him. I am sure your heart will find words that shall ease his suffering. You have always provided such comfort to me."

205

"I hope I can come up with something, honeybunch, but it won't be easy. Think we're each fighting a little touch of fear. Well, all but Merlin and the Elves. Their deadpan expressions tell me they are untouched by the situation. However, I'll see what I can do." He gave her arm an affectionate pinch and walked over to his old friend.

"Hey buddy, how ya holdin' up?" Randy tried to sound upbeat. "Pretty dismal place, huh?"

Tom looked up—his mellow brown eyes teeming with grief. "I suppose I'm doing well as can be expected. Traveling through this ghoulish land is enough to make the dead shudder. However, when I first caught sight of the Manor, it literally ripped my heart to shreds. Thought of Kat being held by that warped piece of dung, is a pain greater than any I could imagine." He heaved a sigh. "Back home, I endured months of Cathy's heart wrenching suffering. It was an inexpressible anguish to watch in helplessness while the cancer destroyed my wife's frail body. Thankfully, the painful torture was relatively brief, and the disease took her within a year's time. She was an amazing mother and extremely devoted spouse. Our many years together were good, and we shared a special bond of love. Ironically, on that fateful cruise, did this bereaved widower think about his deceased wife? Nope, all thoughts were of Kat. Due to the fact only a couple weeks had passed since Cathy's death, I felt fairly guilt ridden. However, you know full well the only *true* love of my life always was, and still is, Kat. Finding her again, having my youth restored, and given the chance to live our lives together for as long as we wish is beyond anything I could have desired or imagined. Fear of losing her forever torments my mind day and night. It's nearly madding." He paused and wiped misty eyes. "What I'm about to say may

206

sound completely bonkers, but if I don't tell someone, I'll explode." The handsome young man walked to a nearby log and sat with head hung low.

Randy eased down beside him. "You know you can always confide in me, Tom. We've been buds a very long time and ironically share the love of a rather *special* girl."

"The past couple days, I can't shake off the sensation that something terrible has happened to her. At first I thought it was only nerves or dumb anxieties' working overtime, but it's getting stronger. It's as though she's not in her own body." Tom edged closer to Randy. "My heart's telling me she's enduring some sort of hideous torture." He looked up into the sunless sky and blinked away welling tears. "I'll never forgive myself for allowing this to happen. If only I had remained by her side. Adera warned me of the impending danger, but did I listen? No. Even McLachen perceived the threat and beseeched me to maintain strict vigilance. Kat would not be in harm's way if I'd listened to either of them, but once again, my bullheaded stupidity placed my beautiful wife, as well as you and our friends, in grave danger. Nobody would be here in this cesspool kingdom risking their lives to save her if I had paid heed— it's entirely my fault."

Randy gripped his friend's shoulder. "Don't beat yourself up like this, Tom. The blame's not all on your head. Every single one of us was thoroughly cautioned, yet none paid a lick of attention. Absorbed in our own moments, we foolishly allowed Tahl to carry out the despicable deed. Merlin's feelin' pretty low and believes if not for his amorous distraction, the abduction would not have happened in the first place. It's time to set the blame game aside and deal with the situation. What's done is done. The past can't be changed. We've made it this far,

207

and we'll keep going. Before long, that feisty lady of yours will be home and probably driving us all nuts."

Tom heaved a sigh. "You're a good friend, Randy. Kat loves you nearly as much as she does me. You two have been through a lot over the years. Wish I'd been there to share some of those adventures. Although, I have to admit, there's a few she's mentioned that might not have been so welcomed."

The two old companions chuckled at the remark, rose, and rejoined the others.

Horace nodded to Tom as the pair walked up. "I see worry weighs heavily upon your brow…you suffer intense reproach. Do not be troubled. All hold some form of guilt regarding Kat's capture, but if truth be told, the blame resides only on Tahl—no one else. With the exception of Adera, this creature's celestial ingenuity and manipulative intellect is beyond compare. Somehow, he would have found a way to achieve the debauched objective. If success is to be met, it is imperative our emotions are set aside, righteous as they may be. Your heart is strong. It overflows with bounteous love and compassion, but for now, do not allow such a powerful force to cloud vital thoughts. When the time is right, make use of this unparalleled weapon. Evil shall be defeated."

"You're right, Horace, and it's about time I get this wooden head of mine screwed back on straight. I'll be alright, now. Thanks. Guess the dismal atmosphere of this crummy land scrambled my brains a bit. But I really pray Tahl gets in my face, just once. Nothing would be more pleasing than to wipe the floor with his *perfect* mug."

Horace grabbed Tom's arm. "Now, *that* is the fervent attitude befitting a true warrior. I am proud to stand by your side and be part of this team."

Charlie and Meeley sat on the lifeless turf nearby and agreed with Horace. "We all love Kat, and if one of us was in her place, you know full well she would not hesitate to come to our rescue," Meeley exclaimed.

Charlie slapped a knee. "Darn tootin'. If I happen to run into that creepy cousin of hers before you do, I'll sure as shoot hold him down until you get there, Tom. It'll be a real pleasure to watch you beat the tar out of that pompous brute."

Faye popped up from beside a decaying log and stood with arms on hips. "Yeah, and I'll help kick the blazes out of him as well."

The sight of the small fairy boasting such a large undertaking brought the troupe to laughter.

Randy walked over and stooped down in front of her. "Little big stuff, we certainly wouldn't want to run up against the likes of you in some dark alley. We might find ourselves in the hospital."

The tiny fairy stomped her foot. "Humph. Keep that tone up with me, Mr. Wise Guy and I'll show you what I can do."

Adera walked over and offered a palm to the small fairy. "Sweet Faye, you have proven to be the bravest among fairies. None shall ever question your zeal. I am sorry to say, the others were merely having a bit of sport with you, which, I must add, is not in good taste. However, please realize that tensions run high at the moment, and a brief touch of frivolity is desperately needed. Do not take offense."

Faye plopped down in the Queens soft hand. "I understand, Highness…no offense taken. The strain on Master Tom's handsome face is pretty intense. He must love her very much."

"Yes Faye, he does. Tom adores my sister, as do we all, and is fearful for her life."

"He shouldn't worry. We will save her." The fiery fairy looked around at the group. "This bunch is a mighty darn brawny lot, Majesty. The Elves are illustrious warriors—highly intelligent beings. Merlin, although rather odd at times, is actually a gifted wizard. The humans are strong willed and resolute. You possess knowledge of Tahl and Odiene and have powers superior to theirs, and you also have me and Punk. We are your *best* secret weapon."

Adera's voice brightened, and she spun around to Randy, nearly unseating the small sprite, "Faye may have inadvertently delivered victory."

Merneos leaped to his feet and hurried over. "I heard what was said and agree wholeheartedly. Tahl and Odiene know nothing of this young lady. Her size will grant unseen observation. Perhaps, our brave little Princess is the chosen instrument of conquest." He turned to the wide-eyed sprite and gave a rare smile. "The appointed tasks shall be incredibly dangerous, but I believe you possess more than enough valor to handle what might be asked."

"Hold on," Tom exclaimed, "I don't want this precious child put in any danger. We'll handle whatever it is that must be done. Keep her out of this."

Faye rocketed from the Queen's palm, hovered in front of Tom's face, waved her petite index finger at him, and spoke using a rather strong, commanding tone, "I am *not* a child, dear sir. My worth has been proven several times through the most complicated missions presented to me. On the other hand, *you* have yet to show an ounce of backbone and done darn near nothing except whine and pout." She flipped her head arrogantly, abruptly spun around, and returned to Adera.

"It appears you have roused this plucky one's temper, dear brother-in-law." Adera giggled and set Faye down on a nearby tree branch. "You shall be our eyes and ears, sweet girl. We do not know what has happened to Kat or where she may be located. I find it unnerving no Qergs have yet been encountered and believe an ambush awaits. Because my aunt and nephew lack knowledge of your presence, any crusade will not be thwarted." She turned to Tom and took his hand. "I would never place our petite friend in danger, please believe me. We are entering a dangerous time and must make use of every available aide. I beseech one and all to hold strong the confidence of my decisions as you have always done in the past."

Randy drew closer to his wife. "Over the years, Adera has never once let any of us down or led us astray. Why would we even begin to distrust this lady's strategy now? Not a single person alive knows Odiene and Tahl better than she does." He gave her a wink and a hug. "Merlin, suppose you could conjure up some sort of cloaked campfire? We don't want the firelight to give away our location, but it's getting a tad cold and we sure as the dickens need some warmth. Being chilled, tired, and hungry will render us significantly inefficient."

The elegant wizard's midnight blue eyes twinkled as he slowly rose. "I do indeed recall just the right spell to meet this wise objective. Gadzooks, another bit of magic has also flowed into my mind. It should provide a suitable shelter and also ample food. I humbly apologize for such tardy lack wisdom. A sorcerer's mind is often fogged by the swirling of so many formulas."

Randy, Tom, Charlie, and Meeley glanced at each other, shook their heads, and shrugged their shoulders.

211

It did not take the ancient sorcerer long to provide a dry, warm campsite. A few more incantations provided a banquet of sorts, allowing the band of friends to replenish their bodies and obtain much needed rest.

A sharp nip on the nose brought Randy out of a sound sleep. "What the heck?" He sat straight up and tried to focus through bloodshot eyes. A nearby giggle brought a baffled look.

Faye fluttered over and perched on his shoulder. "Sorry, Master Randy, but its way past daylight and time to get underway. Punk didn't mean to startle you, but he did do a good job and certainly roused your sleepy head." She covered her lips and giggled again.

Randy looked over at the handsome Barred Owl sitting beside him and began to chuckle. "Okay, you got me. I'll admit it was funny. Scared the daylights out of me, but if he had pulled this prank on someone else while I watched, I would have rolled in laughter. No harm done." He yawned and stretched a bit, nearly knocking Faye off his shoulder. "Whoops, perhaps you should find a safer landing strip, little Princess. Besides, I need to move my fanny and wake up the others. Dang, feels like we just went to sleep."

Charlie stood and stretched. "Sure is hard to tell daylight from dusk in this wretched place. I'll be happy as a bee in a honeysuckle bush to get back to Bowlandria. Hope I never see this land again."

"This was once a kingdom of beauty, Charlie," Adera said. "Only after Odiene and Tahl arrived and eradicated happiness, did Mantalac fall into despair. I have not journeyed to this locale for many years, and my heart is saddened to find it worse than during the prior visit. Such a vile declaration is dire, but my Aunt and Nephew must

212

be destroyed. The populace does not deserve punishment, for they have committed no crime. Father could not have foreseen havoc of such horrific intensity would be inflicted, nor would he wish it upon any being."

Meeley sat down alongside the Queen and Randy. "You said earlier your race is forbidden to kill another of your kind. How are you gonna defend yourself against those two?"

"In defense, the act is allowed, but *only* in defense. However, because they are my blood, the consequence of such an act will be severe. It is the worst breach of our sacred law."

The dragon rider raised a brow. "What will happen if you destroy them, Adera? I mean, it *is* in defense. Those two are pure evil."

Adera drew a deep breath. "Because I shall act against the primary directive of my ancestors, I must relinquish the throne. A monarch cannot justly serve when that individual places themselves above the rules."

"That's bull! You're doing what has to be done for the sake of the entire Realm. These jerks are pure scum. They steal, torture, kill, and do whatever—to whomever. Talk about breaking the rules. No way are you getting off that throne, lady." Meeley looked around at the others, who by now had awakened and hovered near the threesome. "Blast it, Merneos, say something."

The regal Elf King starred with frozen eyes at the benevolent Sovereign. "What would you have me say? Adera is correct." He paused and stepped forward. "She, like I, have been selected to lead, protect, and govern our kingdoms. The laws equally apply to us. One cannot reign with honor when we believe ourselves superior to the masses and chose to live by exclusive regulations.

213

However, a beacon of hope exists. Adera, one of us must destroy Odiene and Tahl in your stead. Our performance of the deed thus resolves you of blame and secures the throne. There is no other solution."

Randy knelt down in front of his distressed wife. "Why didn't you reveal this nonsense before, sweetheart? Merneos is right. Just get us near those creeps and we'll do the dirty work."

Adera lovingly ran a finger down Randy's cheek. "None of you can achieve what must be done. Their powers are too great. Only my supremacy can overcome their abnormal strength." She gazed deeply into his blue eyes and smiled. "Do not be troubled, my dear husband. Kat shall be rescued and sit upon the throne, as she should. My sister will become a great monarch and amply protect all provinces. It will thus allow us more time together to do things we have desired, such as have a honeymoon."

"Well, I certainly can't argue with that bit of logic." He leaned up and gave her a kiss. "First, let's get into the joint and see about rescuing Kat, then we'll figure out how to take care of the other matter."

Tom cleared his throat. "I hate to interrupt you two, but there's something that needs to be addressed." He paused and inhaled deeply. "I want to be the one who takes out Tahl. Adera, I understand Kat is your sister, and you hold great love for her, but she is my life, my love, and my wife. *Lord Monster's* contemptible actions grant me the right of retribution. I know you possess sophisticated powers that will undoubtedly rise above theirs, but this time I'm begging you to lay aside any personal feelings. Give me a chance to fight this brut. Surely you can divulge a method we might employ to circumvent their malicious trickery. Grant me and the others the opportunity to eliminate these two rogues once and for all. Please Adera, we, or rather I, deserve revenge."

She looked around at each member of the troupe, who stood in silence. "I shall do as you ask. Once rendered powerless, my aunt and her son should easily fall prey to your weapons. Merlin, may I hold a private audience? Forgive me, dear ones, but fortification of your armaments now grows imperative. Unfortunately, the alien method employed cannot be revealed. Come old friend, there is much to do." She took hold of the great sorcerer's hand and led him away.

Randy watched the duo vanish into the dense fog. He was proud of his new bride for granting the wishes of their companions, but could see an enormous amount of hurt and trepidation fixed in her striking eyes. *She knows full well that should we fail, Kat's going to die. No power on earth will prevent it.*

"Hey y'all, gather 'round for a second. We need to talk." He drew a deep breath and secretly prayed the right words would be spoken and be effective.

"I think I know my wife pretty darn good, and I'm telling you right now, she's worried sick. If we're unsuccessful, Kat's gonna be eliminated. There's no getting around that fact. However, failure may mean all our lives, including Adera's, will also be forfeit. The Realm will then be at the mercy of Tahl and Odiene. Tom, I sincerely understand your feelings. I'd be plumb out of my mind nuts if Adera was in Kat's place. All I'm asking is we stop and think logically about this endeavor. We're each pretty darn competent fighters. Heaven knows we gained plenty of combat experience going up against Nimue and her ghouls. Unfortunately, this is a whole other ball game." He paused to gather more thoughts.

215

"Odiene is not some trivial descendent of the original travelers, but actually *is* one of them. She's the blood sister of Zuegas. I'm not even sure if our Queen knows the full extent of her aunt's capabilities. They've never directly fought. Merneos, you know about Adera's prior rescue endeavor and how it developed into a horrible disaster. This weighs heavily on her mind. She, and a full regiment, battled against these two and yet were devastatingly defeated. Her powers, although young, were no match. Now, we're going up against this sadistic twosome with a whooping militia of eight?"

Troubled eyes glanced at one another, as though beckoning for a resolution.

A dynamic voice broke the deathly silence, as Horace spoke up, "Is this the once valiant group I so fervently trained? Are you the same warriors who did not fear insurmountable odds?" In anger he reached down, picked up a large rock, and slammed it to the ground in the center of the assemblage. "Perhaps you might prefer to wage war on this solitary piece of stone. Or is that asking too much?"

"We didn't say we won't fight, Horace," Charlie replied. "If any of us claimed not to be scared half to death of what might happen, then doggone sure we'd be lying. You trained this bunch well and think it fair to boast that every single one of us were exemplary students." He stepped to the center of the circle and picked up the rock. "Guys, our concerns need to be laid to rest right now. Let's get motivated and form a winning course of action. We can do this, dudes. The time has come to begin acting like the warriors Horace fashioned us out to be. Heck, we faced overwhelming legions of hideous demons and won. Poor Kat stood up alone against that eighty-foot titan, Ios. Why not buck up and show a little backbone? Yeah, it's true those two jerks are pretty potent, but we possess a crushing weapon…grit, and by golly day we sure have an abundance of that to smack them with."

Slouching bodies suddenly straightened and all stood proud as anxiety slowly faded from troubled faces. Eyes brightened, and a triumphant smile began to form while an enthusiastic response filled the still night air.

A latent fire had been ignited.

Chapter Fifteen
<u>Manor of Misery</u>

S nappishly awakened by the thud of approaching footsteps, large round golden eyes opened and glared in fierce anger as the silver-encrusted handle of the massive oak door turned. Kat leaped to her feet and growled.

Arrogant as ever, Lord Tahl strutted into the expansive quarters. He pulled a short handled whip from his belt and tauntingly ran the leather strips through his fingers. "Mother and I have yet to explain this fractional resistance to my will. Perhaps a bit of flogging will alter such enigmatic impudence." A quick snap of the wrist produced a bone-chilling crack. "You have a choice, cousin, do as I say without hesitation, or have flesh ripped from that hide. Years of practice have made me quite an expert using this handy item."

Kat snarled, baring large white fangs. *I would gladly suffer the whip's pain in order to sink my teeth into your scrawny neck.* She considered attacking, but Cianest's warning invaded her mind. *Much as I would love to rip this jerk to pieces, I must not kill him. That momentary pleasure is not worth remaining in this state for eternity. For now, I'll control my emotions and act the part of an enslaved pet.* Eyes blazed as the prodigious black cat settled into a position of submission.

A pompous grin formed on the cruel captor's face. "That is more like it. From now on, you will do as I direct, regardless of what is asked. Do you understand?"

Kat nodded and lowered her gaze.

218

"Due to your alien blood, what little there is of it, Mother assumes it may take time for the full effect of the collar to take hold. However, be warned missy, should you try to harm me or mother, I shall not hesitate to slit your furry throat. Are these words clear?"

As before, she nodded.

"Good, now follow me." He turned and stepped into the poorly lit hallway.

She paused a moment, but suddenly felt an overwhelming compulsion to do as asked. *Why is this happening? I can't seem to combat its power. Apparently Odiene's thingamajig is finally starting to control my will. I have to find a way to fight it. He mustn't be allowed to rule me. Adera said I have powers that have yet to surface. Oh please, if they truly exist, let them come to my aide now.* The giant feline leisurely meandered into the dim torch lit corridor, and followed in quiet submission behind her vile master.

They traveled a short distance when at last he came to an abrupt halt. "Go to your room and be groomed. Your stench offends me. Perhaps I should change you into a slithering, odor free viper. It might actually be a more fitting and enjoyable solution. Any displeasure or insolence could easily be brought to an abrupt halt by a hearty stomp to the reptile's head." He looked down, and snickered. "It is tempting, but for now, this form pleases me. When properly bathed and perfumed, return to my quarters. Now, get out of my sight."

Before Kat could move out of the way, he kicked her hard in the side. Anger shot to the surface like a raging wind. She raised a paw to lash out, but found herself unable to follow through with the attack.

Lord Tahl threw his head back and laughed. "That's a good kitty. It appears the wild beast in you has at long last

219

met its match. Aw, don't look so disappointed, precious. The wait to enjoy my person is nearly ended. Continue to follow all demands and this form will be terminated. Then, you will squeal with delight as unmatched passion is given. Soon, you will know what it is like to be a woman serviced by a divine prince."

His disgusting and pitiless words hung in the air like a heavy mist. Golden eyes overflowed with abhorrence as Kat stood alone in the icy passageway. She turned and focused, trying to figure out the way to her room. *Holy Crickets, it's amazing how intense my eyesight is now.* She giggled…humored by the dippy statement. *Yikes, better watch myself. Someone might hear me. Sure hope Brandi will be my attendant. It'll feel mighty darn good to vocalize for a bit.*

The door to her room was slightly ajar, making entrance easy for the large predator.

"Who's there?" Brandi peered out from behind the ornate dressing screen. The sight of the colossal cat delivered a loud blood-curdling scream.

"Brandi, it's me, Kat. Don't be afraid. I've been transformed and promise not to harm you. Please, stop screaming. You'll bring the Qergs running, or worse, Tahl."

"W-what kind of demon are you? Get away from me." The terrified girl backed up against the wall. "Y-you are n-not Kat. She is human. Stay back."

Unsure of what to do, Kat laid down. "I swear to you, it's really me. Tahl used his mother's amulet to alter my appearance. I'm puzzled by this ability to talk, but nevertheless, I can. The stupid clown doesn't know it, so I can't say a peep around anyone else except you and Ibby. Trust me, I am Kat."

"Prove it. Tell me something only she would know."

220

"Okay, Ibby can speak. No one else knows that. You also told her and me about Cianest before she was transformed."

The meek servant girl blinked and edged away from the wall. "Sweet mistress, what has that deranged monster done to you?" She took a few steps forward and stopped. "Are you absolutely positive you won't eat me?"

Kat began to chuckle. "No, it's perfectly safe." She stood and slowly strolled over to Brandi. "You can pet me if you like. I believe my coat is quite soft." A queried look showed on her feline face. "Wow, can't believe I just made such a lame comment. Sorry, this fiasco has my brain so scrambled it's not funny."

The ecstatic servant ran up and hugged the big cat. "It *is* you. No one else would speak in such a manner."

"I'm supposed to get groomed and then go back to dumbo's room. I have no idea why. He certainly can't seduce me in this state." She let out a growl. "Oh dang blast it. Sometimes my human voice gets mixed up with this cat like one. Have you heard anything from Ibby or seen her?"

"No my lady, not since you left. Why?"

Kat paused and sat down. "The poor little thing was thrown in the cell with me and was to become my meal. Of course I didn't harm her, but she needed to get the blazes out of there before it was discovered. Using a bit of ingenuity, we managed to set her free. Ibby was going to try and locate my sister and husband. I sure pray she's okay. Tahl's out of his flippin' mind, and no telling what the pompous twerp would do if he found out the truth."

"I understand, my lady. Do not be troubled. Dear Ibby is extremely crafty and am certain she is fine. Let's hope, for all concerned, her trek is successful. Why don't you come into the bath and let me wash the soil from your

221

coat." Her odd words brought a wince. "I apologize, mistress, but there is no other manner in which to address your condition."

"It's okay. Like it or not, I'm cloaked in fur. To be honest, a nice clean one would be welcomed. The dungeon in this Manor of misery is nothing more than a filthy hellhole. Thought of poor Cianest living day in and day out in such squalor breaks my heart. She doesn't deserve the inhumane treatment forced upon her."

The devoted caretaker carefully bathed Kat, making sure every bit of stench was washed from the ebony pelt. She then built a blazing fire so the noble creature might dry in toasty warmth. Much was discussed as the pair sat and conversed. Brandi promised never to disclose the secret of Kat's vocal ability, knowing full well the wrath it would incur. However, their jovial banter was cut short when the door unexpectedly swung open.

Gog's gruff voice boomed, "Lord Tahl wants the cat to come to his room at once."

Brandi leaped up and dashed to the intruder. "*Mistress* Kat is ready and will accompany you at once." Eyes welled as the melancholic onyx feline lumbered from the room.

What joy had been obtained conversing with Brandi quickly vanished as she entered Tahl's quarters and viewed him lying bare-chested on the garish bed beside a scantly clothed young woman.

"Ah, the awaited audience arrives." He rose, walked over, and sarcastically patted her head. "That's a good kitty. Now, get up on that walnut dresser and lay down—facing me. From now on, you will come every evening to my room and alight upon this furnishing. It is desired you witness all the pleasures so eagerly cast aside. Now, watch and weep, dear cousin."

222

Unable to resist the demented commands, Kat sauntered to the oversized elaborately engraved piece, leaped up, and settled down.

Obviously amused at the perverted request, the ancient prince dismissed Gog, and proceeded to primitively seduce the helpless female.

Kat heaved a sigh and lowered amber eyes, unwilling to further observe the travesty. *Please hurry, Tom. I don't know how much more I can endure.* A crystalline tear slowly trickled down her pelted face and fell upon a velvet-coated paw.

Tiny feet swayed aimlessly from the barkless limb of a withering Elm as the young fairy edged closer to her feathered champion and eyed the sleeping group below. "They sure are an odd bunch, Punk." The great Barred Owl ruffled his feathers and shook. Faye gave off a muted giggle and stroked his chest, "My thoughts exactly." She reached around and gently began to whisk bits of debris from her resplendent fairy wings. Their brawn would be put to the ultimate test in a short time and needed to be in pristine condition. Odium Manor was a vast maze of shadowed corridors. The precarious undertaking would place enormous demands upon the delicate appendages as the miniature warrior searched for her quarry.

"Excuse me, Princess, my Lord wishes a word with you."

Faye leaped into the air and hovered inches above the limb. "Horace, your stunt scared a toad's life out of me. Don't sneak up on a fairy like that. Have you completely lost your mind? Why, I might have hurt you." Tiny feet touched solid wood and wings folded back in place as she eased from the air. "Such a foolhardy endeavor could have lost us a vital member of this group. Don't do it again. You hear me?" She shook her finger at the wide-eyed Elf and huffed.

Obviously taken aback by the tenacity of this minute foe, Horace momentarily stood in silence. Soon, an uncharacteristic curl to the lips began to form a feeble smile. "I shall be more cautious in the future, Princess." A courteous bow was presented. Although small in stature, Faye was nevertheless royalty. "Lord Merneos has requested a private audience, my Lady. What he has to discuss must not be heard by other ears. He awaits your presence deep in the forest. May I offer a ride?"

The effervescent sprite stomped her foot. "I am perfectly capable of traveling on my own, thank you. These wings can move me along a lot faster than those big feet."

Horace snickered. "Forgive me. The offer was not intended to insult such unique abilities. I realize the appointed task might be rather arduous and only wished to preserve every ounce of strength you possess. We would not want anything to happen to such a daring soul and valiant companion."

The petite fairy blinked in disbelief at his remarkable gallantry. "Well, you present a valid point, Sir Elf. Last time I ventured into that awful place, Punk transported me a good part of the way to save energy. Sure isn't gonna happen this time." She sighed and fluttered to his shoulder. "Gee, you are kinda boney, but I'll force myself to endure the hardness. Don't think for a single minute I'm going to enjoy the lift…just complying to conserve my vigor."

Horace hastened into the decaying thicket of trees, far away from earshot of the others, where King Merneos waited.

"What's wrong with him?" she whispered as they neared. "His face is drawn tighter than a bowstring."

"A most unpleasant obligation has been assigned to my Lord should the need arise. It is one he does not take pleasure in performing."

The noble King remained expressionless as the duo approached. "I thank you for coming, Princess Faye. Please, allow my hand to act as your seat so we may better converse."

It was apparent something deeply troubled the great sovereign—a worry that propelled a chill down the small sprite's spine. She accepted the offer and lit upon his outstretched palm.

The King spoke low and soft, "There are times we are each obliged to perform a difficult task, but none greater than what has been delegated to me. You need know nothing more concerning this fact. Upon your return, I implore you to report directly to me before a solitary word is uttered to any other. Deliver to me, and to me alone, the status of Kat. It is imperative I be informed immediately and secretively. Queen Adera and Tom suspect she is enduring intense anguish—a mystery that has yet to surface. Can you act in accordance with this meager request?"

A worried look engulfed Faye's face as she peered into icy blue eyes. "Yes, I can do as you ask, but why?"

"It is not necessary for you to obtain the reason," the tone of his voice was firm.

Faye was puzzled. *What the frazzledump is going on? Something smells rotten.* Suddenly, eyes widened, and fear surged into her heart. "You mean to kill Kat, don't you? No, I won't allow it. You can't slay her. I will not support such a despicable plot."

225

Merneos drew a deep breath. "It is not of my doing, but a direct request from the Queen. I have pledged my allegiance. If Kat suffers the fate of Cianest, and the spell remains unbroken, our Princess shall endure a life no mortal should be forced to live. I do not wish her harm, but also do not desire to see such a tender soul live in eternal agony. Believe me when I say this, the act shall be one of last resort."

The young fairy stared into the faces of the two Elves, unsure of what to say. She despised the thought of Kat being destroyed, but also knew he was right. It would be a gruesome act of kindness to end her torture. "I will help, but only if you swear an oath to me that Kat will not be harmed if only the *tiniest* shred of hope remains."

"I solemnly vow it shall be so. If merely the wisp of a hairs chance for salvation is found, she will not be harmed."

Horace bent down on one knee. "Little Princess, the declaration of King Merneos is a pledge that will never be broken. He does not desire this loathsome task come to fruition, and will do all in his power to see it does not transpire. However, he has also assured Queen Adera, that should no other choice arise, he will indeed carry out her wishes."

Faye nodded. "It's obvious you speak the truth, and I feel in my heart the correct decision will be made. I'm not sure how as yet, but I'll relate my observations to you prior to alerting the others. Now, if you don't mind, I'd like to leave. It's nearly time for me to head to the Manor. However, heed my warning, sirs. Should I find either of you have lied or deceived me in any way, or should Kat be slaughtered senselessly, vengeance will be mine. I may be small, but don't underestimate my powers."

King Merneos placed the spirited fairy on Horace's shoulder, backed off, and bowed. "Rest easy, little warrior, I shall not go against my given word. Let us be off, Princess."

None of the group had yet stirred as the trio returned. Faye took wing and perched next to Punk, while the two Elves covertly nested by the smoldering fire.

She realized it was near time to get underway. "Better wake all these lazybones up, Punk. Think you can manage it?" She giggled as he fluffed his wings and prepared to dive.

The majestic owl swooped down mere inches above the sleeping companions. At times, the tips of his enormous wings would snap at their faces as he passed.

Merlin leisurely strolled into the awakened camp carrying a feathery bundle in his arms. "I happened upon this pitiful creature in the woods. She claims her name is Ibby and has come in search of Adera." He set the quaking little hen down and backed away.

"This chicken can speak?" Randy exclaimed as he drew near. "How is such a feat possible, Merlin?"

"I believe she may be a mortal who has suffered a curse. Her vocalization is a mystery. It is a bit odd and seldom occurs. Try as I may, my powers have been ineffectual to restore her former likeness."

Adera strolled over and knelt down in front of Ibby. "I am the one you search for. Are you human?"

The disheveled fowl looked up into the benevolent Sovereign's face and nodded. "Yes, the wizard is correct. I was once human. Lord Tahl used his mother's amulet to transform me in punishment for aiding Kat."

The mention of her name brought everyone to attention.

227

Ibby let out a loud squawk when Tom rushed over and scooped up the little hen. "You've seen Kat? Is she okay?"

Adera stepped toward him and placed a hand on his arm. "Tom, this young lady is frightened. Allow a moment. We are all equally anxious. Please, set Ibby down and give this child time to adjust."

Tom drew a breath and did as the Queen suggested.

"I-I was Kat's handmaiden. She is a wonderful person and does not deserve the treatment placed upon her. Tahl is almost insane with rage."

Randy sat down alongside the trembling changeling. "Rest easy, Ibby, you are among friends. No harm will befall you within this camp. We have come to rescue Kat. Queen Adera is her sister, and that goon, who so abruptly snatched you up, is her husband, Tom. Can you tell us what has happened to her? Is she okay?"

Ibby glanced around, her beady eyes wide with fear. After a few minutes, she fluffed her feathers, eased down, and seemed to relax a bit. "She is well, but does not appear as you knew her. Kat would not give in to Tahl's lust. In a fit of anger, he transformed my Mistress into a panther."

Adera let out a shriek and cast a fleeting glance at Merneos, who inconspicuously nodded and looked away.

Faye hunkered close to Punk. "This is really bad," she whispered. "I can't explain it to you at this moment, dear friend, but unless that deed can be undone, Kat is in grave danger."

Tom reached for his weapon. "That's the proverbial straw. I've had it. Grab your things and let's go get my wife." His advance was halted by a firm grip on his arm.

Randy's tone was forceful, "No Tom, this has to be handled carefully or the entire venture will meet failure. For pity sake, give Adera time to grasp hold of herself and

228

sort things out." He turned back to the little hen. "What else can you tell us, Ibby?"

"Kat is safe for now and is in no immediate danger. However, I did overhear him say she will remain transformed until she decides to do as he asks. I know the spell can be reversed because I have seen it happen."

The Queens expression lightened. "Do you know where she is being held?"

"Yes Highness, I do."

"Randy, Tom, our despair has been vanquished. Perhaps, with the assistance of this brave maiden, Faye might be led to Kat and a vital message delivered. Information of our propinquity will again fortify my sister's resolve. Ibby, it is imperative Kat know a rescue attempt is forthcoming. Would you be willing to lead one of us back into the Manor?"

The downy hen ruffled her copper hued feathers. "It's going to be difficult and dangerous for one of you to slip by discreetly, Highness. My undersized stature allows freedom to move about in the shadows undetected. Without knowing the present situation, a person of your size will surely be discovered. Such a feat cannot be accomplished safely."

Faye flew down and landed directly in front of Ibby. "Oh yes it can, and I'm the one who can do it, too. Just lead the way."

Adera smiled. "As you see, dear Ibby, there *is* one who meets the requirement necessary to perform such a precarious venture. Are you willing to guide this daring fairy to my sister?"

"Hi Faye, perhaps you don't remember, but we've met once before. You delivered a most welcomed message to Kat not long ago. That certainly was some feat."

229

Faye slapped her leg. "Well I'll be a goose neck. I didn't recognize the name. Kat called you Isabelle. Splozits, you sure look different. What made you want to become a chicken?"

Ibby snickered. "Believe me, this was not by choice. Queen Adera, Faye is small enough to make the task feasible. My escape was possible thanks to the accidental discovery of a long forgotten passageway. It is never occupied and pretty sure it will remain that way."

Horace cleared his throat. "Excuse me, might we inquire about guards?"

"Tahl ordered them all inside. They have been strategically placed throughout the Manor. No one can enter the halls without being noticed. Apparently, he's aware of your presence. Qergs patrol in pairs, but if Faye could discretely fly ahead and report their location, it might be possible the entire group could slip past them as you covertly move about the corridors."

"The stars are on our side at last," Horace declared. "Once Kat is informed of our plans, this duo should be able to safely lead us through the Manor. Victory is in sight."

Charlie jumped up excitedly. "It's brilliant and just might work. Lord Toilet Paper knows nothing of our secret weapons—Faye and Ibby. Using their guidance, we can do this, dudes."

Adera stood quiet, her face taut. "Let it be so."

Faye clapped her hands and soared up to Punk. "Keep watch over this group for me and don't let anything happen to them. I'll be fine and be back in the wink of an eye." She gave him a little hug then fluttered to King Merneos, perched on his shoulder, and whispered, "I believe the information requested has been delivered, Sire.

230

Kat can, and will, be saved. The deadly assignment has been officially *cancelled*." A quick flip of the wings brought her back to Ibby. "Okay, I'm ready. Let's get going. Uh, would you mind if I hitch a ride for a portion of this trip? It might help conserve a bit of wing strength." She looked over at Horace and gave a devilish wink.

"Sure," Ibby replied. "Jump aboard."

With an exuberant wave goodbye from Faye, the uncanny pair sped off, quickly vanishing into the fetid mist.

Chapter Sixteen
An Elf's Heart

Rays of diffused light flowed through the gothic stained glass window illuminating the loathsome boudoir. Roused from sleep, Kat yawned and peered around. Tahl, and the young maiden who unwillingly occupied his chamber, had obviously departed. *Good, at least the warped jerk is out of sight for the time being. I've never hated anyone as much as I do him. My heart breaks for that poor girl. You can bet your boots her fate has already been decided.*

Kat leaped down from the top of the walnut dresser and began to pace the tomblike marble floor. She was unsure of what to do next or when her disgusting captor would return. The door had been left slightly ajar, but fear of a trap halted escape. At last, unable to contain insatiable curiosity, a stalwart paw tugged at the herculean wooden barrier, revealing an eerily unoccupied corridor. She inched into the comfortless gallery and cagily moved along...her cat eyes and ears vigilant.

At last, a Qerg was spotted moving toward her. She hunkered down, bared teeth, and hissed—her sleek black coat bristling.

The repugnant guard glanced down at the large predator, grunted, and walked on.

Something's not right. Why didn't he come after me? She was puzzled by the monster's bizarre reaction.

Suddenly, a nearby door was thrust open. Tahl stepped out and stood in front of her with hands on hips. "Well, it appears my pet has decided to prowl. Be my guest. The collar around your precious neck will thwart any chance of

232

flight. Enjoy the day, Princess, for I shall once again enjoy the evening." He threw his head back and burst into impious laughter, administering a pitiless kick as he passed.

Rabid eyes remained fixed on her depraved cousin until he vanished from sight. Dagger sharp claws dug at the menacing leather restraint in a desperate attempt to remove it, but the endeavor proved futile.

She looked around, trying to gather some sense of bearings. *I have no dang idea where the blazes I'm at. This part of the Manor is totally unfamiliar. Somehow, I have to find my way to the dungeons and speak with Cianest. Perhaps she can give a bit of welcomed advice. All this malarkey has my poor brain a frazzled mess, and I can't think worth diddly.* Saddened eyes stared into space as visions of the Queen and her beloved Tom flooded a distressed mind. *Okay Kat, get your big girl panties on and buck up. Feeling sorry for yourself isn't going to solve a thing.*

An hour or more passed before the familiar entrance to the clammy underground prison was discovered. She stood outside the first cell and listened for movement, indicating the mysterious creature was awake. "Psst, Cianest, it's me, Kat. Are you okay?"

"Yessss," she hissed. "I have been inssssane with worry, dear one. Have you been harmed in any way?"

"No, not really, however, I might never erase some crummy images burned into my conscious last night." The ebony cat reared up on its hind legs in a desperate attempt to see inside. "Dang blast it, I'm still too short. I wanted to speak to you face to face, but can't quite reach. Maybe if I jump a little and grab hold of the bars."

The pounding of cloven hooves echoed off icy granite walls as the cursed being rushed to the door. "No Kat, you mussst not view me in this form. I beg you to cease trying. Pleassse do as I ask, child."

233

"Okay, if that's what you want, but the sight of your present body isn't gonna alter my feelings one tiny bit. I realize the real Cianest is a far cry from the creature imprisoned here. Shoot, I'm a far cry from looking like myself, but I'll honor the request. By the sound of things, your body apparently has hooves and the hissing suggests something facially serpentine. Have to admit, the serpentine part rattles me somewhat…never have liked snakes."

Cianest began to chuckle. "You lift my spirits, little one. It is a rare pleasure. My appearance is a grotesque compilation of various creatures, each more hideous than the next. You do not need this nightmare added to your dreams."

The sound of movement in the next cell startled Kat. "Cianest, we're not alone. Whoever it is now knows I can speak. What should I do?"

"Do not be concerned. The new captive was brought in during the night. When the moon grows full, my lethal thirst shall return. This poor subject is to be sacrificed. I would rather suffer death than inflict such wrath upon these innocents, but the choice is not mine to make. Perhaps, you might free her."

"I don't know how, but I'll try. It's not easy doing things in this condition." Kat strolled over to the secured unit and again rose up in an unsuccessful effort to see inside. "Hello in there, my name is Kat. I'm a friend."

Moments passed in silence before a reply was given. "Friendship does not exist in this place. Leave me." Although edgy, the feminine voice was uniquely melodic.

Ears perked up. "I sense you have the heart and voice of an Elf."

"How would you know such things? Are you Elvin?"

234

"No, I'm human—or was human. I've been abducted and enslaved by Lord Tahl. Much as I hate to admit it, he's my dimwit cousin. A short time ago the creep grew intolerant of my insubordination and transformed me into a panther. The big jerk claims he'll reverse the spell once I learn to obey him—which will be…*never.*"

Kat's brash comment brought a restrained chuckle. "You amuse me, human, but my question remains unanswered. How do you know I am Elf kind?"

"That's a simple question to answer. Some of my best friends are Elves."

"Ridiculous. We do not associate with such beings. Your race is inferior and cannot be trusted."

"Well, sorry to burst your bubble, lady, but I share a kinship with many Elves. King Merneos of Durmeleigh is one. So take that and stuff it in your hat." Kat huffed and began to turn away.

"Wait! I know of who you speak. He is an honored King. How is such an acquaintance possible?"

"Enough of thisss idle banter, Kat. Reveal to her who you are," Cianest hissed.

"Jiminy Crickets, don't blow a gasket." Kat drew a deep breath. "I am the sister of Queen Adera of Bowlandria. My human companions and I were brought into this world many years ago. One of them, Randy, was recently married to the Queen. When the Realm was threatened by Nimue and her demonic army, all of us traveled to Durmeleigh for training. We fought side by side with the warriors of that land and have since grown close."

"Knowledge of this valiant endeavor is legend. Forgive my lack of respect. I am called Nia. Our clan was once large in number, many thousand in fact, but now only two survive. My sister, Nerak was initially captured. I sacrificed myself to free her."

"Holy smokes, what on earth happened to all your people?" Kat positioned herself comfortably in front of the door, anxious to know more.

"It began when Lord Tahl and his mother came to this Kingdom. In time, they grew curious about the lands outside of their boundaries, and eventually ventured into Elladraine. Eons ago, my clan formed and built our beautiful kingdom. For centuries we lived in peace, free of the outside world. At first our King and Queen accepted Tahl and Odiene, honoring their distinguished bloodline. We had no reason to suspect the pair's motives were evil. Soon, children mysteriously vanished, followed by many elders. For months the bizarre occurrence remained uncloaked. One-by-one our home was decimated until perhaps a hundred dwellers remained. We had little choice and were forced to turn away from tranquility and become avid warriors—men, and women alike. Existence depended on this conversion. She-Elves fought as men, willing to sacrifice their lives for the good of the residents. I excelled in my duties and was soon elevated in rank."

A mournful sigh breeched in the dank air. "Eventually, war arose. Tahl and his Qergs descended upon our land like a rainstorm from hell. Nearly all of my people were slain, including our King and Queen. Both were savagely slaughtered…their mangled bodies hung from the kingdom's most sacred building as warning to those who escaped. After the desecration and plundering ceased, nothing recognizable remained. In time, the handful of us who survived were either captured or killed, leaving only my sister and myself. We are the lone survivors. Before long, I fear Nerak will be all that remains of a once great nation."

"Leapin' lizards, I had no idea any of this happened, and I'm positive Adera knew nothing of it either. My sister would never have allowed this twosome carry out such heinous acts." Kat shook her head. "I seriously doubt even King Merneos is aware of such a travesty. There is no way on earth that nobleman would have ignored your plight. He would have helped in some manner. What's happened to Nerak?"

"I do not know, but believe she is not far off. Tahl and Odiene's reign of terror must be brought to an end. Their continued destructiveness will spread like a blistering flow of lava, until every bit of this land falls prey to them. Unless liberation is provided, it appears all is forsaken. "

Kat was silent as fear gripped her soul. *What if Adera isn't coming because she feels my aunt and cousin cannot be defeated? Have I been abandoned like Cianest?* She shuddered and drew a breath. *No, I refuse to even consider that option. She will come. I must remain strong and trust my inner feelings.*

The Ebony captive stood and snarled. "My sister will save us, I feel it. Don't give up the ship just yet. Right now, hope is about the only parcel of sanity we possess. The full moon has just passed, Nia. Cianest will do no harm. Of course, I can't say the same about dimwit Tahl. Elves are historically known for their attractiveness, so that blasted dude might take a fancy to you like he does every other good-looking female. His advances could prove to be a fate worse than death." She sniggered and moved back in front of Cianest's chamber door. "I know you heard all our chatter and can understand why I have to try to figure something out. Perhaps, it may come down to me destroying my aunt and her deranged son after all."

237

A pair of clawed, scaly hands grabbed hold of the bars. "No Kat, I forbid such an act. Have patience. Adera will not fail. She shall conquer thisss evil. Please, you must hold fast."

The exquisite panther stared momentarily at the cobbled floor. "I'll wait a little while longer, but my tolerance is wearing mighty thin. Guess you could say patience is *not* one of my virtues." She heaved a sigh. "I have never hated anyone as much as I do these warped relatives. Every bone in my body wants to rip his lovely throat out and shove it up his mother's bu…"

"Kat!' Cianest cried out, "Do *not* speak in such a manner. Remember, you are a princess and the royal daughter of Zuegas. Mind your manners."

"Listen lady, I've been drugged, kidnapped, abused, ridiculed, starved, and turned into a dang blasted cat. I think I've darn well earned the right to say whatever the heck I want, so…butt, butt, and *butt*." She snorted and pawed the floor. "Sorry, didn't mean to spout off like that, but I've just about reached the end of my stick. I need to release a bit of this frustration before my dang blasted head totally blows."

Airy laughter erupted from the nearby cell. "I am impressed with your spunk, human. Perhaps some exist who are not so bad after all. Should I survive, it will be intriguing for us to meet face to face."

"Well, right now my face is a tad covered with fur, so best we wait until I become presentable. Of course, being an Elf, you might like this appearance better. Think it's getting to be time for me to get out of here before I'm spotted. I'll try to come back soon." She snickered, slowly turned, and slinked up the winding stairwell.

Faye was bouncing around like a dry cork in a water-filled washtub as the little hen sprinted along the pathway. "Bongles Ibby, will you slow down. I feel like my head is attached to my feet. I'm more winded than you. Maybe I should fly from this point on."

The transformed maid immediately reduced the hurried pace which allowed the flustered passenger to somewhat catch a breath. "I'm sorry, Faye, but unfortunately this is how a chicken runs. Relax. We're not far from the secret entrance, but think it's best to wait for the shroud of darkness to descend. I'll hold it to a nice slow, easy walk from here on out, okay?"

"Shroud of darkness?" Faye exclaimed. "When has it not been dark here? I think the sun is afraid to show its face in this miserable excuse of a kingdom."

Ibby came to an abrupt halt and nearly unseated the feisty rider. "Mistress, I do not wish to sound rude, but Mantalac is my homeland. Please do not speak so ill of it. Our kingdom was much different in days past. The barrenness you see is the makings of Lord Tahl and Odiene. Their evil ways stripped all happiness from every corner and brought about the utter desolation now witnessed. The elders tell of a time when our land was warm, sunlit, and cheerful. Luxuriant trees and colorful, fragrant flowers dappled the sumptuous grassy landscape. Birds and abundant wild life scampered about in carefree play. It was a far cry from the misery you now view."

Faye leaned forward and gave the little hen a robust hug. "I'm sorry, Ibby. I didn't mean to sound so disrespectful. Please, forgive me. Ironically, our kingdom is separated from Mantalac by just a wee bit of a brook.

One side is absolutely beautiful, while the other grows more inhospitable by the day. It's sometimes hard to comprehend how two lands can be so close, yet so dissimilar."

The tiny fairy drew a breath and looked around…eyes brimming with sadness. "My friends and I will destroy that fiendish pair before long, and your home will once again be as it was. Queen Adera won't allow this desolation to continue. She had not realized the severity. To have something of such magnitude strike Drealon would cripple the heart of my people, as I'm sure it has done to yours. I will never again speak out rashly as I did. Information of the past remains unspoken among the Fairies. Most believe the two kingdoms have always been as they now are. Well, it will get fixed. The sun's going to shine bright as fireball before long. Mark my word. Tahl, Odiene, and their fiendish guards have a clandestine date with destruction."

Ibby nodded. "Thank you, Mistress. I believe this declaration holds truth. Once the spell upon me has been broken, I will give you the biggest and strongest hug you've ever had."

Faye began to giggle. "Hey, I'm just a little thing so don't make it too big or you'll crush me."

The pair snickered and slowly continued on toward the menacing black stone abode as the veil of night plunged them farther into blackness.

Faye gasped at the incredible magnitude of the structure as they neared. She had only viewed it from the air and not realized its enormity. "Splozits, this thing is huge. How the dickens will we get in? I can fly, but not sure my wings will carry me much further after such an endeavor."

"The secret entrance is just around the corner, Princess. For many years, it has not been used and remains void of occupants, other than perhaps a few mice or rats." Scaled legs sprinted toward the ramshackle opening and swiftly ducked inside.

"Hey, it's blacker than night in here. Now what'll we do? If a hoppy toad landed on the tip of my nose I'd never be able to see it." Faye slowly eased off the back of the fluffy bird, but did not venture from her companions side.

"Rummage around the floor and try to locate two smooth round stones. If you slap them together, they will supply us with a bit of light," Ibby directed.

Although mumbling about digging in the vermin-infested dirt for some dumb rocks, Faye complied and at last located two of the mysterious orbs. A quick rap together produced a rather subdued glow, yet sufficient enough to illuminate the passageway. Afraid of becoming separated and lost, the nervous sprite held the stones in one hand while maintaining a firm grasp on Ibby's wing feathers. "This place already gives me the jeebies. Do you actually know where you are going?"

"Yes Mistress, I have scouted this route many times before. We will soon arrive at a partially rotted door and can easily slip through the decayed crevices into an isolated dust-laden chamber. From there on, however, caution must be employed. Eyes will be everywhere."

Once they entered the dimly lit derelict room, the rocks were no longer needed. "Guess I can toss these babies to the wind now." Faye naively heaved them into the air, causing a thunderous clamor to permeate the deathly stillness as they struck the paved floor.

"Faye!" Ibby whispered, "Stealth must be utilized and a sound not made. Qergs hear the slightest noise and will come running. For goodness sake, be quiet."

241

Eyes widened and the little fairy blushed. "Sorry. I wasn't thinking. I'll be quiet as a mouse. Well, they sometimes aren't so quiet. In fact they can be outright noisy at times. I remember...hey!"

A ruffled wing momentarily covered her mouth. "Be *quiet* —stop jabbering. Now, follow behind me and don't so much as utter a peep. Understood?" Ibby whispered.

"Fine, I won't say another word. But what if something was important and you needed to be informed about it? Am I supposed to just zip it and not mention that an ogre is about to have you for dinner? Or would you prefer to be its main course?"

Ibby rolled her beady eyes and turned to face Faye. "Look, if you need to alert me for some unknown reason, just tug on a feather and point, but for goodness sake, remain quiet!"

Faye opened her mouth to say okay, but quickly closed it when she spotted the vexed look being given by her clucky friend. Instead, she gave a thumb up and nodded.

The duo proceeded cautiously through the eerie labyrinth of shadowed corridors. An occasional Qerg was encountered, but the quick thinking couple managed to remain obscured until safe passage was granted.

Once upstairs, they began the search for Kat, only to find her room vacant...obviously not slept in for some time. The former maid peered around—eyes troubled with apprehension. "I don't like the looks of this."

Suddenly, the door creaked open. "Ibby. You're back." Brandi rushed over and scooped up the startled hen. "I'm so happy to see you again and know you're okay. Did you find Queen Adera?"

"Yes I did, and also met several others who have come to free Kat." She directed her glance over to the fireplace.

"Uh, the little creature peeking out from behind the tattered green footstool is Faye. She's a fairy and a key member of the troupe."

Brandi began to snicker. "How could a fairy be so significant? What good can such a tiny being do against the likes of what wanders these halls?"

"I heard that remark and will have you know I can do a lot to help. Ibby can attest to my abilities." Faye fluttered out and stood with hands on hips alongside the little red hen.

"I am so sorry and offer a most sincere apology, Mistress. It appears you may be small in stature, but enormous in bravery." Brandi cast a playful wink at her feathered friend.

Faye flipped her head in proud acknowledgement of the complimentary statement.

Ibby began to giggle. "She's a handful, Brandi, but truly vital to the success of the group. Where is mistress Kat?"

Brandi drew a deep breath as eyes saddened. "Most times she is by the side of Lord Tahl. A mysterious collar has been set in place and which demands obedience and prevents escape. Knowing his captive cannot flee, Tahl has allowed her to roam freely within the walls. I often observe our poor mistress sitting alone by the large east-wing hall window staring out into the bleakness. Many times piteous sobs break the morbid silence."

"Faye, we must hurry and deliver Adera's message. The moment has arrived for you to fly ahead. Qergs will surely be everywhere from this point forward."

"That is correct," Brandi exclaimed. "I don't understand why, but all of the gruesome beasts were removed from their former stations. They now patrol these hallways in great numbers. Some are difficult to see and appear to be hiding, ready to leap out in ambush. It is rather odd."

Faye heaved a sigh. "No, it's not odd at all. I suspect Tahl and his despicable mother await the arrival of Adera and the others. They've apparently set traps throughout their ghastly domicile. However, this is where I come into play. The sinful duo is totally unaware of me. I can flutter about without detection and report the findings to Queen Adera. As the rescue party begins to wind through the halls in search of their quarry, I'll scout ahead to insure the path is clear."

Brandi smiled. "Ah, now I see why you are so valued. Such ability will truly be a great asset. I wish you both safe travels and pray this misery is soon brought to an end. Many suffer the horrors of Tahl and Odiene's brutality." She strolled to the door and motioned for the two companions to come forward. "Hurry, the hall appears clear. Please, be careful. Danger lurks in every corner."

Faye soared into the air and flitted into the leaden corridor. Ibby thanked Brandi and hurried behind. They had barely traveled halfway down the hall when the progressive thud of weighty footsteps was detected. As before, the quick thinking twosome managed to hide and remain unnoticed. Curious, the tiny fairy darted about like a bee, peering into each room as they wandered along. Ibby frequently chastised her overzealous companion, warning of ever-present danger.

"Psst, Faye, come here."

The little sprite landed next to the coppery-feathered hen, her face dancing with uncomplicated enthusiasm. "What is it? Did you spot Kat?"

"No, but this door leads into Odiene's chamber. She seldom leaves it and is surely inside. Be extremely quiet and stay alert."

Unable to contain childish inquisitiveness, Faye squeezed through the partly open door granting entry and a glance around. The room was immense. Animated candlelight skipped around pale blue walls while the flicker of a roaring fire further speckled the decorative plaster ceiling. A black figure on the epic four-poster bed suddenly reared its head, rose slowly, and slinked to the edge of the overstuffed mattress…intense violet eyes glowering.

"Hey look, it's a kitty," Faye excitedly exclaimed as she hurried toward it. "Hi there, I'm Faye."

Ibby dashed to the naive fairy. "This is not an ordinary feline, Faye. He's Odiene's pet. Remain silent and slowly back away." She grabbed hold of Faye's tunic with her beak and tugged.

"Oh geez, don't go bustin a plume, Ibby. I somehow sense this precious creature won't harm us. Kinda hard to explain, but there's actually something familiar about him. Splozits, I know what it is. When I first came here to rescue my two friends, this brave creature helped us escape. Without his aid, we would have been captured." She tore from Ibby's grasp, rushed over to the bed, and boldly stood on the floor looking up at the feline perched directly above. "Remember me?" She whispered. "We met in the dungeons a while back. You sure have pretty eyes, Master Cat. Mine are nice, but nothing compared to those peepers. Are you a captive like so many others in this place?"

The black cat nodded, glanced over at the door, and pointed a paw at it.

Ibby inched up alongside Faye. "He's telling us to leave. Odiene's napping, and if she wakes, we will perish."

245

"Can you believe how pretty this creature is? The cats back home would be pea green with envy after seeing the likes of him. Our poor little things aren't even as big as his whiskers. Wonder who he could be?"

"Faye! Stop blabbering. Let's get the dickens out of here," Ibby's voice was hushed, but the tone was purposeful.

"Oh, okay. Don't get your down jumbled." Faye smiled at the ebony feline, waved bye, then turned and scurried out of the room.

Once they were out of imminent danger, Ibby reprimanded her lacy-winged ally in a most severe manner. "That foolhardy stunt could have caused this entire endeavor to fail. We were appointed a royal task, and you better start taking things a bit more serious, young lady."

Faye hung her head and lowered her wings in submission. "I'm sorry. You have every right to be angry. I won't let it happen again. I'll be more careful from now on and follow your instruction." She lovingly stroked the hen's head. "I swear I don't know what gets into me at times. Mother has tried to break my habits, but they just seem to surface without warning."

"I truly understand your youthful exuberance, but it's imperative we find Kat, deliver the communication, and return to the group. Should we fail, many will suffer." She gave the little fairy a gentle nudge. "Let's head toward Tahl's room. This wing is eerily void of occupants."

As they made their way along, a sinister shadow emerged and crept steadily toward them. They quickly slipped behind a nearby curtain and cautiously peered out as the slinky silhouette drew close. "Its Mistress Kat," Ibby exclaimed and rushed forward.

After an overwhelming greeting between the threesome, the ever-important message was at long last delivered.

Kat sighed. "Thank you," she whispered. "Again, sweet Faye you bring soothing news. My mind is somewhat at rest knowing a rescue is imminent and loved ones will soon come for me." Large golden eyes welled up. "Convey to my sister how much I wish to see her again and that I love her. Also, tell my sweet Tom his love is always held close. I miss each and every one of them more than words can say and will count the hours until we are united once more. I cannot express the gratitude I hold for your valiant venture. These words have lifted my soul and fortified a weakening mind. Now, get the tar out of here before you two are spotted. Use extreme caution upon your return. Tahl's goons are everywhere and many hide from sight. Oh, and be sure to tell King Merneos and Horace there is a captive Elf being held in the dungeons. Nia is a warrior and might prove to be an unexpected blessing. Go quickly and be safe."

The pair nodded and headed off. Faye cast a brief glance back at the giant predator forced to remain behind…alone in the dismal dwelling of evil. Thought of such a sweet person so horribly imprisoned pierced the bounteous heart of the fairy princess. More than ever, she was determined to help free Kat, Ibby, and many others who were being tortured by the vile ancients.

Once outside the walls, Ibby suggested she climb aboard and hold on. Tiny legs pumped like iron pistons as they sped back to camp.

Chapter Seventeen
Day of Reckoning

Randy looked down at his exquisite wife who slept cradled in his arms. He tenderly brushed a wisp of golden hair from her forehead and smiled. Outwardly, she presented herself as being brave and determined, but he knew below the hardened surface beat a worried and broken heart.

Tom noiselessly eased up alongside and spoke just above a whisper, "First time I've seen Adera get this much rest in days. It should do a world of good. Heaven knows, before long, we'll all need to utilize every ounce of strength we can muster."

"Afraid you're right about that, Tom. Once Ibby and Faye return, I seriously doubt anyone will be able to hold Adera back. She's gonna want to get underway immediately. Our date with the devil draws closer by the hour. Hey buddy, appears you're sportin' some bodacious bags under those peepers. Might not hurt you to grab a few winks while it's still possible. I doubt even a stupid catnap will be obtainable before long."

"Nah, contrary to my looks, I'm really okay. Besides, there's no blasted way I can get any sleep. Thoughts of Kat rip through this bonehead brain the second I close my eyes. I want her back, Randy. I wanna hold my wife safely in these arms. Until I do, rest is impossible." He stared out into the gloomy mist. "You suppose Faye and Ibby are okay?"

Randy nodded. "Yeah, I believe so. Those two are pretty resourceful. I've never known anyone called Ibby before. Suppose it's one of Kat's *famous* nicknames?"

Tom snickered. "I wouldn't doubt that for a second. Sounds like something she'd come up with."

"Of course she came up with it, you dorfenberries, and I like it."

The unexpected vocalization from behind sent a shockwave of fright through both men. Tom slipped off the log backwards and Randy leaped up, causing Adera to shriek as she tumbled from his lap onto the decaying turf.

The boisterous outburst wakened the others who jumped up and rushed over with weapons drawn.

Randy helped his disheveled wife to her feet, then turned and faced Faye who mischievously giggled while hovering in mid air.

"That stunt was not funny, little miss, and definitely not appreciated." Randy's voice was void of humor. "I should clip your wings for pulling such a stupid prank."

Faye quieted down, but eyes continued to give off an impish gleam. "I'm sorry. Sometimes I just can't help myself. Mother gets upset over such trivial antics and is forever telling me I am far too impetuous for my own good. However, I fail to see a problem. Splozits! A girl needs to have some fun now and then. I remember the time—uh, guess you don't want to hear about that time, huh?" The sight of the entire group standing with arms angrily folded rendered Faye silent, at least for a few seconds.

Adera shoved Randy aside and faced the little fairy. "Where is Ibby? Was the venture successful? What news have you brought? Speak child."

249

"Whoa, slow down, sugar," Randy, cooed. "Let's not forget the fact she's just a youngster. Faye, I suggest you land and better inform this bunch before someone *does* clip those pretty wings."

Faye winced, slowly descended to a tall stump, and sat down. "I'm sorry, Adera."

Intense turquoise eyes softened and a faint smile formed on the Queen's porcelain face. "No, please forgive *me*, little one. Fear and stress momentarily controlled tattered emotions. Where is your companion?"

"I'm right here, your Majesty." The fluffy red hen jogged in…sides heaving. "I just could not keep up with Faye. She's really fast."

Ibby let out a sharp squawk as Merlin walked over and scooped her up. "Perhaps you will find a bit of water and some tasty morsels adequately refreshing, Mistress Isabelle."

The pretty fowl's eyes widened. "Oh, how lovely it is to hear my proper name spoken, sire. I appreciate the nickname placed upon me by Kat, but often miss this given title. Thank you."

Tom brushed off his clothes and knelt down near Faye. "Okay, time to spill it. Is Kat alright? Was the message properly delivered?"

Faye smiled. "The lady is fine, sir. Lonely and I believe frightened, but remains out of harm's way for now. The message was given, and I have replies." One by one she conveyed Kat's responses. "During our search, we managed to scout a great portion of the Manor. Hate to be the bearer of bad news, but her rescue is going take us down a rather difficult road. There are Qergs everywhere. We were lucky and didn't encounter Tahl and Odiene, but you can bet your toenails those two are somewhere within

250

the fortress and apparently know our whereabouts. Kat said to be very careful. Oh, I nearly forgot. King Merneos, the lady said to inform you and Horace that an Elf is being held captive in the dungeons and needs to be rescued. Her name is Nia and she's a warrior. Mistress believes her talents will be of great help in our fight."

Merneos and Horace glanced at each other, apparently finding the disclosure rather unsettling. "We will see to it she is set free," the Elf King coolly replied.

Randy wore a puzzled look. "Merneos, we weren't aware there were other Elves in this Realm. Did you know about them?"

"Of course, several clans remain scattered throughout the land. What I find distressing is the fact one has been captured. All Elves are talented and disciplined combatants—it is inherit to our kind. To be apprehended is a near impossibility."

"It is not so *impossible* when only two of your kind remain." From the pitch-black forest, a melodic voice caused swords and arrows to be drawn. "Do not be alarmed. Secure your weapons. I come in peace."

Charlie moved in front of Meeley to shield his sleepy-eyed wife. "We will sheath our weapons only when we feel there is no need for them. Come into the light, so we might make that decision."

Slowly, a willowy shadow presented its true form…a female Elf. She was tall, appeared young, and had chocolate brown hair neatly braided into one long tress. A royal blue tunic and fitted black trousers covered a rather svelte body. Dangling from her small waist was a sheathed jewel handled sword, while a fearsome bow draped squared shoulders. Striking blue-gray eyes traveled from one

251

member to the other and at last focused on Horace and Merneos. "You are Elfin?"

Horace stepped forward and bowed. "Yes. I am known as Netho by my kin, but also answer to the title of Horace which is used by others not of our race. Allow me to present King Merneos, Sovereign of the Kingdom of Durmeleigh."

Nerak placed a clenched fist over her heart and nodded politely. "Your legendary home is renowned throughout the colonies. I stand humbled, my Lord."

Merneos took her hand and stared into a sullied, tear stained face. "You stated only two of your clan remain? Thousands once resided in Elladraine. What has become of your Kingdom's populace?"

She drew a breath. "In the deep of night, Lord Tahl and his army of demons descended upon our land. Their numbers were overpowering. Our King and Queen, our warriors, and the greater part of my people were heartlessly slaughtered. A few of us managed to escape, but in time most were found and taken to Odium Manor, never to be seen again. My sister and I wandered for months in hopes of locating others who may not have perished. Sadly, we encountered none."

The great Elf King's face grew tight and a delicate nose flared angrily. "This is an outrage. Extermination of our kind will *not* be tolerated. The lives of Tahl and his mother must be forfeit."

Adera and Randy looked at one another and clutched each other's hand. "I've never seen Merneos this infuriated," he whispered.

"Nor have I," she replied.

Charlie slammed his sword to the ground. "Oh, now a fierce rage develops, Merneos. You sure as heck didn't

252

show a great deal of fuming emotion when a human or some other poor creature was butchered or abducted. Why the blazes did you trudge along with us anyhow? Was it because you feared your friendship with Adera would be in jeopardy? To be perfectly honest, your royal lordship, I believe if it had been one of us humans kidnapped by Tahl, I doubt your lily-white fingers would have been lifted to help."

"I assure you, Charlie, your statement is far from the truth," Horace interjected.

"Yeah, well it doesn't look that way to me. This pompous attitude turns my stomach. Put 'em up, elfboy. Let's see if you can stand up to a real man—a human one." Charlie rushed up to the Elf with fists drawn. "

Suddenly, both were roughly shoved away from each other as Meeley stepped in between them.

"That will be quite enough from the two of you, and I mean it! You're both acting like a pair of juvenile schoolboys. Knock it off before I *knock* your thick heads together." Eyes blazed as she glared at the feuding duo. "I've been relatively quiet this entire trip, even though there were times I wanted to scream. We're all on edge and emotions are frazzled, so just stop it. Now is not the time to flap your lips at each other. It has to cease right this second. Do I make myself clear?"

Charlie lowered his eyes and relaxed a tense body. Horace did the same.

"Now, apologize to each other, which includes you Mr. Elf. Don't dare let me hear one single excuse, or both will suffer the consequences from one rip snortin' irate female. Get my drift, boys? No bloomin' excuses. Shake hands and stop the foolishness."

253

Charlie kicked gingerly at the dirt. "I apologize Horace, and also to you King Merneos. Sorry. Hope you'll forgive me. Don't have a clue of what caused me to flip my wig like I just did. I know better. You two have been as close and good to us and anyone could ever expect. Really don't know what the horsefeathers got into me. I'm sincerely sorry and pretty much embarrassed by my cap snappin' actions." A sheepish grin formed on his reddened face as a hand was extended.

"I accept the apology and beseech you accept mine. We have been friends for many years and hope to remain such for many more. Forgive me, my brother." Horace countered the gentlemanly gesture as their long time bond of fellowship was vigorously renewed.

Merlin cleared his throat. "My lords and ladies, I fear this passionate flare-up was brought about by the toxic gas. I suggest we each, including the Elves, partake in a bit more elixir. Alas, had we not been detained for this length of time, what was ingested prior would most likely have sufficed." The wise wizard passed out an adequate portion of his remedial cocktail to each member, including the she-elf, Nerak, who oddly appeared unaffected. "Dear lady, I find your imperviousness to the ever present toxins most intriguing. It is a well-known fact that Elves possess a resplendently stalwart constitution, but your resistance is astounding. Even our two valiant warriors have experienced a few distressing moments."

"My sister knew of the danger and brewed a tea prior to our arrival. It neutralizes the noxious vapors. However, the effects do appear to be waning."

The ancient conjuror clapped his hands as eyes brightened. "I must indeed meet with this talented creature. It appears we have much to discuss."

"I entered Mantalac to save my captured sister, Nia. May I inquire the reason an uncharacteristic band of mixed breeds tread upon such unclean turf?"

King Merneos cocked an eyebrow at the discourteous statement and gestured to Adera. "Perhaps the Queen of Bowlandria might best explain the mission, lest I speak wrongly. Come Nerak, join us, and converse."

Randy stoked the fading embers of the dwindling fire as the group formed a circle and were comfortably seated.

Following a swift introduction, Adera promptly clarified all questions. "We would be honored to have you enlist in our quest. Many victims require deliverance, including your beloved sister. What say you? Will my offer be accepted?"

Nerak's piercing eyes trailed around the ring of friends. "Yes, I accept and offer my services. Once Nia is liberated, we are duty bound to repay the debt. In gratitude, we shall fight alongside this group to insure success."

Randy stood. "Then it's settled. At first light, Ibby and Faye will lead the way into the Manor. Although it might be a tad difficult, I suggest everyone try to catch a few winks. Something tells me we're gonna need our meager brains to function at full steam from here on out. Faye, perhaps it might be best to have Punk remain behind. His flight is stealthy, but unfortunately we can't risk him being seen. Sorry. It's for his safety, and ours."

The little fairy nodded in agreement then flew to her feathered knight and lovingly stroked his head.

A slight smile crossed Randy's handsome face as he watched the small maiden snuggled up to the owl's soft downy chest and close her eyes. "Looks like tomorrow's gonna be Tahl's day of reckoning, Adera."

255

"Let us pray your words are realized." She drew in close to him. "I do not know if my mind can embrace slumber, but I shall try. You must also seek rest, my sweet husband."

Randy wrapped his arms around her and nodded. Worried eyes glanced around the camp as loyal companions made an effort to obtain a moment of needed rest…a near impossible feat to accomplish as the unyielding stillness swallowed up the night.

Muted rays of light spewed across the barren landscape as dawn approached. Hours had passed like mere seconds. One by one the diverse assemblage woke and quickly prepared to get underway.

To everyone's surprise, Ibby and Faye proved to be rather proficient guides. Barely an hour passed before the group arrived at the clandestine entryway.

"This tunnel looks mighty small, Ibby." Charlie scratched his head and peered into the chamber's dusky opening. "I'm not too keen about going in there. We might get stuck."

"No sir, do not fret. The scope of the area is far greater than it appears. My chosen route would not have been suggested had I felt you could not easily travel along without incident. Although it's a bit hard to imagine at the moment, I am human and aware of your size."

They had only traversed a few feet when their progression was quickly thwarted. Dissolving light had transformed into complete darkness within the clammy stone structure.

Meeley shrieked and frantically wiped a large mass of cobwebs from her face. "Okay, that's it, blokes. I've had enough. Wandering about in such blank obscurity is utter nonsense. We can't see a hand in front of our face, and it's

256

getting worse as we move forward. I for one am not taking another step."

"Merlin, might you provide a small beacon of light?" Adera whispered.

"Had I a stick, my Lady, the task would be possible. Alas, there is no material to work with."

Suddenly, a sharp crack echoed through the tomb-like burrow, and a soft glow began to illuminate the path. "Oh for the love of mushrooms, Merlin, it's a rather uncomplicated matter to figure out." Faye rolled her eyes and plunked a pair of the smooth blue rocks into Randy's hand. "Here, use these to locate more. If two are smacked together, they'll produce light. You shouldn't have a problem finding others—the floor is littered with them. The larger they are, the more light they'll emit. Just be careful you don't pick up some rodent droppings by mistake. The darn place is overrun with tons of that disgusting debris. Mice and rats are such unclean pests."

Ibby ruffled her feathers. "I take offense to that remark, Faye. You know full well my sister, Jewell, as well as many others, were unsympathetically transformed into these pitiful mammals. They scurry about the unclean halls of this miserable place in utter helplessness."

The feisty fairy rocketed to the ground and boldly stood in front of the small hen. "Maybe they were changed, and maybe they were not. I've seen no actual proof of any such occurrence. Nevertheless, I stand by my statement and find rodent droppings disgusting. So take that and stick it in your beak."

Merlin stepped in between the feuding duo. "Ladies, ladies, once again it seems we are plagued by disagreements between each other. This meager fellowship must hold strong, or it shall end in failure. I believe no calculated

257

offense was intended, Ibby, but also suggest you think a tad more wisely before speaking, young Faye."

Randy cleared his throat. "Ahem, how 'bout we all just cool our jets a bit. Frustration is running sky high right now, so let's lay aside any annoyances and tend to the task in point. Everyone has an important part to play in this venture. Without Ibby's guidance, we would not have penetrated these walls, and your ability to travel ahead undetected is also of great value, Faye. Remember, we're a team. Each of us better dang straight work together or dance with death. Now, shake hands, uh, feathers and hands, and let's continue on." He snickered slightly as the two did as they were told. "Okay y'all, scour about for more of these dad-gum rocks so we can light up the joint." Within seconds the tunnel was fully illuminated and another barrier vanquished.

The group moved along in silence and soon arrived at a large, dilapidated wooden door, clearly indicating the tunnels end had been reached.

As Randy placed a hand on the door, he was abruptly halted by Ibby's snappish intervention. "Sir, stop! Great vigilance must be used. When Faye and I left, the room beyond had been abandoned. However, that may not be the case at the moment. Qergs were being stationed everywhere within the Manor, and I suspect a sentry might now stand guard at this site to prevent entry or escape."

Horace drew close. "What she says is most likely valid, Randy. First of all, I suggest we douse our lights to avoid inadvertent detection. Next, it would be advisable to dispatch Faye to stealthily scout ahead. We do not know what waits beyond this obstruction."

"You're right, Horace." He motioned to Tom, who quickly joined them. "The three of us will accompany Faye

258

to the door while Merneos, Charlie, and Merlin remain a safe distance behind guarding the women."

Nerak bolted forward and forced her way between them. "You are most presumptuous to think of me as some helpless female. I am a skilled warrior. My talents can, and should be, made use of."

The three men gave a quirky glance at one another, apparently taken aback by her brash and unexpected declaration.

Randy heaved a sigh. "Dang, forgot she's an Elf and has radar hearing. Suppose we should allow her to tag along?"

"It's fine with me," Tom replied. "I for one am not about to argue with a well trained woman bearing arms." He chuckled and playfully nudged Randy.

Horace coldly stared at her. "I see no reason to disallow the request, as long as Nerak understands *we* are in charge and our rules are to be obeyed."

"My word is given. I shall follow all commands." She gave a gracious nod and strategically positioned herself behind them.

Once the others were informed of the plan, the five edged close to the crumbling ligneous obstacle. Randy took a moment to carefully ascertain all feasible options and determine the next proper course of action. "Faye, can you squeeze through the cracks and check to see if the chamber is clear?"

"Of course I can. Those gaps are so wide I could fly Punk through them."

"I want you to be very careful, young lady. Do not flit around the room or go into the hallway. We only want to know if the path is safe to proceed. This is merely a scouting task. Do you understand me?" Randy used a firm tone.

259

The bouncy fairy giggled and took wing. Moments passed in silence and nerves mounted as they waited for her return. Soon, the flutter of tiny wings was heard. "Oh Master Randy, there is a giant Qerg blocking the doorway into the Manor. We cannot proceed."

"Is there only one, or more, Faye?" Randy's eyes grew worried.

"I saw only one, sir. The big oaf is leaning against the wall, back to us, and appears to be half asleep."

Randy signaled for everyone to join them and gather close. "Listen, we ran into a slight problem. There's a Qerg guarding the doorway. We can't proceed until he's taken out. It'll have to be done quietly so we won't alert others. I'm open to any suggestions, y'all."

Merneos spoke up, "An arrow to the head should clear the path."

Horace interrupted, "Pardon my boldness, Majesty, but the brute may bellow prior to death. In addition, the sound of his spear and body armor clashing against the floor will most likely bring reinforcements."

The Elf King nodded in agreement. "My noble warrior is correct in his assessment. However, a method must be formulated to unobtrusively remove this hindrance." He bent down and softly set the fading light-stones on the floor. Suddenly, vivid blue eyes widened. "We have become blinded by the obvious. The answer is right before us—a rock. Propelled at the precise angle and speed, it would instantly render the Qerg unconscious without fear of sound."

Randy winced. "I understand what you're getting at, but there's a tiny problem, Merneos. When the rock falls to the floor, it's gonna echo down the halls like a turkey shoot gunshot. Plus, we still would have the earsplitting problem

260

of his weapon and armor. I'm afraid it's close, but no cigar."

"Point well taken, my friend, but a solution is at hand," Horace replied. "The rock must be bound in cloth, rendering the fall noiseless. If my calculations are correct, and be assured they are, the rest of us can rush in and hinder the creatures fall, thus, making the attack relatively silent."

"Are you kidding me? No way can we pull off such a stunt." Randy shook his head. "Sorry, there has to be another way. What you're suggesting is plum insanity. One slip and we'll have more Qergs than we can handle. It's too risky. Not even the best computer could determine the proper timing."

The fêted Elvin warrior gripped his friend's shoulder. "Have we not dealt with more complex issues in the past? Where is your faith? I once knew a proficient and fearless combatant. Has he been lost?"

Randy gazed into frosty blue eyes, and then cast a glance at the others. "My inner self feels mighty unsure, but to be fair, I'll leave the final decision up to the group. The warrior you trained and fought beside remains, Horace, only he's become a bit more cautious. Married life tends to do that to a man." He chuckled, winked at Adera, and heaved a sigh. "Okay gang, it's up to you. All in favor of Horace's idea raise their hands."

Without a second of hesitation, all hands except his were lifted

"Well, looks like the overwhelming answer's yes, Horace. Sure as blazes hope you know what you're doing, buddy. Our lives, and Kat's, are at stake here."

The unemotional Elf nodded. "Do not be concerned, Randy. The initiative will not fail. I require cloth and binding material."

"Allow me to contribute a parcel which should sufficiently meet your cloth necessity." Adera ripped a piece of hem from her tunic and handed it to the Elf.

Meeley stepped forward and offered a long, soft leather shoestring. "This oughta truss that rock, Horace, but I'll need it back once the deed is done. I'm sure as heck not about to trot through those halls barefoot."

"Thank you ladies, these shall suffice." He looked around and unearthed a somewhat large oval rock, sharply pointed on both ends. "Ah, this shall serve the purpose well." Moments later, the makeshift weapon was ready. "Please, line up single file behind me. The instant this projectile is unleashed from my hand, burst forth through the door. Do not hesitate. King Merneos, we possess the greater strength and shall tug at the monster's garments, forcing a backwards decline. Once he begins to slump, the rest must hamper the sound of his fall. Merlin, your task will be to secure his lance. Under no circumstance must it be allowed to hit the floor. Silence is vital. Also, be wary of the tip. The commandeered article shall become valuable, for its lethal effect also applies to Qergs."

Once everyone was in place, he covertly eased the door ajar, just enough to have access to his prey.

Randy edged up close and whispered, "Horace, you're only going to get one shot. Make it count."

The incomparable cavalier cupped the rock in his palm, took aim, and without the slightest display of exertion, launched it toward the Qerg with the velocity and precision of a high caliber bullet.

A sickening thump was heard as the pointed tip of the bound stone penetrated the monster's temple, killing it instantly. The entire group dashed into the shadowy room, each attending to their delegated task.

However, Merlin inadvertently tripped on his robes and tumbled into the wall. Disaster was at hand.

Suddenly, the weapon's rapid decline ceased and it eerily began to float downward. Miraculously, entry into the Manor had been successfully cleared of its first deadly obstacle.

"Hey, will someone get this darn thing off me." The sound of a tiny voice from under the giant spike breeched the stagnant air. "Ouch. There must be a gazillion stones down here. Bongles, my nice clean wings are all dirty now from waddling around on this filthy floor. Hello? Is anyone out there? Will someone please get this dinglerideen thing off me?"

Adera rushed over and gently lifted the Qerg's spear. "Faye, my dear child, have you been injured?"

The little fairy wiggled free, stood, and dusted off her clothes. "No, I'm fine, but that silly thing is heavy. At least I stopped it from falling. Merlin, you are such a clumsy oaf at times. Splozits."

Merneos rushed over and knelt down on one knee. "Ladies, hush your voices." He looked at the flustered sprite and smiled. "Little princess, your bravery is commendable. Without such a valiant endeavor, failure would have been met. We owe you our gratitude."

Round hazel eyes widened and a proud glow formed on the fairy's face. She shook her wings, freeing them of any debris, and soared into the air. "Well, are you all going to plant your feet and gawk at this dead fiend, or proceed on so we can take out some others? Let's move it, guys."

263

Gazes shifted from one to the other of the troupe, who snickered, and followed their feisty companion into the stygian corridor.

The thought of his lifetime friend being held captive in such an abhorrent place propelled an icy shudder down Randy's spine as he ambled in silence alongside his bride. *My heart breaks for Tom. He'll be utterly devastated if something happens to Kat. He loves her more than life. I hope and pray our quest isn't already a failed mission.* He drew a deep breath to fight off the blast of panic that pierced his chest like a dagger of doom. The revelation of Kat's fate drew close.

Chapter Eighteen
Final Retribution

Intensifying dejection spread throughout the countryside like a fetid plague as Mantalac continued its hopeless plunge into the boughs of hell. Any remaining shred of cheerfulness was steadily being devoured by a ravenous evil.

Unable to clearly discern day from night, Kat reluctantly obeyed her master's commands once again and sauntered toward Lord Tahl's quarters to rest. The prodigious door had been left open, granting easy access for the exotic feline. Dwindling candlelight unveiled a muddled form gauchely sprawled out across the bed. *Appears my classy cousin has passed out in another drunken stupor. Well, at least the big jerk won't bother anyone in this condition. Shame he can't remain loaded until Adera and Tom get here.*

She plodded over to the designated chest of drawers and leaped on top. Once settled, sleep was miraculously obtained. The sensation of her beloved Tom stroking a troubled head seeped into an intoxicating dream. Suddenly, reality of actual hands being placed upon her roused the big cat. Golden eyes strained to focus, and at last leered into the smirking face of Tahl. She bristled and hissed as intense hatred overcame any shred of fear.

"You miserable cur, I have had enough of this impertinence." He raised an arm and explosively delivered a violent backhand to Kat's face, nearly knocking her to the floor. Enraged, he picked up a multi-tailed leather flogger, and pummeled the feline's ebony coat—its dagger-like barbs lacerating flesh as they struck. "You will respect

265

and obey me, or suffer the consequences, dear cousin. My tolerance grows dim."

"Tahl stop! Put down that whip."

An airy voice from behind caused him to abruptly pivot around. "Mother, I didn't hear you approach." Seething fury churned in his eyes. "Give me one good reason why I should cease delivering punishment? It is fitting." Crazed with rage, he belligerently hurled the torturous weapon across the room. "What is so important to bring about this interruption? I do not appreciate it," his tone of voice was harsh and raffish.

Violet eyes blazed as she approached and briskly slapped his face. "How *dare* you speak to me in such a manner? Such ungracious insolence will not be permitted. I demand an immediate apology, or you shall feel the swift sting of my retaliation."

Lord Tahl's demeanor weakened as he rubbed a reddened cheek. "I beg forgiveness, Mother. It was wrong of me and will not happen again."

She cast a fleeting glance at Kat, then strolled over to the bed and made herself comfortable. "Come, sit by me, son, urgent and distressing matters require immediate discussion. I do not know how it was accomplished, but Adera and her ignoble band of followers managed to enter our home. Qergs have been dispatched to seek them out and ordered to destroy all but three."

"Three? Why spare a single soul? Slay the entire bunch and be done with it, Mother." Incensed eyes glared at Kat. "That animalistic wretch can join them as well."

The beautiful ancient sighed and shook her head. "At times such as this, I question your preparedness to rule in Adera's stead. Have you learned nothing, Tahl? I do not wish to kill Adera. My conscious remains reluctant to go against the commandments of our homeland. However, it would be a fate worse than death for her to witness the torture and destruction of that vile human she has wrongly taken for a spouse. One of the other mortals is the mate of your *pet*. Order the beast to slay him. I believe such an act should prove to be a more suitable form of retribution, do you not agree, son? Once the deeds are performed, Adera shall also be transformed. Then, both sisters can comfort one another as they share a filthy dungeon cell…for eternity."

Tahl broke into laughter. "Why Mother, it appears you are far more devious than perceived. Even my demented mind hadn't fantasized a more delectable fate for our pompous relatives. I wholeheartedly approve."

Kat yearned to speak, but dare not. Somehow, she had to warn Adera, and the others. *I will never bow down to either of these monsters. No force on this earth could make me obey and kill my beloved Tom. It will not happen. My love for him won't allow such a sickening scheme to be committed. If anyone is to be terminated, it will be you, Tahl. Nothing would give me greater pleasure than to part your throat from that miserable neck.*

"I suggest, my darling son, you gather your wits and prepare to engage the intruders." She turned and sashayed to the door. "Do not linger. Time is of the essence. The enemy prowls the halls as we speak. There shall be ample time for self-indulgent escapades once our conquests are met. Now, make ready." She paused and drew a deep breath. "Tahl, I grow weary of these immature actions of late and find them most troubling. I have serious doubts and concerns in your ability to govern. Perhaps, it shall be best to utilize my astuteness and preside over this monarchy until such time a proper sense of responsibility is displayed, although I fear a lack of mature soundness may be a long time coming." A slam of the door announced her departure.

Tahl momentarily stood silent—his face distorted in rage. "Enjoy your moment of gloat, mommy dearest. Soon, you will kneel at my feet and plead for mercy, but rest assured, none will be given. Your days treading this earth grow short. No one is going to stand in my way…including you."

He stomped across the room and quickly donned battle weapons and armor. As he searched for the rashly lobbed whip, his hate filled gaze fell upon the silent panther who returned an enraged glower. "What did you say, cousin? Sorry, I didn't quite catch those words. Aw, what's wrong? Cat's got your tongue?" Tahl began to snicker…obviously amused by the taunting banter. Laughter trailed as the ignoble Lord exited the room.

Kat waited several minutes before leaping from the highboy. Scarlet droplets of blood oozed from gaping wounds as muscles involuntarily quaked in agony. However, passionate abhorrence toward the aggressor trumped all pain. "I must find Tom and Adera. They are in mortal danger and somehow have to be warned. Odiene and Tahl have gone completely insane."

She plodded to the door as powerful paws vigorously tried to force it open. However, it was tightly bolted and escape was futile.

The group had barely traveled more than ten feet when three Qergs charged forth. Randy, Tom, and Charlie drew their swords and attempted to engage the colossal fiends. Unfortunately, lengthy spears, tipped with deadly toxin, thwarted any significant advance. Suddenly, a sickening thud echoed off stonewalls as the lifeless trio of demons dropped to the floor.

"I thought my skilled students had been better trained and realized the need to be more attentive," Horace announced as he approached. "Are your human ears clogged? We clearly discussed the only method of destroying these beasts, yet you blatantly disregarded all instruction. A well-aimed arrow to the head is the only effective course of action to cut down these brutes. Heed my warning gentlemen—do not make another foolish mistake for it shall be your last. Had Merneos, Nerak, and I not arrived in time, this careless trio of mindless baboons would have been slain. Sheath those swords, and draw your bows—now!" Anger, unlike any they had heard before, flowed from his lips.

Adera rushed to Randy and forcefully grabbed hold of his arm. "I cried out to thwart that foolish attack, but my words went unheeded. Never act in such an unwise manner again. A moment more and I would have become a widow. The thought is unbearable." Loss of sleep and intense anxiety were openly visible on her sullied face.

Randy embraced his bride. "I'm so sorry, sweetheart. It was a reckless mistake and one we won't make again. You can bet the dang house on it. Now dry those pretty eyes, babycakes. Everything's gonna be okay." He turned to the Elves. "It was right to chastise us, Horace. We deserved a darn good tongue-lashing and probably a tad bit more. If not for you three, we might be laying there dead. Thank you. All of you."

Tom and Charlie nodded in agreement.

The wise Elf warrior bowed his head in respect, acknowledging the sincere token of appreciation.

269

"Randy, sorry to interrupt, but we better keep moving," Tom interjected. "It might be advisable at this time to split up."

"You're right, buddy." The handsome South Carolinian peered around. "How about you and I proceed on to see if we can find Kat? Charlie, will you, Meeley, and Merlin head in the opposite direction. Ibby said Odiene's quarters were in the west wing. In the meantime, Adera, Nerak, Horace, and Merneos can find their way to the dungeons to release Nia and Cianest."

Meeley's eyes widened. "Are you some kinda nut? Release that monster! She's a killer."

The benevolent queen placed a hand on Meeley's shoulder. "No, dear friend, she is not. Cianest is the victim of a horrific spell. The full moon has passed. She will not render harm. Please believe what I say."

Proud of his beautiful wife's wisdom and kindness, a radiant smile formed on Randy's face. "Okay, time to move those keisters. Take a lesson from our stupid irrational behavior a few minutes ago and be vigilant. Keep your bows ready. From what I've gathered Charlie, the only problem you might encounter with Odiene is that dang blasted amulet wrapped around her precious neck. Don't allow the witch to grab hold of it, or you will never see the light of day. Pretty sure she'll be heavily guarded, so be ready to fire." He walked over and gave Adera a quick kiss to the cheek. "Be careful, sweetheart. We'll see if we can locate Kat and meet you back in the Hall of Armor. Ibby and Faye, you two come with Tom and me. We need your eyes Faye and your directions Ibby."

Without hesitation, the small band divided and hurried off to their appointed destinations.

Adera's mind raced as they descended the winding staircase leading to the dungeons—her heart torn between two emotions. She was anxious to free an innocent companion, but also held fear of viewing the transformed creature. No one alive had seen or had knowledge of Cianest's grotesque appearance.

All were silent as they approached the lair of the Lamiae. Bowlandria's queen cautiously drew near the stalwart door. "Cianest, it is I, Adera. We have come to free you."

A spine prickling voice broke the eerie quietness, "My sssweet friend, I have long waited to once again hear your voice. Do not look upon me. I am unlike the being you once knew."

"It matters not to me," Adera replied. "My heart will only see you as you were. Do not fear. The moon phase has passed. Are we in danger?"

"No, I have control during thisss time. No harm will befall you or your company. I pledge my word."

The Queen addressed her wide-eyed companions, "Please, hold fast. I prefer to enter alone."

Hands trembled slightly as the latch was lifted. "Come forth, sweet daughter of light." The great Sovereign stepped inside and eased the door closed behind her.

Slowly, the creature emerged from a shadowed corner.

The sight of the hideous monster brought a gasp from Adera, causing the beastly immortal to retreat. "Do not hide, Cianest. Be assured my response was not one of fear. What has been done to you shreds every fiber of a weeping heart. It is far worse than imagined."

A cherubic creature, which once had been lovelier than a spring breeze, was now a nightmarish fiend. The bulk of its body was that of a horse. From the midsection back it was cloaked in putrid green fur...the front section jacketed with reptile-like skin. Her equid rear legs were cloven hoofed... the forelegs little more than protracted, lurid, scale covered extensions of her arms. Feline type paws with spiky talons replaced delicate hands. The multihued head was somewhat human in form, with grotesque raised ridges in place of eyelids. A pair of scalpel sharp fangs, obviously used to drink the blood of her victims, protruded from a serpent-tongued mouth. Repulsive strands of raggedy blue-green hair flowed from her head down a long skeletal neck.

Adera slowly approached and wiped a tear from glowing red eyes. "You will soon be rid of this sordid facade and liberated. Do not dismay, Cianest. *Deliverance* is at hand. Come, join us." The Queen walked to the door and paused. "My friends, I must relay a word of warning. You shall undergo a moment of shock at first glimpse of Cianest, but do not be afraid. What you see is merely a shell. The purest of souls continues to thrive within. She desires to join our quest and I beseech every courtesy be extended. Never forget, the creature which stands before you is not of her doing."

Eyes widened as the duo emerged from the cell, but nary was a sound of dread uttered as Adera graciously introduced one to the other.

Merneos approached Cianest and bowed. "My lady, anguish has been your constant companion, but it shall soon be banished forever. Together, we shall battle and defeat the evildoers who have wronged you and so many other innocents."

272

Cianest nodded. "Wordsss elude me at thisss time. Thank you, all of you. King Merneos, a member of your race residesss in the next cell. I believe she might be a proficient assset."

Nerak rushed to the door and yelled, "Nia, are you inside? Are your alright?"

"Yes, I am fine."

Horace hurried to unlock the door, freeing the stunning, dark haired occupant who dashed into the anxious arms of her beloved sibling. "Nerak, what are you doing here? My demands were to leave and remain safe. Why have they been ignored?"

"Do you honestly believe I would abandon my sister? Such a thought would not enter my mind. Fate brought me to this group, and with their help, we will finally rid the land of the vile malignancy that flows across it. Are you up to fighting with us?"

"I willingly offer my hand to do whatever is required." She turned to Merneos. "I overheard the introductions. It is good to know other exist. My name is Nia. Unfortunately, we are the last of our clan."

"I am saddened to hear of Elladraine's destruction and knew its King well. He was a most admirable warrior and noble ruler. You and your sister are more than welcome to set up residence in Durmeleigh."

"We humbly accept the gracious offer, Highness." Her focus immediately shifted to Horace, who stood next to Merneos. "May I inquire your name?"

An uncharacteristic blush rose in his face, and flamboyant blue eyes brightened. "I am Jetho, but those not of Elven blood call me Horace."

Adera covered her lips to conceal a smile. The instant attraction between the pair was more than obvious.

273

The sight of Cianest brought a sharply drawn breath from the eye-catching she-Elf who backed away—fright obviously engulfing her alluring face.

"Do not fear, Nia, no harm shall befall you." Adera reached out and gently took the hand of the alarmed Elf. "Her hideous disfigurement is the result of a contemptible transformation brought about by my nefarious ancestors to satisfy a psychotic form of entertainment. Upon their destruction, all eyes shall feast upon an immortal of incomparable magnificence...a gentle and pure spirit. Cianest has more than earned the right to fight alongside us."

Horace edged close to Nia. "Queen Adera speaks only truth. Do not be concerned. If my company is acceptable, I would be honored to shield you from any danger, dear lady."

She nodded as hint of a smile formed. "The gallant proposal is satisfactory."

Adera whispered to Merneos, "Our aloof warrior appears enraptured by this striking newcomer."

He leaned in close and replied, "It seems you are correct, Adera, and I must say, it is about time. Perhaps we are witnessing the initial development of a forthcoming joining." He gave a playful wink.

The Queen cleared her throat, "Ahem, it is time to immediately vacate this site and reconnect with our companions." She glanced at the unattractive life form. "Cianest, it may be an impossible feat for you to ascend the stairs. Perhaps it is best you remain behind."

"Do not be concerned, sssweet Adera. No barrier shall be an obstacle. Let usss go."

Merneos led the way, trailed by, Adera, Nerak, Nia, Horace, and Cianest. Before the others could emerge into the corridor, two Qergs charged the Elf King and Adera. Unprepared, their bows could not be utilized. Both instantaneously drew swords and artfully avoided the fiend's lethal spears. Horace and Nerak rushed forward, drew arrows, and aimed. However, the consequent battle prevented a clear shot.

"Merneos, Adera, pull back. We have no open target," Horace yelled. His bellow seized the attention of the larger brute. It broke from the ongoing skirmish, grunted, and rushed at him. An arrow blazed through the air with the speed of a lightning bolt, delivering a deadly blow and felling the beast. Nerak dashed to the left, awarding unobstructed access to the other. Moments later, both Qergs lay dead on the musty cobbled floor.

"They came out of the shadows, hidden from view," Merneos declared. "We must implement extreme caution as we advance."

Adera gathered the one of the two spears. "Nia, can you make use of this lance until a more suitable instrument is located? Be wary of the tip, for unlike their hunting blades, the toxin used is designed to kill."

"I have been amply instructed to utilize such a scepter of war, and shall take care to evade the noxious head." She scanned the lethal implement and frowned. "Might someone shorten the staff to make it more adaptable to my hands?"

"Allow me, my lady." Horace retrieved the spear from Adera, drew his sword, and with one swoop, severed the rod down to an agreeable dimension. He then presented it to Nia and bowed. "I believe this will suffice."

Eyes twinkled as she took the weapon. "Indeed it shall, my lord."

The diverse group of warriors proceeded onward to meet up with their companions in the Hall of Armor. As they wove through a confusing labyrinth of dimly lit corridors, many more Qerg's were encountered—and effortlessly eliminated.

Randy instructed Faye to fly ahead and report any forthcoming danger. He felt a prickle of uneasiness as they approached the demented ancient's den, finding it eerily void of expected resistance. "Tom, something's not right here. We've not encountered one Qerg."

He nodded. "Yeah, my nerves are sending the same signal. Could be a trap waiting for us to enter that room."

"Sirs, I do not sense what you fear resides in Lord Tahl's quarters. He is much too devious for something so obvious," Ibby replied. "A greater conflict has surely been formulated."

"You are probably right, Ibby, but would rather be safe than sorry. We're aware of that jerk's methods and need to remain alert." Randy reached down and patted her feathered head. "Are you absolutely positive this is his room?"

"Yes, I am certain of it. Please be careful." She drew back from the bulky door…dark eyes wide with dread.

Faye fluttered to Tom's shoulder. "If one of you will crack this thing open a wee bit, I'll wiggle in and check to see if it's safe."

Randy winced, but realized it was their best option. "Okay Faye, but promise you won't go hog wild and get reckless."

The timeworn hinges creaked as they raised the bolt and eased the door negligibly ajar. Faye immediately inched in and vanished from sight. It felt as though hours passed before she returned.

"Other than a whopping big black panther, its empty," the small sprite declared with a slight giggle.

"Kat," Tom exclaimed as he pushed past Randy and dashed in.

The exotic feline looked up and leaped from the chest. "Tom!" She bounded into his arms, knocking him down in the process. "I knew you would come."

Randy began to laugh. "Well, she certainly hasn't lost her exuberance." He walked over, knelt down on one knee, and gave a playful pat on the head. "Nice jacket you're wearin', kiddo. Bet it keeps you toasty at night. Actually, I kinda like this new look."

"You dang blasted smart-aleck. If I wasn't so stinking happy to see you, I'd bite your hand clean off." Amber eyes scanned the room. "Where are the others? Where's Adera? Have they been hurt?"

"Whoa, don't blow a gasket," Randy exclaimed. "They're all fine. We split up. Everyone's supposed to meet up in that big hall. Where's the kidnapping slime ball?"

She backed off Tom, allowing him to rise. "I don't know. He left a while ago, but dressed for war. Something's sure as shoot up, but I haven't a clue to what it is. Think we better get the blazes out of here."

As they exited the room, she noticed the little fairy standing by the door. "Hello again, this certainly is a pleasant surprise. I cannot thank you enough for all you've accomplished."

"It was my pleasure. Just wish I could have done more," Faye replied. "Sure couldn't have done much if it hadn't been for Ibby over there." She pointed to the plucky hen that stood silent in the shadows.

Kat roared and dashed to her, "Ibby, I'm so glad you're okay. I've been worried sick that el jerko hurt you in some way. Well, won't be long now. We'll soon put a swift end to his torture. Once he's eliminated, you, and others, will be restored, including me. I've had about all I can take of this new look. Tom, don't *ever* get me a fur coat. I'll knock you to the moon if you do."

Tom chuckled, "I'll certainly remember that, kitten." He reached down and tried to remove the band from around her neck. "Sorry, sweetheart, this contraption isn't about to budge."

"I know, Tom. There's no way to remove it. The darn thing is under Tahl's control. We can't kill him until it's been removed, or I'll be stuck in this lousy necklace forever." She glanced down the corridor. "Better hurry and join the others fast as we can. Where did you say we're supposed to hook up?"

"In the Hall of Armor, wherever the dang heck that is," Tom replied.

Kat chuckled. "Follow me. I pretty much know my way around this joint now and discovered a few short cuts. Faye, you might need to save a bit of energy, so hop on board. Randy, perhaps it would be best if you carried Ibby so we can make some time."

He nodded and scooped up the small red hen. Faye fluttered up on the great cat and nestled into its sleek, ebony coat, with both hands grasping the collar for support. Without a second of delay, they bounded off.

The sound of footsteps from the opposite direction brought the outlandish ensemble to an abrupt halt. A sigh of relief was given when Meeley, Charlie, and Merlin emerged from shaded obscurity. After a short, but jubilant reunion, the group cautiously entered the designated area.

Obviously overwhelmed at the sight of Adera, Kat dashed to her. "Oh Sis, I prayed every day you would come. At times, I feared a rescue was impossible, but my heart held strong. Cianest said you would never abandon me." She glanced over at the gruesome beast that stood nearby. "No one need introduce us, Cianest. It breaks my everlovin' heart to see what's been done to you, but it'll soon be over. Lord Tahl and his loathsome mother are about to meet their maker."

Tears gushed from turquoise eyes as the benevolent queen embraced her sibling. "My darling Kat, no power on earth would keep me from you." She ungraciously wiped her eyes and looked at Randy. "Did you encounter many Qergs? We engaged only a small band, which is most unsettling. I fear danger lurks."

Meeley drew a breath. "The queen's chamber was empty, other than a gorgeous kitty napping on her bed. Perhaps momma and son were unwilling to face this bunch and decided to run. We'd make mincemeat out of them, and they darn well know it."

Adera shook her head. "I am afraid, Meeley, they would not do such."

"No, we would not." Tahl, trailed by Odiene, stepped into the room and slammed the double doors behind them. "You were right, Mother, these morons are so predictable and gathered exactly where we wanted them to. How easy it has been to corral this miserable group of rabble." He gave a guttural cackle. "Their destruction will be boorishly simple now. Don't worry, dear auntie, death will not be your fate. We have a more desirable solution in store. I believe watching all the others be exterminated one after the other, thanks to your vain misjudgment, is a rather ecstatically fitting punishment."

279

Randy stepped in front of his wife. "You no good piece of dung. Back off or I'll slit you from throat to toe."

Tahl gave off a spine shuddering laugh. "Such big talk for such a pitiful excuse of a man. Perhaps I should rid this human affliction first."

"The mortals and pointed-eared creatures you may slay, my son, but keep in mind, you cannot break the laws of our race. Adera and Kat's life must not be taken."

Adera shoved Randy aside. "Why are doing this Odiene? What has caused your heart to turn so cold? The person I knew was once gentle and kind, adored by my father, and a dear friend to my mother."

Violet eyes smoldered with rage. "Adeanra was the cause of this bitterness. She brought about the needless death of my beloved spouse with her foolish exploit…an act I shall never forgive."

"No Odiene, you are mistaken. Mother ventured off to search for medicinal herbs. Your son was deathly ill and required their need. Without them, he would have died. It was an unforeseeable accident, nothing more."

"Lies, you speak lies," Tahl boomed. "Do not listen to that serpent tongue, Mother. It is a ploy of distraction. She means to save her life, nothing more."

Odiene stood silent—a scowl covering her face. "She speaks the truth. You laid near death, my son, unresponsive to any treatment. Adeanra brewed a tonic from the gathered herbs which did indeed cure the affliction."

Tahl turned to her, his eyes blazing. "Do not be swayed by this venom. Adeanra killed your husband and deprived me of a father. Our time of vengeance has arrived. Use the talisman. Transform the others into cockroaches so I may step upon them and end their miserable existence. Do it, Mother. Do it now!"

She reached for the mysterious charm draped around her neck, but paused as violet eyes began to well up. "No, I will not act at the moment, but desire to hear more."

"Enough! Give it to me." He angrily snatched the extraterrestrial trinket from her, breaking the chain that held it in place. "I'll start with you, Elves. Prepare to die." He began the enigmatic incantation, but before three words could be uttered, the weapon of destruction was plucked away.

"Punk," Faye exclaimed, as she excitedly clapped. "Way to go. Bring it to us."

The noble owl soared overhead and dropped the malicious pendant into Randy's outstretched hand.

Enraged, Tahl shrieked for his Qergs to enter and attack then lunged at Randy, knocking him to the floor while trying to retrieve the dreadful ornament.

The group quickly drew arrows and began to launch a barrage of death. Almost immediately, the oversized demons began to fall, saturating the white marble floor with their rancid black blood.

Randy scuffled hand to hand with Tahl, but was no match for the ancient's inexhaustible might. A hard blow to the head dropped him to the floor.

Adera yelled out and ran to her husband, cradling him in her arms as she wiped a threadlike stream of blood that trickled from the open gash.

An evil grimace emerged on Tahl's face. He drew an arrow and aimed it at her. "You make this too easy. I shall slay you both with one strike."

Odiene screamed and rushed toward her niece just as the arrow was released. "No, do not kill her." The

281

projectile penetrated her back, piercing a tortured heart. She collapsed at the foot of her niece and reached out. "Forgive me, child. I have wronged you and my brother."

Adera gently laid Randy's head down and scooped up the woman who sought her annihilation for so long. "There is nothing to forgive, Odiene. Pains of love often cloud our thoughts."

The beauteous ancient struggled to speak as billows of scarlet liquid erupted from her lungs. "You do not know what offense I have committed. The death of your mother was brought about by my hand. I weakened the braid on Pegasus, knowing it would eventually break. It is your right to curse me for eternity. My eyes were blinded by grief. Forgive me, although I do not deserve mercy."

Adera looked down upon the dying woman draped in her lap. "I do not hold blame, sweet sister of my father. Forgiveness is mine to give, and I willingly do so. Go in peace, Odiene. Your sins are absolved."

Moments later, a body fell limp and once vibrant eyes faded as a life ended. Death released all who had been transformed by her as bursts of light flashed throughout the house.

Randy sat up and took the hand of his weeping spouse. "It's okay, sweetheart, she's finally at peace and at last with the love of her life."

Tahl voice thundered with fury, "You caused the death of my mother and shall pay dearly." He rushed toward Adera, but was knocked aside.

"Tom," Randy yelled, "don't do it" Sadly, his plea appeared useless.

"You will not harm another soul. There is a debt to be settled between us, Tahl." Tom drew his sword and attacked. A clash of metal against metal permeated the air as they battled, but like Randy, he was quickly overpowered.

Tahl approached the semiconscious opponent and held the biting point of his blade tight against Tom's throat. "I should remove the head from its worthless body, but prefer a more enjoyable means to your end." He turned to Kat. "I command you to kill this rubbish. Rip his throat out. Do it, now!"

She shook her head and groaned, obviously trying to fight the controlling force. "No, I won't harm him."

Tahl gasped. "What sorcery is this? How did you obtain speech? It is not possible."

Kat sneered. "Oh, but it is possible, Lord Tahl. Ignorance of my ancestry has betrayed you. My body may have been mutated, but your amulet had no effect on other abilities."

"Perhaps so, cousin, but even you cannot avoid the power of the band around your neck. I demand you slay this human."

Round cat eyes welled as she slinked over and straddled her husband with teeth bared.

Randy tried to stand, but was unable. "Kat, don't do this. He's your Tom, the only love of your life. You have to fight back."

Slowly, the ebony head edged closer to Tom's neck. "I love you. Please forgive me for what I am compelled to do," she whispered.

Before her beloved spouse could utter a word of protest, she spun from him and unexpectedly leaped upon Tahl. Strong, fierce teeth grabbed his gullet.

Cianest screamed out. "No Kat, you must not. Stop her, Tom. Death by her hand shall condemn your wife to remain in this form for eternity."

283

Before the impending attack could be thwarted, Kat closed amber eyes and sunk ivory fangs deep into her captor's throat, ripping life from the one she hated.

It was done.

Lord Tahl lay dead.

Suddenly, the oversized room filled with an intense blinding light. The hideous creature, Cianest, had been unselfishly released from bondage. Golden wings slowly unfolded and stretched as the glorious seraph reclaimed her celestial magnificence. Retribution had at long last unchained most from the impious curse.

Alas, one remained. The lethal bite had sealed Kat's fate.

Chapter Nineteen
The Journey Home

Bleak sinister clouds began to evaporate, allowing shafts of life-giving sunlight to trickle across a decimated landscape. Hope flooded the hearts of the oppressed residents as deadly vapors vanished and enslaved loved ones bounded into the welcoming arms of their families.

Kat stood by Tom's side and glanced around the room at her friends. The once sullen Manor was now bustling with glee. She peered up into her husband's handsome face and felt a powerful jolt of reality tear through her body. The love and companionship they once shared would be forever lost. Kat's unstinting act emancipated the souls of the tyrannized, but now doomed her to a life of distress. Agonizing thoughts were disrupted by a delicate voice.

"Why did you not listen, sweet child?" Cianest cooed. "Lord Tahl's death would have come at the hand of another."

"I couldn't take the chance, Cianest. He was overpowering the others and might have killed one of them in the process. The thought of such an atrocity, coupled with intensifying hatred, was more than I could bear. At least everyone's safe and can never again be harmed by the likes of those monsters." Kat fought back tears that pleaded to gush forth and swallowed hard. "You are so beautiful. To see your true self lightens my own burden. I'll be fine. After all, destiny never sleeps, so who knows what it has in store for the future. Right now, I've been dealt a rotten deck, but it could all change with the snap of a

285

finger. Actually, there's no one to blame except me. I knew the consequences and did what needed to be done. Seeing everyone released from their torturous bonds brings a bit of contentment."

Tom's eyes welled up. "I don't know how, but we'll find some way to break these bonds, Kat. I'll never give up hope. Perhaps Merlin can conjure a cure."

"I'm afraid, dear lad, no magic known will undo this travesty," the great wizard stated as he strolled up. "However, I shall endlessly search the land for an antidote and will not rest until one is found, my lady. You have my solemn promise."

Cianest smiled and affectionately stroked the great panther's head. "Fear not, Kat, a force more powerful than the talisman exists."

Ibby, now restored to human form, rushed over and wrapped her arms around the neck of the exotic feline. "Oh mistress, I have never witnessed such selfless bravery. How can I ever repay you?" She rose and waved to a pretty woman standing with Charlie and Meeley, who immediately strolled over. "Kat, this is my sister, Jewell. Once Tahl was slain, she was unbound. We will gladly travel to Bowlandria and serve you in any way possible."

"No Ibby, you both must return to your family. They need you more than I do. Thanks for the gracious offer, but I'll survive. Sure won't be easy, but at least we're all alive. That's what's most important." Golden eyes glanced around the room. "Excuse me, but I really wanna go see my sister."

The Queen stood with Merneos, clearly distressed. As Kat approached, Adera looked down and began to sob profusely.

"Don't cry, sis, it's gonna be okay. I'm fine, honest."

286

"Never has my heart been shattered as it is." She dropped to her knees and embraced Kat. "I pray you will forgive me."

"There's nothing to forgive. My stupid temper brought this about, and now I have to make the best of a bad situation. Hey, we've overcome a lot of things together, and I'm sure something will remedy the situation in time. Now, dry those peepers."

Meeley and Charlie huddled close—their faces overflowing with grief. Horace stood alongside Nia with eyes lowered. Randy, obviously engulfed with unendurable emotion, wiped away a deluge of tears.

Although professed to be in acceptance of the eternal demonic curse, the epic sight of her distraught companions, family, and husband, suddenly overtook Kat with extreme distress. Reality of the situation escalated suppressed emotions. It was an unbearable breaking point. She glanced at Tom, let out a heartbreaking moan, and bolted from the room. He yelled for her to stop, but his pleas were ineffectual. The swift feline tore through the maze of corridors like a whirlwind, exited the Manor, and headed for a distant cliff. At the precipice, she stopped and stared at the rocks below. "I can't allow Tom to suffer a torturous life. I love him too much. He must be set free."

Cianest glided over to Adera, who had collapsed into Randy's arms. "It is time for me to depart, dearest friend. Do not lose faith, for *miracles* often come to those who *believe*." She smiled, bent down, and lovingly kissed the Queen on her forehead. Gold-feathered wings gracefully unfolded and arms stretched upward. Suddenly, an intense shimmering light illuminated the room as the resplendent being faded into nothingness.

Unsteady, Adera slowly rose and struggled to regain emotional control. She turned to Merneos, but let out a shriek upon discovery he was nowhere in sight. "No, my instructions cannot be carried forth. Hurry, we must go after Kat. Her life is in peril."

Randy furrowed his brow. "It's okay, sweetcakes. Tahl and Odiene are dead. All danger has been eliminated. Why are you so upset?"

"You do not know what I have arranged. It must be halted." She pushed away from him and raced out of the Hall of Armor with the rest following."

Once outside, she scanned the area, her eyes panicked. "Where is she? We must find Kat. If we do not locate her post haste, she will needlessly perish. "

Punk soared overhead, screeching excitedly and flapping his wings.

Faye soared to the Queen and pointed to the outlying ridge. "She's up there, Highness, but Merneos is not far away. Perhaps he can help."

Adera let out an uncustomary yell, "Merneos stop! Do not do as I asked."

However, the Elf King did not waver from the avowed task. He loaded an arrow, and prepared to fire.

The look on Randy's face indicated realization of what was about to take place. He also called out, but it was too late. The deadly projectile was released and sped at lightning speed toward the intended target.

An ear-piercing thunderous boom erupted, as though a wayward jet had broken the sound barrier. Suddenly, the arrow, which was a sheer millimeter from striking the raven-coated feline, disintegrated and vanished.

Eyes widened and gasps rang out. Cianest had returned and hovered a few feet above Kat. Never had such an ethereal display been witnessed.

A solitary feather was plucked from one of the heavenly angel's wings, given a kiss, and blown into the air. The glistening golden plume twisted and turned as it slowly drifted downward, gently coming to rest on the head of the unwary panther. There was a dazzling flash of multicolored lights coupled with an earsplitting scream. When the intense brightness ebbed, Kat's human form, free of the garish collar, lay motionless upon the rocky surface.

Tom rushed to his wife, lifting her into his arms. "Kat, please don't leave me."

Amber eyes fluttered as she gradually regained consciousness. "T-Tom. I-I feel strange."

He held her tightly while tears dropped upon her face. "My beautiful Kat, I have you back."

Adera and the others hurried to her side, shocked by the astonishing transformation.

"I don't understand. I'm human again. How did this happen?" Kat exclaimed as she was helped to her feet. "We were told the spell couldn't be broken."

"Boundless love and the unwavering faith of those present provided the means, dear one," Cianest replied. "Never once did you utter words of regret or ask for deliverance. The unselfish feat you so willingly performed, Kat, revived my numinous powers. Out of divine gratitude, you are released from the tormenting bonds so wrongly inflicted by evil. Now, I must take my leave. At long last, I have the power to rejoin my kind. However, even though you may not see nor hear me, I shall always be a mere

289

whisper away. I shall forever be near to protect and remain watchful over each of you until the end of time. My departing blessings are given to this land, and all who have needlessly suffered. May hallowed sanction hold sway over this Kingdom and those who dwell within." She waved her hand, smiled, and vanished.

Almost immediately, leaves began to appear on desolate trees. The scorched earth turned green and flowers sprung forth, permeating the air with their pleasing fragrance. Melodic songbirds darted about the lofty boughs, and woodland creatures emerged from the now lush forest. Mantalac had miraculously been brought back to life.

Kat stood in shock, unable to fully grasp what had transpired. A soft breeze fondled denuded flesh causing an eruption of goose bumps. "Dang, I didn't realize how warm that fur coat was. I'm freezing. Course it might help if I had some blasted clothes on."

Randy began to laugh. "Yep, Kat's back." He removed his jacket, walked over, and draped it around shivering shoulders. "Welcome home, kiddo. Thought for awhile we were gonna lose you."

"Not a chance," she quipped. "You can't get rid of me that easy."

It was unanimously decided they would spend a few days in Mantalac and allow Kat time to regain a bit of strength. The trek home would be lengthy and moderately arduous.

The return to Odium Manor widened eyes. The structure, which had been dark and malevolent, had undergone an astounding transformation. Ashy granite walls glistened in the radiant sunlight. Once shadowy chambers now appeared warm and hospitable. A cheerful atmosphere vanquished one of despondency.

290

Adera dispatched teams to thoroughly explore the palace to insure all loathsome creatures, including the bodies of Tahl and Odiene, were removed, and properly buried. As before, all would reconvene in the Hall of Armor once the unpleasant tasks were completed.

Everyone, except Meeley and Charlie, had rejoined the group, which caused a bit of concern.

"Well, about time you guys decided to show up," Randy exclaimed as the smiling couple entered the room. "We were about to send out the Calvary. Where the dickens you two been?"

"Meeley and I checked out the west wing and found someone rather interesting wandering around Odiene's room." He snickered gave a playful wink. "Hey Faye, you have any idea who this dude is?" Charlie stepped aside, revealing an undersized figure standing behind him.

The small fairy let out a high-pitched shriek, "Poppa, it's my dear sweet poppa." She flew into his open arms as the two shared a tearful reunion. "I thought you were dead."

"No, sweet daughter, my life was spared, although at times death would have been more welcomed. I was to be offered to Cianest, but at the last moment, Odiene decided to extend my suffering and cruelly transformed me into her pet."

"Splozits! *You* were that witch's black cat. Certainly clears up a few things."

"Yes, Faye, it was I. We first met when you nearly became prey to several Qergs in the dungeons."

The excited sprite gave a sheepish grin. "That was pretty foolish of me, Poppa, but I had to save my friends. I do remember feeling a strange familiarity toward that kitty, but couldn't explain it." She gave him another robust

291

hug. "Mother sure is going to be in for a shock. I can't wait to see the look on her face."

He chuckled and glanced around the room. "I owe each of you a boundless debt of thankfulness."

Adera stepped forward. "Nothing is owed, King Larc. Your brave daughter has repaid the debt many times over." She bowed graciously. "It is indeed a pleasure to see you once again. I was only a child when last we met."

The fairy King gave a quirky look. "Forgive my failure to recognize the lovely daughter of Adeanra. I should have realized, for you look so like your beautiful mother. The tragedy of her death touched the hearts of me and my people. She was truly a great lady and loved by all who crossed her path. Upon my return, a grand celebration will be given in your honor."

"The gracious offer is appreciated, but unnecessary, King Larc. Our reward is the glow on Faye's face," Adera replied. "A few days must be given to allow my sister time to recover. Once she is up to the task, we shall depart this land." The distinguished Queen then proceeded to introduce every member of the troupe.

Ibby and Jewell had gathered many others, who appreciatively prepared a luscious and very welcomed dinner for their liberators. After all had eaten, sleeping arrangements were discussed. None, however, would venture near the former quarters of Tahl. His room was to be forever sealed.

Merlin, who had been noticeably absent for some time, excitedly entered the room. "My dearest Queen, your sister and friends requested I utilize my superb talents to prepare a rather unique surprise. Please, take the arm of your spouse and come with me."

Adera and Randy gave each other a somewhat apprehensive glance, but did as asked and followed the wizard. Soon, they arrived at Kat's former chamber. A puzzled look graced their faces for the bulky wooden door had been mysteriously replaced by a rather opulent one.

Kat walked forward, squeezed the hand of the ancient conjuror, and drew a breath. "I sure hope they like what we've done."

Merlin slowly turned the ornate knob and eased the door open. "It is time our newlyweds enjoy a proper honeymoon."

Adera gasped as she peered in. The lackluster room had been lavishly redecorated into a magnificent bedroom fit for royalty. "Oh," she said. "I am without words."

The happy couple started to enter, but was halted by Kat's loud exclamation, "Just hold it right there you two. Randy, load that bride of yours in those lazy arms and carry her over the dang blasted threshold."

He shrugged his shoulders and chuckled. "Better do as she says, sweetums, or we might have to spend the night in the barn." Adera giggled like a child as he scooped her up and they entered the room.

Kat reached for the knob and started to shut the door. "Good night, lovebirds. Pleasant dreams."

Three days passed quickly, and Kat grew stronger by the hour. At last, the time had come to begin the long journey home.

Adera knew Mantalac would need guidance and advised the townsfolk to decide who would reign. To everyone's astonishment, Jewell and Ibby, who now chose to again be called by her given name, Isabelle, were delegated to live in the immoderate palace and act as the kingdom's governing officials. The two ecstatic girls could not believe the honor

293

bestowed upon them and vowed to manage their land with the same kindhearted diplomacy demonstrated by Queen Adera. Tears of joy and sorrow were shed as the collection of friends bid each other goodbye.

Emotions were elevated as the group made their way into the fairy kingdom of Drealon. Queen Fallon dashed from her home as an explosion of cheers thundered throughout the small sovereignty.

Adera's eyes filled with joy as she watched Faye and the fairy monarch reunite. "Mother, there is someone who has waited a long time to see you again." She motioned to Punk, who immediately flew down carrying his charge. At first Queen Fallon stood silent, her tiny body quaking with apparent disbelief.

King Larc dismounted and dashed to his beloved spouse who sped into his arms. "I am home, my wife, and shall never again leave your side."

Faye turned to Adera and the others and began to giggle. "Bongles, this was better than I imagined. For once, *Mother* is speechless."

As predicted, evening brought an unrivaled celebration. Even the Elves partook in the merriment as music filled the tepid night air.

The following morning Kat and Tom decided to search for a quite spot where the pair might enjoy a few moments of private relaxation. They happened upon a blossoming grassy slope alongside the babbling creek that once separated two differing kingdoms and agreed this was the perfect location.

Tom spread a blanket on the supple turf and pulled Kat down next to him. "Is this a little piece of heaven or what?"

He gave her forehead a sweet, tender kiss. "As before, my stupidity nearly lost you. I promise it won't happen again. I'm gonna stick like glue to you from this day forward, baby cakes. The horror you endured is mindboggling and would have never taken place if I'd heeded Adera and McLachen's warnings. I'm so sorry, Kat. Can you ever forgive me?"

She pressed a finger to his lips. "There's nothing to forgive, Tom. I was acting bullheaded as usual and didn't listen either. I know there are a thousand questions you would like me to answer, but for now, sweetheart, I simply wish to enjoy the dreamy ripple of flowing water. I wish to hear the melodic songs of the birds and view the blue sky. I wish to feel the warmth of the sun upon my flesh and listen to the whisper of the wind as it rustles through the trees. But most of all, I wish to fall asleep in the loving security of your arms and remain there for eternity."

He embraced her tightly and sighed. "I'm certainly no wizard, but these are wishes I can easily grant."

For the remainder of the day, few words were spoken as the happy couple savored the companionship of each other.

Over the course of the next two days, the mismatched brigade enjoyed the warm hospitality of the fairies.

Leora and Willa, the lovely tree nymphs, made a brief appearance and expressed their joy at the group's success. "If our assistance is ever again required, Merlin knows how to reach us."

"Adera, did McLachen remain in Bowlandria?" Kat asked. "Sure can't wait to see him again. I really miss Cook and the others as well, even lanky Jerome." She chuckled, "Think it's fair to say I might be a little homesick."

"McLachen is near, dear one. You need only speak his name, and he shall rejoin us without delay. In truth, we require our steeds, for tomorrow we leave for Bowlandria."

Kat's eyes brightened. "McLachen, I'm here."

Half an hour passed with no sign of the great Bayard. Suddenly, the thunder of hoof beats was heard, as the ebony stallion, his son Chendar, and the six bay Arabians burst through the dense brush.

The sight of the majestic horse brought a squeal of delight from Kat. "McLachen," she yelled as she ran to greet him.

"My Lady, you have returned. I have long dreamed of this moment. We shall not be parted a third time. You have my solemn vow," he exclaimed and lovingly nuzzled her soft hand.

Tom walked over to stroke the neck of his wife's noble stallion, but quickly receded when ears were laid back and teeth bared. "Whoa, McLachen, I've learned my lesson. In no way will I ever again allow Kat to be put in harm's way. You have *my* vow on that. Can we be friends again?"

"I will hold you to your word, Master Tom. However, be warned. If your pledge is broken, even for a second, my wrath will be felt and it shall not be pleasant. For the moment, and for the sake of My Lady, I accept your amity."

Kat began to giggle, finding the banter between the pair amusing. She eyed the grazing Arabians and gave a quirky look. "Uh Adera, unless some of us intend to walk, we have a slight problem. It seems there're more riders than horses."

"She's right," Charlie exclaimed. "Not one of us gave a second thought about this dilemma. Okay Randy, put that brainiac head of yours to work."

296

McLachen gave a loud whinny. "Do not worry, My Lady. The solution is quite simple. Bayards and can easily accommodate more than one. I shall carry you and Master Tom, while Queen Adera and Randy ride together on Chendar. Two others must utilize one horse, which will be switched with another steed each day so they will not tire."

"Wow," Randy exclaimed, "That can work. I'm sure Meeley and Charlie won't mind doubling up."

Horace stepped forward. "Pardon me, but if there is no objection, the lady Nia could accompany me in place of our esteemed couple." He cocked an eyebrow and cast a glance at her.

A bit of blush rose in Nia's face. "I do not find the offer objectionable."

The group exchanged glances and grinned sheepishly.

Kat hadn't noticed the apparent interest her Elvin friend had in the she-Elf, but decided it best to keep all comments to herself. "So, it's all settled. Tomorrow we head for home."

Faye fluttered over and landed on Randy's shoulder. "Hey, did everybody forget about me? I'd like to go along. All this talk of your Kingdom has me curious." She pointed to Randy's saddlebag. "I rode in that smelly thing for days and certainly can stand to do it again. A few dried flowers should sufficiently cloak the stench. I won't get in the way, I promise. Punk doesn't need a horse and can effortlessly make the trip. Please, Queen Adera, can I go?"

"I think we have a new family member." Kat snickered and nudged Randy.

"So it seems, kiddo," he replied. "It's all up to you, Adera."

The Queen drew a breath. "If approval is given by Faye's parents, we welcome her with open arms. Kat, perhaps you and I should plead the case for this brave fairy. Faye, you must understand, I shall honor their wishes. If they forbid such an endeavor, I am bound to support the decision."

"Agreed, fair is fair. Let's check with them now. Morning will be here before you know it, and I have a lot of packing to do."

Kat winked at her sister. "We best do as she asks or none of us will get a drop of sleep tonight."

The tiny sprite clapped her hands. "I know you can't enter the city, so I'll go fetch Mother and Father. Be right back in two shakes of a tail feather." Without another word, she soared into the air and disappeared from sight. It seemed barely a minute had passed before she returned with the two sovereigns trailing close behind.

"My daughter said there was urgent need to speak with us," King Larc exclaimed as he, Faye, and his wife perched on a low hanging tree branch. "Has something happened?"

Adera rolled her eyes and smiled. "All is fine. I apologize for this sudden and unexpected conference, but Faye's exuberance is a trifle hard to contain at times. The young lady has declared a wish to return to Bowlandria with us. We would be honored to open our home to such a brave little one, but will do so only with your approval."

"Absolutely not," exclaimed Fallon. "My daughter is a mere child and will not venture off to some unknown land. No, I forbid it."

King Larc patted his wife's hand. "My darling, our Faye is no longer the small child we knew. She has proven exceptional maturity ten times over. Regrettably, it appears the day has arrived to set her free." He put an arm around his Queen and pulled her close. "Our daughter may travel with you, Queen Adera. My permission is granted. Go with our blessings."

Faye leaped for joy and flew over to Adera. "Okay, you've been given the word, so can I go, please, please, please?"

"Yes dear one, tomorrow you shall begin the trek to my Kingdom." She turned to the energetic sprite's parents. "I willingly pledge full responsibility to your loved one and shall become her personal guardian. Do not be concerned. No harm shall befall your daughter. We also extend an open invitation for your visit whenever you like and for however long you desire to stay."

Faye rushed to her parents and embraced them. "I promise to do whatever Queen Adera tells me to do and thank you from the bottom of my heart. I love you both, more than you can ever know. I'd gladly stay, but this is something I truly desire. Why don't we head on home? There's some packing to do. The rest of the night belongs to us and we'll talk till daylight. Bongles, I'm so excited. I couldn't grab ten minutes of rest if someone plopped me on the noggin." She looked up and yelled, "Hey Punk, we're going on a road trip. Pack your feathers."

The noble owl hooted and bobbed his head.

Queen Fallon smiled and turned her glance upwards. "My valiant knight, take care of this precocious young woman for me. Watch over her with the diligence you have always provided."

Little sleep was had by all as anticipation rose in the hearts of the brigade. At first light, the horses were made ready and the jubilant travelers prepared to start out. As in Mantalac, emotions overflowed and tears fell, but soon the group was mounted and the pilgrimage home began. Faye yelled and waved goodbye from the security of Randy's brown leather satchel, bringing a gleeful laugh from all but the Elves.

The long journey was relatively pleasant and exceedingly uneventful. Soon, the great white spires of the Castle appeared on the horizon.

"Well Faye, what do ya think of our humble abode," Randy asked.

"Splozits, that is one big place," the buoyant fairy shouted out with vivacity. "I've never seen anything so grand in my whole life."

"Nor will you, Princess," Merlin exclaimed. "There is none to compare in the entire Realm."

The sound of hoof beats upon the cobblestone courtyard brought a welcoming burst of greeting, as the hefty wooden doors were wildly thrust open.

"Saints preserve us, if it isn't herself and me sweet darlin' Kat home safe and sound. It appears the answers to me prayers have been heard," Cook shrieked as the jolly plump woman bounded down the granite steps. "I've been worrying off ten lives. Tis good to see the likes of ya it tis." She ran to Kat and gave a robust hug.

Tom began to laugh. "Hey Cook, don't break her in two the first day home."

A blush rose in the cheeks of the chirpy woman as she released her stalwart grip. "Well, just look at the sight of ya, lass. Why, I've seen more meat on one of me kettle bones. After a wee bit of cleanin' up, come to me kitchen, Kat darlin'. That goes for the rest of ya as well. There's a nice hearty pot of stew brewin' which should take the hunger from those bellies." The lively woman walked to Queen Adera and took her hand. "What a blessed day this has turned out to be." She glanced over the sovereign's shoulder at the two elfin women and Faye. "Saints preserve us. It seems ya have returned with a few more than ya rode out with. Think I'd better be on my way if you're not minding, me darlin Queen. Appears there's a good bit a cookin' to be done. Tonight you'll feast on a meal the likes you've never seen, and by the looks of the bunch of ya, it's more than overdo." She turned to the stoic butler who stood alongside her. "Well, ya lordship, don't ya just be standing there with yer mouth floppin' down. Get those big feet movin', Jerome, and prepare the rooms."

He scowled and gave a huff. "I am well aware of what needs to be done, Margaret Mary. The Brownies are already making proper arrangements. In addition, every apartment is being filled with delightful floral bouquets, compliments of our garden gnomes, Pudge and Gleek." He turned from the chubby woman and politely addressed the Queen. "Welcome home, Majesty. I am pleased everyone has returned safe." The lanky butler then gave a respectful bow before leaving.

Randy began to chuckle and turned to Kat. "Welcome home, kiddo. See, nothing's changed."

Kat laughed. "It sure feels good to be back. I've missed everyone so much. Feels like I'm almost emerging from some kind of warped dream."

Tom chuckled. "I'd say it's more like a blasted nightmare. Well, it's over, and now the healing process begins. What say we head to our rooms and get spruced up a bit. Think we have a lot of dirt and grime to wash off. Plus, I'll bet my bottom dollar there are two Brownies who are probably busting a corset waiting to see you."

Kat nodded then glanced at the ebony stallion. "Hold on, I need to go talk to McLachen." She walked over and gave the noble horse a robust hug. "Rest easy, my beloved friend. I'm safe now. Think it's time you headed home. I suspect a pretty gray mare named Darcy is waiting anxiously for your return." She rubbed his velvet nose. "We'll have a long chat tomorrow. I love you so much, McLachen, and promise to listen better in the future."

He nodded in agreement and turned to Chendar. "Let us be off, son. Your mother waits." Moments later, they were gone from sight.

The Castle seemed even more elegant than before as Kat made her way into the giant structure. She looked at the glistening white alabaster statue of Cianest centered in the Great Hall and smiled. "This certainly is a gorgeous tribute to our magnanimous Angel, but ironically it doesn't hold a candle to her real beauty in comparison."

Tom eased up beside her. "No, it sure doesn't."

"Never forget, sweet sister, she shall always be near." Adera lovingly kissed Kat's cheek.

The tender moment was abruptly disrupted when an overly energetic Meeley charged up. "Sorry to break up this tender moment, but I really have to go check on Knox. That dragon must be nearly out of his mind with worry. Sure hope my big green hunk o' love hasn't ignited anyone. I'll see you all at dinner."

Charlie shrugged his shoulders as he watched his sparkling wife dash out of the room. "Yep, you're right, Randy. Nothing's changed. I swear I often play second fiddle to that woman's fire breathing puppy."

Later that evening, the refreshed group enjoyed a scrumptious meal, a few beakers of wine, and a good bit of banter. Soon, the weary band of travelers headed to their quarters. A night of tranquil slumber was more than welcomed by all.

The following day, Kat held to her word and spent a good part of it with McLachen.

Merlin offered the use of four flying horses to King Merneos, Horace, Nia, and Nerak to expedite their long voyage to Durmeleigh. The sight of the mystical creatures brought gasps from the two she-Elves. After a few moments of instruction, all were mounted and took to the sky.

At Kat's insistence, Adera and Randy set out to finally enjoy a long overdue honeymoon at Unicorn Lagoon. It not only offered an unparalleled beauteous setting, but also blissful tranquility and uninterrupted privacy…something the couple had not enjoyed since they pledged their vows.

Faye and Punk settled in to their new living arrangements and even managed to make friends with Kat's two Brownies, Meon, and Hoki.

As the week progressed, Kat regained her vitality and even managed to take a quick flight on her magnificent flying horse, Junar. She squealed with delight as the pair rocketed into the misty clouds and soared across a land of beauty.

The horror of days past quickly began to fade from her mind. One evening, while Tom accompanied Charlie to help Merlin with a new batch of flying horse colts, she strolled alone into their quaint courtyard and sat staring up into the starlit sky.

"Having a bit of trouble sleeping, kiddo?"

She leaped to her feet, startled by the unexpected voice. "Randy, you scared the living bejeepers out of me. Dang you! Give a girl some warning next time."

He eased down alongside and put an arm around her shoulders. "Sorry Kat, for once you're right. After all you've endured the past few weeks, I should have known better."

303

She smiled and gave him a playful nudge. "Did you have a nice honeymoon?"

"Sure did. Should I give you a full blow by blow of all the wonderful details?"

"No, don't you dare. That's purely personal. Blast it Randy, don't be such a toad-turning brat. I'm just glad you and Adera finally got to spend time together. The little jaunt you had in Mantalac was not the greatest."

"Say, how bout we take our minds off things around here and see what's happening back in the other world? Have you looked into your globe lately?"

Amber eyes widened. "My globe! Jiminy Crickets, I completely forgot all about the darn thing. What a super idea. I'll go get it. How 'bout we check and see what Tippy's up to these days." Without allowing him another word, she dashed to her room, retrieved the magical orb, and quickly sprinted back, plopping down next to him. "Okay, now slide in close so you can get a good look." She held the beautiful egg shaped sphere in her hand. "I wish to see our friend Tippy." Without hesitation, the golden center started to twirl, and soon an image began to take form. Kat edged closer to Randy as they stared in silence for several minutes. Smiles quickly began to fade and disbelieving minds tried to grasp hold of a harrowing visualization. "Oh Randy, this can't be happening…not to Tippy. We have to do something. Think. You're the dadgum genius here."

"I-I don't know what can be done, kiddo. We're a long way from there. I'm afraid this situation is out of our hands. Sorry Kat, there's no way to help."

The two lifelong friends, saddened by the heart-tugging image, sat with heads lowered. Suddenly, eyes widened as they turned to each other and bellowed in unison, "The Book!"

Welcome to
Cook's Kitchen

Most in the Realm address this bubbly lady simply as Cook, but few know little about the charming and loving woman.

Margaret Mary Mullane was a long time resident of the Emerald Isle. However, she is far from being an average Irish citizen.

Her sweet mother was a petite adventurous red-haired charmer named Briney O'Shea. During one of her travels across the Moors, she happened upon a stranger perched atop a moss covered stonewall. He had hair dark as night, with eyes that twinkled like green stars. The handsome lad leaped down and politely introduced himself as Drustan Mullane. Soon, a fiery love burned deep in both hearts, but sadly, matrimony between the two was forbidden.

She was human—he was Leprechaun.

Months passed and secreted moments of tender bliss were shared. Eventually, Briney learned she was with child. The pair pleaded with the Leprechaun King to allow a marriage, but Brian would not give his blessing. Fearing reprisal from the superstitious villagers, the duo decided to flee. Unfortunately, the plot was discovered, and Drustan became banned from the land of humans.

Fearing for the life of his beloved, the sobbing young lad begged his King to help save her life. Unwilling to bring about the destruction of an innocent child, Drustan was granted an audience with another immortal…Zuegas. He agreed to grant asylum to both mother and child in his newly formed sanctuary. However, as punishment, neither she nor the child would be granted the gift of immortality.

Briney willingly took on the duty of chef and also governess to the Ancients' young daughter, Adera.

Margaret Mary grew like a weed, working alongside her aging mother in the lavish kitchen. It was a chore she relished and took to cooking like a spoon to soup. She and Adera were inseparable, growing as close as sisters.

In time, Briney fell to the fate of all humans…death.

Margaret Mary, now approaching 40, continued her mother's work, finding happy solace in the spacious kitchen as age crept upon her. Her designation was never that of a servant, but one of a family member…cherished and loved. The duties she undertook were completely of her choosing.

One morning, the plump, bubbly woman observed the sovereign's sister pour an unfamiliar potion into Adera's drink. She flung the goblet from the young girl's hand, alerting Zuegas of this suspicious act. The liquid proved to be a deadly poison.

As a reward for saving the life of his daughter, Zuegas graciously awarded Margaret Mary eternal life. From that moment on, Cook, as she was now called, would no longer age nor face death until the time of her choosing.

Adera adored, and continues to adore, this loyal companion. With maturity comes wisdom. The Queen often sits with her friend, disclosing secrets and also asking for support and guidance while sipping on a cup of fresh brewed tea.

A unique touch of magic was miraculously passed on to Cook by her father. She often employs this clever endowment to concoct mind-boggling dishes, making her the most proficient and talented chef in the entire Realm.

It is with great pleasure we were graciously presented with eight of her most treasured recipes. We hope you will try some and enjoy a wee taste of Bowlandria.

Adera's Awesome Baked Grouper

Beautiful Queen Adera finds most seafood dishes irresistible. This is one of her Majesty's favorites, so Cook makes sure this particular concoction is frequently on the menu.

However, the three mermaid Princesses, Maris, Nerissa, and Romey, prefer their serving raw.

RECIPE:

Preheat oven to 350 degrees.

Skin two pounds of fresh grouper, cut in serving size pieces, and set aside. (NOTE: If purchasing in a seafood market, request they skin the fish for you.)

In a bowl, whisk together:
> 1 cup Sour Cream
> ¼ cup Parmesan Cheese
> 1-Tablespoon limejuice
> 1- Tablespoon finely grated onion
> ½-teaspoon salt
> ¼-teaspoon black pepper

Arrange grouper pieces in a single layer in a 12 x 8 shallow baking dish.

Spread cream mixture evenly over the top of the grouper.

Sprinkle with paprika.

Bake until fish is flaky.

Cooks Cherry Sauced Pork Loin

Margaret Mary has a personal favorite, and this is it. Guests at the royal wedding feast were treated to a grand meal, with this being the overall favorite. Merlin, Tom, and Charlie ate so much they struggled on the dance floor and would have preferred a nap instead.

RECIPE:

Preheat oven to 325 degrees.

> 1 Boneless Pork loin roast – about 4 to 5 pounds
> ½ teaspoon salt
> ½ teaspoon pepper
> ½ teaspoon crushed thyme

Rub roast with mixture. Place on a rack in a baking dish and roast uncovered for about 2 – 2 ½ hours or until meat registers 170 degrees.

When roast is done, prepare sauce.

SAUCE:

> 1 cup cherry preserves
> ¼ cup red wine vinegar
> 2 Tablespoons light corn syrup
> ¼ teaspoon ground cinnamon
> ¼ teaspoon ground nutmeg
> ¼ teaspoon ground cloves
> ¼ teaspoon salt

Combine all ingredients in a small saucepan. Bring to a boil on medium heat, stirring to prevent scorching. Reduce heat to simmer and continue to cook for around 2 minutes.

Serve in a gravy boat with roast to pour over sliced meat.

Elven Green Bean Casserole

Everyone knows Elves consume very little meat. They prefer greens and earthy food. Knowing this, Horace's mother, Helen, traveled to Bowlandria and worked alongside Cook to develop this wonderful vegetable dish. It took a great deal of searching to gather the necessary ingredients.

King Merneos, Nirage, and Horace thoroughly enjoyed this casserole at the Royal Wedding Feast. Meeley and Charlie said it was the best thing they ever tasted, so it has been routinely added to the Castle's dinner menu.nts, but the finished product was well worth the effort.

*We have altered Cook's complex version to make it easier on us humans.

RECIPE:

Preheat oven to 350 degrees.

> 2- Packages of frozen French Cut Green Beans
> 3- Large ripe tomatoes- thinly sliced
> 3- Medium onions-thinly sliced
> Mozzarella cheese
> Parmesan cheese
> Basil
> REAL Butter- <u>unsalted</u>
> Salt & Pepper – to taste
> Regular Bread Crumbs

Cook green beans in saucepan. When done, drain well, and add 4 Tablespoons <u>Real</u> Butter. Mix thoroughly.

Spray a square 9 inch pan with butter flavored Pam. Add a layer of the buttered green beans, perhaps half of the amount.

On top of the green beans, sprinkle salt, pepper, and some basil. Then add a layer of thin sliced tomatoes, onions, sprinkle of parmesan cheese, and a good sprinkle of Mozzarella Cheese.

Repeat.

In a bowl, add 4 Tablespoons of melted butter. Mix in a portion of breadcrumbs. Sprinkle the mixture on top of the bean casserole.

Bake for around 35 - 40 minutes.

Kat's Favorite Sweet Potato Casserole

Kat always tells Cook that South Carolina Sweet Potatoes are the best in the world and make it better, but this version comes in pretty close. She says it's like eating yummy sweet potato silk. Jay, Randy, and Tippy loved this casserole nearly as much as Kat. They said it was a hog snortin' Taste of Home.

RECIPE:

Preheat oven to 375 degrees.

Put 3 cups of peeled, chunked, and thoroughly cooked sweet potatoes in a food processor.

*(If you chose to use canned, put in a colander, wash, and drain first before adding to processor-no cooking necessary) Process until smooth which should only take a few minutes.

Add ½ cup of <u>Sweetened Condensed Milk</u>. Process to blend.

Add 2 beaten eggs and ½ cup Evaporated Can Milk. Continue to blend.

*Please make note there are TWO kinds of canned milk...Sweetened and also Evaporated.

While processing, melt ¼-cup REAL BUTTER (in a microwave for ease) and slowly add to mixture while blending - along with 1 teaspoon and a dash more pure vanilla. Continue processing until nice and creamy.

314

Pour mixture in a casserole dish sprayed with Butter Flavored Pam.

Sprinkle a little brown sugar on top (can use Splenda Brown Sugar) and if you like, some VERY fine ground pecans and a little grated coconut.

Bake for around 30 minutes.

NOTE: Fresh sweet potatoes will produce a far better flavor. However, canned will be fine, and adds a bit of convenience. Either is okay. You can also use ground walnuts, but pecans are sweeter and give it a better taste.

Meeley's Crab Quiche

Like Queen Adera, our vivacious dragon rider, Meeley, loves seafood. She enthusiastically worked alongside Cook to develop this savory dish. Catching the crabs usually takes up the better part of a day, but the entire gang enjoys the lively excursion. They know the reward for their toils will be scrumptious.

*As in other recipes, we have added convenient alternatives.

RECIPE:

Preheat oven to 350 degrees.

1 nine-inch pie shell. You can also make your own crust or pre-made, roll out and put in a nine-inch pie pan.

 NOTE: Cracker meal pie shell <u>will not</u> work with this recipe.

Filling:

In a bowl, mix all ingredients together.

> 1 cup plus 2 Tablespoons Half and Half
> 6 oz. grated mozzarella cheese
> 6 oz. grated sharp cheddar cheese
> 3 medium eggs, beaten
> Dash of garlic pepper to taste
> Dash of salt to taste
> 3 chopped scallions – sautéed in a little butter
> 2 cans of lump crabmeat – picked through to remove as much shell as possible
> 1 Medium size can of sliced mushrooms.

316

NOTE:(If using fresh, slice and cook desired amount. One can never have too many mushrooms.)

Blend all ingredients well.

Pour into pie shell.

Bake on a cookie sheet for 30-45 minutes or until an inserted knife come out clean.

Meon and Doki's Fudge Brownies

Our lively little caretakers begged Cook to design a dish named after them. After a day or two of thinking, our plump Irish cook recalled a delectable dish from back home. It was perfect. Everyone agreed this was a keeper recipe, and so 'Fudge Brownies' were added to the menu. Charlie especially loves them, not only for the incredible taste, but for the title.

You see, Fudge is the name of his beloved flying horse.

RECIPE:

Preheat oven to 350 degrees.

Grease or spray with Pam, a 9 x 13 square baking dish.

In a bowl, whisk together all ingredients until smooth.

> 1 ½ Cups All purpose flour
> 2 cups Sugar
> ½ cup, plus 2 Tablespoons Cocoa
> 1 teaspoon salt
> 1 cup oil
> 4 large eggs
> 2 teaspoon pure vanilla extract

Pour into baking dish.

Bake about 30-40 minutes, or until center comes clean when pierced by knife.

Cut into square and place on a serving dish.

Randy's Cream of Carrot Soup

This is Randy's favorite dish and always tells Cook – It's Bowl Lickin' Good! The flavor is not what you may think, but is mild and sweet. The aloof nymph Bagi at first refused to taste it, but at Queen Adera's bidding finally took a spoonful. She rolled her stunning emerald eyes and sat down, finishing not one, but two big bowls.

(The recipe sounds a little complex to make, but it really is easy. Also, butternut squash can be substituted for the carrots to give you another great dish.)

RECIPE:

Simmer in a covered saucepan until tender:

> 3 cups thinly sliced fresh carrots – peeled
> 3 Tablespoons REAL Butter – salted
> 1-teaspoon sugar or Splenda
> ½-teaspoon salt
> Enough water to just cover carrots
> ½-teaspoon nutmeg
> ¼-teaspoon cinnamon

While carrots are cooking, melt on low heat in another saucepan:

> 3 Tablespoons REAL Butter – salted
> Slowly blend in with wire Wisk:
> 2 Tablespoons all purpose flour
> ½-teaspoon salt
> ¼-teaspoon white pepper

319

*Continuously stir over medium heat until smooth and bubbly, but be careful not to scorch.

Remove from heat. Slowly stir in with a wire Wisk:

> 1 full can Evaporated Milk
> 1 full can of <u>whole</u> Milk (just add to empty Evaporated Milk can)

Put cooked carrot mixture in a blender and cream.

When smooth, add to milk mixture in the saucepan, and heat on medium low, stirring constantly. <u>Add</u> 2/3 cup of whipping cream prior to serving.

Tippy's Spinach Salad

While in Bowlandria, Tippy often made her famous salad…a treat everyone enjoyed. She adored working in the kitchen nearly as much as reading. Although our enchanting friend returned home to be with family, Cook often prepared this dish in her honor…a flavorful tribute to a delightful, loving lady.

RECIPE:

Thoroughly wash and drain a bag of fresh baby spinach. Tear into large pieces and put in a large bowl.

Boil 3 large eggs and fry 6 strips of bacon, cooked very crisp.

Set aside the bacon dripping. **DO NOT DISCARD**.

SAUCE:

Mix together in a bowl

> 1 Tablespoon sugar
> 1 small onion grated VERY fine
> 1 Tablespoon of the bacon dripping
> ¼ cup salad oil
> 1 cup mayonnaise
> 1/8 cup white vinegar
> 1 teaspoon yellow mustard
> ¼ cup parmesan cheese

Mix well.

321

Add the sauce to the spinach and toss well.

Chop hard-boiled eggs and crumbled bacon bits. Lightly toss to mix.

Top with garlic croutons if desired.

Glossary of Characters and Terms

Adeanra (ah dean rah)-Elegant mother of Adera. Tall, slender, with long platinum blonde hair. Has same turquoise eyes as Adera. Was a scientist on the lost mission. Extremely kind and gentle. Had an uncanny mental connection with animals. Was killed when she fell from Pegasus.

Adera (ah-deer-ra)-Appointed Queen of Bowlandria-blonde-turquoise eyes-strikingly beautiful-immortal-lives alone in Castle built by the Ancients-has never been married-Fiancé Tanas was killed by jealous sorceress.

Ahren (a-ren)-Demonic warrior appointed by Nimue to train and lead her troops-vicious-has no conscience-larger than other Shankquas-extremely muscular-hates Randy.

Bagi (Badge-gee)-A nymph-long curly red hair-emerald green eyes-beautiful-aloof-dedicated to Adera.

Bayard (bay-erd)-Mythological horses-can speak and carry great weight.

Bowlandria (Bow-land-dree-ah)-First occupied and the most important kingdom in other realm-gateway through the portal-beautiful-peaceful-medieval in appearance-no modern features.

Brandi (bran dee)-replacement maid for Kat when Ibby is transformed into hen.

Brendalyn (bren dal lin), **Chastena** (chas tee nah), and Tabota (ta bow tah)-Queen Adera's personal Brownies.

Cianest (see a nest)-Angelic creature kidnapped by Lord Tahl, transformed, and held captive in a hideous form. Was a childhood friend of Queen Adera.

Deliverance Brigade-Name given to rescue party by Charlie.

Drealon (dree lonn)-Beautiful and mystical fairy Kingdom and home to Faye. Fairies of this clan can communicate with various creatures. Intelligent beings, kind and peace loving. Do not have wings until they prove worthy. Borders are hidden by spells. No outsider can enter without permission. Qergs cannot enter. Most valued law is not to venture beyond the secured boundaries for any reason.

Durmeleigh (derm-ma-lee)- An Elf kingdom-secluded-built in mountain valley-enchanting-private.

Faye (Fay)-Young fairy princess, would be similar to a human around the age of sixteen. Daughter of Queen Fallon and King Larc. Has silky waist long ash brown hair and hazel eyes. Rides her pet Barred Owl **Punk.** Tends to rattle on when speaking and often goes off the subject. Rebellious, feisty, and brave.

Ganieda (Ga-nay-dah)-Magically talented sister of Merlin who entered with him-kind-gentle-beautiful-killed by sorceress Nimue.

Helons (he-lons)-Goblin warriors resurrected by Nimue to fight Adera-toad like appearance-small bat-like wings will not let them achieve flight, but can leap twenty to thirty feet off the ground-cannibalistic-odorous.

Hoki (ho-kee)-Female Castle Brownie who cares for Kat-about two feet high-sharp pointed ears-large light brown eyes-pretty-pixie-like-short cropped light brown hair-delicate frame-shy and most times invisible-loyal.

Horace-Elf name is **Netho** (nee-tho)-tall-handsome-muscular-has strong features-blue eyes-part human-immortal-highly aloof-one of Durmeleigh's best warriors-keeps his gentle heart secret-Elf father is deceased-juvenile brother is Enal-(ee-nall).

Ios (eye-os)-Last of the sea Titans-an eighty foot sea serpent who can travel on land as well as in the sea-vicious-lust's for blood-imprisoned by King Legar for vile deeds-freed by Nimue and is now her servant.

Isabelle (Iz zah bell)-Mantalac captive forced to become servant to Kat by Lord Tahl. Kat gives her the nickname of **Ibby**. In anger, Lord Tahl transforms her into a red hen. Searches for her older sister **Jewell** who was captured prior to her. Becomes great friends with Kat. Gentle and helpful.

Junar (ju-nar)-Kat's personal flying horse-brother to Kiv-a golden palomino with white mane, tail and wings.

Kelsi (kel see) and **Tempi** (temp pee)-Fairies and two best friends of Faye. Young and inexperienced. Follow Faye outside of their Kingdom and are captured by Qergs.

King Legar- (lee-gar)- King of the me-people-handsome-long white hair and beard-icy blue eyes-widowed-has three daughters-meets Nimue in mermaid form, is seduced by her and they soon marry-he and his people become imprisoned by his Sea Queen to be used as slaves—or food for her pet sharks.

King Merneos-(mer-nee-os)-Elf King of Durmeleigh-entered when the Elves time among mankind had ended-aloof-kind-generous-tall-long platinum-blonde hair-penetrating blue eyes-pointed ears-pale skin-mannerly-intelligent-immortal-great warrior-close to Adera and Merlin-bestowed gift of youth and immortality to all who enter realm-detests violence, but will fight when necessary-has close relationship with Nirage.

325

Kiv (Keeve)-Merlin's personal flying horse-brilliant copper-coated chestnut with same colored wings.

Knox (nocks)-Meeley's dragon-enormous yellow eyes-large, leathery bat-like wings of translucent green- around forty feet high-iridescent green scaled body-short legs with long claws-immense sharp white teeth-dragon type head topped with ivory horns-harmless to friends, but protective of realm and those he loves-purr's when happy-fly's at tremendous speed-can breath fire-hatched shortly before Meeley arrived and given to her by Adera.

Larc-King of the Fairy clan. Captured and turned into Odiene's pet black cat known as **Jypsey** (jip sea).

Leora (lee or rah) and **Willa** (will lah)-Mischievous and beautifully unique wood nymph sisters in the Land of Gentle Woods. Homes are within the trunks of trees and can emerge at will. Helpful and harmless. Flirtatious with human men.

Lord Tahl (Tal)-Evil Dark Lord of Mantalac and son of Odiene and Kram. Considers himself a deity and demands worship from villagers. Exceptionally handsome. Has an insatiable lust for women. Favorite past time is watching Cianest feed on victims. Power hungry. Has an angelic face and demon heart. Around six foot four with semi long cocoa brown hair, intense green eyes, short boxed beard and neat mustache. Turns violent when shunned by a female. Has a hypnotic effect on his victims. Loves no one. Intelligent and skilled at riding and swordsmanship. Well spoken and charismatic.

Mantalac (Man ta lack)-Desolate Kingdome 420 miles north of Bowlandria. No happiness can be found in even the smallest corner since being ruled by Lord Tahl and his mother, Odiene.

Maris (maa-rus)-Oldest of the three Mer-Princesses-name is Latin for Of the Sea-waist long dark brown hair-blue eyes-long, wispy flowing tail and fins-scales of blue and aqua-familiar with land above-wise.

McLachen (mick-latch-in)-A magnificent black stallion-the last Bayard-has the ability to speak-is exceptionally close to Kat.

Meeley (meal-lee)-Female pilot who entered realm in late thirty's-has whispery Kansas drawl-tall-gray eyes-somewhat attractive-hearty laugh-takes to the air on her "little green flying machine"-lives in a distant cottage with pet, Knox.

Meon (me-onn)- Female Castle Brownie who cares for Tippy. Appearance is similar to Hoki.

Nalay (nal-lay)- Unicorn stallion-white with exceptionally long curly mane and tail-penetrating blue eyes-magical-intelligent-has brilliant golden horn-tears can render any poison harmless-capable of great speed-gentle-lives with mate Adel-(ah-dell) and baby colt Wister-(wist-ter) at Unicorn Lagoon-shy and secretive-friend to Adera-very close to McLachen-fascinated with Kat.

Nerak (near rack)-pretty sister of Nia. Escaped capture and searches for her sister. Joins the Brigade in their quest. A brilliant warrior. Fearless.

Nerissa (ner-ris-ah)-Middle Mer-Princess-name is Latin for Daughter of the Sea-waist long blonde hair-blue eyes-and has green and yellow scales-impetuous at times.

Nia (nee ah)-Female Elf captive of Lord Tahl. Is scheduled to be sacrificed to Cianest upon next full moon. Tall, pretty, has gray eyes and long dark hair. Wears warrior type of apparel. Comes from the distant **Kingdom of Elladraine (El la drain)**. Qergs killed all by her and her sister. Rescued by Horace and is as intrigued with him as he is with her.

Nimue (nim-u-ay)-Wicked sorceress who entered with Merlin- hates Adera-shape shifter-beautiful-long curly black hair-brilliant green eyes-shapely-murders Ganieda and Tanas then flees into the sea to escape the wrath of Adera-happens across Mer-people-transforms into a mermaid-enchants and marries King Legar to become Queen of the sea-possesses his Trident-builds demon army-longs to control all of earth, including other realm-is control's Ios.

Nirage (near-raj)-Hauntingly beautiful-Elvin sorceress-tall-immortal-slim-mysterious-long white hair-icy blue eyes-has gift of clairvoyance-is very old-wise-magical-

Odiene (O dean)-Sister of Zuegas. Exceptionally intelligent and beautiful. Has long wavy black hair and intense violet eyes. Was friends with Adera, in the early part of their voyage, but the friendship turned to hatred. Blamed the death of her beloved husband **Kram** on Adeanra. Wanted her son Tahl to follow in Zuegas's footsteps and resented the appointment to Adera. Vowed revenge against all, including Kat. Learned the art of black magic from **Yiema** (yee ma) and **Kaiva** (kay vah), two twin sons born from the lust of a dark sorcerer and witch. Possessed an instrument from the crashed vehicle that would eventually be known as the Wand of Circe. Used it to alter the DNA of a mortal and transform them into any creature. Was banished from Bowlandria to Mantalac when Cook discovered her trying to poison Adera.

Odium Manor (O dee um)-Black castle constructed as home by Lord Tahl and Odiene. Cold and unwelcoming. Surrounded by a deadly vile mist.

 Pegasus (pay-ga-sus)-Legendary horse and personal flying mount for Queen Adera- pure white body and wings-is the original stallion brought to Bowlandria by the ancients.

Qergs – Lord Tahl's goblin guards. Large, bulky in stature, with acute hearing and sense of smell. Often grunt. Have no conscious. Thick arms, legs, and overall body, with short neck, long greasy hair, and black lidless serpentine eyes that can see in the dimmest light. Carry spears that can either tranquilize or kill. Leader is **Gog**.

Queen Fallon (Fall en)-Beautiful fairy queen of Drealon. Mother to Faye. Her name is Gaelic for Leader. Is small in stature, perhaps a foot high-has long, narrow, iridescent wings and waist long carrot red hair. Eyes are pale sea-foam green. Her wispy gown is woven from spider web silk-wears an impressive spiked crown of gold and precious gems. Is stern, but fair.

Relar (ree-lar)-Adera's personal coach driver-dark skinned-medium height-strong masculine features-handsome-deep brown eyes-short black hair-very regal looking and acting-has baritone voice with slight Jamaican accent-easily controls the Thunder Hooves-compassionate-extremely intelligent.

Romey (rah-mee)-youngest Mer-Princess-acts much like a young teenager-name is Latin for Sea Dew-waist long red hair-has orange and gold scales-very immature and disobedient-

Savah (saa vah)-Fairy counselor to Queen Fallon.

Shankquas (Shank-qwas)-Horrific water goblins raised up from the bowels of Hell by Nimue to fight Adera-three feet high-donkey like ears-putrid green skin color-cannibalistic-deadly-grotesque-somewhat human in body

329

shape-dagger like teeth-sharp claws-like finger tips-emotionless-soulless.

Sriebonia (Sray bone nee ah)-Home planet of the Ancients. Resides in another galaxy, but is similar to earth in many ways. Has an advanced civilization capable of time travel and mass mind control-Located in the Pleiades star cluster which is also known as the Seven Sisters. To get to Sriebonia, you would need to pass through the center of the cluster to locate their galaxy.

Tanas (tan-nas)-Friend and protégé of Merlin-handsome-fearless-falls in love with Adera and becomes her fiancé-killed at Adera's feet by Nimue.

Wendy-Wife of Charlies friend Howell.

Zuegas (zoo gahs)-Adera's father and also the father of Kat. Adored his wife Adeanra and mourned her death. While grieving, he traveled to our world and met Kat's mother, Madeleine. Was very tall, about six foot six, and muscular. Handsome with amber eyes which Kat inherited. Was captain and leader of the exploratory expedition that became stranded on Earth. To escape the troubles of humankind, he and others developed the Realm. Was made King. Developed the portal and knew how to traverse both realms. Adored both daughters. Trained Adera to eventually rule. Gave Kat McLachen when she was a small child and the Bayard was a young colt. Was kind and wise. When Madeleine and Kat were returned to our world, he could no longer bear the sorrow and decided to end his existence. Was extremely intelligent. Forceful yet highly compassionate and gentle.